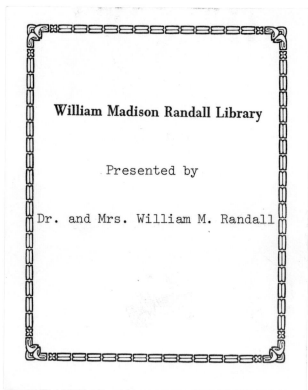

THE GREEK

THE GREEK

A Novel by Pierre Rey

TRANSLATED BY J. F. BERNARD

G. P. Putnam's Sons, New York

To the reader:

The author, in the course of this novel, has occasionally drawn his inspiration from several well-known personages and real events which have been widely covered by the world press.

Nonetheless, it is important to recall that this is a work of fiction and that the situations described, the dialogue, the places, the characters, the reactions and actions of the principal and secondary characters are entirely the product of the author's imagination.

If this novel does in fact constitute a commentary on contemporary morals, or at least the depiction of a certain society of our times, it nonetheless remains a work of fiction. It is not a *roman à clef*, and still less is it a work of biography or of reportage.

PIERRE REY

Part One

[1]

BELOW was a maze of bare rocks bleached white, like bones. Overhead, in a sky of dizzying blue, the sun blazed, and the sea reflected its rays with the violence of an explosion. The Rolls was motionless on an overhang six hundred feet above the water. It hung there in space, incongruous in this place of suspended movement and liquefied time.

The heat was intense, but Niki, sprawled out on the seat of the automobile, shivered and turned down the air conditioner. Mechanically, he smoothed the lapels of the iron-gray jacket marked with the monogram "S.S."

The monogram had been the subject of much comment among the other chauffeurs. They had accused Niki, jokingly, of being branded. He could not have cared less what they thought. He knew that most of them were jealous, because servants, like dogs, measure their respective importance by the importance of their masters. So far as the people who stopped in the streets to stare at the car, they were too impressed by its splendor to register any emotion other than that resigned admiration which served to confirm Niki in his profound contempt for them.

Niki wondered whether he had time for another cigarette before S.S. arrived. His employer was a heavy smoker, but he tolerated nothing less than Havana cigars in his automobile, as though the common perfume of bleached tobaccos would blend badly with the aroma of the Rolls' leather seats. Niki reached toward his pocket, then stopped. He looked at his watch. Noon, exactly. Twice he had tried to get out of the car and walk around, but both times the heat had been like a crushing weight on his shoulders. He tapped his fingers on the seat, wondering how such a godforsaken country could have given birth to a man so rich.

Niki looked up at the sky. A black dot appeared out of nowhere, grew larger. The chauffeur buttoned his jacket and adjusted the knot of his tie. Then he opened the door and leaped to the ground with a display of energy. The airplane was losing altitude along the length of a perfect, imaginary perpendicular line, its propellers spinning in the torrid air. It touched the ground sixty yards from the automobile, then came to a stop. A man in a sport jacket got out. Jeff, probably. He turned and held out his hand. A figure appeared in the doorway of the plane: a small man in black, dressed as though he were going to a funeral—an alpaca suit, black tie, white shirt. His heavy tortoise-shell glasses glistened in the sunlight, and his thick red hair seemed a spot of flame. Niki wondered if S.S. would acknowledge his presence by a nod, a gesture, anything to indicate that he considered the chauffeur more than an accessory, like a tire on the Rolls.

He did not. Socrates Satrapoulos, lost in thought, climbed into the automobile without glancing at Niki. When he was settled in his seat, he said, "To the village, up there."

Niki glanced through the windshield. There was no sign even of a house. He started the engine and moved the Rolls cautiously onto the narrow stone roadway. It was a steep climb, and the automobile had difficulty remaining in second gear.

Two miles up the road, Satrapoulos spoke again. "Turn left here."

Niki obeyed automatically. Now he could see the village, literally perched on the summit. The whitewashed houses, seen from below, blended into the bleached rock of the mountain. Where on earth do they get water? Niki wondered.

"Stop."

Satrapoulos was out of the car before the chauffeur could open the door for him. Niki watched him moving up the steeply inclined path toward the houses. Then he was lost from sight behind a boulder.

Satrapoulos was uneasy. Here he was on alien territory. The trappings of power, acquired so painfully, were behind him. He felt naked, fragile, vulnerable. The sharp stones of the street scratched the leather of his expensive black shoes.

* * *

As a boy, Socrates Satrapoulos had been playing with his friends one day in a vacant lot in a suburb of Athens. Tony suggested a contest, intended to settle, once and for all, the question of which of the boys was able to urinate the farthest.

There was a lengthy discussion concerning the rules of the contest. Socrates, quite rightly, suspected that Tony had suggested the competition because he was certain he would win. And Socrates could not bear the thought that he might possibly lose in a competition of any kind. As the debate among the other boys grew heated, Socrates' attention was absorbed by the problem of finding a way to win.

"I can't piss right away," he announced. "I went only ten minutes ago."

"You're just trying to get out of it," Tony retorted. "You know you're going to lose."

Socrates replied that the contest was not his idea, but Tony's. "Anyhow," he added, "I'm not trying to get out of it. I just want enough time to go home and drink some water. I'll be right back."

Socrates ran across the square adjoining the lot and into his house. His aunt was in the tiny courtyard, hanging clothes on a line. He went into her bedroom.

Socrates searched through her sewing box, scattering spools of thread, pins, and scraps of lace until he found what he wanted.

"What's the matter?" the aunt called.

He did not reply, for he was already in the bathroom—a closet, with a hole in the concrete floor—lost in his own mysterious needs. Once he shivered spasmodically.

When he returned to the arena, Socrates learned that the ground rules of the competition had been laid down. The contestants were to stand with their backs against a wall, and each one was to urinate in turn. The distance of each boy's stream would be measured, with the help of a length of string, by the other contestants who would serve as referees. Socrates accepted the rules, and the contest began.

Then it was Socrates' turn. He fidgeted with his pants. "What's the matter?" Tony asked. "Are you trying to hide your cock?"

Socrates did not answer. Leaning against the wooden wall, he concentrated, computing his chances of winning against the prodigious arabesque of Tony's jet. He seemed to swell up under the effect of two simultaneous and contrary actions, retention and evacuation, both of them violent. He remained motionless for a few seconds more, then released his urine.

5

There were gasps of astonishment which quickly turned to shouted congratulations. Later, a prisoner of victory, Socrates had a difficult time ridding himself of his friends long enough to remove the rubber tourniquet from his penis. It had begun to cut into his flesh.

He had never told anyone what he had done. He wondered now why the episode came to mind. Certainly, many times since then he had made use of much more spectacular ruses.

In which one of these rabbit hutches did she live?

He sensed, rather than saw, a man behind a curtain covering a doorway.

"Athina?" he asked.

The curtain was thrust aside and the man stared at Satrapoulos for a moment, then gestured up the road. "The last house," he said.

A few more yards. Then, perhaps, everything would be resolved. Or it might become more complicated and difficult. There was no way to tell. Satrapoulos was one of the richest men in the world, but his hundreds of millions of dollars and his tens of thousands of employees did him no good here, in this poverty-ridden village. His fleets of tankers, his copper and gold mines were as nothing. And his banks and platoons of lawyers, his politicians and his servants, were powerless in this desolate place.

Now he stood before the doorway. Like that of the house at which he had asked directions, it was covered by a cloth, a piece of torn burlap. From within, he heard the sound of wood being broken. He hesitated, then asked in a voice that he did not recognize, "Is anyone there?"

There was no answer. The sound of breaking wood continued. In a louder, firmer voice he asked again, "Is there anyone there?"

A voice answered, an old woman's voice. "Who is it?"

Satrapoulos pushed aside the curtain. In that instant his features were transformed. A moment before they had been tense. Now they were affable, relaxed. "May I come in?" he asked, smiling broadly.

His eyes had not yet adjusted to the dimness of the house, and he could see nothing. He removed his glasses, and his face resumed the dimensions which it had had at birth. The nose was there, the astonishing celebrated nose which seemed to dominate the face and to reduce the eyes and mouth to mere details. It was whispered throughout the world that Socrates Satrapoulos' nose was proportionate to the size of his penis. This was not entirely correct, but neither was it wholly incorrect. It was simply that no one seemed able to resist the nose-penis analogy. A few friends, intimate enough to ask the question, received as their answer a gesture of dismissal and a few shakes of the head which conveyed a negative response, while Socrates' smile and expression shouted a loud "yes."

His eyes adjusted to the light within, and he saw the old woman. She stopped breaking wood.

"Who are you?" she asked.

Socrates' smile held. "You don't recognize me?"

"What do you want?"

"Well, now—"

"I've already said everything that I have to say."

"To me?"

"To you, to the others—you all come for the same thing."

"Not I. I'm Socrates."

"Socrates? Socrates who?"

"Come on, Mama. You know me."

She stood motionless, puzzled. "It's you, Socrates?"

"It's me, Mama." Socrates' voice had grown gentle, and he was furious at himself for this sign of weakness. Yet this worn-out woman, as thin and brittle as the black kindling that she had been breaking, was his mother. He was astonished that she had not recognized him, that blood had not cried out to blood. Still, on this August day in 1952 it had been thirty-odd years since he had last seen her. A man changes in thirty years.

He looked around the tiny house where he had been reared, in the village of Moutalaski, lost in the ancient Turkish region of Cappadocia. Later there had been another house, in Salonika. He also remembered an apartment at the foot of Mount Piraeus, behind Nikaia, at the foot of Ikoniou Street. There had been two sisters and a brother—all left alone every day as their mother worked as a knitter in a woolen-goods shop. His father, Alexander, had spent his days dreaming of owning a mighty fleet of tankers, while he managed to provide his family with only a hand-to-mouth existence as the employer of a few divers who fished for sponges. There had been another village in Turkey when Socrates was still almost a baby. Some terrible things had happened there. They still preyed occasionally on Socrates' mind, though he could not remember exactly what they were.

"They've been here," the old woman said.

"Yes, Mama, I know. That's why I've come."

"What do they want?"

"They want to use you to hurt me, Mama."

"How can they do that? I can't hurt you. I can't help. I don't even know you."

"But I can help you."

"Well, then, help me break this wood."

Socrates Satrapoulos picked up a few sticks and clumsily tried to splinter them. With a strength unexpected in a woman of her age, Athina jerked the branches from his hands. "Leave it alone," she spat. "I had a son once. He died more than thirty years ago. Even if you were my son, there's nothing I want from you. Not even to see you."

"Mama—"

"Don't call me that. If I were your mother, you wouldn't have waited thirty years to find out if I'm still alive."

"What did you tell them?"

"Why do you want to know? You've gotten yourself into trouble, haven't you? I always knew that you'd end up badly. God knows, I told you that often enough."

Socrates smiled in spite of himself. "Maybe you told me that once too often."

"Did you help your brother? Did you help your father? You didn't even come to your own father's funeral. And me—have you helped me? Look how I live!"

"I tried to help him, but you wouldn't let me—Mama." The word seared his lips. It was a term which stifled him to the point that when his wife had become a mother, she had ceased to inspire any sexual desire whatsoever in him. They had stopped making love.

The woman's voice vibrated in the room. "I don't want anything from you," she shouted. "No one here wants anything from you. Keep your help to yourself. I don't need it. I've learned to do without you, and I can continue doing without you."

"Did you talk to them?"

"I don't have to tell you anything. You wanted to live without parents, didn't you? Well, you don't need me now."

"You still don't understand, do you?"

"Your father used to say that you had crazy ideas. He was right. You drove everyone around you crazy."

Socrates' hands tightened around a small branch that he was holding. He could not break it. Like a child, he stammered, "Mama, please—"

Then his voice rose shrilly and he began to shout, "You never cared anything about me! You always preferred my brother!"

8

The old woman was sobbing now; dry, harsh sobs, strange in that worn throat. "Get out," she said. "Get out! Never come back to this place!"

"Listen to me—"

"Get out!" The woman pointed to the door, searching for a final, devastating word. "You're—you're a degenerate!" she screamed. The term had come to her instinctively. In itself, it signified nothing, but within the framework of the past, the four syllables were transformed in Socrates' mind into a nightmare word, into a symbol of discord and a remembrance of all his rebellions.

He had left home when he was sixteen. For four years, he had been intoxicated by his newfound freedom. He had delighted in taking his father's place, in living his dreams, in succeeding when he had failed. His mother had seemed not to notice his success. Socrates had been disappointed and puzzled by the lack of reaction on the part of the only audience that he wished to please. For a few years, he had indulged in the luxury of sending money to his parents. He knew, in retrospect, that he had done so, not out of filial obligation, but to show them that he had money to spare and perhaps to make them feel the weight of his youthful power.

Then had come the whirlwind: his first love affair, his first ship, his first million, his first wife. What could this old woman understand of his triumphs? How could she understand the man in the black suit whom she insisted on treating as a child? How could anyone who lived as she did imagine the heights to which he had risen? After his first successes, he had begun to consider his family as a weight around his neck. They were a ballast, dragging him downward—especially when, in moments of uncertainty, Socrates wondered whether, like Icarus, he had not climbed too high. And now, after all these years, he was here. His fate still depended on the whim of this old peasant woman, the very memory of whom he had tried to eradicate from his life. Why had he not, like so many other men, been orphaned at birth!

"Get out!"

"For the last time—"

"Get out, I say!" The old woman picked up a sturdy branch and waved it at him. "Don't come back! If I die before you, I forbid you to follow my coffin! My curse is on you!"

Socrates paled. A dozen retorts sprang to his lips, but he could not bring himself to utter them. It would have relieved him enormously to be able to heap insults upon her, but he could not speak. He turned on his heel and strode out into the street. Now he would have to wait for several hours more, until he reached Kallenberg's house in London that evening, before knowing what to expect.

People said many things about Raphael Dun, but no one said that he was not handsome. Tall, slender, his hair gently graying, Raphael had an animal grace about him that drew women to him almost against their will. At thirty-three, he still retained a seductive youthfulness, a studied disarray, about him. At times he wondered how long he could continue to sustain the illusion. Now, standing nude before the vast mirror in his room at the Ritz, he wondered again.

Raphael had always been fascinated by palaces, above all, by that in which he now lived on the Place Vendôme in Paris. Whenever his gambling losses made it impossible for him to live there, he could not bear to be far away, and he would take a small studio on the fourth floor of a modest building in the rue Cambon, just opposite the Bar Bleu. In better times, he had only to ask the Ritz to send a porter for his bags, and, simply by changing streets, he changed worlds.

His identification papers described Raphael as a "journalist," but he was neither a reporter nor a photographer, although he had dabbled in both professions with middling success. He was a polymorphous man, something of a flatterer, a man-about-town whose lack of occupation had rendered him indispensable in a social milieu as polymorphous as he, a milieu in which a certain vagueness was *de rigueur* and in which one did not mention what one was able to do, but only, with a laugh, what one was not able to do. And this, it was generally agreed, meant that one could do anything at all.

Raph's whole life was founded on such ambiguities. He came from a family of tradesmen, jewelers. He himself had never practiced that trade, of course, but he concealed his bourgeois origins as though they were a loathsome disease, out of respect for the sensibilities of his friends who might have been shocked at his modest origins. He had often wondered how he had managed to escape the family trap, and he had never been able to give himself a candid answer. He simply did not know. It was luck, perhaps, combined with an infallible instinct for making exactly the right acquaintance at exactly the right moment. His most superficially spontaneous gestures were calculated with mathematical precision, and every smile, wink and handshake were weighed and bestowed as though they had been doled out by a computer. For Raph, the world consisted of two groups of people: those who could be useful and those who could not. He made a systematic attempt to cultivate only the former. And since he was not burdened with specialized talents, other than a flair for poker, he had made an enviable reputation for himself as a social arbiter. When there was a new film, people always asked, "What does Raph Dun think of it?"

Raph's headquarters were in New York, his watering place was Acapulco, the city he loved most was Rome, and his birthplace was Paris.

It had begun when Raph was sixteen and preparing to follow in his father's footsteps. Then, one day, there had been an accident in the street outside the shop. An expensive automobile had crashed into the back of a delivery truck. Raph immediately recognized the driver of the automobile, despite the blood on her face: Clara Marlowe, the world-famous actress. An ambulance arrived, and the attendants loaded the victim into the vehicle. It was said in the street that despite all the blood, the lady was not seriously injured, only blind drunk.

Raph had not known it at the time, but the accident marked the turning point of his life. An hour later two handsome, confident young men arrived at the shop and introduced themselves as reporters from *France-Soir*. They asked Raph—whose name at the time was not Raphael Dun, but Paul Gueffier—for details of the accident. "Come have a drink with us," they said, "and you can tell us all about it."

They had gone to a bar where, over whiskey—Raph's first taste of it—they had extracted all the information they required. "You have a good eye," they told him before leaving. "You'd make a good newspaperman. Well, we have to go. We're expected at Cannes tonight."

That was all it had taken. Thereafter, when his father scolded him for his preoccupied air while serving customers, Raph retorted with lofty words about his "bent" for journalism.

"Are you through admiring yourself?"

The question brought Raph back to earth. He had forgotten about her. Without turning, he glanced at her in the mirror. She was stretched out nude on the rumpled bed, a statuesque blond, in her mid-twenties, a fine chain of gold around her waist and another, smaller, around her left ankle, her body too perfect to be really exciting. They had been sleeping together for three days, but since both were in love with themselves, neither had been able to take full advantage of the other.

"Why don't you get dressed, sweetheart?"

"My name is Ingeborg. Not 'sweetheart.'"

It was the most difficult moment of a relationship. It was time to part company, without either partner knowing quite how to go about it. Raph began gently enough. "Your husband is going to be worried about you," he said.

"Why?" She laughed. "He knows I'm with you."

"Still, you haven't been out of the hotel for three days."

"You managed to get out for a whole day."

"My work—"

"What work?"

"I told you, I had to go to Greece."

"Do you expect me to believe that?"

Raph shrugged. They were all alike.

"Show me your passport," she demanded.

"If you like."

He got it from his suitcase and handed it to her. She examined the customs seals.

"Now do you believe me?"

"Was she pretty?"

"I won't dignify that with an answer."

He smiled at the thought of the old woman he was supposed to have visited the day before, in an impossible place, a village lost in the wilds. Instead, he had chosen to remain in Athens, where friends had organized a most extraordinary game of strip poker. An obscure associate, a native, had been dispatched in his place and, by all accounts, had acquitted himself perfectly in all respects, returning with information whose value he did not suspect. Dun had paid him most generously out of his own pocket and everyone had been content.

The young woman misread his smile. "You find my question amusing? You steal me from my husband, lock me in the Ritz, and the next day fly off to Greece to meet another woman, and you have the nerve to smile?"

This time Raph laughed openly. "Ingeborg, you're ridiculous. Women are really extraordinary creatures. As soon as a man leaves you for a few hours, you assume that he's meeting another woman."

"You said yourself that you were meeting another woman."

"Yes. But a very old woman. And it was business. In fact, I didn't even see her."

"You run off a few hours after we meet to visit an old woman, and it's part of your job? You must think I'm an idiot."

Raph hesitated between anger and laughter. His sense of humor won out. He threw himself across the bed and said, "Listen, I swear to you that she was at least eighty."

"Eighty? Is she your rich old aunt?"

"Yes, something like that—only better."

"Are you her heir?"

"I'm afraid not. But I expect to get something out of her when the time comes."

"When will you know?"

"Tonight, maybe."

"She's going to die tonight?"

"Die? Where did you get that idea?"

"But you said— Well, explain it to me again."

"I can't tell you any more right now. Seriously, sweetheart, it's a secret."

"I guess I'm condemned to spend my life with a man of mystery," Ingeborg sighed.

Raph felt a touch of panic. "Condemned to spend my life," she had said. At precisely nine o'clock that evening, wearing his new Cardin dinner jacket (three fittings under the eye of the master himself), he must be in London, at the fabulous Kallenberg House, the opulence of which put Buckingham Palace in the shade. Meanwhile, how was he to get rid of Ingeborg? He had promised that they would have dinner at Maxim's that night.

She read his thoughts. "How do you want me to dress tonight?" she asked.

There was no way out. "Ingeborg," he began, "we'll have to change it to tomorrow evening. I can't tonight. I have to leave for London, in two hours."

"For London?"

"Yes, London."

"Another old woman?"

"Listen, it has something to do with what we were just talking about. I'm supposed to spend the evening at Kallenberg's—"

"Take me with you."

She must be out of her mind, Raph told himself, aghast. The most beautiful women in the world would be there, and the wealthiest, bearing the most resounding titles. And this little tramp wanted to be invited, to join that splendid gathering, to move in that exalted circle—a circle into which Raph had worked so hard to be admitted. It was too much.

"Look, be a good girl and get dressed, will you, sweetheart?"

She turned on him with a ferocity of which he had not thought her capable. "Raphie," she spat out, "let's see which one of us is really the sweetheart. If I was good for you in bed, I'm good enough for your friends. Don't try to argue with me. I've made up my mind. I'm going with you."

"That's enough," Raph replied icily. "I've tried to be nice, but I can see that I was wrong. So kindly get your ass out of my room. Now!"

"That's your final word?"

"That's it."

"All right." She got out of bed and began arranging her hair before the mirror.

That was easier than I thought it would be, Raph thought and congratulated himself. She was furious, of course, and that was to be regretted, for Raph prided himself on keeping on good terms with his former mistresses. But it couldn't be helped. He watched her finish her hair. A superb body, there was no doubt about it.

His amused admiration turned to alarm as Ingeborg walked toward the door, still nude.

"Where do you think you're going?"

"I'm leaving. That's what you want, isn't it?" Then she opened the door and vanished into the hallway. A surge of panic sent Raph in pursuit. He looked down the corridor and saw Ingeborg walking casually, as poised as though she were fully clothed. It was a potential disaster. Raph was well known at the Ritz, and the management tended to overlook the fact that his bills were often not paid until months after they were presented. He could not afford a scandal at this point.

He hurried after her, whispering her name as loudly as he dared. "Ingeborg! Ingeborg!" As though in a dream, he seemed unable to catch up to her. She maintained the distance between them, her lovely posterior moving in the same steady, stately rhythm as her long legs. Then the dream became a nightmare. Down the corridor, bearing a tray of food, came Marcel, the floor waiter. Simultaneously, Ingeborg reached the elevator and pressed the button.

Marcel, a servant of the old school, was magnificent. He walked past Ingeborg without even glancing in her direction, and he greeted Raph with his usual air of deference: "Is there something wrong, Monsieur Dun? May I be of service?"

It was then that Raph realized he was wearing only a robe. With a shrug of despair, he pointed silently to the naked woman waiting for the elevator.

"Do not concern yourself any further, Monsieur Dun. I will take care of it."

But it was too late. The elevator door slid open, and Ingeborg, without deigning to look at the two men whispering in the corridor, entered the car.

"Madame! Madame!" Marcel shouted, hurriedly depositing his tray on the floor.

The door closed noiselessly.

"I'll try to get her in the lobby," Marcel shouted to Raph, and then plunged down the service stairway.

To himself more than to the waiter, who was no longer within earshot, Raph said, "Something to cover her with. She'll need something to wear. . . ."

Suddenly terrified at the prospect of having to explain a nude Ingeborg to the management, Raph ran into his room, hastily pulled on pants and a sweater, seized the suitcase which had been packed for his trip to London, and followed Marcel's lead down the service staircase. He would take refuge in his studio in the rue Cambon until the impending storm had blown over. He had no intention of allowing Ingeborg's madness to interfere with the evening at Kallenberg's house.

Little Spiro sat in the yard of his house, under an olive tree, cracking almonds. He held a jar of honey on his knees. To his right were the unshelled nuts; to his left, those he had already shelled. When there were enough of the latter, he would use a stick to stir them into the honey. He looked up, suddenly aware of three simultaneous phenomena: there were red ants on the side of the honey jar; there was a green lizard basking in the sun on a rock less than three yards from where he was sitting; and there was the sound of an automobile engine growing steadily louder. It had been three months since he had seen an automobile, and now this was the third one in twenty-four hours. That was not even counting the two helicopters (his uncle, who had been in the navy, had told him what they were) he had seen the day before. In great excitement, Spiro threw the shelled almonds into the honey, set the jar down under the olive tree, and rushed to the edge of the rocky cliff. Three hundred feet below, he saw the automobile moving up the slanting mountain roadway. This time he could not see who was inside. The day before, he had twice witnessed the arrival of strangers who had come down from the sky in helicopters and climbed into automobiles. The cars had come to the village. Awhile later they had returned to the same spot below, the helicopters had retrieved their passengers and disappeared into the sun. His uncle's information had been limited to the nature and function of helicopters. Beyond that, he had nothing to say; indeed, he had ordered Spiro to forget what he had seen. Now Spiro watched the car until it vanished from sight. When he returned to his almonds and honey, he found the jar filled with ants.

Lena Satrapoulos glanced covertly at Mark. They had not spoken for the past ten minutes, each of them pretending to be totally absorbed by the food on their plates. Lena, out of habit, had removed her left shoe under the table, but Mark's foot had not moved to touch hers. Through the door which opened onto the terrace, Lena could see the Hôtel de la Monnaie beyond the Seine, set into perspective by the automobiles moving across the Quai du Louvre. The calls of exotic birds floated into the restaurant from the cages of the shop next door.

Lena searched desperately for a way to break through the wall of hostility which had sprung up between them, running from the mustard jar to the base of the bottle of Château-Laffite and ending at Mark's lighter. How strange, she reflected, that the same objects in a different context took on a totally different meaning. Her husband's silence had signified that she was free to live a life of her own. But that of her lover caused her heart to fill with love for him.

She remembered perfectly the first time she had seen Socrates Satrapoulos. It had been almost four years after the death of her father, and she had still been a child. She had gone into her mother's office in search of one of her schoolbooks. There was a man sitting in one of the enormous armchairs reserved for visitors. He was smoking a cigar, and his black shoes were the shiniest she had ever seen. He had risen. A small man, with strange, rust-colored hair, and a nose—not a ridiculous nose, but a nose completely out of the ordinary. Gentlemen of forty with big noses, were beyond her range of interests. She made a brief curtsy, took her book, and returned to her English governess. (Governesses in Greece were always English, since English was the language in which it was easiest to count.) If anyone had told Lena that she would marry this strange little man, she would have laughed.

Lena had later pieced together a part of what had happened from what Satrapoulos himself told her, a part by comparing that version to the one related by her own mother and the rest by guesswork. After she left the room, Satrapoulos had remained standing, motionless, lost in thought. Then, suddenly coming to himself and embarrassed by the puzzlement on Medea Mikolofides' face, he had asked sharply, "How old is your daughter?"

"Thirteen. Why do you ask?"

"I—I find her ravishing," the Greek had stammered.

Lena's mother had quickly changed the subject.

The following day Satrapoulos, contrary to his custom, signed a contract with Medea Mikolofides which was not to his obvious advantage. When Medea did not query his motives, he volunteered: "You know, I am far from unaware of where my true interests lie in this matter—"

Medea interrupted him with a gesture. She was the richest shipowner in the world, a woman accustomed to command. It was intolerable that a newcomer, no matter how talented, should presume to address her with such insolence. "Explain yourself," she ordered in a harsh tone.

Instantly, Satrapoulos was transformed into a model of humility. With much stuttering, he explained that he was stricken with love for little Helena.

"Do you realize that she is thirteen?" Medea asked, shocked. "And you—you—"

"I know," the Greek replied. "I am thirty-eight. But in four years, she will be seventeen, and I will be only forty-two. And that is not so terrible a difference. I ask only one thing: that I be allowed to wait for her."

The widowed Medea had sensed his sincerity. Gently, she attempted to make him realize that such a proposal was unthinkable; that she could not decide such a matter alone; that Helena herself, when she was of age, would have to be consulted.

But Satrapoulos persisted, unshaken by her arguments. Finally, Medea, touched by his determination, said, "Listen. Let us speak frankly. I have three daughters, and the other two are as beautiful as Lena. If you want to marry into our family, then choose one of Lena's sisters. Not Melina, of course, since she is only fifteen. But why not Irene, who is nineteen?"

The Greek shook his head slowly. "Madame Mikolofides, I will wait as long as I must, but I will wait, nonetheless, until Helena can become my wife."

He had waited four years. Then they were married. Lena, meanwhile, had turned into a breathtaking beauty, although she seemed totally unaware of it. The delicate bones of her face, the transparent skin, the huge eyes, the tiny, rectilinear nose were the incarnation of that perfection which, five centuries before the birth of Christ, anonymous Greek artists had conceived and then engraved on terracotta. And Satrapoulos, conscious of having acquired the rarest jewel of his life, was transformed into the perfect husband, a man who was at once a father and a lover.

The marriage lasted one year, before nature reasserted itself. Between Lena and the Greek, there was henceforth a telephone—on the dinner table, next to the bed, even on vacation. There were sudden trips to the four corners of the globe, each more hurried, more demanding, and more unbearable than the last. Lena, who had become accustomed to Satrapoulos' tenderness, now felt naked, abandoned. She had passed, directly from the arms of her father into the bed of her husband, and she had considered the Greek a second father, who, incidentally, made love to her. Now she was an orphan once more, despite a pregnancy which had begun two years after their marriage, at a time when she saw Socrates Satrapoulos only occasionally—between a meeting in Cuba on market conditions and a board of directors' meeting on the Saudi Arabian coast. To her everlasting astonishment, she had given birth to twins, a boy and a girl, whom she named Achilles and Maria. She was not only an orphan, but also a child-mother. Thereafter Lena withdrew into herself, only vaguely conscious of her offspring's existence. She spent most of her time alone, listening to phonograph records, as isolated by her fortune, her mother's fame, and her husband's increasing celebrity, as if she were on a desert isle.

Before her marriage, her sisters had spoken jokingly of her "fiancé," touching their noses meaningfully and then bursting into shrieks of laughter. They had been right. It was only a game. Her marriage was a game, and her children, a bad joke. She had met Mark during a cruise, a year after her sister Irene had married Kallenberg. She had already seen him several times, in the semidarkness of the room where her mother occasionally screened the latest American films.

Unfortunately, Mark's wife, Isabelle, kept him under constant surveillance. Even when she played bridge—and she was a fiend for it—she played with one eye on her cards and the other on her husband. She called attention to her exclusive proprietorship constantly using "we" in place of "I": "We have a headache, so we'd better lie down," and "We hate Modigliani, but we adore Cranach." As though the proprietary "we" were not sufficient to establish ownership, Isabelle insisted on always placing Mark's devotion in evidence. "My husband absolutely *insists* upon accompanying me to the bathroom." She giggled. "He's such a child. When he's away, anywhere in the world, he telephones me several times a day—that is, if for some extraordinary reason I haven't accompanied him."

Worse yet, in her certainty that she could not be dethroned, Isabelle made a practice of pointing out to Mark, with appropriate commentaries, women whom she thought he found attractive. And Mark, poor idiot that he was, toed the line drawn by Isabelle without suspecting that her maternal solicitude and constant hovering would castrate him more surely than the keenest scalpel.

Lena felt deep pity for Mark. She saw him as a helpless captive in the clutches of an ogre who took advantage of his gentle disposition to compensate for her own inadequacies. She also felt something else. Although she could not explain the impulse, Lena sometimes experienced a physical need to touch Mark. It was so strong that when she spoke to him, she could not resist patting him on the hand or, sometimes, on the thigh. These were innocent gestures, unnoticed except by women like Isabelle, women who were expert in discerning concupiscence in other women. Isabelle, indeed, had caught the scent of lust in the air at the very beginning of the cruise aboard the *Pegasus*, but she was unable to bring herself to believe that this little bourgeoise, attractive as she might be, was a serious rival. Lena, to her, was too insignificant and too colorless to make an impression on Mark. And Socrates Satrapoulos, complaisant as any husband, saw nothing. He was too certain of his place in the world to believe that any man would dare try to take what was his.

On the first morning of the cruise, Lena was coming out of her cabin as Mark appeared on deck from a dip in the sea, his lithe, muscular body dripping water. Lena would never forget the smile he gave her. (At the time, Isabelle's attention was engaged by a noted bore whom she had fleeced the night before at the card table.) The smile offered more than a promise. It offered a certainty. Soon they would be together.

It happened on the fifth day of the cruise, off the Greek islands. Isabelle was on the aft deck, playing for heavy stakes against a famous statesman. She was absorbed in her game, but at ease, since she had just seen Mark swimming alone near a rubber raft to port of the *Pegasus*. Satrapoulos was in his cabin, his telephone to his ear, his files clutched to his chest. Neither of them saw Lena slip into the water on the starboard side and swim silently around the yacht. When she reached the bow, she raised her hand and waved at Mark. He waved back, silently inviting her to join him. She began swimming slowly in his direction. Then she appeared to change her mind and swam along the hull of the yacht until she had reached its prow. There she waited in the shadows, floating lazily on her back. Mark, meanwhile, was allowing his raft to drift so as to remove himself from Isabelle's line of vision. The operation was carried out in perfect silence, as was its sequel. When Mark was close enough to Lena to touch her, she dived. At a depth of fifteen feet, she righted herself and looked toward the surface. Above her, Mark's body seemed almost translucent, surrounded by an aureole of sunlight refracted mysteriously in the slow swell of the sea and the foam of the waves. With a thrust of her legs, Lena rose toward that luminescent halo, forgetting that she was married, that her husband was in the vessel above her head, a small man enclosed in the womb of his own yacht, surrounded by cunning seamen, bored guests, and legitimate spouses. No one, nothing existed; nothing, other than the glistening form toward which Lena moved.

She broke the surface next to Mark's raft and laid her hand next to his on the raft. They were under the forward deck of the yacht, in a blue-tinted shadow, weightless, moving gently in the warm water. Mark's hand came to rest lightly on Lena's shoulder, then moved down her back. She felt it slide into the trunks of her bathing suit. Then his fingers were inside her. She gasped, clutching at the raft to steady herself. Mark pressed himself to her, and she felt his organ hard against her back. Orgasm came with an intensity which she had not dreamed possible. It lasted only a minute, but it was so total and all-encompassing that it seemed to contain the explosive dilation of all the time already lived and of all the years yet to be lived. Now she was certain: God existed, and he had Mark's face. Now she could die without regret. She had experienced all things, lived all things, learned all things. She clung limply to the raft, nodding feebly when Mark's whisper came to her through a fog: "I'll signal when the coast is clear." He disappeared noiselessly beneath the surface.

Mark had been on deck for some time, briskly toweling himself under Isabelle's approving eye, when Lena climbed wearily aboard and made her way to her cabin. After locking the door, she threw herself across the bed and slept.

There had been other times since then, but never had the ecstasy of that first encounter been equaled. Mark was able to arouse her with a facility which alarmed her, but her pleasure had always been tempered by the realization that he was generous neither with his time nor with his body. When a rendezvous had been arranged, he seemed to take pleasure in discovering obstacles to it, and he delighted in postponing it upon the slightest pretext.

Last night again, using the excuse of Kallenberg's dinner in London, she had flown to Paris with the intention of surprising Mark. She arrived, joyful at the prospect of the night they would spend together. But nothing had gone as planned. She had been unable to reach Mark at his house at Saint-Cloud. She had telephoned twice, and on both occasions Isabelle had answered. Lena had put down the receiver without a word. At dawn, after calling several nightclubs in a vain attempt to locate Mark, she swallowed three sleeping pills and fell into a restless coma. She awoke several hours later, exhausted.

Finally, at noon, she reached Mark at a studio where he was working on the dubbing of an American film. He seemed pleased neither at the sound of her voice nor at the knowledge that she was in Paris. Finally, almost reluctantly, he consented to meet her for lunch, explaining that he was very, very busy and that he must, without fail, be back at the studio by three o'clock. Lena had masked her disappointment under a bantering tone. She would have endured any humiliation rather than forego the pleasure of seeing him. When they met, Mark was distant, even brusque, despite her efforts to draw him out. It occurred to Lena that he might be upset at the two anonymous telephone calls to Saint-Cloud which Isabelle had no doubt reported to him.

"Are you angry?" she asked.

Mark stared at the table, drawing designs with the point of his knife. Finally, without looking up, he answered in a hollow voice: "No."

"Well then, what's wrong?"

"Nothing."

"You're not pleased to see me?"

"Yes, yes, of course."

"Well?"

He looked at her. "Well, what?" he asked harshly.

"I don't know what's wrong," Lena said softly. "I don't understand. I came to Paris especially to see you. I spent a good part of the night trying to find you. And now you're angry with me. Have I done something wrong?"

"I would be grateful if you'd let me know beforehand the next time you plan to come to Paris."

"I was only able to get away at the last minute. I wasn't even sure that I would be able to come. I thought I would surprise you."

"Well, you succeeded in surprising me. And I'd appreciate it if, in the future, you would not, as you say, spend a good part of the night trying to find me."

"Is that what's bothering you?"

"Yes, that's it. I work for a living. I work hard. I need my rest."

"Did she say something?"

"Of course she said something. You called twice and hung up on her twice. Did you think she wouldn't notice?"

"You're afraid of her, aren't you?"

"I don't give a damn about her. I just want to keep her off my back, and you're not making it any easier."

"What did you expect me to do? I had to get in touch with you—"

"Why? How can I arrange to see you if you don't even let me know that you're coming?"

Lena made an effort to preserve her calm. Nothing ever went as one expected it to. So much the worse. She had only one goal, and that was to get Mark to make love to her. Her single thought was to hold him in her arms, to have him to herself for the remainder of the afternoon. The chauffeur from the Paris residence would pick her up at the Plaza at 6 P.M. to drive her to the airport. It was now 2:10. She had almost four hours before leaving for London. She would spend them with Mark, no matter the cost to her pride. "Mark," she said softly, "you're perfectly right. I was wrong and thoughtless. I should have let you know I was coming. Don't be angry. I did it only because I've missed you so."

"All right, all right."

"I thought Isabelle was staying at the Eden Roc."

"Well, she's not. You found that out last night."

In the face of Mark's continued hostility, Lena made a final desperate effort. "I'm sorry, Mark. I won't say anything more about it. The only thing that matters is that we're together, with a whole afternoon before us—"

He looked at her sharply. "What whole afternoon? I have to get back to the studio."

"Surely it won't make any difference if you don't go back this afternoon."

"Come on, Lena. You know how we work. I'm not alone. I work with a crew. If one of us is not there, the others are stymied."

"Well, telephone them—"

"You're joking."

"—tell them you're tired. . . ."

"Listen to me, Lena." Mark spoke with the exaggerated patience that doctors use in addressing a sick child. "Sometimes you act as though you're twelve years old. I have to explain everything to you, and still you don't understand. Now listen. I am not married to Socrates Satrapoulos. I am not a billionaire. I am rich, but in a perfectly ordinary way. I have money, but I must work for it. Now, can you understand that?"

"No. I don't understand anything."

"I mean, how can you think that I am a possession of yours, to be picked up and put down at your sole convenience?"

"What about her? Aren't you a possession of hers?"

"Helena, Helena"—he called her Helena only when he was truly angry—"why don't you go back to your hotel, make yourself beautiful, and enjoy the evening at your brother-in-law's party. Then, on your way back from London, call me. I'm sure we'll both see things much more clearly in a couple of days."

Lena knew that she had lost. Her need of him would remain unsatisfied. Her desperation was transformed into rage and resentment. "In two days? Add those two days to all the others that I've spent waiting for a sign from you so that I could come running. How many days does that add up to? Do you think I can go on like this? Do you?"

Mark looked at his watch. "I'm sorry, but I have to get back to the studio. They're waiting for me."

"So they're waiting for you, too," Lena said, her voice rising. "The whole world is waiting for you."

Mark glanced around the room in alarm. His work in films had made him a celebrity. His face was known around the world, especially in Paris. If anyone recognized him, if a single informer telephoned a newspaperman, if a line were printed about this ridiculous scene, he would be lost. Isabelle would make his life a hell on earth.

Lena's voice had climbed to a near shriek. "Well, go home! Go home to Mama! After all, you're married to her!"

Lena had drawn blood. Mark, losing control of himself, shouted back, "Then why don't you go home to Papa?"

Before Mark realized what was happening, Lena stood, upsetting the wine bottle, rushed out of the restaurant onto the sidewalk, and started across the street. Simultaneously, a few hundred yards away, a traffic light changed from red to green. A moment later, brakes were screeching, horns blaring, curses shouted. Lena, instinctively, leaped back onto the sidewalk a second before she was run down by a large truck. Mark found her there, surrounded by a crowd of curious onlookers, an expression of utter ferocity on her face. She saw him as he drew near. "Don't come near me! Don't touch me!" she screamed, her eyes moving in a frantic search for a means of escape. Then Mark was upon her, struggling to hold her and whispering hoarsely, "Lena, Lena! Relax! Please!"

With a violent jerk, Lena freed herself and ran into the pet shop adjoining the restaurant. Mark followed her, and he, the proprietor, and a clerk watched in alarm as Lena seized a hooked wooden pole used to raise and lower the shop's awning, and began swinging it in a wide circle. Mark, in an attempt to snatch it from her grasp, collided with a large tank. A second later, the shop was awash in an assortment of tropical fish ("our specialty") from the waters of the Indian Ocean. The customers in the shop stood, transfixed in astonishment, as the water swirled around their feet, and Lena, raised to new heights of fury by the sight of their stricken faces, began using her pole against anyone within reach, the proprietor as well as Mark, the customers as well as the clerk.

Finally, Mark was able to grasp one end of the pole and jerk it from her hands. But Lena had not yet finished. Frantically, she began opening cages. In a few seconds, the shop was filled with barking, yelping dogs. These were followed by two gray foxes and a crowd of small Malaysian monkeys. A flock of doves filled the air while, below, innumerable hamsters, rabbits, white rats and chickens scurried across the floor and out onto the sidewalk, where they were greeted by the screams of mingled delight and horror from the crowd gathered to witness the spectacle.

There was a moment of near silence as Lena emerged from the shop and disappeared into the crowd. No one tried to stop her.

Mark came out of the shop an instant later. As he did so, a tiny old lady approached him timidly and touched his sleeve. "Monsieur Costa?" she whispered.

Mark glanced at her.

"Monsieur Costa? Mark Costa? I've seen all of your films. . . ."

Mark did not answer. The woman held out a tattered notebook and a ball-point pen. "Would you give me your autograph? It's not for me, of course. It's for my granddaughter."

[2]

The boy passed his hand over the girl's thigh. The sail luffed as the tiny boat began to turn into the wind.

"Stop!" the girl said and laughed. She moved her leg an inch or so. "Those sailors are watching us."

"Let them watch. They're just jealous." Nonetheless, to the girl's chagrin, he replaced his hand on the tiller. "Look at that boat," he said admiringly. "What I wouldn't give to have something like that!"

"What would you do with it?"

"I swear I'd never set foot on land. I'd spend my whole life sailing around the world."

"And what about me? You'd leave me behind, I suppose."

He laughed. "Sure. Without even looking back." He moved his hand to her thigh again.

They had rented the sailboat a half hour earlier. Now, a half mile from the beach, they had a clear view of the boat riding at anchor in the open water. It seemed so perfect as to be unreal.

"Let's go closer."

"All right."

"How do you suppose people like that get their money? What kind of work do they do?"

"Work?" the boy replied. "People who own boats like that don't work. Other people do their work for them. All they do is eat caviar for breakfast, drink champagne, and give orders to the crew."

"How many people does it take to run a boat like that?"

"That boat? I guess it must be two hundred and fifty or three hundred feet long—probably forty men."

"That many!"

"Sure. A boat that size doesn't run itself. When I'm rich—"

"You! You don't get to be a millionaire by cutting people's hair."

"The guy who owns that boat had to start somewhere, too. When he was my age, he was probably a barber or something like that."

Now they could see the deck perfectly. Several sailors in white uniforms were leaning against the rail watching them.

"Can we go closer?"

"Why not? The ocean's public property, isn't it? Besides, I want to see her name."

When they were within fifty yards of the yacht, a voice boomed across the water: "What do you want?"

Involuntarily, the boy let the sail luff. Then, angry at himself for allowing himself to be intimidated, he shouted back, "What business is it of yours?"

"Get out of here!"

"Let's go," the girl pleaded.

"I'll be damned," the boy said angrily. "Who the hell do you think you are?" he shouted toward the yacht. "This is public property!"

There was a hurried conference on the deck of the *Pegasus*; then two sailors moved toward the gangplank. A moment later a white launch pulled away from the yacht and headed toward the sailboat.

"Come on, let's go!" the girl said.

The boy forced a laugh. "What can they do to us? Do you think they're going to torpedo our boat?"

"Let's go!"

The boy did not answer. His attention was focused on the launch, which was now twenty feet off the sailboat's starboard and moving slowly parallel to it.

"You're right, friend!" one of the sailors yelled. "The water is public property!"

With that, the launch suddenly accelerated and shot ahead of the sailboat. When it had attained full speed, it turned and headed straight for the small craft. The boy and girl watched in terror as it bore down on them.

"They're going to ram us!" the boy exclaimed. And, as the girl screamed, he threw his arms around her and, in the same motion, jumped into the water, dragging her with him.

The launch did not turn until it was almost upon the sailboat. Then at the last second it veered, raising a wake which caught the tiny craft broadside and upset it.

"You see?" one of the sailors shouted as the launch headed back toward the *Pegasus*. "Didn't I tell you the water was public property? Enjoy it!"

"Those bastards," the boy said through his teeth. "They could have drowned us." Then, with one arm around the sobbing girl, he swam toward the overturned sailboat.

Wanda was playing a game with herself before the only mirror which she had not yet broken, that in the bathroom. It was a strange game. She would move slowly past the mirror, in profile. The point of the game was to spy herself in the glass without turning her head, then to shut her eyes at the first vague glimpse of her own body. Occasionally, she varied the game by walking backward toward the mirror, then spinning around and closing her eyes at the precise moment her white form became visible in the glass.

After several minutes of these unrewarding maneuvers, she clenched her fists and bit her lips with the effort of forcing herself to stand still before the mirror to take a good long look at her reflection. She could not bring herself to do it. Her aversion was stronger than her will.

She returned to the bedroom and threw herself on the bed, facedown, sobbing, beating the pillows and the mattress with her closed fists in a rage mixed with tears. She was wearing only a white dressing gown, embroidered with a single letter: *P*, for *Pegasus*.

An hour earlier Wanda had sent her maid ashore on a transparent pretext. She had foreseen the intense depression that would take possession of her. Socrates had left her on board, alone, and there was no chance of escape. These seizures had recurred regularly since her childhood, and neither success, nor wealth, nor the perpetual homage paid her had a deterrent effect on their onset. Invariably they left her empty, ravaged, a stranger to herself. Her peerless body, which had aroused the desire of the millions who had seen her dance, now seemed an object of revulsion. She could not bear the sight of herself in a mirror.

Wanda did not particularly like herself. Rather, she hated herself, and everyone who did not hate her. The more people told her she was beautiful, the more intense became her wish to hide herself, even to die, as though to escape the crush of an intolerable insult. Of the twenty films that she had made, she had consented to see only one. And on that occasion she had fled from the screening room in terror.

Since then she had never seen herself on the screen and as far as possible had refused to allow others to see her in life. She shunned public exposure to the point where she refused to walk the streets or to enter shops. For years, journalists had lain in wait for her outside the various hotels in which she stayed according to her whim or to the seasons. She had not danced for many years, yet her legend survived and would probably survive until she was in her grave.

Now she was near fifty (that, at least, was the age indicated by her passport), and the thought was sufficient to send her into a fresh paroxysm of tears. Ironically, she was terrified of losing that physical perfection which had been the source of all her unhappiness. She could not understand why, just at the point when time was prepared to gift her with a new appearance, she wished so desperately to retain the old.

Finally Wanda rose to her feet, let the gown fall to the floor, and returned resolutely to the bathroom, determined to know the worst. She approached the mirror. Yet at the last second, in spite of herself, she averted her eyes. Slowly, she returned to the bedroom and picked up the one object which had become an integral part of her public image: her heavy sunglasses. She put them on, patting her hair over her ears to repair the disorder, and started toward the bathroom again, only to stop once more. It was useless. Again, she was filled with rage. She crumpled to the floor, writhing as though in agony. Finally, she rolled onto her back, raised her legs, and slowly brought her feet toward her shoulders, until her knees were on either side of her face, framing it and touching the floor. She remained in that position for a long while, motionless.

Gradually, her body seemed to come to life again. She shivered, and her legs returned to their normal position. At last she rose to her feet and once more moved toward the bathroom. This time she walked directly to the mirror with her eyes closed, imagining what she would see: a tall, bony woman, the whiteness of her body accentuated by the absolute blackness of the pubic area, her eyes hidden by enormous sunglasses. She stood before the mirror, gathering the strength to open her eyes.

There was a knock at the door of the cabin. Wanda, her anger mingled with relief, turned from the mirror and opened her eyes.

The knock came again, now more insistently. She did not move. She bit her lips and pressed her hands against her ears. There was silence. Then the knocking again.

"What is it?" she shouted angrily.

"Your eggs, madame."

It was Ceyx, Socrates' personal servant, a man whom she both feared and hated without quite knowing why. Perhaps it was his equivocal air, his sly look. He watched her constantly as he served her. She could not bear him. Socrates had told her that in Greek mythology, Ceyx had been a man who, through love of his wife, Alcyone, had been transformed into a girl. If only that could happen to her, Wanda had thought. If only she could fly away.

"Leave them outside the door," she ordered.

She did not remember having asked for eggs. She waited in silence, hoping that the intruder would go away. He did not. Instead his voice insinuated itself into the cabin again. "Madame, they will be cold."

Wanda was certain that when Socrates was not aboard, the staff deliberately tortured her. "All right, all right," she shouted. "Come in." Nervously, she pulled the lapels of her dressing gown together.

Ceyx entered holding a tray. She searched his face for a hint of mockery which would enable her to complain to Socrates. There was none. The waiter's face was expressionless, his eyes neutral. How horrible it was to see him standing there, the tray in his hand, and to know that he was judging her. She was overcome by anger and anguish.

"Show me these famous eggs!" she demanded.

Ceyx raised the heavy silver cover.

"Look at them," Wanda spat. "The yolks are soft. You know I can't stand soft yolks!"

"Madame, the chef—"

"Get them out of here! I don't want soft yolks!"

The door opened behind Ceyx and Satrapoulos entered the cabin. At first, Wanda thought that he was exhausted, but when he spoke to Ceyx, she realized that he was all but exploding with fury.

"What's going on?" he demanded.

"I don't know, sir," Ceyx stammered. "Madame—the eggs—"

"Well, what about the eggs?"

"The yolks are soft," Wanda answered despairingly.

After the insults he had just sustained from his mother, the Greek was ready to vent his repressed fury on anyone who came within range. "Let me see," he ordered.

His face reddened as he examined the plate. "What's the meaning of this?" he shouted, his voice filling with the frustration and rage which he had been obliged to contain within himself for the past hour. "What am I paying you for? Have you looked at these eggs?"

"But, sir, the chef—"

"The chef! You can't mean there's a chef aboard! Isn't there anyone on this boat who can cook an egg?"

"Socrates, please," Wanda interjected. "It doesn't matter. I really don't want any eggs."

"Do you hear that?" Socrates screamed at Ceyx. "Madame Deemount cannot even eat the food that you serve her! What do you think this is? A hamburger joint?"

Since words alone could not relieve his anger, Socrates plunged his hand into the eggs and crushed them. The yolk and the oil dripped from his fingers, spotting the sleeve of his shirt. "Look at that!" he roared. "Do you call these things eggs?"

He waved his dripping hand before Ceyx's eyes, an inch from his nose. The man was certain that his employer's next act would be to smear his face with the eggs. Instead, Satrapoulos abruptly wiped his hand on his employee's white, starched jacket, covering it with oil and egg yolk. Ceyx glanced imploringly at Wanda, asking her to bear witness to the humiliation to which he was subjected so unjustly.

"To the galley!" the Greek roared.

He took Wanda by the hand, uncaring that she was not dressed, and pulled her out into the passageway. Ceyx followed in their wake. On deck, they passed several officers and seamen, who stared at them in covert astonishment but moved hurriedly out of the path of their enraged employer.

The Greek burst into the galley. "Who prepared these eggs for Madame Deemount?" he roared.

The chef, who had certain illusions of grandeur, waved aside his assistants and presented himself before the master. "I did, sir. Is something wrong?"

"Everything is wrong! When I hire a chef, I do not expect to have to teach him how to cook."

The chef, taken by surprise, gaped.

"All right," Socrates continued. "I want you to explain to me exactly how you prepared these eggs. Step by step. Go ahead!"

The chef scratched his head. "Well, it's very simple—"

"No, it is not simple! The simple dishes are the most difficult to prepare. Go on!"

"First, I take a round skillet into which I put two drops of oil. I heat the skillet—"

"How do you heat it?"

"Over medium heat."

"Go ahead."

"Then I break the eggs. Using a fork, I scoop the whites over the yolks. I leave the eggs on the fire for a minute; then I remove them and add salt and pepper."

There was a long silence. All eyes were on the Greek. His lips set in a small, bitter smile.

"No. No. I regret to have to tell you that you are talking nonsense. That is not the way to cook eggs."

Satrapoulos looked down at his black alpaca suit, then turned to one of the busboys. "You! Give me an apron."

The boy took one from a stack and handed it to his employer. The Greek tied the strings behind his back. Stamped across the skirt of the apron, in large letters, was the legend "I am a sweet baby." No one laughed.

Socrates took a small skillet from a row of pots and pans. Carefully, he turned on a burner on the gas stove, then adjusted the flame as low as possible, until it was barely visible.

"Give me two eggs."

Someone handed them to him.

"Butter!"

Holding the butter in his hand, Satrapoulos began his lecture. "First of all, you must never use oil with eggs. Use a pat of butter."

He dropped the butter into the skillet, then placed the skillet over the fire.

"When the fire is low," he continued, "the butter doesn't burn. It melts slowly, and it retains the taste of fresh butter."

Everyone watched fascinated.

"As soon as the butter has melted, remove the skillet from the fire. Then break the eggs into it. One, two. Now you add salt and pepper" —he glared at the chef—"not after the eggs are cooked, but before they are cooked. Then cover the skillet, and place it over very low heat."

He turned toward the chef. "And now, when I remove the eggs from the fire, the yolk will be firm and covered with a thin, white, translucent layer."

He removed the skillet from the stove, lifted the lid, and thrust the skillet toward the chef.

"Smell!" he ordered.

The delicate and appetizing aroma of fresh butter wafted through the galley.

"And that, gentlemen, is how one cooks eggs. Curnonski himself gave me the recipe." He looked at Wanda. "I hope you will enjoy them, my dear."

Satrapoulos removed his apron, then placed the eggs on a plate. He brushed aside Ceyx, who tried to take the plate. "Leave it there. I'll carry it myself."

He left the kitchen in great dignity, Wanda on his left arm and the plate of eggs on his right.

Peggy Nash-Belmont was in seventh heaven. In one hour, her chauffeur would drive her to Idlewild—actually not her own chauffeur, but her stepfather's, since she always shunned any outward display of wealth. Except for a few intimate friends, no one knew of her sumptous Park Avenue penthouse. She was determined not to give her co-workers cause to be envious, for envy was detrimental to good order in the office. For that reason, her office relationships were maintained on a purely professional basis, and Peggy rejected, gently but firmly, all attempts by her associates to cultivate her socially.

Of course, everyone knew that she had money. In New York, the name Nash-Belmont was practically synonymous with money. It symbolized the dynasty of bankers which, along with the Morgans and the Rockefellers, held financial America in the palms of their hands. And when her mother had divorced her father, twelve years before, it had been to marry into an equally eminent family, the Beckintoshes, whose members occupied two pages in the New York *Social Register*. There had been a Beckintosh on the *Mayflower*. Beckintoshes had fought in the Revolution and had subsequently served their country with distinction as statesmen and scholars.

Peggy's father, Christopher Nash-Belmont, was quite mad, of course, but he was the handsomest and most engaging madman on the American continent. Handsome as a god, he had always been surrounded by the attention and homage of women. Peggy's mother had captured him after he had managed to preserve his bachelorhood for thirty-seven years. Her strategy had been simplicity itself.

She had steadfastly refused to become his mistress, confident that she would one day be his wife.

At the time Janet and Christopher, both British subjects, had lived in London. Janet herself was the daughter of a prominent banker, and two years earlier she and her two sisters had formed the most striking trio among London's gilden youth. Their father had given them each a new Bentley, the three cars identical in all respects except for the horn. Doris' horn sounded on *do*; Janet's on *re*; and Juliet's on *mi*.

The wedding was the event of the year. Janet had had twelve bridesmaids, and her Molyneux wedding dress had a train twenty-five feet long. Two huge rooms had not sufficed to hold the gifts which arrived from all over the world, to say nothing of the thousand guests invited to the reception. The honeymoon began with Paris and continued through the capitals of Europe, leading eventually to the Bahamas and finally to New York. There the couple had been the lions of the season, and no hostess of repute would have dreamed of having a party without inviting Janet and Christopher.

When the time came to return to London, Janet had discovered that she was madly in love with New York. "Why don't we live here?" she asked Christopher. "You could open a new bank."

"Darling, you're incredible! I didn't dare suggest it myself!"

It had been that simple. They fell into each other's arms, and that very day they bought a splendid house just off Park Avenue. Two years later Peggy had been born. Janet, when she awoke at the hospital, had taken the child into her arms and cried out in horror, "What an ugly thing! She doesn't look like a baby at all. She looks like a little old woman. Do you think I've waited too long to have her?"

Since Janet had just celebrated her twenty-first birthday, the question provoked a gale of laughter among the assembled nurses and doctors.

At five, Peggy won her first horse race. At eight, she completed a book of poems of which the first part, in free verse, was a paean to nature and the second, in alexandrines, a declaration of love to her favorite pony, Jolly Beaver. At ten, she tasted the sorrows of love when a certain blue-eyed aviator dared throw her over to marry a horrid girl twelve years her senior. Despite such disappointments, her life had been a series of fairy tales set in sumptuous surroundings, with immaculate parks, smiling servants, long black automobiles driven by liveried chauffeurs, and blond, serene Austrian governesses.

Peggy's nurse was a Frenchwoman named Anne-Marie, and no one could say for certain whether the infant's first word had been spoken in French or in English, for she always claimed both as her mother tongue.

Her fourth year had been a difficult one. Her mother, after a three-week absence, returned home with a baby in her arms. Smiling happily, she said to Peggy, "Come and see your new sister. Her name is Patricia."

Peggy, whom no one had thought to inform of the event beforehand, came, stared at the infant for a moment and gave her mother an incredulous, accusatory look. Then, bursting into tears, she ran to her room. Her father had followed her. He attempted to explain that having a baby sister was the most wonderful thing that could happen to a little girl. But Peggy would have none of it, and Christopher retreated in defeat after having promised that Peggy should have a dog.

The very next day Peggy's "family," which had included Jolly Beaver and a raggedy-ann doll named Pamela, took in a new member: a black three-month-old Scottish terrier named Sammy. The only other change was that Pamela's name was changed to Patricia and that she was beaten daily.

As soon as Peggy learned to write, she began a daily journal in which she recorded her impressions of the world as well as caricatures of her governesses and tutors. At the same time, she devoured *Little Lord Fauntleroy* and *The Adventures of Tom Sawyer*. When she was eight, she mentioned to her mother that her favorite story was one about a man who threw himself over a cliff for the sake of his lady-love. After many questions, her mother had elicited the information that Peggy was reading Dostoevsky.

"Do you understand all the words?" Janet asked in astonishment.

"Yes. All except one: roulette."

Peggy was twelve, and had read *Gone with the Wind* four times, when the thunderbolt fell. Her parents were divorced. Peggy could not, or would not, understand what had happened. Two years later, when Janet married Arthur Erwin Beckintosh, Peggy politely presented her with a bouquet of flowers after the ceremony, then locked herself in her room and cried for twenty-four hours. When her eyes dried, she went to live with her mother and stepfather at Merrywood, the Beckintosh property on the banks of the Potomac in Virginia. Her summers were spent at Greenwood, in New England, sailing and lying on the deserted private beaches belonging to Arthur Erwin Beckintosh.

Heaven was on Sundays and school holidays when Peggy and Patricia visited their father. In their eyes, Christopher Nash-Belmont was a god who could create pleasure at a whim. He regarded it as his duty to worship all that his daughters worshiped, and he took it upon himself to teach them to love the things that he himself loved. The rule at his household was: do whatever you like. Better still, he encouraged the girls to do all the things that they were not allowed to do at their mother's house. They climbed trees, threw cream puffs at each other, rode their bicycles without touching the handlebars, and, as their governesses watched in horror, ate ice-cream cones five minutes before dinner.

The years had not diminished Christopher's passion for Peggy. Even now, his fabulous gifts were the talk of New York. And Arthur Erwin Beckintosh felt obliged, in self-defense, to rival Peggy's father in the extravagance of his own gifts to her. Peggy accepted all these with serenity, without really wanting them and without realizing that they had become indispensable to her. Yet, because she had received so much without once having had to ask, she had experienced an overwhelming desire to make something of herself, to do something independent of her name and her fortune.

Under the pseudonym of "Scarlett," in honor of her favorite heroine, she had entered an essay contest organized by *Harper's Bazaar*, which was intended, according to the publicity, "to favor the development of young talent," but which, in fact, aimed at nothing more than increasing the magazine's circulation. The subject of the essays was to be "A Day in the Life of a Truck Driver," and Peggy had won first prize. She owed her success to imagination and hard work. She had spent a week going from truck to truck, working, loading fruits and vegetables, talking to the truckers. While the other contestants had racked their brains to find poetry where there was none, Peggy had described reality in harsh, even crude terms: the truckers' girls along the highways, the drinking when extreme fatigue kept one awake, the ways of cheating on freight tonnage, and the hundred other things that respectable young girls never dreamed existed.

The prize was a job at the magazine, which Peggy modestly accepted. The editor expected to meet an angular, bespectacled girl, probably wearing slacks, and she had prepared a little speech of welcome composed of the clichés customary on such occasions. But when

Peggy appeared in her office, the editor felt compelled to abandon her rhetorical flourishes. She knew perfectly well who Peggy was. Astonished at Peggy's explanation that she had entered the contest in order to get a job, she had asked, "But I know your family very well! Why didn't you just come to me directly?"

"I prefer it this way," Peggy had replied. "I wanted to be hired on my merits rather than on the basis of my name and family."

Then she had gotten down to work.

It had not been easy. She had run the gamut of journalistic chores, from the beauty-aids column ("What cream should I use on my face at night?") to pieces about keeping dogs from being killed by automobiles or, rather, since the *Bazaar* appealed to a very special audience, to pieces on how to prevent "the dear little companion of your life" from being run over by automobiles.

It had taken two years of grinding labor, but finally Peggy was regarded as the magazine's star, as she had always been the star of everything she attempted. It was satisfying. But it was even more satisfying that she was earning her own way.

Peggy glanced at her watch. Julian, her stepfather's black chauffeur, was late. Mentally, she reviewed the list of dresses she had packed and smiled at the amount of luggage that she required for one evening in London: three large suitcases, two handbags, and a cosmetics case. But what an evening it would be. And what an extraordinary idea it was to celebrate Christmas on August 13! Jennifer Cabott, the editor of *Bazaar*, who had not been invited, had seemed aghast at the idea and had instructed Peggy to spare no one in her piece covering the affair. "Most of these people," she had explained to Peggy, "are uneducated gangsters. They think they can do whatever they want simply because, instead of breeding, they have money. Don't try to be easy on them."

Peggy knew Kallenberg only by reputation, but that reputation was not entirely pleasant. He was a *nouveau riche* who had gained power through deceit and bluff. He was German by birth, a shipowner by profession, a womanizer and dowry collector by inclination. He seemed to draw his inspiration from a determination to surpass his brother-in-law, Socrates Satrapoulos, in every way: ships, finance, women. Peggy's friends had described his house to her. Titians and Rubenses in the dressing rooms, Tintorettos and Cranachs in the bathrooms.

The doorbell rang. It was the chauffeur, finally. The maid helped him carry the luggage to the service elevator. Ten minutes later Peggy was in the back seat of the black Lincoln, explaining to Julian that he must make good time to the airport. It was 8 A.M. in New York; 1 P.M. in London.

She glanced at her watch again. "Julian, can't you go any faster?" The heavy automobile leaped forward, and Peggy settled back into the cushions. At that instant, there was a dull impact, as though something had glanced off the car. The Lincoln swerved as Julian braked frantically, then steadied itself. Slowly, the chauffeur brought the automobile to a halt on the shoulder of the highway.

"It wasn't my fault," he said. "He got out of his car just as I was passing—"

Peggy turned. Through the rear window, two hundred yards down the highway, she saw a dark shape lying motionless on the concrete. Other cars were stopping. A crowd was beginning to form.

Julian's voice rose in near panic. "It wasn't my fault! I tell you it wasn't my fault!"

"Calm down, Julian. No one has said it was your fault," Peggy said quietly.

"Madame, please stay here. I have to go back there—"

But Peggy had already made her decision. "Stay where you are!"

"Madame—"

"Be quiet! Is the car all right? Can it be driven?"

"Yes, but—"

"Then drive it!"

"But I may have killed him—"

"I said drive."

"Mr. Beckintosh—"

"Mr. Beckintosh is not your passenger. I am. And I order you to start this car!"

As Julian obeyed, Peggy lifted the telephone receiver concealed under a mother-of-pearl panel and dialed. Julian glanced at her through the rear view mirror. "Are you calling the police?"

"Just drive, please." Then, into the telephone: "Hello? I want to report an accident, three miles from Idlewild. There was a pedestrian in the middle of the road. My chauffeur couldn't avoid hitting him. . . . I have a plane to catch. A Lincoln—hold on a minute."

She leaned forward in the seat. "Julian, what's your license plate number?"

"72 87 NY 11."

Peggy repeated the number into the telephone. "Peggy Nash-

Belmont. . . . No, it belongs to my stepfather, Arthur Erwin Beckintosh. . . . That's right. . . . No. I've already told you, I have a
plane to catch. . . . You can send someone to see me. . . . 326 Park
Avenue. Good-bye."

Peggy broke the connection and immediately dialed another number. "Mr. Beckintosh, please."

Julian had now brought the Lincoln to a halt before the International Airlines terminal at the airport.

"Hello, Arthur? I'm afraid we've had an accident on the highway.
Some man practically threw himself in front of the car. . . . I don't
have time now. Julian will tell you about it. Please take care of
everything. I know I can count on you. I'll see you Tuesday." She
hung up.

"Julian."

The chauffeur was standing beside the car with the suitcases.

"I want you to find me a porter. Then go back immediately to the
scene of the accident. The police will be waiting for you. Don't worry.
I've spoken to Mr. Beckintosh, and he will take care of everything.
Now get me that porter."

After all, Peggy reflected, there was no reason for her to miss her
flight because some idiot had decided to stand on the highway and
because another idiot had not had sufficiently good reflexes to avoid
hitting him. It was too bad if the man died, but it was really none
of her business. Thousands of anonymous people died every day all
over the world. But there was only one Kallenberg, and he celebrated
Christmas on only one day of the year, the night of August 13.

The room could have been a classroom or a conference room, but
it invariably made visitors think of a chapel. Before a table covered
with an orange cloth stood five rows of chairs occupied by the twenty
privileged beings who were allowed to approach and be received by
the Prophet: ladies and gentlemen of a certain age, all well dressed
and meticulously groomed. From time to time, one of the audience
rose at a sign from the Prophet, who then said, "I am listening."

Interviews with the Prophet invariably began and ended with such
a ritual. And the Prophet, once he had spoken, listened to his
supplicant without uttering another word himself. Yet despite his insignificant appearance—remarkable only for the fact that he resembled a composite of human types—his charisma was such that his
interlocutor was able to forget the presence of the others and, often
to his own astonishment, describe, publicly and without shame,

thoughts so intimate that he had never before admitted them even to himself. Then, the ordeal over, the speaker returned to his seat, stunned at the enormity of what he had just done, and was again transformed into an anonymous listener.

It was Tuesday, the day which the Prophet called his "Poor Day." Every week he devoted an afternoon to a free collective séance for those who were not wealthy enough, or famous enough, to merit a personal interview. Ordinarily, the séance lasted from 2 P.M. to 6 P.M. Judging by the number of people who had been waiting for months to be admitted to the Presence, the Prophet's silence was all to the good. His clients spread the word of his power throughout Portugal —the very word which the Prophet himself never uttered.

The other days of the week were devoted to more serious business, to clients willing to part with any sum in order to spend an hour with the Prophet of Cascais.

Now a man of about sixty years, tall, of distinguished appearance, stood before the table.

"I am listening."

The man stood silent for a moment. Then he began in an unexpected fashion. "I am an asshole," he said.

The Prophet nodded once, indicating that he had noted the man's words.

The man, as if finally free of years of accumulated guilt, explained in great detail the reasons for his statement. His life lay in ruins. His wife had left him, and his children hated him. Yet he had worked hard all his life for their sakes.

In the middle of the man's discourse, the Prophet saw Mario, his butler, appear in the doorway and signal to him.

"Why," the man continued, "have I been such an asshole? Why did I spend my life working, rather than enjoying myself the way others do? Why?"

The Prophet silenced him with a gesture, then beckoned to Mario. The butler would not have interrupted the séance without a good reason. Perhaps a journalist had managed to insinuate himself into the audience, despite the careful screening to which all of the Prophet's clients were subjected.

Mario whispered into his ear. The Prophet nodded, then whispered back a few words.

Mario turned to the audience. "The Prophet," he announced, "asks that this room be cleared."

There were no protests. The audience rose with a discreet scraping of chairs and filed out the door, with the man whom the Prophet had interrupted in midsentence bringing up the rear.

When he was certain that no one remained, the Prophet walked out of the chapel into the courtyard which separated it from the main house. He glanced out at the sea, a sight of which he never tired. How far he had come, he reflected, from his lowly beginnings. His clients were kings and grand duchesses, giants of the financial world, and the arbiters of the destinies of nations, none of whom would consider issuing a single order or signing a single decree until they had consulted the Prophet.

He walked into the main house, pushed open the door of the library, and held out his hand to Socrates Satrapoulos. "My dear friend," the Greek began immediately, "I have a terrible problem."

The Prophet disengaged his hand, smiling. "Yes, I know," he said.

"He has found my mother. He's trying to use her. If he succeeds, I will be ruined!"

"The tarot cards have already informed me of all this. Do calm yourself."

"He's even sent newspapermen to see her. Somehow they found her in that godforsaken village. What should I do?"

"Don't torture yourself. The signs are favorable to us. We will return to the sender the bomb which he intends for us."

Satrapoulos stopped pacing the room. The Prophet's use of the plural "we" and "us" was strangely comforting. The Greek was no longer alone.

"Are you sure that it's not too late?"

"I am certain of it."

Satrapoulos fell into an armchair, suddenly freed of the weight he had carried all day.

"How should I proceed?"

"I want you to begin by telling me everything in detail—and calmly. Then I will consult the cards. When they have spoken, I will know what you must do."

A strange man, Socrates mused. He costs me millions, but he has brought me billions in exchange. And he has never been wrong.

[3]

"Robert, do you have your flash?"

"That's the fourth time you've asked. Yes, I have it."

Jean-Michel fell silent and devoted his full attention to driving. In the back seat, behind the two Frenchmen, the interpreter smiled. With what these foreigners were paying him for one day's work, he would be able to live for a month. They merely wanted him to translate a conversation with a peasant woman who lived in a village that Skopelos had never heard of. The two reporters had not been very clear about the purpose of the interview—something about an inheritance—but, as Skopelos would have been the first to admit, that was none of his business. His business was to take a French word and turn it into Greek, and vice versa, and, of course, to collect for his pains.

The photographer tested his electronic flash equipment, and the result was like a miniature sun in the car. The other man, Jean-Michel, had already run several tests on the tape recorder. Skopelos had heard his own voice on the tape and had not recognized it.

The two Frenchmen seemed nervous. Perhaps it was the heat.

"Skopelos, do you understand what you're supposed to do? You're to translate our questions. From time to time, tell me what the old woman's answers are. Then, when we get back to the port, you'll translate everything from the tape. All right?"

"Yes, I understand."

"Good. We're almost there. I can see the houses. Let's leave the car here."

The three men made their way on foot toward the row of white-washed houses glistening in the sun. A man emerged from one of the buildings, and Skopelos asked directions to Athina's house. Silently the man pointed to the last house at the end of the street, then turned and disappeared into his doorway.

"Not very talkative, is he?"

Skopelos grinned. "They're a backward people in this part of the country. No newspapers, no radios. The only thing that's important to them is their goats."

"And their women?"

"They're only seen in public once: on their wedding day. In the old days, the girl's family had to pay as much as a half million of your francs to have their daughter marry the man her father selected. Once they're married, they're cloistered, like nuns. They bear children, take care of the goats, and run their households."

"*La dolce vita*," Robert remarked. "We should send our women here to be trained."

They had reached the last house. Robert pushed aside the curtain and looked inside. He could barely distinguish the form of an old woman, digging in a sack.

He turned to Skopelos. "Ask her if she is Athina Satrapoulos."

The woman nodded in reply to Skopelos' query.

"Good," Jean-Michel said. "All right, Robert, let's get to work. Skopelos, translate what I say."

He spoke to her, in French, loudly, as though he expected that she must be deaf. As he spoke, he thought: so this is the mother of the great Socrates Satrapoulos! What a scoop this is going to be!

"Madame Satrapoulos, we've come to talk to you about your son, Socrates—"

Before Skopelos had finished translating the sentence, the old woman began speaking rapidly in Greek.

"What is she saying?"

"She says," Skopelos replied, "that she is not deaf, and she would like you to stop shouting."

The woman spoke again.

"She says," Skopelos began.

"Stop saying 'she says,'" Jean-Michel ordered. "Just translate."

"All right. She says: 'What has he done now?'"

"Who does she mean?"

"Her son, obviously."

"Ask her how long it's been since she's seen him."

"Thirty years."

"What does she think of him?"

"She says that he's a good-for-nothing."

"Does she know that he's rich?"

"She says she knows nothing about him."

"Does he send her money?"

"No, never. Instead, he has taken money from her."

"What kind of child was he?"

"A dirty little thief."

The old woman nodded vigorously as Skopelos translated these last words.

"Did he love his father?"

"He never loved anyone but himself."

"Was he a good student?"

"He was thrown out of every school he ever attended. None would keep him more than a week."

"Why?"

"Because he was already full of evil."

"Hasn't he ever tried to help you?"

"No, never."

"Does he have any special reason to avoid you?"

"He can't stand people who knew him when he was weak, including his mother. Once he struck me."

"When did that happen?"

"He just jumped on me and started beating me. His father had to drag him away."

"How old was he when that happened?"

"Thirteen."

Jean-Michel looked at Robert in triumph. Raph Dun certainly had a talent for turning up fantastic subjects. He might be a snob, but he had an infallible instinct for a story.

Robert told Skopelos to ask Athina if they could photograph her bedroom.

"Yes. But this is the bedroom. I sleep here with my goats."

Jean-Michel quickly computed how much he could get for this story about the unknown mother of the world's most celebrated billionaire.

"All right," he said to Robert. "Let's stop for a while. Take her outside and get some color shots of her standing in front of this shack. With her goats, if you can. Try to make the whole thing look as poverty-stricken as possible."

He turned to Skopelos. "Tell her we'd like to start from the beginning again. And ask her for the exact date of Socrates' birth. I want the whole story, day by day."

In the Mikolofides family, avarice had been so cultivated that it increased with each succeeding generation until, in Ulysses Mikolofides, it became a pathological obsession. Ulysses had decided that he would have no heir, for he could not bear the thought that someone would come after him to enjoy what he possessed. Moreover, it did not entirely displease him that he would be the last in a glorious line.

Unfortunately, his wife had another view of the matter. Even though generally submissive to her husband's dictates, Medea Mikolofides rebelled and insisted that her husband provide her with a child. With the passage of time, her desire to have children became monomaniacal. She tried lying to Ulysses about her monthly cycle; but he did not believe her, and on those rare occasions when he joined her in the conjugal bed, he outfitted himself with the latest in preventive devices.

After three years of marriage, Ulysses realized that he faced a difficult choice. Medea must either bear a child or lose her mind entirely. Already he had surprised her several times, knitting infants' clothing or reading books and magazines on child care. On such occasions, she had not reproached him, even with her eyes. She had continued working on her blue booties or her pink sweaters, until, one night, he was unable to bear her silence any longer.

"Go up to your room," he shouted at her. "I'll give you your blasted child. And God help you if it's not a boy!"

She gave him a look of utter adoration and climbed the stairs so rapidly that she almost fell, prattling all the way, "Oh, Ulysses, thank you, thank you!"

A month later nothing had happened.

Ulysses was angry in spite of himself, and he set himself to the task with increased vigor.

Still nothing happened.

He found a specialist who assured him that he was not sterile, and then he insisted that Medea undergo a similiar examination. No one could find anything wrong. There was no reason, they were assured, why they could not have a child.

Thereupon Ulysses was transformed into an insatiable lover, cursing the gods who refused to give him what they conferred so liberally on the poorest of men.

Neither Ulysses' efforts nor his curses were of any avail. Medea's stomach remained as flat as a board. Meanwhile, she wandered through the house with a distracted air, barely eating, interested in nothing but the children of the servants, whom she showered with extravagant gifts.

Two more years passed before Medea could bring herself to speak of adoption, and then she met with obstinate refusal on her husband's part. If he had not been enthusiastic about having a child of his very own, he was not about to let someone else's little bastard inherit his fortune.

It was at this stage that Medea's sister, Nina, died in childbirth, having previously admitted to her horrified family that she did not know who the father was. Now she was dead, and the infant was alive.

Medea threw herself at her husband's feet, imploring him to adopt the baby.

"It's out of the question," he replied. "If it were a boy, we might at least discuss it. But a girl—"

Thereupon, he left on a trip, ostensibly on business, but in fact to escape his wife's lamentations.

When he returned, there was a cradle in his wife's room.

Medea threw her arms around her husband's neck, delirious with joy. "Look at our child," she exclaimed. "I've named her Irene!"

There was nothing he could do. His wife was herself again, after so many years. And the child was already there. He consented, muttering that the infant would surely be the ruin of them all.

Ulysses had just resigned himself to the role of reluctant father to Irene when he was stupefied to learn that Medea was pregnant. This time, he was certain, she would make up for everything by giving him a son, a son who would be his own extension in time and space and whom he would name Ulysses, after himself.

Seven months later Melina was born.

Two years later there was another child: also a girl, whom they named Helena.

Ulysses went from despair to resignation. It was God's will, he told himself. His duty was clear. He must guard the family fortune with new vigilance so that it would not be dissipated by these "castrates," as he called them in his own mind when he was angry.

Irene had not had an easy adolescence. Her mother reported to Ulysses that the child had hair on her arms earlier than in her pubic area. She had always been a timid child, but now, beset by repeated instructions as to what she was to do and not to do, she became withdrawn, silent, almost sullen. She locked herself in her room and applied dipilatory creams to her arms, determined to come to terms with her femininity.

No one had ever told Irene that she was an adopted child. Therefore, socially and psychologically, she was indeed the eldest child of Ulysses and Medea Mikolofides. Yet she had been made to feel that she was only tolerated, that she had been a disappointment, and that it would have been better for everyone if she had been born a boy.

Later, under the double impact of prayer and electrolysis, the hair on her forearms had disappeared. But by some sort of biological compensation, it grew abnormally thick in the pubic region and on her thighs and even brought a permanent shadow to her upper lip. With horror and shame, she overheard a maid refer to her "mustache." She took some consolation from her eyes, which were large blue-black orbs, lined with very long lashes.

When Melina was born, Irene was told that she should be happy. She did not understand why, and suspicious by nature, she foresaw that henceforth she would be required to share her father's affection, meager as it was, with this newcomer.

One night, two years later, Irene discovered something that brought her great joy. It was near midnight when she suddenly awakened in the bedroom which she shared with Melina. She lay in her bed, staring into the darkness, turning over in her mind the plan that had occurred to her only a few days before.

She turned on the lamp—which was strictly forbidden—and tiptoed over to the cradle. Melina was sleeping, her mouth open. Irene had looked at her for a long moment. Then, with trembling hands, she reached into the cradle, raised the covers, and removed Melina's diaper. With her heart pounding in her chest, she looked.

There was nothing.

Nothing. Therefore, there was no reason for her parents to love Melina more than they loved Irene. There was no difference between them.

Overcome with relief, Irene covered the baby with kisses. And Melina, of course, awakened and began to cry.

Medea rushed into the room, accompanied by the nurse. "Look." She laughed. "See how Irene loves her little sister." The next day the story was repeated throughout the household. At the age of six, everyone said, Irene was already behaving like a real little mother.

THE GREEK

When Ulysses took Irene upon his knee to stroke her hair, the child was not deceived. She knew that this special favor was being conferred because she had been discovered kissing Melina. Therefore, she concluded, she would have to continue pretending. She would have to simulate exaggerated love for everything that her father himself loved.

Irene was barely over the shock of Melina's appearance when Helena was born. By a singular act of injustice, Lena, as she was called from the first, was a strikingly beautiful infant. Visitors went into ecstasy over her blue eyes, the perfection of her tiny nose, the color and abundance of her hair. And thus, Irene was brought to the realization that her true rival was not Melina, but Helena. Nonetheless, she loudly acclaimed the miracle that was Helena, surpassing everyone else in her simulated worship of the infant. She insisted on helping bathe Helena, although when no one was watching, she would pinch her fat thighs and arms savagely.

And so it continued through the years, with Irene's ambivalent hostility toward her youngest sister taking its toll, not only of Helena, but of Irene herself. At sixteen, she suffered her first nervous breakdown, which had the effect of reinstating her in the forefront of her parents' attention. How delightful it was to watch her worried family hover over her bed, to see them at the mercy of her mood, grateful when she smiled feebly to demonstrate how courageously she bore her afflictions. Henceforth, she would know how to recapture their sympathy and affection. She had never forgotten the lesson. Whenever she felt the need of love, she took refuge in the comfortable fortress of her sickbed, where she allowed an army of distracted doctors to ply her with tranquilizers or vitamins or stimulants.

Three days before his fortieth birthday, Ulysses Mikolofides died of a heart attack. Irene watched as his body arrived at the house in an ambulance. He had been stricken in his office—"he died at his desk," the official version had it. Unkind associates told a less edifying tale, whispering that he had expired from an overdose of aphrodisiacs in an attempt to preserve the illusions of a nineteen-year-old secretary.

After the funeral the first matter to be settled was that of Ulysses' holdings. It was a question that Medea herself settled in straightforward fashion. She convened her husband's various boards of directors and announced that all authority now lay in her hands. When the news became known, there were smiles in the offices, and a number of cutting remarks. But Medea had not been Ulysses' wife for nothing. Anyone who questioned her authority or her judgment was dismissed immediately, and discipline was reestablished forthwith.

The companies with which Ulysses had done business soon discovered that they would gain nothing by his death. Medea, who had always lived in her husband's shadow, now emerged as a peerless businesswoman, with a talent for making instantaneous judgments and an infallible instinct. In three years she doubled the capital—already unprecedented—inherited from Ulysses' estate. And during this period, her three daughters pursued the normal course of their lives with varying results.

Irene, by the time she was twenty, had not yet received an offer of marriage her mother considered worthy of her station. She therefore set about ridding herself of her virginity in a way that no one had foreseen, with a Greek soldier who was obliged to raise his skirts in order to expose his organ. The soldier had been provided as a guard during one of Medea's receptions. He was a farm boy, ignorant of the ways of polite society, naïve enough to think himself irresistible. Irene, who had been stationed outside the house to await the arrival of an unloved aunt, became conscious of the soldier's stare. Disdainfully she inquired as to the reason for his attention.

"It's your ass," the soldier replied. "It's magnificent."

His words reduced Irene to silence. Her eyes, her intelligence, her sense of responsibility—these things had been universally praised. But her behind, never.

She was not displeased. During the reception, she could barely bring herself to respond to compliments on her eyes. She had already reached a decision concerning the soldier.

She met him at eleven o'clock that evening. He took her to a dark corner of the garden, leaned his antique musket against the wall, raised his skirt, and proceeded to make love to her, military-style, standing upright. Irene could not decide whether the sensations she was experiencing were pleasant or otherwise. It was a bit like eating oysters for the first time, she told herself. In any event, the whole thing bore no relationship to any situation that she had ever been able to imagine.

The soldier, once he had ejaculated, withdrew. Without stopping to catch his breath, he spun Irene around and, still standing upright, made love to her a second time, Greek-style.

Then he adjusted his skirt, with the sly air of a transvestite, and burst into laughter.

Irene, who already felt slightly ridiculous, asked why he was laughing.

"It's because I'm happy," he replied.

Irene decided to interpret the remark as an insult. She slapped him, then fled among the trees.

Later that night, in bed, she tried to analyze the encounter. One aspect of it commanded her attention with irritating persistency. It had to do with clothes. She had been wearing a black silk pants suit with very loose trousers, while the soldier wore a skirt. In order to expose herself, she had lowered her pants. And he, to expose his organ, had raised his skirt. Why, Irene wondered, did that seem so important?

A year later she had met Herman Kallenberg for the first time, on the occasion of Helena's marriage to Socrates Satrapoulos. The German shipowner enjoyed a solid reputation as a womanizer ("Bluebeard," those who knew him well called him). He was a year younger than Satrapoulos, but he was already on his fourth wife: an American, the widow of a steel magnate, whose capital Kallenberg had invested in his own maritime enterprises. Immediately following the ceremony, Kallenberg and his wife had had a violent argument. The truth was that he was already tired of her. She was older than he, and the victim of an obesity which had resisted the best efforts of dietitians and reducing salons alike. He sensed that she reduced his stature in the eyes of Satrapoulos, whom he regarded as his archenemy. For the Greek, not content merely with possessing a seventeen-year-old beauty, was now posing as the heir of the colossal Mikolofides empire.

When Madame Kallenberg, pale with shame, fled the reception, Kallenberg pretended not to notice. She had never understood that a man sometimes needs to be alone. Now that she was gone, Kallenberg felt like himself again. He made a beeline for Melina, but the wall of young bachelors surrounding her forced him to beat a retreat before he had been able to launch an attack. Irene, who had taken refuge in the least frequented corner of the room, watched him. She understood perfectly what Kallenberg was doing, and she knew what the outcome would be. She waited, listening with half an ear to the semicircle around her, which consisted of two frayed priests and three well-scrubbed Kallenberg employees who had been invited in an excess of charity.

A few minutes passed before Kallenberg caught sight of her. He smiled broadly and picked his way through the crush of people. He bowed before her and begged the honor of a dance. Medea Mikolofides, who had missed nothing of the drama being enacted, frowned. Irene ignored her. She was not really attracted to the blond colossus who had just taken her hand. He was too sure of himself, his voice was too loud, and he made even an invitation to dance sound like an order that would not permit discussion. But he was famous, and he had publicly chosen her, and for that, she was grateful. They moved onto the floor, and she was surprised to find herself trembling as he took her in his arms. The authority and confidence which he exuded overwhelmed her, and a wave of warmth broke in the pit of her stomach. She felt his huge, rough fingers press into the soft flesh of her hips and linger there a moment.

By the time the dance ended everything had been settled. Irene had found her master, and she was determined that he would remain such so that she could make him repay for the emotion he had awakened in her. Kallenberg, for his part, could have asked for nothing more to his choosing. Why, he wondered, had he not noticed this one before? If he married into the family, he would be in the doubly advantageous position of being able to control both Satrapoulos' intrigues and Medea Mikolofides' finances.

Having decided, he acted. A month later, he began divorce proceedings, charging mental cruelty—his American wife's, not his own.

Meanwhile, the Widow (as Medea was generally known) gave much thought to this turn of events. On the one hand, she was delighted at the prospect of Irene's marriage, for she had feared that the girl would become an old maid. On the other, she was disturbed at the thought of having not one but two sons-in-law trying to wrest control of the Mikolofides empire from her hands. Still, there was something to be said for having a couple of these new generation gangsters in her stable. They would know how to deal with others of their ilk. Finally, she opted for the political solution, deciding not to oppose the marriage, but assuring herself that she would keep a vigilant eye on her two formidable sons-in-law.

There was an investigation of Kallenberg, of course, before the engagement was announced, an investigation conducted with the same thoroughness as that of Satrapoulos which had preceded his marriage to Helena. Irene had made herself privy to the results of the investigation of Kallenberg, somewhat unofficially, by listening at keyholes. She found a number of things in the report which had surprised her and which she prudently stored in her memory for future reference. She intended to confront her husband with these nuggets of information immediately after their marriage, so that there might be no possible doubt as to who was to wear the pants in their ménage.

She had been disappointed. Kallenberg was like an egg of steel. Nothing she had said made the slightest impression. He was invulnerable because he was insensitive to everything outside himself. On the wedding night, when she had done her best to bring him to heel, he left the house without a word and did not return until dawn the next morning. In the interim, Irene's expert makeup had run, her transparent nightgown had taken on the appearance of a wrinkled rag, and she had been obliged to swallow a handful of tranquilizers to keep from exploding with rage. When her husband finally returned, she was virtually comatose, but, instinctively, she turned her back on him.

He undressed and stretched out on the bed next to her. Irene pretended to be asleep. He turned her toward him by grabbing a handful of her hair and jerking violently. She pretended to waken and to regard his brutality as a caress, smiling in the darkness despite a pain so intense that it brought her to the verge of tears.

"So," she said, "you're here. I was asleep."

His reaction was a surprise. "Wake up, bitch, and show me what you can do with your ass."

It was the second time Irene had heard a man use that word, and hearing it freed her from her inhibitions. There followed a fantastic race for pleasure, with Irene concentrating upon the memory of her Greek soldier and Kallenberg straining after his own personal fantasies. Each of them was making love to himself, in a sort of violent masturbatory exercise.

Kallenberg's moans were accompanied by frequent blows, which Irene accepted as a love offering and which increased her excitement. When Kallenberg finally penetrated her, she suddenly knew all, understood all the sources of his violence, the motivations which awakened his overriding desire for power, for Herman Kallenberg's penis was laughably small. It was rendered all the more ridiculous by the giant body to which it was appended. Here, she told herself, is something of which I can take advantage. But, once again, she was mistaken. Kallenberg was perfectly aware of the diminutive size of his organ, and he compensated for it ferociously by an unrelenting aggressiveness, an aggressiveness which expressed itself in his Homeric delight in victory, his sudden rages, his thirst for conquest and domination, his desire to humiliate.

THE GREEK

The relationship between Irene and Kallenberg was therefore established under the double banner of hate and submission, destruction and sarcasm. Irene quickly entered into the spirit of this unremitting battle which could end only with the death of one of them and the survival of the other. Sometimes, she feigned surrender so as to lure Kallenberg into lowering his defenses; then, when he was vulnerable, she attacked, coldly and pitilessly. And sometimes, when she was weary, she surrendered herself wholly to his yoke and drew her pleasure from that submission.

The plain fact was that she hated Herman Kallenberg. The idea that he had conceived of celebrating Christmas on August 13, for example, was as grotesque as it was blasphemous. But since he was determined to do as he wished, she was left with two choices. She could either go off on a trip, which would cause a storm of rumors that Kallenberg was estranged from his fifth wife, or she could remain in London and pretend that the whole thing had been her own idea. In either case, the vandals who would be guests in her historic house on the Mall were certain to leave few of her possessions intact.

She was lying in her bed now, wondering which course to adopt. Next to her, within easy reach, on a tray of massive gold which had been a gift on her second anniversary, was an array of multicolored pills, intended to induce various effects. Her pills were with her always. Even a momentary separation from them threw her into a panic.

The house telephone tinkled softly. She picked up the receiver and heard: "Listen to me, you fat pig. You will buy yourself a sexy dress for tomorrow. I'm sick of those grandmother outfits you wear. It's bad enough that you bore everyone to death. You don't have to look like an old cow in the bargain."

Irene knew how to translate Kallenberg's words. They meant that he probably had a whore in his office—he was very fond of whores —and wanted to make certain his wife was in her room. She smiled to herself. The whore was in for a surprise.

Irene poured a glass of milk and began swallowing her pills according to the proper ritual. First the blue ones; then the pink pills, the yellow pills, and the green pills. The white pills were last.

She stretched out on the bed again and dreamed that she was gorgeous, and a prostitute, and that she was making Herman suffer.

Kallenberg had never admitted it to anyone, but his secret dream was to be a public executioner. The greatest happiness he could imagine was to be able to kill people without running the slightest risk oneself. But people were hypocrites. Who except Herman Kallenberg would have been strong enough to recognize the existence of such a desire in himself? People had been weakened by morality, castrated by religion.

He poured several ounces of whiskey into his glass and held it out to the girl.

"Here, pig. Drink!"

She made a face and looked at him oddly.

Here's another one who knows, Kallenberg told himself.

"What's the matter? Don't you like alcohol?"

"It depends on what kind of liquor and who I'm drinking it with."

"Then what do you like?"

"Money."

"I've paid you."

"Who said you didn't?"

"What would you do if you had a lot of money?"

"I'd make people like you toe the line."

"You're a strange one. You like to see people crawl?"

"Yes."

"People like me?"

"Yes."

"Why? Am I ugly?"

"No. In fact, you're rather handsome."

"Then why?"

"Because you make me want to vomit."

He slapped her across the face, twice, hard. The imprint of his hand appeared in scarlet on both of her cheeks.

"Now," he said, "does that make you want to vomit, too?"

Boldly, the girl faced him, marshaling her strength to keep from crying.

Kallenberg, in a calm voice, spoke as though nothing had happened. "What would you do to get money?"

She remained silent, unflinching, like a mouse attempting to stare down a ravenous cat.

"I'll tell you what you'd do," Kallenberg said. "You'd do anything."

Still she was silent.

"Look," he said, reaching into his pocket and withdrawing a roll of bills. "There are several thousand pounds here. All I have to do is hand you a few of these pieces of paper and, if I want you to, you'll dance, crawl, show me your ass, or lick my feet. Now, how do you want to begin?"

"I'd like to have my purse."

"Answer me! How shall we begin?"

"Please give me my purse."

The girl was frightened now. She was no longer concerned about saving face. She had already received her fee, and he had already made love to her—in his own way, by slapping her. They were even. All she wanted now was to be allowed to leave, quickly.

"Here's your purse, cunt! Take it!" Kallenberg threw the purse on the floor, onto the marvelous Chinese carpet which he had acquired, for its weight in gold, from a shady gentleman who specialized in objects stolen from museums.

The purse lay there, a hideous little white plastic object, incongruous on the unique red of the carpet, more offensive than if it had been a pool of spittle or dog excrement. The girl bent over, retrieved her purse, clutched it to her chest, and waited.

"Well, get out! And get that look off your face. I'm going to send for you one of these days."

Kallenberg pressed a button and one of the panels of the bookcase swung open. Behind it was a steel door which he opened by dialing a coded combination. He stood in the doorway, gigantic, frightening, waiting for her.

"Why don't you go?"

She dared not go near him, and her obvious fear was a pleasurable supplement which Kallenberg had not anticipated in their bargain.

"Hurry," he snapped. "I have work to do. When you get to the bottom of the stairway, tell the guard that you were with me and he'll let you pass."

She looked at him, still hesitant, as though he were a bridge which she was certain would collapse under her feet. Then suddenly she gathered her courage and ran past him. With a roar of laughter, Kallenberg gave her a mighty slap on the rear which sent her stumbling down the first steps on her high wooden heels. "Disgusting as I am," he shouted to her, "you're lucky I'm in a good mood!"

Then he slammed the steel door and locked it. The paintings in his office were worth an estimated four million pounds and had been gathered by his agents from the four corners of the globe. Sisley, Renoir, Pissarro, several Monet sketches of the cathedral of Chartres, two Degas studies of the dance, three Lautrecs, four Van Goghs, a magnificent Modigliani nude, a masterpiece from Gauguin's Tahitian period, and, to balance the moderns, a *pietà* of Raphael, a breath-taking line drawing of Leonardo's, and a Rembrandt self-portrait which was the equal of the "Man with the Golden Helmet" in the Munich museum.

These covered two walls of the room. The other two walls exhibited Kallenberg's collection of engravings depicting the famous merchantmen from the days when sailing ships were preparing to surrender to the onslaught of the age of machines. There was the *Washington*, an iron steamboat launched in 1865 and converted, three years later, into a ship with two engines and three masts. There was the *Lafayette*, launched the same year and also a steamboat, and the *Pereire*, a three-master which had been given an engine and re-named the *Lancing* by the British, who bought her in 1888. Kallenberg knew the history of each of these ships by heart, the dates of their launchings, the details of their service, and the stories of their deaths twenty-five to forty years later. The engraving of the *Ville de Paris* signified nothing to Kallenberg's visitors, no matter how erudite they might be. But Kallenberg saw, in his mind, the ship's eight-hundred-horsepower engines carrying her slowly through the Pacific. He saw every detail of the transaction in which she had been sold at Bremen in 1888 and then converted into the four-masted *Bischoff*, which later sank in the Elbe. To Kallenberg, a ship was not a carcass of metal, canvas, or wood, but a living thing which was destined to ply the seas forever, bringing fame and fortune to those who owned her. His true delight lay not in art, but in ships. In his soul, he was a Viking. It was his custom to study the models of his tankers at great length before giving the order to the shipyards to begin construction. He ran his fingers over them, caressing them tenderly, and in his mind's eye, he saw them as they carried his colors over the waters of the earth.

One day, in Egypt, Farouk had said to him, "I'll buy your entire fleet, if you want to sell it. But tell me, what would you do with the money?"

In the final analysis, the same question remained today both for Kallenberg, who could buy whatever he wished, and for the whore from Soho, who could only sell.

"With the money," he had told Farouk, "I would buy a new fleet and become your competitor."

He had answered instinctively, without thinking. Today, if someone had asked him why he was so enamored of competition, he would not have known how to reply. It was not important to know why one entered a race, but to race and to know how one was racing.

Kallenberg's family in Hamburg had been pirates for centuries. As far back as one cared to go, there had been a Kallenberg on the bridge of a ship, pursuing a victim. Herman Kallenberg's father, however, had developed an itch for respectability and had determined to break with tradition. His son, he decided, would become a diplomat, and he spared no effort to assure that his decision would be implemented. Thus it was that Herman had been exiled to Switzerland as a student, an irony of which he alone appreciated the bitterness. But even there, he never lost sight of his ultimate goal, which was one day to rule the world's oceans. His friends at school were the sons of emirs and of bankers.

Later his father sent him to school in England, to Oxford. Here, at least, he was on an island, among a seafaring people. It was true that he could not see the ocean; but he could imagine it, and instead of pastures inhabited by grazing cows, he visualized white-crested waves and mighty ships. His favorite reading material was the stock market report, and the market's fluctuations, which he learned to predict, made his heart pound in his chest. He already spoke German, Greek, French, English, Spanish, and Portuguese, but he insisted on learning Arabic, for he sensed that this language would be of paramount importance in building his empire.

He had long resigned himself to the unpleasantness to which he was occasionally subjected because of his particular physical deficiency. In the showers, after a game, he insisted upon covering himself with a towel until he was safely hidden by the steam. But even with these precautions, there had been occasional sarcastic remarks which made him blush to the roots of his hair. On such occasions, he replied contemptuously that his tormentors knew nothing about it; that the size of an organ in repose bore no relationship to its dimensions when erect; and that he, Herman Kallenberg, could put them all to shame.

Obviously, such bombast was unsuitable in the presence of the girls whom he honored with his attentions. The young ladies in question usually kept silent on the subject, which wounded Herman more deeply than any of his fellow students' remarks. Only one girl —a little redhead whom he met at a dance at the university—had dared allude to it. "For heaven's sake"—she laughed—"you're hung like a mouse!"

He had not been angry. Indeed, he preferred her candor to the silence or whispers, and he did his utmost, subsequently, to make the redhead forget such details as the size of his penis.

When he had completed his course of studies, his father asked him how he wished to begin his career. The old man already saw his son as third secretary in some distant South American republic. Coldly, Herman informed his father that he had no intention of embracing diplomacy. At the same time, perhaps to console him, he also announced that he planned to marry the wife of a certain ambassador.

It was perfectly true. Kallenberg had met her at a tea. She was thirty years old; he, twenty-two. She had been captivated by his giant physique; he, by her excellent connections.

Immediately following the wedding he took all her available assets and used them to buy two old ships destined for the scrap heap. With what was left, he hired a crew of workers and set them to the task of making the two wrecks look like ships once more. The disintegrating hulls were covered with so many coats of paint that the hulls' loose plates were virtually welded in place. There remained only for Kallenberg to organize a maritime transport company, to insure his fleet, and to find a customer.

Kallenberg did not follow the practice common among his more unprincipled associates in the shipping business. He did not hire experts capable of pulling the wool over the eyes of insurance agents so they would insure a battered old wreck for a hundred times its true value. Then the ship would be towed out into the open sea, where the seamen opened large holes in her hull, sent out an SOS, and allowed themselves to be saved by the maritime authorities.

Kallenberg could not bring himself to scuttle a ship. Not even for profit. He signed on crewmen, found clients by charging far less than his competitors, and his ships invariably managed to perform according to contract. With the profits from these first voyages, Kallenberg bought more seaworthy ships, although he reserved a part of his capital to buy overage trawlers about to be retired. At twenty-four, therefore, when his classmates at Oxford were still discussing their choice of professions, Herman Kallenberg was already a rich man.

At the summit of the pyramid which Kallenberg was determined to climb stood the untouchable Ulysses Mikolofides. Along the way, however, was a man his own age, Socrates Satrapoulos, over whom everyone was making a great fuss. Kallenberg knew that the Greek was not beyond reproach, that he occasionally employed professional help to sink his ships. But he was a true rival, and the prospect of cutthroat competition between the two of them excited Kallenberg.

It also irritated him that Satrapoulos enjoyed a head start. It was as though the Greek had had the same ideas as Kallenberg himself, but earlier. Yet Satrapoulos had neither the same advantages as Kallenberg nor the same education. His manners were unpolished. He was small, ugly, and myopic to boot. All he had was a kind of genius for smelling out a profitable deal, usually one on the fringe of legality.

Bluebeard had first observed this during the Spanish Civil War, which was a godsend to all shipowners. Everyone had converted their fleets of fishing vessels into carriers of war matériel to both Loyalists and Republicans. Whenever Kallenberg heard of a profitable venture, it seemed that Satrapoulos had been there ahead of him. Fortunately, customers were not difficult to find, and Kallenberg reaped huge profits, which he immediately invested in other ships. He also speculated on the market, with a daring that made less aggressive investors shiver. His rivals attributed his success to luck, whereas in fact, it was the result of systems which, while apparently illogical, were completely valid in an unorthodox sort of way.

One of Kallenberg's secrets was that he never invested in a "sure thing." He knew that sure things never remained sure for long and that they must inevitably drop in value as they attracted large groups of investors. It was in this spirit that Kallenberg had approached the Emir of Baran. Baran, which lay on the Persian Gulf, was no more than a stretch of desert without a tree or a drop of water to its name. It was inhabited by a million fanatics who dressed in rags and were dying of hunger and an overdose of religion. The emir, Hadj Thami el Sadek, who claimed to be a prophet, was a political atavist. He preached the holy war against infidels, since his emirate had no oil to sell to them. When Kallenberg delivered a shipload of guns to the emir, he was astonished to discover that Satrapoulos had done the same thing before him and never demanded payment for purely tactical reasons. Apparently, Herman's brother-in-law had wasted neither his time nor his money on the deal.

The Emir of Baran, with the backing of a handful of sun-crazed soldiers, had rapidly gained the ascendancy by his perpetual references to the Koran, by invoking Allah as the prime mover in all his actions, by practicing a scrupulous asceticism, and by imposing his word and the strength of his convictions by force of arms. His policies were a model of consistency. He demanded that all the sheikhs and emirs of the Persian Gulf recognize him as their religious leader and accept his moral authority, for, as he pointed out, only he was beyond suspicion of base material motives. One ruler after another accepted this proposal, for their confrere of Baran was, as he claimed, very poor indeed and therefore above corruption. His authority spread, and in time he came to be regarded as a general arbiter of all disputes. Foreign ambassadors came to pay him court, knowing that nothing could be signed without his blessing. In a short time, he had become, to the dismay of those whom he represented, the official spokesman for every domain along the Persian Gulf. Conscious of his power, he doubled his religious fervor and held himself up as a model to the subjects of other sovereigns: a kind of Arab Gandhi, a dry prince afloat in a sea of oil.

After a number of secret contacts, Kallenberg succeeded in reaching the emir, displaying great humility and devotion, which were intended to bring him a fantastic prize: a contract to carry the millions of tons of crude petroleum which flowed from the emirates of the Gulf. The Emir of Baran was enchanted with this man who spoke Arabic so well, who was so well informed as to his accomplishments, and who could recite verse after verse of the Koran by heart. Yet he resisted Kallenberg's propositions, saying only that he would make his decision when the proper moment presented itself. When the emir mentioned Satrapoulos' name, Kallenberg pointed out that the Greek was a man without religion, an atheist, an agnostic. What a pity it was, he observed, that so gifted a man was so devoid of the virtues sacred to Allah. Then, frantic at the thought that so rich a prize might fall to his enemy, he threw caution to the winds.

"Highness," he said, "your motives are so pure, so noble, that I feel I must enlighten you concerning the man who is called Satrapoulos. I know him well. He is the husband of my own wife's sister. I fear that, if you choose him over me, your followers will ultimately discover certain things concerning him which will reflect upon your choice."

"To what things are you referring?"

Bluebeard's bluff had been called unexpectedly. Until then the conversation had been purely rhetorical. But now this old zealot was asking for practical details.

"Well," Kallenberg stammered, "there are women—"

Hadj Thami el Sadek smiled. "If the love of women is a sin for you Westerners," he observed, looking Kallenberg in the eye, "then you also must be a great sinner."

Kallenberg was thoroughly disconcerted. It had never occurred to him that the emir would inform himself on his private affairs. He would have to think of something else, something stronger. Suddenly, he was inspired. Why had it not occurred to him sooner?

"I was not speaking of women in general, Highness, but of a particular woman. Let me explain. In London, some newspapermen came to see me. They wanted to write an article on a woman—the only woman truly worthy of respect: a mother. Satrapoulos' mother. I learned that that good woman is literally in danger of starving to death. Satrapoulos has not given her one obol in thirty years. If this news becomes known, if the scandal breaks, many people will be shocked, even in financial circles. Newspapers around the world will pick up the story. Satrapoulos has not many friends. His methods of doing business have angered a great number of people. It would take very little to turn everyone against him. If this happens, he will be discredited, and his associates with him."

"Has this article been published already, or do they intend to publish it in the future?"

"It has already been written, though it is not yet published. I have seen photographs of the unhappy woman who is his mother."

"May I see them?"

"I will have to find the men who showed them to me."

"Surely that will be a simple matter for a man of your resources. Let me see them. Then we will speak again."

When Kallenberg returned to his plane, his head was throbbing. Like everyone else, he had heard vague stories about Satrapoulos' mother living in poverty somewhere in the mountains of Greece. But were the stories true? Or were they merely part of the Satrapoulos legend? But what if they were not?

There was a way to find out. Kallenberg thought immediately of Raph Dun—a nobody, to be sure, but nonetheless a man who went everywhere and knew everyone. He remembered Raph because once at a cocktail party the man had had the presumption to invite him to his suite at the Ritz for drinks. Kallenberg would surely have refused had it not been for the fabulous creature hanging on Dun's arm at the time. He had accepted Dun's invitation, and Dun, in return, had given him the girl to warm his bed. Since then he had encountered Dun on several occasions, in the most unexpected places, and each time Dun had conducted himself in the most disgusting manner, as though he and Kallenberg were accomplices of some kind.

As soon as Kallenberg reached the Hilton at Djibouti, he called his Paris office and gave instructions to locate Dun and take him to London. The next day the two men were sitting in Kallenberg's office, and

Kallenberg, overflowing with amiability, had asked Dun if he were capable of protecting his sources of information. Raph had answered by placing his hand over his heart.

"Very well, then," Kallenberg went on. "In that case, I am in a position to give you a real scoop."

He told the story of Satrapoulos' mother, justifying his own conduct—the Greek, after all, was his brother-in-law—by pretending that he was seeking revenge for a grievous wrong done him by Satrapoulos.

"Of course," Kallenberg said offhandedly, "I will take care of your expenses. The first thing to find out, obviously, is if Madame Satrapoulos is still alive. If she is, I want to know everything about her. I could have asked my own investigators to handle this; but absolute discretion is essential in this matter, and I know I can rely on yours. When you have the information I want, bring it to me. Then I'll tell you what to do with it. I may not be in a position to allow publication immediately, but you can be sure that you'll be well paid for your work."

Three days after the meeting, Kallenberg had the answer to the first question. Satrapoulos' mother was indeed alive, living in a remote village. Dun had seen her with his own eyes. It remained only to call in specialists to complete the second phase of the project. This had been done, and Kallenberg now had in his possession a fantastic collection of photographs and a tape containing many startling revelations—all of which were now safely locked in the vault of his bank.

Kallenberg could hardly contain his excitement. For a long time now, Socrates Satrapoulos had deserved a lesson. And tomorrow night, August 13, he would give it to him. What a Christmas it would be! And what presents! He himself would have the Greek's head after he had placed prints of the photographs in Satrapoulos' stocking.

Overflowing with joy, Kallenberg took down his favorite painting, a Lucretia by Cranach, which depicted her piercing her breast with a knife, and kissed the painting, passing his tongue over the tiny, bleeding breast.

No matter what Satrapoulos did now, he was lost. If, after the publication of the documents, he continued to press for the contract with the Emir of Baran, the scandal would alienate the emir. It would therefore be to his advantage to withdraw from the competition and leave the way open to Kallenberg, his brother-in-law. In any case, whether or not Satrapoulos withdrew of his own accord, there would be no chance of his getting the contract. He had lost.

Moreover, as Kallenberg knew very well, Satrapoulos had ordered construction begun on three giant tankers. They were being built at that very moment in Norwegian shipyards. How would Satrapoulos get out of that one? Unless he used them to haul bananas, the huge ships would have to remain idle. The thought made Kallenberg roar with laughter.

He stopped, struck by a thought. With Satrapoulos effectively out of the running, only his mother-in-law, Medea Mikolofides, remained as a real competitor. Only she would stand between him and the pinnacle of the pyramid. If she were eliminated, he would reign as undisputed lord of the earth's seas.

[4]

The inhabitants of London are universally regarded as a jaded people, incapable of surprise. Yet from eleven o'clock on the morning of August 13, a mob of people had been milling about before the gigantic Kallenberg house on the Mall. In truth, the spectacle was calculated to awaken the curiosity even of the most unrelentingly British among them. In the suffocating August heat a crew of workmen had raised two Christmas trees, each thirty feet high, before the portals of the house. Late in the afternoon a BBC truck had arrived, disgorging a flock of technicians who unrolled giant spools of cable, set up cameras, and made strange marks on the sidewalk with pieces of white chalk. By eight o'clock it was growing dark as engineers tested their lighting and their cameras. The crowd of spectators, now comprising several hundred persons, emitted loud "Ohs" and "Ahs."

Four men appeared and unrolled a strip of plum-colored carpeting from the doorway of the house to the curb. Above it, they erected a majestic canopy. Then three refrigerator trucks arrived. Huge mounds of snow were unloaded and arranged in a semicircle around the entrance to the house, while workmen activated several enormous fans which had been installed on the stairs. Soon a miniature snowstorm raged before the Kallenberg house, covering the Christmas trees with shining white crystals of ice.

Shortly, ten giants from the Royal Guard appeared, on horseback, and took up their stations alongside the trees. And finally, two bearded Santa Clauses, appropriately fat and jolly, emerged from the house to stand on either side of the portal.

At exactly 10 P.M., the first Rolls, bearing a diplomatic license plate and flying the flag of Kuwait, drew up before the house. Two men, clad in jellabas and wearing dark glasses, debouched onto the carpet. The chauffeur stood stiffly at attention in the swirling snow, one hand holding the door of the automobile open and the other clutching his cap, as the dignitaries made their way under the canopy to the steps, where they were met by two bewigged and liveried footmen bearing flaming torches. The crowd applauded enthusiastically.

A Bentley moved to the curb, and the crowd recognized Betty Winckle. There were murmurs of admiration as she emerged, clad in a creation of glittering white covered with diamonds, on the arm of her escort, an anonymous bronzed giant. The photographers cried, "Betty! Betty!" and the star smiled and posed accommodatingly. Laughing, she lifted her dress so the train would not touch the snow, and to the people who shouted her name, she called back, "Merry Christmas!" A roar swept over the crowd.

The street was jammed now with vehicles waiting to discharge Kallenberg's invited guests. Inevitably there were a few incidents. A very fat bejeweled lady lost her footing in the snow at the precise instant that a voice from the mob cried, "I'll bet they're paste!" The woman sprawled on the carpet, and since she was unable to rise on her own, several other guests attempted to raise her, amid general hilarity. Finally, two footmen came to the rescue and succeeded in hoisting her to her feet. Sputtering in indignation, the lady made her way up the steps on the servants' arms, as the onlookers good-naturedly cried, "Merry Christmas!"

The parade of guests continued uninterrupted, the ladies venturing courageously into Kallenberg's midsummer snowfall, their coiffures protected by umbrellas, the gentlemen laughing and calling to one another, gesturing, brushing the snow from their dinner jackets.

A shirt-sleeved passerby stopped and stared for a moment, an expression of utter astonishment on his face. "What the bloody hell—?" he muttered to himself, then turned and disappeared into the sweltering August night.

"Do you want to make some money?"

The young man turned. His face was pale, his eyes wary. Despite his youth, he had about him the look of a man just out of prison. He rapidly took stock of the two men before him, concluding from past experience that they were not policemen.

"What makes you think I need money?"

"I didn't ask if you needed money. I asked if you wanted to make some."

"How?"

"Look, let's not play games. Do you want to make some money or don't you?"

"Doesn't everybody? But it depends on what I have to do."

The two men exchanged a brief glance. One, the taller of the two, was named Percy. The other, short and stocky, was called Wise. They looked like what they were: small-time hoodlums who made their living along the London waterfront. In that respect, neither of them was particularly conspicuous among the clientele of the Anchor Tavern, one of Bankside's most popular pubs.

Percy answered, "We want to play a joke on a bunch of nobs, to put some life into their party. A friendly joke."

"Why didn't you tell me it was a joke? I need a good laugh. How much are you paying?"

"Ten pounds."

"What do I have to do?"

"Just come along with us. We'll give you the details in the truck."

The young man tapped the counter with a coin to attract the bartender's attention. Wise, with an expansive gesture, threw five shillings onto the counter. "Forget it," he said. "It's on us."

They emerged from the bar onto the docks. Nearby an anonymous delivery truck was parked.

"Come on," Wise said. "Get in. I want you to meet some nice people."

There were about ten men in the truck, seated on two benches, smoking, passing around a bottle of Seagram's, drinking, wiping the mouth of the bottle on their sleeves. For the past two hours—since shortly before the first of Kallenberg's guests had begun to arrive—Percy and Wise had gone from pub to pub, collecting men. They were all young. Had it not been for their hard looks, they could have passed for students.

Percy and Wise worked for Bill Mockridge, who was connected with International Shipping Limited. International, in turn, was the British affiliate of a Panamanian shipping concern. Wise was sufficiently astute to suspect that Mockridge's real employer was, in fact, Socrates Satrapoulos, the famous shipowner. But since Wise was neither curious nor talkative, and since Mockridge had got him out of jail by posting a heavy bail, he had mentioned his suspicions to no one, not even to Percy, his closest friend and his business associate. The two men had undertaken a number of unusual assignments for Mockridge, assignments dealing with such matters as union elections and strikebreaking. Occasionally, they had been asked to beat up men whom they did not know and against whom they had nothing—save Mockridge's assurance that the victims were not "regular guys."

In this particular instance, their assignment was to gather some hundred strapping young men, pay them ten pounds apiece, and deliver them to a certain house on the Mall with orders to disrupt a party. It was an easy job: push around a few of the guests and create a rumpus—just enough to make someone call the police. Then, of course, they were to disappear before the police arrived.

Wise wondered whether his men were right for the job. What if he could not control them? Well, he would see. Meanwhile, he would explain what was expected of them, then give them their money.

The truck came to a halt before a huge deserted warehouse. Within, the other men Percy and Wise had recruited waited. This was the last load.

Wise looked at his watch. Sixty minutes to H hour.

Raph Dun instructed the chauffeur of his rented Cadillac to drive past the house on the Mall. He had seen the mob of onlookers, pushing and shoving one another to get a better look at the guests, to ask for their autographs, to see them in the flesh. The automobiles of the arriving guests were lined up three deep along the curb. All these things had made Raph decide to postpone his arrival. Above all, he did not want to be merely one of a group of guests. He must arrive in solitary splendor, his chauffeur holding open the door of the black Cadillac so that he might emerge into the snow, a stunning girl on each arm, and receive the plaudits of the crowd.

"Raph, is it real snow?" one of the girls asked.

"Yes, my dear. Everything in that house is real. The jewels, the paintings, even the snow."

"Gina," the second girl said, "is my hair all right in the back?"

"It's perfect. Lend me your compact."

Kallenberg had told him, "Bring whomever you wish. Your friends are welcome in my house." He had radiated warmth following delivery of the documents.

Raph had taken advantage of the invitation to ask two actresses of his acquaintance to accompany him: Gina, who had just arrived from Rome, and Nancy, a Frenchwoman who was shooting a film in England. They had surpassed themselves this evening. Nancy, the blonde, was in white, and Gina, a brunette, was in black. Together, they looked like the two sides of a domino.

Raph knew from long experience with gatherings of this kind that at a certain point during a protracted evening the skin of the youngest women faded; that of the not-so-young curdled, like an overripe soufflé; and that of the older women appeared, like wrinkled parchment, through cracks in the veneer of cosmetics.

The Cadillac had now circled the block three times, but circumstances were not yet entirely suitable for Raph's entrance.

"Go around again," he told the chauffeur.

"Is he really as rich as everyone says?" Nancy asked.

"Richer than everyone says."

"Even richer than Satrapoulos?"

Dun smiled. "Let's just say that one is as rich as the other. But, you know, business is unpredictable. A lot of things can happen to a man. One little disaster and, pouf!—a man's fortune can disappear."

"Nancy, do you know him?" Gina asked.

"Know who?"

"Kallenberg."

"No. Do you?"

"No. Is he married, Raph?"

"Yes, he's married. And don't think that you're going to be the next Madame Kallenberg. He plays around, but he doesn't marry." He burst into laughter. "All right, girls. Are you ready for your grand entrance?"

The chauffeur was able to get into the second spot in line. Not bad, Raph told himself.

Then there was a cry: "Stand back! Stand back!" A siren sounded in the street, and an ambulance, its lights flashing, drew up behind Raph's Cadillac. The chauffeur had no choice but to make way for it, and the car moved forward before Raph and the two girls were able to get out. It stopped twenty feet farther on, at a point where it was surrounded on three sides by other automobiles and on the fourth by the mob.

"Stay here," Raph ordered. "I'm going to see what's happened." He leaped from the car in time to see two attendants run up the stairway carrying a folded stretcher. Five seconds later, they came out of the house surrounded by a knot of men in dinner jackets, straining under the weight of a very large, diamond-encrusted woman lying on the stretcher, her face contorted in pain.

"It's the fat one who slipped in the snow!" someone shouted on the sidewalk, and the spectators burst into laughter. Hastily the attendants loaded the stretcher into the ambulance, as another voice cried, "Next time, lady, bring your skis!"

Very funny, Raph said to himself, furious that his entrance had been spoiled, laugh at her if you want to. You'll all be asleep in your hovels when this party is still going strong.

Then, angrily, he pushed his way through the crowd toward his car.

Amore Dodino did not fit the time-hallowed image of a tenor. He was a singer, but he was not stupid. In all fairness, however, it should be noted that he was not a great singer. He was, in fact, mediocre. Moreover, he looked remarkably like a horse—albeit a handsome horse. His long, bony face, his magnificent, manelike hair, his rigid posture and large, semicircular posterior—all contributed to the illusion. When he started, at a gentle gallop, to throw himself upon an acquaintance and bestow the ritual triple kiss on each cheek— right, left, right—one almost expected to hear him neigh. Instead of equine noises, however, what invariably issued from his lips was a totally unexpected, sometimes shocking observation, usually at the expense of the friend in question. Or else, when Peter and Paul arrived together, he rushed to embrace Paul (right, left, right), whispered a calumny about Peter, and then, hurling himself at Peter (right, left, right), murmured some atrocity about Paul. Invariably, both victims laughed, knowing that each of them was the object of the other's amusement, but feeling nonetheless that they were even.

Paradoxically, Dodino's victims worshiped him, for, as everyone knew, he bestowed his insults only on the best people, and his silence was the equivalent of a death sentence in international society. For Dodino, without really trying, had been accepted as the high judge of that society, the grand master of the order, with the power of arbitrarily accepting or rejecting bids for membership. Woe betide anyone who crossed him. With a single word, he could open an old wound or inflict a new one, at which his accomplices would pick, by their laughter, until it proved fatal. He was adorable, pitiless, unpredictable: the ultimate homosexual. No one knew, from one day to the next, where one stood with Amore Dodino.

For the moment, he had fixed his attention on a striking young woman who was laughing uncontrollably at one of his sallies. "My dear," he said, "my poor words are the only means I have of provoking you to spasms of any kind."

Peggy Nash-Belmont was thoroughly entranced, and Dodino's sallies to people entering the room were "absolutely fantastic." Dodino, of course, knew his *Almanach de Gotha* by heart, as well as his various *Social Registers*. He was perfectly aware of who Peggy was. He knew her name, her antecedents, her net worth, her relatives, her mother's marriages, the given names of her two grandmothers, her sisters' nicknames, the identities of her couturier and her hairdresser, and the kind of perfume she used. Yet he behaved toward Peggy as though he had never heard of her. And Peggy, delighted at being "discovered," allowed herself to be deceived.

"Excuse me a moment, my dear," Dodino whispered to Peggy, moving toward Raph Dun.

"You, of all people," he accosted Raph. "Kallenberg is *not* very discriminating tonight. Introduce me to the two heavenly creatures with you." He lowered his voice to a hoarse whisper. "For God's sake, Raph! They let you in with those two *sluts?*"

"Amore, this is Gina, and this is Nancy."

"They're lovely! You see that enormously fat creature over there, the one who looks as though she's about to bear an elephant—even though she has the reputation of being androgynous—well. . . ."

As Dodino spoke, he passed his hand with loving insistence over Dun's posterior. Dun smiled. "A return to affection, Dodo?"

"Hardly, my dear. A return to middle age. I'm going through menopause. And don't look at me like that. You look as pregnant as that other one over there. Doesn't he, girls?"

Gina and Nancy laughed loudly. They both knew Dodino by reputation, and they were prepared to laugh at anything rather than
have it said that they did not understand.

A troop of footmen passed, carrying caviar canapés, followed by
bewigged children with champagne and glasses.

In a corner of the room, Satrapoulos was teasing his wife, who pretended to be absorbed in a Rubens hanging on the wall above her
head. "So," Satrapoulos was saying, "you love birds so much that
you go into pet shops to open their cages and set them free. . . ."

Not far away, beneath a Giotto Madonna, Isabelle Costa dug her
fingernails into Mark's hand. "I'm not going to let you go until I find
out," she hissed, "what were you doing in the pet shop with that little
tramp!"

"Isabelle, listen to me. . . ."

Before a raised platform on which a chamber orchestra was holding forth, Irene stood receiving her guests, allowing her hand to be
kissed, acknowledging compliments, and never taking her eyes from
a young Scottish lord, or at least never taking them from that portion of his muscular, solid legs which was visible between the tops of
his stockings and the bottom of his kilt. How she would have loved
to lift the hem of that male skirt. . . .

She sighed lasciviously. A massive dose of tranquilizers she had
taken that morning, after a sleepless night during which Kallenberg
had beaten her with a belt in a vain attempt to get what he wanted,
had enabled her to spend a quiet forenoon. Since 6 P.M., she had
been seeing the world through a blue haze induced by amphetamines
and black coffee. It was not a disagreeable view. It erased the wrinkles
from her guests' faces, leaving them smooth, if somewhat ill-defined.
However, she was able to see their teeth with surprising clarity, and
these she counted, mechanically, when anyone smiled.

A sudden change in the atmosphere of the room brought her out
of her lethargy. The orchestra had stopped playing, and Kallenberg
mounted the platform. He raised his arms for attention and began
speaking.

"My friends—"

Applause.

Satrapoulos, standing behind Lena, made a face.

"—since today is Christmas"—(laughter)—"I have a gift for you!"

With a theatrical gesture, he pulled back a square of cloth covering an object propped up against the piano. There was a long cry of

admiration at the superb Degas canvas depicting two dancers at the bar.

"It's for you," Kallenberg said.

"It's an auction!" someone shouted.

Kallenberg smiled good-naturedly. "No, no, my friends. It's not an auction. It's a door prize! And one of you is going to win it. On the reverse side of your invitation card, there's a number—"

There was a rustle in the room as everyone searched frantically for his card.

"I've won it," Countess Lupus cried, "except that I've lost my invitation."

Everyone laughed.

"And now," Kallenberg continued, "to pick the winning number, I need a hand. An innocent hand."

No one stirred. The host moved down the three steps of the platform and, with an air of authority, took Lena by the hand and led her onto the podium.

"Of course, Lena Satrapoulos is my sister-in-law, but surely Caesar's wife is above suspicion!"

Helena's liaison with Mark Costa was no secret to many of Kallenberg's guests, and a number of surreptitious looks were directed toward Satrapoulos. The Greek's face remained impassive.

"So, Lena, would you please draw a number? Just one number."

Kallenberg held out a large silver urn, and Lena removed several slips of folded paper. She retained one, allowing the others to fall back into the urn, and handed it to her brother-in-law.

"Ninety-three," Kallenberg announced.

There was silence for a few moments; then, a shout: "It's me!"

"Come up here," the host ordered, and Peggy Nash-Belmont made her way through the crowd and up the steps of the platform. Kallenberg took her hand, gallantly kissed the tips of her fingers, embraced her, and gestured toward the Degas. "It's yours," he said.

When the applause had abated, the host concluded: "To one and all, a Merry Christmas! And now, let the feast begin! To the table, everyone!"

At the far end of the room, a gigantic rosewood panel slid back to reveal another room, as large as the first. Through the floor rose dozens of small tables, decorated with flowers and shaded lights, and covered with gastronomic delicacies.

Gina gasped with admiration. "It's like something from the *Arabian Nights!*" She had read a book or two in her time.

"Not at all, my dear," replied Dodino. "It's pure Walt Disney. The *Fantasia* of the plutocrats."

The orchestra, playing Christmas carols, led the way into the dining room, and the servants bustled about seating the guests. Dun, who had seen many such celebrations, judged that this was indeed one to remember.

Between compliments from her guests, Irene stole away to her apartment. She had made a blunder which she must correct at any cost. Her honor was at stake. In all innocence Helena had asked her sister what Kallenberg had given her for "Christmas."

"Come up to my apartment in ten minutes, and I'll show you," Irene had answered without thinking.

Her immediate problem was that Herman had given her nothing. Usually, he missed no opportunity to flood her with extraordinary gifts of all kinds—fabulous jewels, paintings of the masters, luxurious clothing. These were not, as Irene knew, manifestations of affection. Rather, they were proof that Kallenberg regarded her as his personal property and that, as such, she must serve to heighten his prestige. Moreover, since his marriage to Irene, Kallenberg had waged a sort of war of gifts with Satrapoulos, a competition which had gone to ridiculous extremes. So intense was the competition between the two men that as soon as he learned of Satrapoulos' latest extravagance, Kallenberg immediately set out to outdo his brother-in-law, and vice versa. On the other hand, Kallenberg sometimes made violent scenes simply because Irene forgot to turn out a light, insulting her and accusing her of trying to drive him into bankruptcy.

So far as her jewels were concerned, they emerged from the vaults of Herman's bank only when there was a party, for Kallenberg swore that Lloyd's refused to insure jewelry when it was not locked in a safe. Still, for everyday use, Irene had managed to hide away a few baubles worth, all told, two million dollars. She kept these pieces in a safe hidden behind the fine copy of Titian's "Venus and Adonis" which hung over her bed. Now she slid the painting aside, dialed the combination, and nervously removed a few items: a pear-shaped pendant, a few diamond rings, topaz earrings, a ruby necklace. Her hand came to rest on a magnificent bracelet of turquoise and diamonds. In the dim light from the safe, it harmonized marvelously with the Chanel creation of cerulean silk that she was wearing.

Irene tried desperately to remember whether Lena had ever seen the bracelet. But it was too late. There were two soft taps, and Lena entered. Irene would simply have to take the risk.

"Here, look."

"Just a second. I look absolutely ghastly."

"Nonsense, you look lovely. Here—"

"Irene, please, just a second. I have to fix my face."

Lena disappeared into the bathroom. Irene fidgeted with the bracelet for three interminable minutes, until Lena reappeared.

"Now, show me."

Irene threw the bracelet onto the bed.

"Cartier?" Lena asked.

"No. Zolotas."

"Pretty. I have two of them, very much like this one, but from Tiffany's."

"I don't remember seeing you wear them."

"I don't have time to wear them. Socrates has a mania about bracelets. He gives them to me one a week, at breakfast."

"He doesn't have much imagination."

"You think so? Three days ago, on the twins' first birthday—you'll see, this is funny—my maid opened the windows in my room about nine o'clock in the morning. I looked out, and there was a gigantic package of some kind directly outside, completely blocking my view. I asked my maid what it was, but she ran out of the room, giggling.

"Well, you know that my room is on the third floor. I looked at the thing again. It was about twenty feet long, just hanging there in the air. I looked down, and there was an orchestra on the ground. As soon as they saw me, they began playing *sirtakis*. Then the package— it was on a crane—began moving down toward the ground. I ran down into the courtyard and tore off the wrapping. It was a Rolls!"

"You already have three Rolls—"

"But this is a *white* Rolls."

"A white—"

"Let me finish. This is the funny part. In the front seat of the Rolls, half asphyxiated, was a chauffeur in livery—a real Filipino! He was part of Socrates' present."

Irene, thoroughly irritated, cut her off. "By the way," she snapped, "what about Mark?"

Lena looked at her innocently. "Mark who?"

"You know very well who. Mark Costa, the actor. He's downstairs right now."

"Oh, Mark? What about him?"

"Lena, don't play the fool—"

"Show me your new jewels," Helena begged, certain that Irene's vanity would win out over her malice.

Irene went to the open safe. "Look at this ring," she said, holding out an enormous blue-white thirty-carat stone mounted on a simple band of gold.

"It's superb! Why don't you ever wear it?"

"Because, believe it or not, it's so heavy that after an hour I can hardly lift my arm."

Lena laughed. "That's terrible," she said. "Come on, let's join the others."

Kallenberg and Satrapoulos were alone in the study. Despite the soundproofing, the sound of voices, women's laughter and strains of music drifted into the room. Kallenberg, a grave look on his face, paced the room restlessly, stopping occasionally to look at a painting. Satrapoulos sat motionless, his huge glasses masking his eyes, watching his brother-in-law's every move, wondering when the attack would come.

"I can't understand," Kallenberg said, "why you've never wanted to collect paintings."

The Greek did not answer.

"I mean, even if you have no appreciation of art, paintings are an excellent investment."

"Did you ask me up here to give me a lecture in art appreciation?"

"No, of course not. It's more complicated than that. I'm afraid it's quite disagreeable."

"You have a problem? Irene?"

"Irene is quite all right, thank you. It's not Irene. It's you."

"Me? How can I help with this problem of yours?"

The Greek's tone irritated Kallenberg profoundly. "It is not I who need help," he growled, "but you."

"I? Why on earth would I need help?"

"I'll lay my cards on the table. I know that you're interested in the Emir of Baran."

"Is there a reason why I shouldn't be?"

"Not at all. You're certainly within your rights. I'm interested in him too, and that is my right, also."

"You don't mean it!"

Kallenberg made an effort to control himself. He recalled that he held all the cards, that the result of the game was already certain.

"I don't know why you're being so defensive," he said in an injured tone. "I'm only trying to tell you what I know. It's very hard to say it—"

"Well, then, just blurt it out."

"I'm very upset about this. It's not just a matter of money, but of honor, a matter than can affect the good name of the entire family."

"Family?"

"In case you've forgotten, I'll remind you that we married sisters and that we're brothers-in-law."

"That's correct. But what has all this to do with the Emir of Baran?"

"You have enemies, Socrates. So do I, for that matter. We have power, fleets of ships—"

"I still don't see the connection."

"I'm coming to it. For reasons that I ignore, but which you may know better than I, a group of French journalists are determined to ruin you."

"Ah. How do they propose to go about this?"

"Your mother."

"What about my mother?"

"They've found her. She talked to them. It's not for me to judge you, Socrates, but she told them that you've left her in poverty, that you've never given her a cent. They've documented the whole thing —tape recordings, photographs, everything."

"So?"

"So, they intend to publish the story."

"How do you know?"

"They thought that we were rivals and that I would like to see the documents."

"How much?"

"How much what?"

"How much did you pay them?"

Kallenberg was the image of injured innocence. "I'm trying to help you, and you insult me. You know very well that the slightest word about either of us is picked up by every newspaper in the world. If either one of us is involved in a scandal, the other one also suffers."

"But what is the scandal?"

"Have you taken leave of your senses? Do you think that a man in your position can leave his mother to starve and get away with it?"

"I don't understand. Has my mother died?"

Kallenberg's blood boiled in his veins. He stormed to his desk—the very desk at which Talleyrand had signed the treaty concluding the Congress of Vienna—picked up an envelope and threw it onto Satrapoulos' lap. "Here, look at that!" He flicked on a tape recorder. It was a mistake, Kallenberg knew. The presence of the tape indicated premeditation. But he could not resist playing his trump card.

Athina's voice filled the room: ". . . thrown out of every school he ever attended. None would keep him more than a week."

"Why?"

"Because he was always full of evil."

"Hasn't he ever tried to help you?"

"No, never."

"Does he have any special reason to avoid you?"

"He can't stand people who knew him when he was weak, including his mother. Once he struck me."

"When did that happen?"

With a brusque movement of his hand, Kallenberg shut off the recorder. "Is that enough?" he rasped. "It goes on for more than two hours. And the photographs. Have you looked at them? Do you recognize her?"

Satrapoulos shuffled the photographs, then fanned them out like playing cards. The expression on his face was that of a man who knows that his opponent holds a royal flush.

"Not very well, no."

"Surely that doesn't surprise you. How long since you saw her?"

Satrapoulos did not answer.

"I'll tell you how long. Thirty years! That's on the tape, also. One changes in thirty years, especially when one lives in a pigsty."

"One changes in thirty years even when one does not live in a pigsty," the Greek murmured. Then, in a louder voice: "All right, what is it that you want?"

"Only to warn you of the danger. That's all."

"Is that really all? What about Hadj Thami el Sadek?"

"That should be obvious. You know very well that, for political reasons, he can never sign a contract with a man whose morals are not above suspicion. Or rather, I should say, with a man whose honor has been compromised by neglect of the most sacred familial ties."

Satrapoulos could not restrain his laughter.

"What amuses you?" Kallenberg bristled.

"Tell me," the Greek answered, "where is your mother?"

"I beg your pardon?"

"I am asking you to tell me where your mother is."

"She's dead, as you know."

"I'm sorry. I had forgotten. How lucky you are."

"I will not be the one to cast the first stone, Socrates, but I can tell you that she never wanted for anything so long as she lived."

"Let's get back to the business at hand. If I understand you correctly, you are trying to blackmail me into giving up the contract with the Emir of Baran."

"That is your way of putting it, not mine. I have simply informed you of a plot against you. What you decide to do about it is your own affair."

"Who will profit from this crime?"

From below, shrieks of laughter reached the room. The guests, their inhibitions dulled by alcohol, were enjoying themselves enormously.

"If there has been a crime, I am not the one who committed it. I repeat that my own mother never wanted for anything."

"Yes, I know. You've already mentioned that. Tell me; these journalists, do you know them?"

"No. I merely received a photograph of your mother in the mail, with a note explaining who she was."

"How much do you think this exposé is worth to them?"

"I really don't think they can be bought."

"At any price? But didn't you tell me that they wanted to sell you this material? What do you suggest I do?"

"I have no idea. I'm not you. Do you really want this contract with Baran so badly?"

"Do you?"

"I have no reason to believe that I will be the one to get it."

"Who else has a chance?"

"There are a dozen others: Livanos, Niarchos, Onassis, Goulandris, the Norwegians—anyone at all, so long as the Arab gets what he's asking for. Our own mother-in-law could carry it off. Or the Americans, the French, the British. So, you see, it's not really just a matter between you and me."

"Yes, I see that. Tell me, Herman. What would you do in my place?"

"First of all, I'm not in your place. But if I were, I would stop and think. If this material is published, you're going to lose the contract. That much is certain. And you know it."

"Yes, yes. That's true. I'm afraid I wouldn't have a chance."

"I think you're being very sensible. The only thing to do is to give up the contract."

"Give up the contract? Who said anything about giving up the contract? I'm damned if I do, and I'm damned if I don't, so I have nothing to lose. I don't know what your own situation is right now, but a part of my fleet is in port right now, without cargo, and I have to find some freight for them. And I have three giant tankers under construction at Oslo."

"You're going to let this terrible scandal break over our heads?" Kallenberg asked in a shocked voice. He told himself that Socrates was surely bluffing. What gall the man had!

In a gentle, resigned tone, the Greek countered: "Well, you yourself assured me that there was no way to buy off these newspapermen. I'd rather have them carry out their threat than let it hang over my head for the rest of my life. Let them publish! I'll still take my chances with the emir."

Kallenberg felt his face go scarlet with rage. "You don't think they'd really publish, do you? They're only trying to put pressure on you! There's someone behind them. They wouldn't dare publish!"

"Who is behind them?"

"How should I know? But I can try to work something out. I can try to find out who it is."

The Greek rose from his chair and brushed imaginary ashes from his trousers. "If you should happen to see any of the people involved—I know it's very unlikely—tell them for me that I don't give a shit for them. Tell them that I run my business as I please. And tell them that I don't like to be threatened."

"You're wrong, Socrates! Wrong! You don't realize what you're saying! Think of me! Think of Irene! And think of Lena!"

"I have thought of you, and it's all taken care of. If anything should happen to me, or if you should lose everything and be in want, like my mother, I've arranged to have a pension paid to you for as long as you live."

"What you're doing is idiotic! A disaster!"

"We'll see. Well, I must go find Lena. And, Herman, I'll never forget what you tried to do for me tonight. Thank you, thank you. And Merry Christmas!"

Before Kallenberg could think of a way to keep Satrapoulos from leaving, the Greek had disappeared through the doorway into the cacophony of songs, shouts, and laughter rising from the ground floor of the building.

Kallenberg looked at his Cranach for a few moments, but found no peace. He rose and switched on the tape recorder. Athina spoke:

"He just jumped on me and started beating me. His father had to drag him away."

"How old was he when that happened?"

"Thirteen."

Suddenly, Kallenberg made his decision. So Socrates Satrapoulos wanted war, did he? Very well. It would be war. And the war, Kallenberg had determined, would begin with Satrapoulos' own Pearl Harbor.

He would have preferred that the Greek simply acquiesce and withdraw from the competition in Baran. But since he was too stubborn to see reason—well, so much the worse for him.

Kallenberg walked toward the door.

After the icy atmosphere of his encounter with Kallenberg, the warmth and noise from the lower floor struck Satrapoulos like a blow. The meal was over. The Dom Pérignon and the Cliquot rosé 1928, imprudently mixed with the whiskey and the vodka which appeared, as though by magic, in the hands of the guests, had done their work. A jazz combo had replaced the chamber orchestra, and a mob of guests moved about to its rhythms. The Greek looked around for his wife. He pushed his way through the dancing couples, an almost anonymous figure in the crowd which he considered nothing more than extras hired to lend a note of authenticity to the drama that had just been played out on the upper floor. Only Dodino, whom nothing escaped, took note of Socrates wandering about as though in search of something.

"The proletariat has returned to us," he said to the young man at his side.

"Who is he?"

"My dear boy! Are you just off the boat? Must I tell you everything. Well, let me explain. . . ."

He squeezed the young man's hand and undertook his worldly education, as a preliminary to undertaking his sentimental education.

Where would Lena be? Behind the platform, Socrates found a door opening into a corridor. There were other doors off the corridor, most of which were closed. Behind one of them, he heard the sound of voices. Cautiously, he turned the knob, and immediately caught the sickly sweet odor of marijuana. In the room three boys and two girls, all very young, were passing around a cigarette. One of the girls was lying on the bed, her skirt around her hips, and two of the boys were investigating her charms. None of them noticed Socrates. He closed the door and opened another. The room was in total darkness, but the sounds emanating from it left no doubt in Satrapoulos' mind as to the kind of activity which it sheltered or the number of persons participating in that activity.

As Socrates moved to return to the salon, he came face to face with Irene. She had just emerged from a door at the foot of the corridor —probably a service stairwell, the Greek decided. He opened his mouth to speak to her, but she brushed past without seeming to recognize him, giving him a mechanical smile, and continued on her way. Satrapoulos wondered where she had been. He walked to the end of the corridor, opened the door and peered in. There was a staircase leading to an upper floor. And coming down the stairs was a Scotsman, magnificent in traditional highland dress. The Greek stepped aside to allow this apparition to pass. The kilted lord gave him a haughty look, as though the great Satrapoulos were a servant, nodded once, and disappeared down the corridor.

Satrapoulos shrugged and followed him to the salon, still in search of Lena. He found her, finally, in animated conversation with the girl who had won the Degas. With them was a tall, handsome man whom he did not know. He brushed Helena's bare shoulder with the back of his hand, apologized for interrupting, and said, "Lena, I think it's time for us to go."

She turned to her companions. "May I present my husband? Miss Peggy Nash-Belmont, Mr. Raph Dun."

The girl's name struck a familiar note. "Are you by any chance related to Christopher Nash-Belmont?"

"He's my father."

"And one of my very good friends. I'll tell you a secret. You and I once enjoyed a brief flirtation. I met you at a horse show. You were with your father, and you could not have been more than six or seven years old."

"Well, Miss Nash-Belmont," Raph said, "you obviously make a deep impression on your admirers, even at that age—"

Satrapoulos surreptitiously pressed Helena's hand. They took their leave of Raph and Peggy and moved along the wall toward the exit.

"What about Irene?" Helena asked. "I haven't even said goodnight to her." She was normally completely indifferent to the amenities so far as her sister was concerned, but she hoped to be allowed to make a final tour of the salon so as to catch a glimpse of Mark. She had deliberately stood close to him several times during the evening, but with Isabelle exercising an even more diligent surveillance than usual, he had not dared raise his eyes to her.

"There's no point in trying to find her," Satrapoulos said. "She has a headache."

"Who told you that?"

"Her husband. I had a long talk with him, in his study."

"With Herman? About what?"

"Paintings. He was trying to convince me to start a collection."

They were in the vestibule, before the massive double doors which led to the street. Two footmen swung open the panels.

"Well," Lena said as they moved toward the sidewalk, "I'll see her in New York next Tuesday."

"You're going to New York?"

"One of those charity things. It's only for three days."

Satrapoulos was no longer listening to his wife. His mind was occupied with thoughts of Kallenberg. His brother-in-law might be able to engineer a snowfall in August, but he, Socrates Satrapoulos, had arranged for fireworks the likes of which Kallenberg and his guests had never seen.

Bill Mockridge had explained to Percy and Wise that their project must appear to be an unpremeditated prank: something youthful, exuberant, undertaken by a group of fun-loving students. In the warehouse on the docks, Wise had given final instructions to his men, then dispatched them, in groups of eight or ten, to mingle with the crowd of spectators gathered before Kallenberg's house on the Mall. There, suddenly, they merged into a single mass with the unpredictable spontaneity of a crowd. The two policemen still on duty and the servants who had been stationed outside the house saw a large band of young men move quickly up the steps and push their way into the house, while the people on the sidewalk shouted encouragement. "Go on in!" someone cried. "If you're lucky, you'll get some caviar!"

One of the bobbies sensed danger and tried to block the horde of youths, shouting to his more complaisant partner, "John! We have to stop them! There's going to be trouble!"

John shrugged. His partner tended to take everything too seriously. What did it really matter? The party was almost over, and what was left of it could certainly do with a bit of excitement.

The youths—none of them was over twenty—were now inside Kallenberg's house, laughing, shouting, pushing aside everyone in their path, guests and servants alike. Within, there had been a moment of stupefaction at this invasion; then the Countess Lupus' piercing voice rose above the din:

"Why, they're charming! Dodino, ask one of them to dance!"

To the laughter of the intruders was joined that of the ladies in the room as some of the youths took them roughly into their arms and led them in a wild dance to the accompaniment of the band. Couples formed, separated, and re-formed as husbands, legitimate and otherwise, pretended uneasily to enjoy the spectacle.

Then, unexpectedly, the forced bonhomie ended. The enormous Countess Lupus, whom a thin young hoodlum was leading in a frenetic jig, declared that she was tired of "dancing." Her partner refused to release her and began spinning her around wildly. After a few seconds the countess succeeded in disengaging herself and gave the boy a resounding slap, as she would have done if he had been her husband. But it was not the housebroken count with whom the lady was dealing. The youth turned pale, then lowered his head and butted the countess in the breasts with all his strength. Then he grabbed great handfuls of her hair and tugged violently.

It all happened so quickly that no one had a chance to react. The countess' magnificent hair suddenly, magically, was stripped from her head, exposing a bald pate from which rose a few scattered tufts of gray. It was a stunning apparition. The countess, still breathless from her involuntary jig, did not even protest when her partner grasped her dress at the shoulder and, with one mighty pull, ripped it open to the floor. There was a horrified silence—even the musicians stopped playing—at the sight of this gigantic woman, shorn of her wig, standing in her slip, stripped of the defenses that she had created against the world.

"There, bitch!" her assailant snarled and struck her across the mouth with the back of his hand.

The countess clumped to the floor with a dull thud, like the sound of a sack of flour striking the ground. The count now rushed to her aid, knowing well that there was nothing he could do other than attempt to wash away the affront to his honor. With the desperate courage of the weak, he threw himself upon the youth, trying awkwardly to strike him in the face.

Meanwhile, the Scotsman—Irene's Scotsman in kilts—stepped forward and, with one mighty blow, sent the countess' attacker sprawling unconscious on the floor. But almost simultaneously, he was assaulted by two of the youth's companions.

Now everyone understood that this was no mere prank and that the danger was real. And everywhere brawls broke out among scattered groups of intruders and guests as Percy, at the head of an assault group, stormed up the grand staircase to the second floor, smashing furniture, ripping precious canvases, destroying everything within reach.

It happened that, at this moment, Kallenberg was in his study with Raph Dun. When he heard Percy and his men on the stairs, he threw open the door. Immediately, two of the invaders were upon him. He was pulled into the hallway and thrown to the floor. He rolled once and, as he twisted, launched a gargantuan kick at the nearer of his assailants. The man screamed and pivoted once before his shattered leg collapsed under him. By then Kallenberg was on his feet again. Without stopping to see what damage had been done, he rushed toward the door of his study, on the way almost instinctively crashing his fist into the face of the second assailant, smashing the man's nose and shattering his cheekbone.

Dun, in terrified silence, watched as Kallenberg threw open a drawer of the desk and took out a Beretta automatic.

"No!" Dun cried, "Don't!"

"No? Watch me!" Kallenberg spat as he charged toward the door.

Dun heard two shots. Then Kallenberg's voice boomed: "Dun, you idiot! Call the police! What are you waiting for?"

Raph, hand trembling, dialed 999. In a voice so calm that it astonished him, he began, "This is the Kallenberg residence on the Mall, number seventy-one. . . ."

Meanwhile, downstairs, the mob continued its work of demolition. Count Lupus, after his impulsive assault upon his wife's partner, had been attacked by three of the ruffians. He had tried to fight them off, but already exhausted by his first encounter, he decided that his only escape lay in flight. He ran up a staircase, his short legs moving with surprising speed, and found himself at a dead end, on a terrace where several guests and musicians had already taken refuge. A moment later his three attackers were upon him, determined to wreak vengeance upon this helpless prey. Lupus looked about wildly for a means of escape. There were none. He begged those already huddling on the terrace to help him. The women screamed, and the men tried to calm them; but no one moved toward Lupus. The three youths came toward him now in semicircular formation, forcing him back until he was standing against the railing of the terrace. He could go no farther. Terror-stricken, he heard one of the men say, "Pick him up by the legs and throw him over."

Lupus wanted to scream, to struggle, to pray, to call his wife, to do something, anything to escape. Instead, he remained standing, petrified by fear. He felt the youths' hands upon him and felt himself being raised into the air. Desperately he clutched at the hair of one of his assailants, and with the other hand, grasped the railing. By then his legs were over the parapet. He felt himself sliding. . . .

"Stop!" A woman's voice rang out, harsh in the night air. "Don't let him go! Pull him back!"

Lupus heard the voice fade, for he was now sliding irretrievably over the balustrade. He felt something brush against his body and clutched at it with all his strength; then he lost consciousness and released his grip, allowing his weight to rest upon the branches of the Christmas tree. They bent as Lupus' inert form continued its descent, then snapped back to their original position, throwing a shower of snow into the air.

At the moment that Lupus struck the ground, Wise was signaling to his men to retreat. He had heard the sound of police sirens in the distance. But the battle was not yet over. The Scottish lord, unwilling to concede defeat, was on the floor of the salon, struggling with two youths who were trying to hold him down. The battered youths, exasperated at his strength and enraged by their injuries, heard Wise's signal. But they were bent on vengeance. One of them pulled a knife from his pocket, and the blade flashed in the light of the precious chandelier overhead. "Hold him!" the man shouted to his companion, as the Scotsman rolled on the floor to avoid the knife. The second man threw himself on him, while the first raised the victim's kilt and, with a single stroke of the knife, severed his penis from his body. The Scotsman screamed once, horribly, doubled over on the floor, and fainted.

Percy ran up to the man with the knife, kicked him viciously, and simultaneously grabbed the other youth by the shoulders and pushed him toward the door. "Get out!" he shouted. "Police!"

At that moment, Kallenberg fired at them three times and missed.

The guests watched helplessly as the mob of intruders fled onto the street and the police sirens drew rapidly nearer. Dodino was hunched over the inert form of the Countess Lupus, tapping her cheeks gingerly, as a wary fisherman would tap the flank of a putatively dead whale. Then the vast salon seemed filled with policemen. Women wept, while stunned men tried to comfort them with meaningless words. A group had formed around the fallen Scotsman.

The police pushed their way through with a stretcher. Next to the victim his bloody organ lay on the plush carpet.

In the middle of the shattered room, towering above the broken bottles and splintered wood, stood Kallenberg, his Beretta still in his hand. To a policeman who approached him, he said, "Upstairs, in the hallway. I think I killed one of them."

[5]

Little Spiro had just herded his goats into the stable. It was dusk. Usually, he returned home earlier; but today the black goat had had something wrong with one of her hooves, and he had had to carry her.

He lingered at the top of the hill, lying on his back, a bit of straw between his teeth, looking at the blue sky until he grew dizzy, as though he might see, written across the heavens, the answers to the questions that preoccupied him.

The life of a young shepherd is a simple one. He has only to be concerned about his animals, a place to sleep and food to eat. Only rarely does anything occur to disturb his routine. Yet Spiro was troubled. He could not discover the meaning of the things he had seen. The constant coming and going of automobiles in a village where no automobiles were ever seen; the helicopters plunging from the sky, landing briefly, and then disappearing without a trace—these things both intrigued him and disturbed him. They constituted the unknown, and the unknown is always frightening.

Several times he had tried to question his uncle, but the latter apparently was determined not to answer. Why?

Spiro hooked the gate of the goat enclosure and walked into the roughly plastered room where he and his uncle ate their meals. Sometimes the uncle made a hot soup, but usually they ate a few olives, a piece of white cheese, and raw onions. Twice a year they killed a goat and roasted whole quarters of it in the fireplace.

On the wooden table were two glasses. One was full to the brim with a heavy wine that tasted of resin. The other, smaller, was filled with milk. Spiro, at his uncle's behest, had tasted the wine, and despite his desire to be a man, he had been obliged to spit it out. Perhaps, he told himself, when he was older, he would drink wine.

He sat to the left of his uncle and, without intending, or even wanting, he asked, "Why did Athina leave?"

The man did not raise his eyes from his plate. Thinking that he had not heard, Spiro rephrased the question: "Where have they taken her?"

"Eat your food."

That same evening, in all the capitals of Europe, the newspapers carried the story of Kallenberg's party on their front pages. Earlier in the day the shipowner had made dozens of telephone calls in an effort to have the story killed, believing that so tragic an event would irreparably harm his public image and his business. He had been astonished at the responses to his request. "You are too modest, Mr. Kallenberg," the editors had said. "You are a hero, and there is no reason to pretend otherwise."

It had been otherwise with the telephone call from his mother-in-law, which had come at dawn. God only knew how she had heard the news so early. Medea had been wild with rage, commanding him to send Irene home to Athens immediately, until the scandal had died down. Kallenberg had acquiesced humbly. If he had known then what the reaction of the newspapers would be, he would have hung up on her. In any case, what business was it of hers?

To be sure, the stories did not per se glorify Kallenberg, but then many things called attention to his courage and his reflexes. He read, again, the headlines of the *Daily Express*: SLAUGHTER ON CHRISTMAS NIGHT. Obviously, the word "slaughter" was hyperbolic. There had been only one person killed.

What a satisfying experience it had been to shoot the man. He had pressed the trigger, as he had a thousand times before while hunting. The youth had somersaulted to the floor. How different from shooting a duck.

On several past occasions Kallenberg had had to restrain himself
from giving way to his desires, especially with women when he had
his hands around their necks or when they had cringed at his feet
and he had felt an almost irresistible impulse to grind his heel into
their faces. Instead, he had joked with them, helped them rise by
winding his fingers in their hair, wondering sometimes if they did
not suspect how close to death they had been.

The *Sun* was hardly more subtle than the *Express*. MASSACRE AT
MILLIONAIRE'S HOME read the headline. The story, however, was written in an impersonal, emotionless style. It lacked the reality of the
screams, the blood, the smell of gunpowder, the blue smoke which
had twice risen from the barrel of his automatic. Who would have
thought that Satrapoulos, by sending in his crashers, would have
given him the opportunity to do what he had always wanted to do: to
kill with impunity?

His brother-in-law's name had come to him almost spontaneously.
Had Satrapoulos really engineered the whole thing? Kallenberg felt
certain that he had. What puzzled him, however, was that Satrapoulos had obviously planned his revenge before he had been attacked, even before he had known that he would be attacked.
Something was amiss. What could have moved Satrapoulos to turn
the party into a "massacre" as the *Sun* called it? He reread the article:

> In the course of an exclusive private party, celebrating Christ-
> mas on August 13, a band of ruffians invaded the London
> residence of Herman Kallenberg, the shipowner, terrorizing his
> guests and injuring several persons. Mr. Kallenberg, after sum-
> moning the police, courageously confronted the armed intruders
> and killed one of them. No identification was found on the dead
> man, but subsequent investigation has revealed that he was Bedel
> Moore, an unemployed seaman and a fugitive from justice who
> was being sought by the police. The intruders' arrival, organized
> to appear to be a student prank, did not unduly alarm Mr. Kal-
> lenberg's guests. . . .

And farther on:

> Count Lupus, the Ruhr steel magnate, is under sedation, after
> having been thrown from a third-story window by the intruders.
> In another encounter, Lord McIntyre was gravely wounded when
> he was set upon by three men who were under the influence
> of drugs.

Kallenberg, who had long regarded himself as possessing a monopoly on violence, was stunned to discover that the Greek was as willing as he to make use of it. Be that as it might, he swore Satrapoulos would pay for his insolence, and very quickly.

The first thing that morning, Kallenberg had drafted a long letter to the Emir of Baran, informing him of the methods which had been used in an effort to compromise him. He had then dispatched Wolf, his confidential agent, to Baran on a chartered flight. In the briefcase which he had handed to Wolf were prints of the photographs taken at Athina's house and a copy of the taped interview with Athina herself.

"Unfortunately," Kallenberg said in his letter, "it is no longer in my power to prevent the scandal, or rather, it has never been in my power to do so. I know, on unimpeachable authority, that the documents confirming my brother-in-law's actions are about to be published. As God is my witness, I have done all that I can to spare my family this ordeal. I myself informed Socrates Satrapoulos as to what was planned. To my surprise, he did not seem unduly affected by this knowledge."

Once the letter and documents had been confided to Wolf, Kallenberg showered and telephoned Raph Dun. Dun, who was staying at the Westbury in New Bond Street, was just drifting off to sleep when the telephone rang. He was exhausted. He had been compelled to go to police headquarters to give his version of events, which had corresponded in all respects to that given earlier by Kallenberg himself: the shipowner had been pulled from his study by two men brandishing knives. He had struggled with his assailants, broken away, seized his Beretta, and fired. Yes, Dun had seen the whole thing with his own eyes, since he had run into the hallway to help Kallenberg after calling the police. The police had thanked him politely for his help. When Dun returned to the Westbury, he had found Gina and Nancy, both frantic with worry, waiting for him. He had bathed, allowed the two actresses to massage his back, and caressed them in turn until his rising pleasure had enabled him to forget the evening's terrifying events.

Now, lying peacefully between Gina and Nancy, the last thing in the world he wanted was to answer the telephone. He tried to ignore its persistent ringing; then, irritably, he picked up the receiver.

"Whoever you are, can't it wait for a few hours? I'm dead on my feet."

Kallenberg's voice had come back, coldly. "I want you to be here in fifteen minutes. If I can do without sleep, so can you."

Dun was obliged to climb out of bed, over the bodies of his protesting playmates, and dress hurriedly.

"Try to get some sleep while I'm gone," he told Gina and Nancy. "I'll be back in an hour."

He stopped on the way to the Mall long enough to swallow two cups of very strong black coffee.

Kallenberg was waiting for him, freshly shaved, wearing a light gray suit, bursting with energy—the image of a man who, after eight hours of undisturbed sleep, had just enjoyed the attentions of a masseur. He went immediately to the business at hand.

"Last night's events have made me decide to go ahead with our project sooner than I had planned. When and where do you plan to publish those documents?"

Dun, half-asleep, made an effort to respond with precision. "First, we must inform the daily newspapers. I know a press agent who will take care of circulating the information simultaneously to the morning and evening newspapers. Then, of course, there are the weeklies. We'll have to allow a certain amount of delay for color publications—"

"Do you have black-and-white prints?"

"Yes, of course—"

"Let me have them. What about radio?"

"I was just coming to that. I'm going to contact a friend at the BBC and ask him to play a section of the tape this evening."

"What about the other stations?"

"Unless I give BBC an exclusive, they won't use any of it."

"Now listen to me. This is too important for it not to be exploited to the maximum. I want the whole world to know what's going on, and I want them to know it simultaneously."

"I'll do my best."

"That's what I want: for you to do your best."

"I don't want to have to sell this material cheap because of haste—"

"Don't worry about losing money. If you lose anything, I'll reimburse you ten times over. And of course I'll pay whatever expenses you've incurred."

Kallenberg's words were music in Raph's ears. He would have enough to go to Monte Carlo or Cannes, to recover all that he had lost in the past few months—

"I'll go back to the hotel and sleep for a few hours," he told Kallenberg. "Then I'll get right to work."

Kallenberg suppressed a surge of exasperation. With so much at stake, this little bastard could think of nothing but sleep.

His voice was soft, almost a whisper, masking his excitement. "Mr. Dun, if I occupy the position that I do today, it is because, whenever necessary, I have been willing to ignore my personal needs. Now I want those documents published with the least possible delay. Are you willing to undertake this on my behalf, or do you prefer that I find someone else to do the job?"

Before Raph's eyes rose the specter of his many creditors, his pile of unpaid bills, and the Ferrari that would undoubtedly be repossessed.

"I understand perfectly, Mr. Kallenberg," he said. "As soon as I leave, I will begin."

"That is kind of you. I want hourly reports on your progress. Sixty minutes from now, I will expect to hear from you concerning the reaction of the daily newspapers."

"Well—I don't know. The managing editors are probably still at home, and my press agent may not be able to reach them."

Instinctively, Dun knew that he had gone too far, and Kallenberg's response proved his instinct to be correct.

"Ah, then, Mr. Dun, wake them up! Wake them up! There are moments when I sense that you are not fully awake yourself—"

Raph tried to retrieve the situation by a feeble attempt at humor. "That's not possible. I haven't been to sleep yet." Then, seeing that Kallenberg did not smile, he added hastily, "Well, I'm off. You'll hear from me in one hour."

Raph was back in the Westbury before he remembered that his room was occupied by a pair of sleeping starlets. He would have to turn them out, he decided. He opened the door. The two girls were dead to the world.

"All right!" he said, shaking Nancy. "Let's go. It's time!"

"Time for what?" the girl mumbled.

"Time to go. I have work to do."

He shook Gina, but the brunette groaned loudly and hid her head under the covers.

Nancy scratched her shoulder. "What time is it?"

"Six o'clock in the evening."

"God! I feel like I've only been asleep for ten minutes."

"Wake up your friend, or I'll get a bucket of water from the bathroom."

"Raph, seriously, is it six o'clock?" She reached for her watch. "You bastard! It's only ten o'clock in the morning!"

Raph, overcome with fatigue and nervousness, lost his temper. "God damn it! I want you to get your asses out of here! I have work to do. I have to use the telephone—in private. Do you understand?"

Gina was awake now. "No one has ever spoken to me like that in my life," she said haughtily. "What a fine gentleman you are."

"There's a first time for everything," Raph observed.

"Where do you expect us to go," Nancy asked, "in evening dresses, at ten o'clock in the morning?"

Raph picked up the telephone. "Desk? This is Raph Dun, in 429. Do you have a vacant room on this floor?"

"Just a moment, sir. I'll see."

The clerk was back in a few seconds. "Yes, sir, 427. When are you expecting your friends?"

"They're already here."

"Ah. How long will they be staying?"

"Only for today. And send up a maid, will you? My friends will go to their room immediately."

He hung up. "All right, you heard," he said to Gina and Nancy. "You have a whole room all to yourselves. You don't even have to get dressed. It's next door, and you can go as you are."

The memory of Ingeborg, naked in the hall at the Ritz, brought a smile to his lips.

"Now he's making fun of us," Gina pouted.

Raph fell into the bed, on top of Nancy, and kissed Gina on the corner of her mouth. "No, my love, I'm not making fun of you. Something has just happened—something fantastic—but I must get to work on it immediately. A minute can mean the difference between life and death. Tonight I want to take you both to dinner with Zanuck. No, I'm not joking. It's my way of apologizing. Now, you two go off to bed, and as soon as I've finished my work, I'll come wake you up."

"It's true, this business about dinner with Zanuck?" Nancy asked skeptically.

"I swear it. We're supposed to meet him at the Mirabella, at nine sharp."

There was a knock at the door, and a maid thrust her head into the room. "427 is ready, sir."

When Nancy and Gina were on their feet, Raph slapped their posteriors amiably. Then he passed the tip of his tongue over Gina's breasts, while using his hand to pat Nancy's stomach. "You won't be sorry," he assured the two girls. "Tonight we'll celebrate the fortune I'm going to make from the story I'm working on!"

Yawning, the two girls put on terry-cloth robes supplied by the Westbury. Raph, his impatience difficult to conceal, held the door open for them. "Until later, girls. Sleep well, so that you'll be beautiful this evening!"

With a sigh of profound relief, he closed the door behind them, picked up the telephone, and said to the girl at the switchboard, "This is Raph Dun. First, I want you to send up some coffee, eggs, toast, marmalade—everything. You decide. Then I want you to stand by. I have about fifty urgent calls to make. The first is to Victoria 25-03. Then—"

Raph gave the switchboard the list of numbers while he evolved his plan of attack. When he had finished, he asked the operator, out of habit, "By the way, are you a blond or a brunette? No, wait! Let me guess. I can tell by your voice. I've got it. You're an ash-blonde!"

"You're wrong," the operator replied laughing. "I'm completely bald."

"Fantastic! I prefer bald girls. What time do you get off?"

She cut him off. "Here is your first number, sir."

Raph was instantly alert. If he played his cards right, he had a fortune in his pocket. After five rings, his agent answered. "Hello, Mike? Raph Dun. Wake up, and listen carefully—"

Raph ignored the stream of obscenities. "I don't give a goddamn about your sleep," he snarled. "If I can do without sleep, so can you."

My God, Raph told himself, I'm even talking like Kallenberg.

"Listen, Mike," he continued, "I have the most incredible, fantastic story. The scoop of the century. You'll thank me for calling you. With what you'll make from this, you'll be able to take a two-year vacation!"

Édouard Fouillet had been manager of the Paris Ritz for almost six months. Before that, he had held a similar position at the Ritz in London. He had been delighted to leave England, to be away from the staid old hotel with its silent, vast rooms and its clientele of distinguished septuagenarians. In France, at least, there was life!

Even during his sojourn in London, he had always arranged to spend his weekends at Enghien, where he had been born and where his mother and his stepfather still lived.

He had not been disappointed in his expectations. The hotel on the Place Vendôme was infinitely more lively than that in Piccadilly. There were many more transients, a truly royal clientele, an outstanding restaurant, and frequently, before dinner, brilliant cocktail parties.

Still, there were certain things that were not quite what they should have been. Silverware had a way of disappearing into the garbage cans, where it was recovered by accomplices. Linens vanished with equal facility. A celebrated sommelier in his old age developed a regrettable fondness for sampling the wines that he was supposed to serve the hotel's guests, and Fouillet, of course, had had to discharge the man summarily. These little nothings all added up to such considerable sums that the Ritz was operating well in the red.

There were other things, too. Some guests were so distinguished that one did not dare insist on their paying bills promptly—this would never have happened in London—and, moreover, were so busy that they could not be bothered with such administrative details. Their obligations, therefore, accumulated from one visit to the next, and if one asked them to pay, they were indignant at the impertinence of it all.

There were problems, also, with the children of the rich and the famous. Some of them were in the habit of bringing a half dozen girls at a time to their rooms, which had a deplorable effect upon the hotel's personnel. Others delighted in organizing parties which went on till dawn. At one such gathering, in one of the Ritz's most luxurious suites, Fouillet had had to intervene to break up a gambling spree.

All these people, obviously, brought a great deal of revenue into the Ritz's treasury. Yet, Fouillet reflected sadly, how times had changed from the days of the grand dukes. Fouillet himself was too young to remember those days, but he had often heard his older colleagues speak of them. Nowadays, it seemed, especially since the war, the most incredible people had money. Loud, vulgar, ill-mannered cattle barons who shouted for caviar at an hour when civilized people were drinking tea. Fouillet, who had risen through the ranks of the hotel hierarchy, was aware of the one eternal truth of his profession: that the guest was always right. Yet there was a point beyond which one could not go, a boundary beyond which lay madness.

He turned toward his assistant manager, who was waiting silently for his superior's decision.

"Be frank with me, Albert. What is your opinion?"

"I have already given it, sir. It seems difficult to go against the wishes of Monsieur Satrapoulos, who is one of our best customers, as well as one of the most generous."

"How much business does he give us?"

"He rents the large apartment on the top floor on a yearly basis. He is here two or three months a year, and he literally deluges the employees with tips."

"Still, there is the matter of our reputation. . . ."

"But who would know?"

"If a single informer tells a columnist, we'll be the laughing stock of Paris."

"There are no informers at the Ritz, sir."

"And chambermaids and waiters? Are there none of those?"

"I think that if I speak to them myself, we can be assured of their complete discretion. Some of them have been with us for twenty years, and certainly none of them wants to be dismissed."

"Can you guarantee that no one will know of this?"

"I think that I can."

"Very well, then. I leave the entire matter in your hands."

"Thank you, sir. I will give orders to vacate 504 immediately."

"504? But why 504? I thought that Madame Satrapoulos was in 503."

"She is, sir. But her—let us say, her guest is in 504."

"This is unheard of! Do you know this Satrapoulos person? When he is in London, he does not stop at the Ritz. He stops at the Connaught. What kind of man is he?"

Albert meditated the question for a minute. How could one describe the Greek? He made the attempt.

"He's a small man, red and black, between forty and fifty years old. Very generous. How can I put it? He is the sort of man whom one would never notice, but who nonetheless has a certain presence about him. It is apparent even to those who do not know who he is. I might say that he is so ordinary as to be extraordinary."

"Does he have special tastes? I mean, does he drink? Does he bring girls up to his room? Does he like boys? That sort of thing."

"I have never heard a word of gossip about him."

"Yet there is this request of his—"

"There is really nothing unusual about it. He has simply asked us to let his mother have whatever she wishes and to deny her nothing. He was very precise. We are to satisfy 'her slightest whim.'"

"Thank you, Albert. I acknowledge that you are right. You have convinced me. All I ask is discretion. Have Madame Satrapoulos', ah, guest, use the service elevator."

"Very well, sir. I'll take care of it."

Albert left his superior sitting silently behind his desk, uneasy with the decision that had just been made. It really goes against all my personal principles, Fouillet lectured himself, as well as against the principles of sound hotel management.

Athina Satrapoulos was gifted with a rigorous constitution and strong heart, even at the age of seventy-six. Otherwise, she would never have survived what had happened to her.

She had been sitting in her shack, drinking a cup of milk, when the men burst in. They were foreigners. She would have been able to tell that, even if they had not been wearing white shirts. What did they want?

They told her, in Greek, that everything was ready, that all she had to do was follow them.

Follow them where? She had not been off her mountain for three decades. Bluntly, she had ordered them out of her house. It was time for dinner, and she did not want guests.

Her words had no effect. They listened gravely, expressionless as statues, nodding benevolently.

Irritated as much by their smiles as by their silence, Athina had snatched up a poker and threatened them with it. For years now, her mind had functioned by stops and starts, each start providing sufficient light to illuminate a specific problem: eating, sleeping, being cold or hot. But she could not understand where these men could possibly want to take her, or why. She was perfectly comfortable in her shack, and she had no wish to leave it. How did she know what, if anything, existed beyond the walls of this house?

Brandishing her poker, she ordered them out again. But instead of being frightened, the two men exchanged a signal of some sort, and moved toward her, one from the left and the other from the right. Not knowing which of them to strike first, Athina had suffered a moment's distraction. They took advantage of it to remove the poker from her hands and seize her securely under the arms.

"My goats!" she had cried. "I haven't fed them yet!"

They assured her that "someone" would take care of her animals. Then they dragged her outside. It was dusk. The sky was still pink in the west, and to the east, one could see the first evening stars.

Strangely, despite Athina's screams, none of her neighbors had looked out of his door. Helpless, she was carried past the village's dozen houses without seeing a familiar face. Beyond the last house stood a huge black vehicle, its doors bearing a red cross. Athina recognized it as an ambulance, and her anger surged. "Let me go!" she screamed. "Let me go! Are you crazy? I'm not sick! Let me go!"

A large white-clad blond woman smiled at Athina, as though happy to see her. "We won't hurt you, Madame Satrapoulos. All we want is to send you on a nice vacation. We know you'd like that."

Athina almost strangled with rage. Her mind was functioning clearly now, as though the long years of vacuity had prepared her to defend herself in her moment of need.

"A vacation?" she shrieked. "In an ambulance? Let me go!"

She called out the name of Alexander, the dead husband of whom she had not thought in a decade, as though imploring his protection.

Her two abductors lifted Athina into the ambulance, grimacing at her stench, and closed the door. The blond woman held out a glass. "Here," she said, "drink this. It will relax you."

Athina took the glass and gulped. Then she spat the mouthful of liquid into the woman's face.

"Why, Madame Satrapoulos," the woman said. "That's not very nice."

Her moderation increased Athina's wrath. Yet something in the woman's eyes alerted her. Behind her back, something was going on, something that concerned her. The thought had no sooner crossed her mind than she was seized from behind. One of the men held her arms; the other her legs. The blond woman pushed back Athina's sleeve and plunged a needle into her arm.

"Bitch!" Athina screamed before she lost consciousness.

"My God, what a stink! It's nauseating."

"I see that you've never taken care of old people. Go on, leave me with her. I can handle her."

"If you need us, Maria, just call. We'll be outside."

The nurse waited until the two men were out of the room. Then she began the task of undressing Athina.

Through the open door, she heard the water running into the bathtub. She had filled the tub with pine and lavender salts, hoping that a single bath would suffice to rid Athina of the violent animal odor which had doubtless clung to her for years. The old woman's legs, when the patched stockings were removed, were surprisingly white, except where the dirt was so thick as to form almost a solid crust.

Athina groaned, opened her eyes, and stared around the room. She opened her mouth and spoke a single word: "Water."

Maria, with a broad smile, handed her a glass of ice water. "Here, Madame Satrapoulos, drink. Afterward we will have our bath."

Athina emptied the glass and, mechanically assisted the nurse to remove her dress. "Are you going to wash me?" she asked.

"Yes," Maria answered. "First, we'll bathe you, so that you'll look beautiful and smell nice. Then we'll do some other things—all nice things that you'll enjoy. You'll see—"

"Things I'll enjoy? What things do I enjoy?"

"When you do them, you'll enjoy them. Now, stand up. I'll help you. Your bath is ready."

Maria supported the old woman as she moved toward the bathroom. She talked continually, smiling, despite the stench. After all, she told herself, old age might be a misfortune, but it was not a sin. One day, God willing, she herself would be old. Who would care for her then?

The two women reached the door of the bathroom. Athina looked questioningly at Maria. The nurse nodded reassuringly.

"Come, madame. You'll love this." She led Athina toward the tub, filled now with a mountain of bubbles. The scent of pine and lavender rose like a cloud, clashing with the old woman's odor.

Athina, naked, felt helpless, stripped of her defenses. But she had no wish to defend herself. The blond woman seemed so kind. So she sat on the rim of the tub and, with the nurse's help, slid under the mound of bubbles. She remembered that in the old days she had bathed herself. But one had to have a reason for being clean, and when one lives alone, it serves no purpose.

Once in the water, she relaxed, recalling a plunge into the warm waters of the Mediterranean when she had been a girl of twenty.

Maria soaped Athina's back, gently, fighting her rising disgust, reciting to herself the reasons she should not run out of the room and never return.

"And now, madame, your hair."

Maria spread the shampoo over the dry, brittle tufts of gray. "It stings!" Athina cried.

"Close your eyes, dear, and just relax."

It does feel good, Athina told herself as she felt the nurse's fingers massaging her scalp.

"Where are we?" she demanded.

"We're in Athens."

"What are we doing here?"

"We're on our way to Paris. You'll see. You're going to have beautiful dresses and all sorts of jewelry—"

"Jewelry? Why am I going to get jewelry?"

"To make you beautiful."

"I'm not beautiful. I'm old. What's your name?"

"Maria."

Maria smiled proudly. In less than an hour she had soothed the savage beast. She had been right to argue that gentleness could work miracles with humans and animals alike.

"My name is Athina," the old woman said. "They call me Tina."

"Yes, Madame Satrapoulos, I know."

"What do you want with me?"

Later, wrapped in an immaculate white robe, Athina inspected the dresses that Maria had removed from an armoire.

"Would you like to try them on?"

"Me? Try them on?"

"Of course, you. They're for you!"

The nurse had spread several of the dresses on the bed. The old woman approached them warily. She touched them gingerly. Her rough, worn hand lingered on the fabric, then withdrew. Then she reached out again, this time more boldly, and her hand caressed the dresses. She lifted one of them from the bed and held it before her eyes, her lips moving in a silent litany.

Then came Maria's real victory. Athina, without a word of encouragement from the nurse, moved toward the mirror, holding the dress before her. Magically, the old peasant woman's innate femininity had reasserted itself after lying dormant for decades. She stared into the mirror for several minutes, surprised to see an image she had long forgotten. She knew it was an image from the distant past, but its name was still what it had always been: Athina Satrapoulos.

Maria took her hand. "Shall I help you try it on?"

Athina allowed the nurse to remove her robe. But, when she was naked, she averted her eyes from the mirror. Deftly, Maria passed a dress over her head.

"Stand still," Maria whispered. She ran to a chest, removed something from a drawer, then returned to Athina. "There," she said, fastening a string of pearls around the old woman's neck. "Now sit on the bed so that we can put your shoes on."

She picked a pair at random and placed them on Athina's feet. "Now look at yourself. You're lovely!"

She guided the old woman toward the mirror.

Athina stood silent before the unrecognizable form in the glass. For a long moment, her face was expressionless. Then she burst into laughter. She laughed until the tears rolled down her cheeks.

"Don't you like the dress?" the nurse asked, puzzled.

Athina's laughter ceased as suddenly as it had begun. She glared at Maria and said, her voice accusatory, "What have you done with my clothes?"

"But, Madame Satrapoulos, they were so worn that I threw them away."

"You threw them away?" Athina screamed. She moved toward the nurse, her hand raised threateningly.

Maria could think of nothing better than to stretch out her arms in a gesture of appeasement. Athina's hand shot out and scratched her cheek, drawing blood. The nurse touched her cheek, saw the blood, and called out in the direction of the door, "Come here for a moment, please. Quickly!"

The door opened, and the two men appeared. They seized Athina and held her. "Well, what do we do now?" one demanded.

Maria, her hand still on her wounded cheek, watched as the old woman struggled to free herself. "No, no, Madame Satrapoulos," she said. "You mustn't do that. It really isn't nice. . . ."

"Why did you leave me alone so long?"

The Greek stifled an impatient retort. He was tired, and he was concerned with the ugly scandal Kallenberg had unleashed. He had chosen to spend a few hours aboard the *Pegasus* so as to find peace and quiet, not to subject himself to this woman's reproaches. Even at the best of times, Satrapoulos did not tolerate such presumption.

"Why didn't you come to London with me? I asked you to."

"You know how I hate parties. You look worried. Is something wrong?"

He peered at Wanda and saw nothing but genuine concern on her face.

"There is a great deal wrong."

He took her hand and kissed it gently. "You were quite right not to come. The whole thing ended in the most unbelievable row. You'll read about it in the newspapers. But tell me about yourself. What have you been doing?"

"Oh, I was bored the whole time. I read, and I looked at the sea. . . ."

He held her hand as she spoke. With him, she was like a child, and yet, so long as men had memories, she would remain the most beautiful woman in the world. He had known her for five years, and he had done everything possible to keep her near him. He showered her with gifts, which she accepted indifferently. He sent airplanes for her, to carry her to him.

At first Lena had resented Wanda Deemount. But as time passed, she had grown accustomed to her presence. To her, the dancer was a living legend rather than a person, a myth rather than a rival. And it was true that the relationship between her husband and Wanda was one which any average man would have considered strange. He had seen her for the first time in New York, just after the war, walking from her hotel to a waiting car. That very day Satrapoulos had taken an oath that he would meet her, conquer her, and hold her captive. He learned that she lived in a tower apartment at the Waldorf, and for an incredible sum, he persuaded the management to rent him the adjacent apartment. Then, feverishly, he had consulted the Prophet to discover when he might approach her with the least chance of being rebuffed.

On the proper day, as H hour approached—he had bribed the maid to discover at what time she left her suite—Satrapoulos had paced his room, terrified at the thought of venturing into the hallway. How would she react when he spoke to her? And what could he possibly say?

He knew a great deal about her already, intelligence gathered on every continent by the army of men in his employ. Yet he could hardly bear the thought of approaching her. He had resisted the temptation to lavish expensive, anonymous gifts upon her, but he had succumbed to the impulse to send her flowers, daily, without a card, telling himself that this was not a woman who would be impressed by his name, his power, or his wealth.

He glanced at his watch, and gathering his courage, he ventured into the hallway. Should he pretend to be waiting for the elevator? Or would it be better if he appeared to be on the way to his suite?

He had covered half the distance to the elevator when he heard a door close, and she was there. Panic-stricken, Satrapoulos forgot completely whether he had decided to be arriving or leaving when he encountered her. He stood rooted in the middle of the hallway as she came toward him wearing a very plain dress, a light coat of tan linen, and her eternal sunglasses. She swept past him like a luxurious liner encountering a rowboat and disappeared into the elevator. Satrapoulos had not known it at the time, but it was to be his last glimpse of her for a year.

"What are you thinking about?"

"I was thinking about you; about how I tried every way to meet you before I knew you."

Wanda laughed lightly. "Did you exist before you knew me?"

"Sometimes I wonder," he answered gravely. Releasing her hand, he stood. "I'm exhausted. I'm going to bathe and change."

He returned to his own quarters, thoughts of Wanda Deemount filling his mind. A few minutes later, in the shower, he recalled their meeting, in Rome, a year later, at the home of friends to whom he had confided his passion for her. To all his previous uncertainties another had been added: the awareness that he was a good head shorter than she. As their hostess had introduced them, Satrapoulos, mumbling pleasantries, had tried desperately to back toward the stairs so as to be able to stand on the first step. If he reached it, he told himself, he would be saved.

Moving backward, like a crab, as he launched into an elaborate monologue, he had drawn Wanda after him, foot by foot, until he had felt the banister under his hand. Then, tapping with his foot, he had searched for the step behind him, found it, and placing all his weight upon his right foot, balanced himself precariously as his left moved toward the step. The problem of getting the right foot to the same level was solved when another guest accidentally lurched against him, and he took advantage of the heaven-sent opportunity to position himself, not on the first but on the second step.

The Greek had immediately felt his confidence return. Now it was she who was compelled to raise her eyes to him. But could she see him? Through those dark glasses, it was impossible to distinguish her eyes.

Wanda had not moved all during Satrapoulos' maneuvering. She had missed nothing of his gymnastics, but she was not displeased. Rather, she was touched that so powerful a man could behave so childishly. She wanted to put him at ease.

"Should we go out onto the terrace?" she had whispered, standing on tiptoe so as to place her mouth level with his ears.

They had sat in the cool night air, she with her astonishing profile toward him. Satrapoulos knew that he should speak, but he could think of nothing to say. His mind had been emptied by the fulfillment of his desperate desire to meet her.

"Tell me about yourself, Monsieur Satrapoulos," she had said.

At once he regretted having let her take the initiative.

"What can I tell you?" he asked, feeling that he was making himself appear ridiculous in her eyes.

"Tell me things that you have told no one else. All I know about you is what the newspapers and magazines say, and I know from my own experience that they are not to be trusted. Why don't you begin by telling me who you are?"

He could not reply.

"I know that you are a shipowner," Wanda continued, "that you are married, and that you are very busy. But what kind of life do you lead?"

He almost replied: I live the life of an idiot. But that definition was not exactly what he had in his mind. What should he say? No one had ever asked him who he was. Words came to his lips, but he would not speak them: sentences that explained all—his travels, his battles, his perpetual and inexplicable compulsion to move ever further ahead, his loneliness, his need for someone to talk to, who would understand him without having to pretend, as Lena did.

Instead, he said, "I am often very much alone."

Wanda was moved by the humility of his admission. Behind it, she sensed many things that she herself had experienced. She, too, was alone, terribly alone, among thousands of admirers, none of whom had ever succeeded in understanding her.

Softly, she said, "I understand you very well, Monsieur Satrapoulos. Do you believe in the stars?"

"I beg your pardon?" he said stupidly.

"I asked if you believe in the stars."

The Greek was unwilling to reveal himself completely. He had learned that in love, as in war, one must always keep something in reserve. It often happened that a fallen adversary made a final, desperate attempt to reverse the course of events. Thus he did not dare admit that he believed only in destiny and that his most trusted counselor was the Prophet.

"Do you believe in them?" he countered.

"Of course!" she replied, as though surprised at the question. "How can we not believe in the stars? The greatest men who ever lived have believed in them. We are so small—"

He listened in silence, astonished that so famous a woman could be so vulnerable. Wanda interpreted his silence as doubt. "Everything is predestined," she said. "Don't you believe that?"

"I believe everything that you choose to say."

"You are right to do so. I never lie."

"Never?"

"Never. I am incapable of lying."

She spoke English with a rough accent which made the blood pound in Satrapoulos' temples.

"What is your first name?" she asked.

"Socrates. Behind my back, my employees call me S.S.—my initials. My competitors refer to me as the Greek."

"Are you really Greek?"

He smiled. "I must be, since I am a shipowner." Then, awkwardly, he plunged ahead: "I've seen all your films—those you made when you were still dancing. . . ."

He saw her stiffen almost imperceptibly. It was too late to take back his words, and there was nothing to do but go on. "You don't like people to mention your films?"

Then he had been unaware that had anyone other than he asked that question, she would have fled into the house. Instead, she had answered without hesitation: "No."

There followed a silence which neither of them seemed able to break. Satrapoulos cursed himself for his stupidity in touching on so sensitive a spot.

At length she was the first to speak. "Would you like to tell me about your ships or about your business affairs?"

"I'd rather not, if you don't mind."

"Why not?"

"Because my ships and my balance sheets have never disrupted anyone's life."

"Neither have my films."

"You told me that you never lied."

Wanda moved, as though to rise, but Satrapoulos placed his hand on hers. "No, please. I'm sorry if I've offended you."

She withdrew her hand. "You could not have been moved by my films because there was nothing of me in them. What moved you was an image. It was not really me."

Suddenly, there were other people with them. "Socrates," he heard his hostess say, "I'd like to present. . . ."

The enchantment of the moment was lost. Once he had fulfilled his obligations to his hostess, Satrapoulos had gone in search of Wanda. She had disappeared.

Without hesitation or compunction, he deserted his hostess and her guests and hurried in pursuit. He found her in front of her hotel, but she was distant and seemed almost not to recognize him. He did not know that he was about to spend the most exciting night of his life in her company. Like any virile, self-respecting Greek, Satrapoulos normally boasted of his conquests, describing them in intimate detail to his friends. But who would have believed him this time if he had told the truth? And how could he dare to tell the truth?

There was a knock on the door of his quarters, and a crewman of the *Pegasus* called, "Madame Deemount would like to know if you are ready."

Paradoxically, he felt momentarily irritated at the way Wanda's moods depended on his presence. It was a responsibility he was reluctant to assume on this particular evening. "Tell her," Satrapoulos replied, "that I'll be with her shortly."

Simultaneously, he decided that he would spend the evening drinking with Epaphos, an old seaman who had a nightclub of sorts in an alley behind the docks at Piraeus. There a man could be himself. No newspaperman was allowed to set foot within Epaphos' door, and when the orchestra began to play, one could forget one's troubles.

He hurriedly put on a shirt, a jacket and a pair of pants, stuffing his pockets with money which he would distribute among the musicians. Some of it would be used to pay for the broken dishes when the evening was over.

To hell with Kallenberg! Socrates told himself as he moved softly across the deck. There were two seamen on guard at the gangway ladder. Satrapoulos issued his orders for the evening by placing his finger to his lips in a significant gesture. Instantly, the men were rendered blind and dumb. Their employer crept down the ladder and leaped into the launch like a man of twenty. To hell with the whole world! he said to himself as he sped toward the lights onshore.

* * *

It was seven o'clock in the morning. Jack Robertson, private secretary to the manager of the Tate Gallery, stirred his tea as he spoke to his wife. "Eve, would you see if the newspaper has come?"

His wife shrugged. In her soiled housecoat, she went to the door, opened it, and walked across the flagstone porch to the mailbox. With only a quick glance at the copy of the *Daily Express*, she returned to the living room.

She was not in the best of moods. She found it intolerable that her husband should be so thoughtless as to make so much noise this morning, while her mother was asleep in a room on the ground floor. She and Jack had had words on the subject before, but she could swear that he deliberately made as much noise as possible simply to irritate her. After all, this was her mother's house—an important point even after thirty years of marriage. If it were not for her mother, where would they go? Jack had never been able to save enough for them to be able to buy a place of their own. Then why couldn't he understand that he was merely a guest in this house and that, in return for shelter, he had certain obligations?

She threw the newspaper onto the table next to him.

Jack pretended not to notice her irritation. He unfolded the paper and looked at the front page with an air of complete detachment, holding the cup of tea in his right hand. His glance lingered on a three-column photograph of an old woman standing in front of a shack, holding a dish of some sort which the goats around her seemed to covet. The caption read: "The mother."

Whose mother? Jack wondered. It always angered him that newspapers used such captions to entice their readers, then compelled them to read half the newspaper to discover what the article was about. It was particularly exasperating that, in this instance, the article was not even on the same page as the photograph. "See article on page 8," ended the caption, in very small print.

Grumbling, Jack put down his cup. He would have to use both hands to turn to page 8.

"Well," he said when he had found the article. "Well."

"What?" Eve asked.

"How unbecoming!"

"What, for heaven's sake?"

He looked at his wife, his eyes shining with indignation. "This billionaire, this Greek, Satrapoulos."

"What about him?"

"It seems that his mother is starving to death."

" 'Unbecoming' hardly describes it. It's absolutely criminal."

Jack Robertson glared at his wife over the paper. Except for an occasional glass of ale, his only pleasure in life was to outrage his wife. "I was not alluding to that," he said softly. "Surely, every man is free to do whatever he wishes with his mother. I meant that it is most unbecoming for a newspaper to publish gossip about an individual's private life."

It was noon in the rue de Lourmel. A woman held out a coin to the vendor and took a copy of *France-Soir*. She stuffed it into her shopping bag, between two heads of lettuce, then walked into a nearby bistro, leaned on the counter, and ordered a cup of coffee. A waitress brought it to her. "Good morning, Madame Thibault."

"How are you, my dear?"

Madame Thibault put three lumps of sugar into the cup—the manifestation of a mania dating from the war and engendered by panic at the thought of a possible shortage—stirred carefully with her spoon, then swallowed the coffee in a single gulp, as though it were a shot of whiskey. She placed the cup in its saucer, lighted a cigarette, removed her newspaper from her bag, and began leafing through it until she found what she was looking for. She tore out that page, exercising great care not to damage it, then distractedly crumpled the rest of the paper and let it fall to the floor. She removed a pencil from her hair, between the nape of her neck and her left ear, and studied the lineup for the sixth race at Auteuil that afternoon. Finally, she made her choice.

She walked across the room toward a man sitting behind a marble table.

"How is it going, Émile? Here, put this on Boule de suif in the sixth." She handed him a bill.

The man wrote a few words and held out a ticket which Madame Thibault took and placed in her pocket. Then she returned to the counter and ordered another coffee.

Into this cup, she put four lumps of sugar. As she stirred, she became aware of something on the sole of her shoe. She raised her foot and saw a cigarette butt attached to the leather by a piece of gum. "*Saloperie!*" she exclaimed, wiping her shoe on the copy of *France-Soir* which lay on the floor.

The newspaper tore. Madame Thibault glanced down, and a photograph caught her eye. She used her foot to turn the paper toward her and read the caption: "Her son is a billionaire, but she lives on charity."

With an effort, the woman bent down and picked up the newspaper, groaning all the while from her chronic lumbago.

This ragged woman is the mother of one of the world's wealthiest men, the billionaire shipowner Socrates Satrapoulos. Our reporters discovered the poverty-stricken woman living in a mountaintop village in a remote area of northern Greece. Her only food is goat's milk and a few rabbits. Her son, whom she has not seen for thirty years, has never contributed to her support (continued on page 4).

She shook her head, lighted another cigarette from the butt of the first, and said to the waitress, "What bastards the rich are! A woman kills herself wiping their asses when they're children, and as soon as they've made a little money, they forget all about her. They don't even send her a little money to buy food for herself!"

In Athens, at eight o'clock that morning, Medea Mikolofides was lying naked on a table in her room. Every morning she placed her enormous body in the hands of her masseur. It was not an attractive body. Medea had hair everywhere, not only on her stomach, chest, and arms, like everyone else, but also on her back. Under that black down, her skin was spongy, unhealthy. The masseur's fingers sank into it without discovering even an indication of elasticity. It was like meat that had been deprived of daylight for too long, for Medea, like many Mediterranean folk, avoided the sun.

As the masseur worked, Medea groaned and gasped.

"Not so hard, Michael," she pleaded.

Medea was thinking of the scandal in which she was involved. Why on earth did her son-in-law feel it was necessary to give parties? Whom was he trying to impress? She herself never gave parties, and she was one of the world's richest women.

"Michael, would you mind turning on the radio? I'd like to hear the market report."

It was an old habit. Yet this morning the widow's mind was elsewhere. She was thinking of her telephone conversation with Herman Kallenberg. She had not minced words. She had said all the things that she had wanted to say for so long. He had let her talk, allowing himself to be scolded like a child. He did not even object when she had ordered him to send Irene back to Athens. "I'll be happy to," he had answered. "And she can stay there for all I care." Then she had demanded to speak to her daughter.

After a long delay, Irene had come to the telephone. She had been bathing, or at least so she said, as with each passing minute the toll for the call to London mounted with mathematical regularity. Why were children so eager to waste money that their parents had managed to scrape together?

Irene had categorically refused to come to Athens. "Absolutely not, Mama," she said. "My husband has problems, and I can't leave him now."

Her husband, indeed! An ambitious fop with a big mouth, incapable of approaching anything methodically, pressing his luck until one day he would fall on his face.

The masseur had switched on the radio.

". . . discovered in the north of Greece. She was living on goat's milk and roots, and she has stated that her son made no attempt to assist her. . . ."

Who was the man talking about, Medea wondered? "For God's sake, Michael! Not so hard!" she complained as the newscaster went on:

"Thus far, Socrates Satrapoulos has been unavailable for comment, but you will now hear the accusations his mother has made against him."

The Widow sat up as though she had been a viper slithering over Michael's hands. Michael too had been listening. Both of them remained silent, waiting for what was to follow.

". . . kind of child was he?"

"A dirty little thief."

"Did he love his father?"

"He never loved anyone but himself."

"Was he a good student?"

"He was thrown out of every school he ever attended. None would keep him more than a week."

Medea turned toward Michael, who was listening eagerly. She reddened.

"Well, what are you waiting for? Massage me! That's what I pay you for, isn't it?"

Michael bent over her, but she pushed him away angrily,

jumped from the table, and ran toward the door. "By God!" she shouted. "I'm going to find out what this is all about—"

Michael interrupted her as she reached for the doorknob. "Madame Mikolofides, at least take a towel. You're stark naked!"

[6]

As the plane landed at Baran, the Greek gave his instructions to the pilot: "I don't want you to leave the airplane. Stay by the radio. These people are quite capable of stealing the plane or of taking it apart and selling the pieces."

On the runway, Satrapoulos saw an automobile approaching the plane: a Rolls, flying the flag of Baran. He pinched his nostrils shut and exhaled to unstop his ears.

The Rolls screeched to a halt on the asphalt runway, and a man emerged from the car to hold the rear door open for Socrates.

The Greek, as soon as he had seen the morning papers, had telephoned Hadj Thami el Sadek and asked to see him immediately. Socrates was in Rome at the time, where he had just sold eleven battered tankers to a consortium of Italian businessmen. Lena, after the party in London, had gone directly to Saint-Jean-Cap-Ferrat for a long weekend with some French friends. Which friends? She had not told him. He would not see her for several days since, from Saint-Jean, she would fly to New York.

"Did you have a nice trip, sir?"

Satrapoulos looked at his companion, who, he knew, was an influential adviser to the Emir of Baran. He was dressed in traditional Arab clothing. His English was impeccable. Satrapoulos surmised that he had studied international law in London and then returned to Baran to make a few laws of his own.

"Excellent. Thank you for asking. I spoke to the emir this morning, and I was happy to hear that he is in perfect health."

"Yes, perfect, even though he drives himself mercilessly."

"A remarkable man, the emir, and a remarkably well-informed sovereign. I wish we had such men in Europe."

The Arab smiled. "Surely there is no lack of great men in Europe."

"They are great men only so long as they are not in power. Then they become demagogues so as to be reelected to office. How can greatness survive such a system?"

"You seem to regret the demise of the monarchical system."

"Not at all. I merely deplore the fact that democracy inevitably leads to the rise of the demagogues."

The Arab laughed. "My word! In the old days your rulers made courtiers out of the people. Now the people make demagogues out of your rulers. It would seem that corruption has merely shifted from one side to the other."

The Greek smiled but did not answer. The car had almost completed the six-mile run to the city of Baran, and Socrates could see the dozen or so modern buildings lining the main boulevard.

"The emir instructed me to take you to your residence," the councillor informed Socrates, "and to tell you that he is anticipating the pleasure of seeing you whenever you wish."

"I regret I cannot take advantage of the emir's hospitality. I have work which cannot be neglected, and I must return to Athens this evening."

"As you wish, sir."

The Arab gave orders to the chauffeur, then turned back to Satrapoulos. "We will go directly to the emir's residence."

The emir's residence! What a genius he was, this emir! His residence was a bare, unfurnished cabin, without even a bed. There was only a straw mat on the dirt floor. There Hadj Thami el Sadek received his subjects so as to preserve the legend that he was a holy man. Sometimes the emir remained in the shack for weeks on end, a prisoner of the image that he had created for himself, eating only a few dates and drinking tea and milk. It was hard to resist the temptation to bring him a few groceries or a bottle of good wine.

The emir's guests, on the other hand, after making the mandatory visit to his shack, were housed in a fairy-tale palace of pink marble, the courtyard of which contained a pool strewn with water lilies and orchid petals and fed by murmuring fountains. The pool was surrounded by flowers, and trees heavy with oranges, lemons, dates, and exotic birds in cages of gold. The palace's apartments were filled with sublime carpets, precious marbles, and rare works of art. The massive fixtures in the huge bathrooms were of solid gold. Guests were attended by bare-chested Nubian slaves wearing wide Moorish pants, and every morning, upon waking, they were visited by masseurs. Socrates was conscious of the expense it had taken to make such a palace rise from the sands of Baran and to provide the water for it in this desert where water was worth ten times as much as oil.

The Rolls halted, and Satrapoulos descended into a narrow alley, half of which was in the sun and half in the shade. Half oven and half dungeon, he told himself, entering a nondescript house with cracked walls. He walked down a hallway between a row of natives motionless in their jellabas: the personal guard of Hadj Thami el Sadek. No weapons were visible, but Satrapoulos knew that the folds of their garments concealed the latest in automatic pistols. They had probably been delivered by one of his own ships. Before a small wooden door, two of the guards bowed and stood aside to let him pass. For the second time in his life, Socrates Satrapoulos was within the Holy of Holies, a narrow cell, bare except for a mat on the floor and a few cushions reserved for visitors.

The emir stood to greet him, holding out his arms for the ritual embrace. "I hope that my brother has had a pleasant voyage," he said in English. "I am honored that he has come so far to greet an old man." His voice had a curious, hissing quality, and his accent was bizarre, as though he had learned English without ever hearing it spoken.

"Highness," the Greek replied, employing the flowery rhetoric customary in the East, "it is I who am honored by the favor of an audience. I would not have dared solicit such a favor if it were not that that which I cherish most in the world, after your own friendship, is threatened."

The emir smiled faintly and spread his arms in a gesture of conciliation.

"Of what do you speak, my friend?"

"Of my honor."

Now that the preliminaries were over, one could discuss business. Satrapoulos had prepared himself as carefully as any student ever prepared for an examination, by poring over the relevant documents to find an approach which would enable him to turn the emir into an ally. He believed he had found one, but he was quite prepared to extemporize if it became necessary to do so. The end would justify the means, and means were something Socrates Satrapoulos had never neglected. First, he would offer an explanation and then attempt to turn to his advantage a situation which he, following the advice of the Prophet of Cascais, had deliberately manipulated to the magnitude of a public scandal.

The Greek opened his briefcase and removed a pile of fresh newspaper articles.

El Sadek held up his hand. "I have already seen these documents."

Satrapoulos was surprised. He would not have believed that the emir's intelligence was so efficient. Taken off guard, he could only stammer, "You've seen them all?"

The emir smiled broadly. "Yes, all of them."

"Then I am certain your Highness has not been deceived by these libelous and defamatory reports."

The emir made a vague gesture, intended to convey nothing and everything, but which Socrates interpreted as meaning: continue with your explanation. I am interested, and I am waiting for you to make your point.

"Unhappily," Socrates went on, "one often finds one's worst enemy in the bosom of one's own family. I have no doubt whatever that these articles represent an attempt to compromise me in the eyes of your Highness."

"I was unaware," the emir murmured, "that you placed such high value on my opinion of you."

Satrapoulos was el Sadek's equal as an actor and indeed was his superior in one important respect: he possessed the ability to believe his own lies. In delicate negotiations, he seemed to be wired to some mysterious current which enabled him to be completely convinced of whatever he said, to live literally the situation that he had invented, and to forget the premise from which he had begun. Often this talent served to create doubt in the minds of his partners, doubt which compelled them to lower their guard. And that was the moment of which Satrapoulos' genius allowed him to take advantage.

Socrates took a deep breath, felt the mysterious current course through his body, and began.

"Highness, we live in a hard world, a world in which we all sometimes forget that we were once children. Our lives are dictated by self-interest, and we forget that which is most precious within our-selves: our sense of dignity.

"My relations with you are of a commercial nature. So be it. When I first met you, business was foremost in my mind. I admit it."

The emir listened in silence, his small, cunning eyes never leaving Socrates' face.

"Then," the Greek continued, "I had the happiness to meet you. I had heard the rumors concerning the way in which you live, your plans for the future, your political aims, your wisdom. At that moment, I realized something. Business is a commodity that a man can pursue every day of his life, while men like you are encountered only once in a lifetime. The self-interest which prompts me to seek your good opinion is as nothing compared to the admiration I feel for you. If you believe that these words are mere flattery, I am sorry. I am not an orator, and I am a man of little education. I cannot express myself eloquently. I merely open my heart to you, clumsily perhaps, but in all sincerity."

Satrapoulos stopped, moved by his own words.

"You spoke of a family," the emir said softly. "What family is this?"

"Highness, it is very hard for me to speak of it."

El Sadek's expression was one of amusement. "And yet you have come in order to speak of it." Then, very gently, he added, "Now, then, tell me of this family."

Socrates saw that the emir was determined to spare him nothing. Very well. He would cross the Rubicon. "My own family, Highness."

"You are telling me that a member of your own family has tried to injure you?"

"That is precisely what I am saying."

"Who, then?"

"Herman Kallenberg."

"I did not know that you were of the same clan."

The Greek felt that el Sadek was going a bit far. "Your Highness is too well informed not to have known it. It has merely slipped your mind. Kallenberg is my brother-in-law. His wife is the eldest sister of my wife."

"Yes, perhaps I had forgotten. But just how is your brother-in-law your enemy?"

"It is Kallenberg who is responsible for this vicious and absurd newspaper campaign against me."

"This is truly shocking. I assume that you have proof of what you say?"

"Of course. Kallenberg himself told me what was planned."

"Is it not possible that he wished only to warn you of the scandal? A scandal that would injure him as well as yourself?"

"Impossible. If he informed me of it, it was with the intention of letting me know that he alone possessed the means to stop it."

"If I understand correctly, you are saying that Kallenberg first lighted the fuse of a bomb intended to destroy you and then suggested to you that he might extinguish the fuse?"

"That is correct, Highness."

"But why should he do such a thing?"

"So that I might withdraw from competition for a market that he wished to have for himself."

"Truly? Which market is that?"

"The transport of crude oil from the emirates of the Persian Gulf which are subject to your moral authority."

"I fear that you and Mr. Kallenberg both give me credit for a power I do not possess." There was a lengthy pause before the emir continued. "This conversation between yourself and Kallenberg, where did it take place?"

"In London, on the very evening of his party—the party which ended in a manner of which you may have heard."

"Yes, I have heard of it. So have my advisers, who, I fear, are 'more royalist than the king,' as you say in Europe. Certainly, the news of this party, added to the newspaper campaign directed against you, is not very good publicity for your family. You say that this conversation with your brother-in-law took place in London. Were there witnesses?"

"Highness, an attempt to blackmail does not take place in the presence of witnesses."

"You are right, of course, but it is regrettable. Very unfortunate, really."

"Am I to understand that your Highness doubts my word?"

"By no means, my friend. I have never doubted it for an instant. But I am not alone. There are the others."

The old fox! Socrates wondered whether he had not underestimated the emir. Had he already signed a contract with Kallenberg? But what could Kallenberg offer him that Satrapoulos could not? So far as scandals were concerned, he and Kallenberg were on a par. What sort of game was el Sadek playing? Was he merely trying to boost the bids?

"Ah, my friend," the emir spoke. "How sad it is to see families disunited."

His tone was chiding, and the Greek, wishing to free himself from blame, fell into the trap. "The gamble of marriage, the risks which arise from a woman's whims—these things do not really form what one may call a family. The members of one's family are those who share the same blood."

El Sadek closed the trap expertly. "But that is what I have always believed! When I spoke of a disunited family, I was referring only to your relationship to your mother. Of course, I have no wish to involve myself in your affairs or even to know the things for which you are being blamed."

Satrapoulos forced himself to remain calm. He nodded in agreement. "Highness, as you say, I have read the things of which I am accused. If they were true, I would be a monster. A man has only one mother, and if he abandons her, it would be better he were dead. However, the reports you have read contain not a particle of truth. They are proof how the lust for money and power can corrupt a man. At the very moment that these so-called photographs of my mother were taken in Greece, my mother—my only mother—was at the Ritz in Paris with two companions and her nurse. Look at these."

He drew a folder of documents from his briefcase and opened it. "Look at that woman in this newspaper photograph, and then compare her to my real mother in this photograph."

Socrates held out a photograph of an elderly woman, elegantly dressed and bejeweled, her features calm and composed. (In order to photograph her, Athina's two "companions" had had to stuff her with tranquilizers.)

"Highness, do these two persons have anything in common?"

The emir studied the photographs, catching the smell of a swindle in the air without knowing precisely what form it would take and yet, at the same time, enjoying himself enormously. Two of the wealthiest men in the world were competing for his favor, and the outcome would depend on his pleasure and also, of course, on the amount of money that each of them was willing to pay for the contract. He pretended to examine the photographs with great care.

"You are right. They do not seem to be the same person."

"Tomorrow, Highness, the whole world will know of this despicable plot to ruin me."

"What do you intend to do?"

"I will file suit for libel against all the newspapers—all of them—which have carried this story. And I will make them publish a retraction, as prominently as they featured this libel. My lawyers are already working on it."

"When will your reply be published?"

"In the daily newspapers tomorrow. So far as the magazines are concerned, in their next issue. Tonight Europe's radio stations will broadcast my mother's press conference from Paris."

"How sweet is vengeance—"

"Not vengeance, Highness, but justice. I insisted that you be the first to know so that this act of treachery would affect neither the friendship with which you honor me nor the esteem in which I am held by your people."

"I am grateful to you for having considered that aspect of the problem and also for having provided me with the means to justify you in the eyes of my subjects. You understand, we have retained a moral code which is inflexible, almost medieval. It would have been extremely difficult, perhaps even impossible, for me to continue our relationship if the accusations made against you had been true. My subjects would not have tolerated an association with a man who does not meet his obligations to the sacred person of his mother. The fact that you are here, in Baran, is evidence of my faith in you."

"Highness, I have a great favor to ask of you."

"Speak."

"I have several ships which are not presently being used to their full capacity. I would like your Highness' permission to establish a shuttle service with my tankers, to bring millions of tons of fresh water to Baran. It is not just that a country as beautiful as this should have no trees."

"Ah, Mr. Satrapoulos, this is a serious problem—"

"And, naturally, in addition to this shuttle, if you will allow it, I will have drilling undertaken—"

"To find more oil?" the emir asked in horror.

"Not at all, your Highness. To find water. With your permission, fifty of my engineers will be ready to begin work in a week."

This was the sort of language that el Sadek understood. Smiling, he nodded his agreement to the proposal, and Satrapoulos' hopes soared.

"But tell me," the emir said, "if your ships carry water in their tanks, how will you manage—in the event that we sign a contract—to take on the oil from the various emirates under my control?"

Satrapoulos' heart beat wildly in his chest. Was he about to win the game?

The emir continued in a half-bantering tone. "Of course, you did know that your brother-in-law has made me an offer higher than yours?"

"Higher? By how much?"

"By some ten percent."

"That is a great deal of money."

"Indeed, it is, but then there is a great deal of profit involved. However, since the party in London, it would be difficult for me to sign a contract with Mr. Kallenberg. There are also offers from America—"

"For the same amount as Kallenberg's?"

"I fear for even ten percent more."

"Then, of course, I will offer ten percent more than the Americans."

"Are you sure you can do no better than that?"

"Not so far as the bid itself is concerned. However, long before this deplorable incident with the newspapers, I intended to surprise you—if you will allow me to do so, of course. If you consent, it will be a good omen for the future."

"I am listening."

"Your Highness, I believe that within ten years, all our present ideas on shipping will be outdated. We will carry more tonnage with fewer ships. And the larger the cargoes, the lower the freight charges. Until now, the largest tanker has been ten thousand tons. I intend to have far larger ships built. Three are actually under construction in a Norwegian shipyard, and one of them is a giant, the largest tanker in the world. I would like your permission to christen it the *Hadi Thami el Sadek*."

The emir had expected a business proposal over which he was prepared to haggle like a rug merchant. Satrapoulos' request took him completely off guard. He was both enormously flattered and impressed. The largest tanker in the world, named after himself! It went beyond anything he had ever dreamed.

"I am honored beyond words that you will allow me to be god-father to your ship. I accept, with all my heart."

"Thank you, Highness. But that is only half of the favor I request." Satrapoulos had kept the best part of the offer for the final moment: an offer which no government could possibly refuse. "If our collaboration should become a reality, I would plan to place three-quarters of my fleet under the flag of Baran."

Despite the aged emir's iron self-control and cunning, it was evident that he was all but overcome with delight. To hide his confusion, he pretended to reflect on the Greek's offer. "Noble friend," he said finally, "your flattering proposal entails both advantages and disadvantages. I cannot make such a decision on my own. I must refer it to my council."

It was all Socrates could do to keep himself from laughing aloud. The emir's council consisted of a few ragged men who responded to el Sadek's slightest whim and who accepted his orders in worshipful silence. The emir had fallen silent, however, and Socrates realized he was daydreaming. Socrates could guess the subject of his dreams. Ten percent plus ten percent plus ten percent equals thirty percent. . . . The largest tanker in the world, bearing the name of Hadj Thami el Sadek . . . dozens of ships carrying the flag of Baran to the four corners of the earth, *his* flag. . . .

The Greek's proposals opened up a new horizon before Hadj Thami el Sadek, a horizon that included, perhaps, recognition of the state of Baran by the United Nations. This, in turn, would allow the Emir of Baran to derive maximum profit from the various governments to which he would lend his vote in various matters. As things now stood, it was impossible for el Sadek to undertake this kind of extortion. He was able, at most, to flirt first with one side, then with the other, without showing a preference for either. He had no intention of offending the Americans by favoring the Russians or of being quarantined by the Europeans for doing business with the Japanese. Therefore, his only recourse had been to deal with private shippers who were powerful enough to supply him with arms and rich enough to assure him financial independence. From the very beginning, he had sensed that Kallenberg was not such a man. He was too vain, too preoccupied with himself and with the impression that he made on others. Satrapoulos seemed cleverer, maturer, more competent. Had he not just demonstrated those qualities by taking a bad situation and turning it to his advantage? It was Satrapoulos, therefore, on whom Hadj Thami el Sadek must lean until he was strong enough to dispense with his services and to assume his proper role in world affairs. Then, when he had united all the Arabian emirates under his banner, they would see a true sheikh.

The emir, when he returned to solid earth, had forgotten his feigned reticence, forgotten that he had intended to keep the Greek in a state of uncertainty for a while longer. "Of course," he said, "you will make payment in dollars to a Swiss account whose number I will give you."

"Highness," Satrapoulos answered joyfully, "it shall be done as you wish."

"Good. Then it is all arranged. And now, my brother, if you wish to rest, your apartments are ready."

The Greek was taken aback by the unexpected invitation. He had planned to return to Europe that very evening—to Geneva, where he was meeting with his bankers the following morning.

El Sadek seemed to sense his hesitation. He insisted. "You will do me a great honor by accepting my hospitality."

Satrapoulos could not refuse without offending his host. Well, he thought, to hell with the bankers. A deal like this one was worth any number of missed appointments. He bowed. "Highness, nothing could be more welcome than your invitation. It is I who am honored to accept, and I do so with joy, since you have judged me worthy of your hospitality."

When the Greek emerged from the ridiculous little house, almost overcome with pleasure at his victory over Kallenberg, he had an almost irresistible impulse to dance a *sirtaki* under the very eyes of the emir's councillor who was standing next to the Rolls, holding open the door for his master's honored guest.

In the eyes of the world, Socrates Satrapoulos was undoubtedly Wanda Deemount's lover. Only two people knew that in all their years together he had never once made love to her, and those two were Socrates himself and Wanda. Neither had told anyone else, for neither could do so without exposing the other's fault—a transitory, almost unique one on Socrates' part, but a permanent one on Wanda's.

The special nature of their relationship had first become apparent long ago in a suite in Rome's grandest hotel, after a party at which Socrates had "discovered" Wanda in attendance, then briefly allowed her to escape him. When he had encountered her a short time later at the hotel, he had pretended surprise that they were both staying at the same place. Even more astonishing, they had adjoining suites —an accident which Socrates had paid an exorbitant price to arrange.

Determined to risk everything on one throw of the dice, Satrapoulos had invited Wanda to join him for a drink. Unexpectedly, she had accepted.

"I'll be happy to," she said. "Meet me in a half hour. I want to change."

Thirty minutes later, when he rang at her door, she answered in a nightgown.

"Come in," she said. "Come into the bedroom. If it's all right with you, I'll lie in bed."

He followed her, his heart beating violently, as she went into the adjoining bedroom and stretched out on the bed.

"Well?"

She looked at him questioningly.

Satrapoulos did not answer. He was concentrating on deriving the maximum pleasure from that moment.

"Would you like to lie down next to me?" she asked.

He was stunned. He had dreamed up a hundred schemes to get her into bed, and now, in a few words, she had made it all unnecessary. His state of mind was that of a boy visiting a whorehouse for the first time. He did not know quite what to do. Nonetheless, he realized that he must do something. He moved to the bed and lay down next to her.

"Would you like to remove your shoes?"

Placing the tip of his right shoe against the heel of the left, Socrates divested himself of the latter and let it drop to the floor. Then he used the toes of his left foot to remove the right shoe. He noticed that he was having difficulty breathing normally. He had effectively abandoned the offensive.

"Why don't you make yourself comfortable? Look, I'm not dressed."

She opened her robe. He saw that, indeed, she had nothing on underneath. His eyes rested on her breasts, for he did not dare allow them to stray downward toward the dark pubic triangle.

"Take off your shirt. . . ." She unbuttoned it for him slowly. The Greek allowed her to do so, near panic at the realization of his own sudden paralysis, incapable of speaking or of taking the initiative in any way. He was suddenly aware of the chasm which existed between the two expressions "to take" and "to be taken."

"Why don't you take off your clothes? I won't be embarrassed."

Suddenly, Socrates Satrapoulos discovered that he was modest. He, who had always been proud of his attributes, now could think of nothing but finding a way to conceal them. It did not seem right to exhibit them. It was beyond belief—as though he were the virgin

119

of the two. In great embarrassment, he drew the sheet over his body and removed his clothing.

"Was that so difficult?"

"With you, yes." Somehow he had regained the power of speech.

"What is there so special about me?" Wanda breathed.

"I don't know. It's very strange—"

Even the touch of her flesh against his gave rise to a surge of panic in him.

"I thought you wanted me. Was I mistaken?"

He found the courage to look into her eyes. She was not making fun of him. On the contrary, she was almost too serious.

"Yes, I want you."

"Then take me, make love to me."

He put his arms around her, felt her body against his, did all that a man customarily does in such a situation. Nothing happened.

He caressed her, mechanically, for ten minutes more, in rising panic. His body refused to function. He had been reduced to impotence. For him to restore himself, it would have been necessary to shake her, to insult her. It would also have helped if she had bitten him. But none of those things happened. She lay there, allowing him to do as he wished, with no sign of response.

"Socrates. . . ."

He pulled away from her, his eyes averted, burning with shame, miserable, crushed by the singular catastrophe which had overwhelmed him for the first time in his life.

"You see, it's not easy. Yet—" She stopped.

"Yet?"

"I would have liked to, very much."

Socrates heard himself say, in a whisper, "So would I."

"You're different." Her voice was low, sad, poignant.

"Different? How?"

"It doesn't matter. There's something wrong with me. I had hoped that, with you. . . ."

"I don't know what happened to me. It's never happened before. I can't understand it."

"It really doesn't matter. Tomorrow you'll be yourself again. You'll be able to perform, with someone else."

"Not with someone else. With you."

"No. I am the one who cannot. If you had been able to go any further, I would probably have made you stop. I've never made love before, you see. . . ."

"Never?"

"No, never. Not with a man."

There was a long silence. He had already noted that silences between them were necessary to give meaning to their words.

"I can't bear to be with men," Wanda explained. "You—you're the first."

Timidly, he took her into his arms again. She did not try to stop him but lay her head against his shoulder.

"I'm ashamed to admit it," she whispered in his ear, "but I've only been with women. I can only do it with women."

"But that doesn't mean that we can't be friends."

"No. I would like very much to be your friend."

Since that day, he had not once attempted to make love to her. Nonetheless, the bonds which united them, based as they were on their common consciousness of a forbidden act, were indissoluble. Thus it is, Socrates reflected, that love dies while friendship endures. In friendship, a man does not satisfy all his desires; something is always withheld. In love, one is too quickly sated.

It was a truth he had learned at great cost to his vanity.

Peggy Nash-Belmont arrived in New York in a vile humor. She had wanted to return with her Degas under her arm, but her new European friends had dissuaded her, pointing out that she would have to pay an import tariff so exorbitant as to defy the imagination. She had had to resign herself to leaving the painting in the vault of the Chase Manhattan Bank's London branch. Later she would try to get it into the country by passing it off as a copy, but first, she would have to find out how it could be done.

She had hardly closed her eyes for the past forty-eight hours, but the residual excitement of Kallenberg's party banished all thoughts of sleep. She had passed the flight editing the notes for her article on the party. She had a particular slant in mind—an original approach that had nothing to do with the sensational aspects of the party with which the dailies would regale their readers.

She looked for Julian at the immigration desk, but did not see him. She caught sight of him a few minutes later, standing just outside the customs enclosure. With him, unfortunately, were two men, neither of whom she could abide. Both of them, at one time or another, had made advances to her. One was Heath, an editor at *Bazaar* and a fop thoroughly imbued with a sense of his own importance; the other was a photographer, a small, pale man with an over-sized rump.

As soon as Peggy had passed through customs, Heath came toward her with a smile which he obviously believed to be irresistible.

"Hello, Peggy!"

"Hello," Peggy answered tonelessly. She turned to the chauffeur. "Julian, here are my tickets. Will you get my bags, please, and take them to the car."

"Peggy—"

Peggy disliked his calling her by her first name. "Yes?"

"Jennifer Cabott asked me to tell you—"

"Not now. I'm exhausted."

"But this is important—almost a matter of life and death!"

"Don't be ridiculous."

The photographer drew nearer, eager to see this snob debutante draw blood from his superior.

"Peggy, this man has to be interviewed, and he's leaving New York in three hours."

"So let him leave. I'll see him tomorrow, wherever he is."

"Peggy, we have a deadline in two days. We've tried everything, and he absolutely refuses to see anyone. You're the only one who can handle it—"

"Don't try to soft soap me, Heath. I'm tired."

"Jennifer is counting on you. It will be a real *coup!*"

"Who is this man that he's so special?"

"He's a politician."

"What's his name?"

"Baltimore."

"I've never heard of him. There are hundreds of Baltimores all over this country."

"Scott Baltimore, the son of Alfred Baltimore the Second," Heath said reproachfully.

Peggy smothered a laugh. Heath would have to get up very early in the morning if he intended to give her lessons in the genealogy of American society. She was perfectly familiar with every branch and twig of the Baltimore family tree.

She assumed an expression of astonishment. "What's the angle on this—this Scott?" She spat out the name as though she were clearing her throat.

"He's twenty-two years old, and he's really just getting into politics. He's just founded a new party, the New American Party."

Peggy spoke to Julian. "Please take my bags home." She turned to Heath. "All right. I'll give you one hour, and not a minute more. I'm dying for a hot bath."

"Thank you, Peggy! Thank you!"

Heath regretted expressing his gratitude as soon as he saw the look of utter delight on the photographer's face. He should have told the bitch to go screw herself. Still, it wasn't every editor who had a chance to work with a Nash-Belmont.

Maria was a bundle of nerves. She had not slept. Her instructions were most specific that she was not to let Athina Satrapoulos out of her sight, day or night, and she had no choice but to share a room with the old woman. So whenever she felt herself growing drowsy, she had made a determined effort to keep her eyes open. The scratch across her cheek was a reminder that her patient could not be trusted.

During the morning, Athina expressed a desire to knit, and the servants brought her needles and yarn. Maria's eyes were riveted on the peasant woman's gnarled hands as they moved the needles rhythmically. Those same needles could become formidable weapons. Without taking her eyes from Athina, Maria spent much of her time at the telephone that morning, arranging for the arrival of Madame Satrapoulos' guest. The whole idea was at once comical and absurd, she told herself. Everyone would die laughing.

Finally, everything was settled. The guest would arrive in one hour, by chartered plane from Greece and helicopter from the airport, accompanied by her attendants. A group of blue uniformed workmen were working frantically to prepare the suite next door for the expected guest. Through it all, Maria had sensed Satrapoulos' power in the alacrity with which she, the humble interpreter of the whims of the shipowner's mother, was obeyed. There were moments when Maria wondered if Satrapoulos were not the actual owner of the Ritz, with the manager as well as the workmen at his beck and call.

Édouard Fouillet, seeking to disguise the disorder caused by Athina's demands, had flooded the suite with flowers, delivering them to Maria personally with a wide, hypocritical smile. Maria had smiled back, knowing very well that the manager stood between the devil and the deep blue sea. Either he acceded to Athina's every wish or he would face the Greek's wrath.

Maria herself felt that she was nothing more than a tool in the staging of the spectacle which was soon to begin. She sensed that beneath the farcical aspects of the situation, something else was going on, something quite serious, the precise nature of which she was unaware.

She shrugged. She was simply an employee, paid to do as she was told. Indeed, she hoped to gain a permanent advantage by proving herself compliant in every way. Madame Satrapoulos obviously would need a permanent nurse.

Maria heard the sound of furniture being moved next door. Voices rose. One of the workmen was obviously outraged at some aspect of the redecoration.

Athina crossed her needles with a loud click. Instantly, Maria was on guard. But there was no trouble. The old woman continued knitting peacefully. What a difference there was between this smiling, neatly groomed elderly woman and the struggling, screaming, stinking peasant whom Maria had first encountered only forty-eight hours earlier. Yet, the transformation was not entirely to be trusted. There might be other lapses, as violent as the one which had occurred the preceding day.

God, Maria prayed, let her behave herself during the press conference. Everything had been arranged for 6 p.m., which gave Maria time enough to prepare her patient for the ordeal. Then, as the interpreter translated the questions and answers, Maria would stand behind Athina prepared for anything.

It was very possible, of course, that nothing unexpected would happen. Maria had dissolved two tranquilizers in Athina's coffee that morning, and at 1 p.m. she would give her two more. Athina had to be sufficiently alert to answer any questions, but not alert enough to cause a scandal.

There was another loud noise from Suite 504, and more voices. Maria decided to investigate. She glanced at Athina. The old woman sat like a portrait with her knitting in her lap and the balls of yarn at her feet. Maria smiled gently. "I'm going next door for a second to see what's happening. They're preparing the room, you know. You just stay where you are."

Maria opened the door of 504 and peered into the suite. She could not restrain herself from laughing aloud. She shut the door very quickly so as not to be heard. Then she opened it again, just a crack. One of the workmen was in open rebellion. "You must think I'm a fool!" he shouted. "There are some things that I can't do!"

Maria quickly and soundlessly pulled the door shut again. She turned. Athina was standing behind her, less than three feet away. She had just urinated, standing, through her dress and onto the Oriental carpet. In her hand, she held one of the long knitting needles, and she was staring absently at Maria's neck.

The Pontiac stopped before the Metropolitan Museum, at Fifth Avenue and East Eighty-first Street, directly across from the Stanhope Hotel.

"All right," Peggy told Heath. "You can go."

She got out of the car and slammed the door. "Follow me," she snapped at Benny, the photographer.

With an air of determination, she strode into the lobby of the hotel, Benny trotting at her heels. Heath had painted the picture so darkly that the assignment now seemed a challenge. Where others had failed, Peggy would, as usual, succeed. She had thought of a way to get past the two gorillas standing guard at Baltimore's suite and she was not sorry that there would be a witness from *Bazaar* to spread the story of her ingenuity.

"Just a minute," she snapped at Benny. She stopped at a marble writing desk, opened her purse, and took out her checkbook. Making certain that Benny could see what she was doing, she quickly made out a check payable to Scott Baltimore for one hundred thousand dollars.

"Say, that's pretty good." Benny grinned. "Think it'll work?"

Peggy glared at him without answering, then shrugged. On a piece of paper, she wrote a note: "A contribution to the New American Party, from a devoted admirer who would like to congratulate you in person." She scribbled "Scott Baltimore" on an envelope, placed the check and the note inside, and sealed the envelope.

"Let's go up."

The elevator took them to the eighth floor. There they got off, and Peggy said to Benny, "Stay out of sight for ten minutes; then come in."

She turned a corner in the hallway and saw what was undoubtedly the door of Scott Baltimore's suite. Two giant bodyguards were before it, fighting off a concerted attack by a number of reporters and photographers.

Peggy strolled up to one of the guards, her face expressionless, and held out the envelope. "Would you hand this to Mr. Baltimore personally, please? I'll wait for an answer."

"I'll give it to his secretary."

"No. To him, personally. And immediately."

The guard was a man accustomed to taking orders, and he saw the look of authority flashing in Peggy's green eyes. He held a whispered consultation with the other guard, then disappeared into the suite.

He was back a moment later with a surprised look on his face. "Please come in, miss."

There was a loud chorus of protests from the reporters and photographers. "What about us?"

"You're just reporters. She belongs to the party."

Benny, peering around the corner, saw Peggy enter the suite. He looked at his watch and began counting the minutes.

Scott Baltimore looked even younger than his years. So young, Peggy told herself, that it was almost a pity to see him dive into the shark-infested waters of American politics. He was tall, slender, with light-blue eyes and a beguiling smile. A handsome man. And one who had an air of disconcerting honesty about him.

He was holding Peggy's check in his hand. "I'm Scott Baltimore," he introduced himself.

"Peggy Nash-Belmont."

Neither of them could tear their eyes from the other. From the other side of the door, voices rose in heated discussion.

"I've seen you ride."

"I know people who know your father."

There was a pause; then Scott held up the check. "Is this a joke of some kind?"

"No. It's a contribution—payment for ten minutes of your time."

He made a face. "I see. You're a reporter?"

"The *Bazaar*. Does that shock you?"

"No one was ever shocked by a hundred thousand dollars." He laughed.

My God, Peggy said to herself, how attractive he is!

"What do you want to know?"

"Everything you'll tell me. Your age, your astrological sign, what you eat for breakfast, what brand of shaving lotion you use, the color of your pajamas—"

"No, seriously."

"I've never been more serious. Five million women read our magazine every month, and they all vote."

He smiled, devastatingly. "How about you? What kind of perfume do you use?"

"Heure Bleue, by Guerlain."

"And your pajamas?"

"That's none of your business."

"You see? It's not that easy to answer questions. Are you married?"

"What does that have to do with anything?"

The voices in the other room grew louder.

"I'm sorry, I have a plane to catch in two hours, and I have a lot to do. Listen—" He thought for a moment. "I'm going to St. Louis, but I'll be back late tomorrow night. Will you still have time for your article if we get together then?"

"Yes, that would be fine."

"Would you like dinner?"

"I'd love it."

"How about Barbetta's, at eleven?"

"All right."

"The food is terrible, but the place has atmosphere."

"Good. I hate eating."

"Thank you again for the check. But I think you'd better take it back." He held it out.

Peggy took it without hesitation.

"What if I hadn't given it back?"

"I would have stopped payment as soon as I got downstairs."

They both laughed.

"I don't know how you are as a journalist," Scott remarked, "but you'd make one hell of a politician!"

Peggy fought her way back to Benny through the mob of reporters in the hallway. "We're going to meet tomorrow night. I'll call you and tell you the name of the restaurant where we'll be around midnight. You can get your pictures then."

A secret shared is no secret at all, she told herself as she watched the photographer walk away.

In the elevator, she tried to think of a word to describe Scott's eyes. Amazing, she told herself. Utterly, absolutely amazing.

[7]

Édouard Fouillet had spent thirty years in hotel management, and he had never seen anything even remotely comparable. At the service entrance of the Ritz an enormous cage stood before the elevator, with a black goat with small white markings just above its hooves inside. Around the cage fluttered Monsieur Fouillet himself and his assistant manager, Albert, both in overalls.

One of the workmen was shouting, "He's nervous, I tell you. He wants to get out. If we don't let him out, he's going to stink up the whole goddamn hotel!"

"Are you out of your mind? We can't have a goat running around loose in the Ritz!"

Albert saw a way out for himself. "Sir, if you don't mind, I'll get back to my desk. I'm responsible for greeting our guests—"

Fouillet's rage quickly turned on his subordinate. "Precisely! You will show this goat the same courtesy that you show our other guests! After all," he added acidly, "when a guest pays sixty thousand francs a day, we must take good care of him."

The goat had now begun butting its head against the bars of its cage.

"You'd better make up your mind," one of the deliverymen told Fouillet. "Should I let him out or not?"

The manager looked at Albert in despair. The assistant manager manfully tried to accept his responsibilities. "Can you guarantee that it won't run loose in the hotel?"

"I can't guarantee anything. We're supposed to deliver the goat to the service entrance, and that's it. According to union rules, we shouldn't even set foot inside this building. We'd like to help you out, but you're going to have to decide what you want to do."

The manager held up his hands in surrender. "Albert," he ordered, "please take these gentlemen to Suite 504."

With a pair of pliers, one of the deliverymen removed the nails holding a side of the cage in place. Immediately, the goat bolted for freedom, only to have the other deliveryman alertly slip a rope around its neck and give it a tug. The Hairy One—as Athina had christened the animal—freed itself with a mighty thrust of its rear paws and trotted to M. Fouillet to sniff warily at his hands. The manager turned away in disgust, then froze. Coming down the service stairs was one of the Ritz's most valued clients, Lord Seymour, followed by a very young lady. The aged nobleman was obviously unwilling to exhibit his ladylove in the lobby of the hotel. And no wonder, Fouillet reflected, since Lady Seymour, who had been in London for the past week, was due to return to Paris the following day.

There was an embarrassed silence on both sides.

Fouillet, expressionless, bowed.

Lord Seymour turned to his companion. "You see, my dear, the Ritz, in addition to its other virtues, has a remarkable restaurant." Then, pointing to the Hairy One, he addressed Fouillet, "Do keep a haunch for me, old man! For dinner tomorrow."

As Seymour led his friend away, Fouillet heard her whisper, "John, darling, how can you possibly be so cruel? That poor animal!"

Helena was sunning herself beside the pool at the Eden Roc when a man near her unfolded a copy of the Paris *Herald Tribune*. Immediately she saw her husband's name in headlines on page one.

When the man abandoned his paper for the water, she picked it up and scanned the story: "Abandoned mother of Millionaire Socrates Satrapoulos," she read. So Socrates had a mother. Somehow the idea had never occurred to her. She could not imagine him as a child, and he had never spoken to her of either his family or his youth. Did he have a father? she wondered. He was truly a man who lived only for the present and the future, ignoring the past as though it had never existed. It was almost as though he had the power to be reborn every morning, to carve a new life for himself with each new dawn.

She looked at the photograph of the old woman. How old was she? Seventy-five, eighty? The photo was fuzzy, and a drop of something or other had fallen on the woman's face.

It struck Helena that she knew almost nothing about her husband —where and when he had been born or in what circumstances. How could he leave his mother in such poverty—if, indeed, the story were true—while he himself had so much? Socrates owned houses which he never even visited, in any one of which his mother could have lived in comfort. Why had he never spoken of his mother? Was it possible that he was ashamed of his family's poverty? Yet he was certainly aware that Helena attached no importance to his wealth.

What a pity, Helena told herself. It would have been such a pleasure to know her mother-in-law, to make a second mother of her, to talk to her of her son. . . .

In London, at Kallenberg's party, Socrates had made several allusions to the pet-shop incident in Paris. Did he know of her affair with Mark? Or did he merely suspect and was therefore fishing for more information?

After five years of marriage, Helena was tired of Socrates. In the beginning, she had worshiped him devoutly, as though he were a god. He had represented the lifting of all restrictions in her life, the door which led from childhood and its duties into adulthood and its freedom. The honeymoon had been heaven. Socrates had been patient, gentle, and loving, and Helena had been at once a docile and passionate pupil. She had not known that Socrates had arranged to be absent from his business for six months or that there would be an end to the voyages, cruises, and parties. Then, one morning, at Portofino, he had jokingly said that the vacation was over, that he would have to "get back to work so that I can support a wife."

Beginning the next morning, she no longer saw Socrates except when he was between business trips or between continents. She had questioned him about his business affairs, trying to share that part of his life, but he had told her nothing. A man, he explained, had responsibilities to meet, work to do. "Look at your father," he had said. "How often did you see him?"

Now suddenly, Helena had discovered that she had a mother-in-law, a mysterious person who had appeared out of nowhere. She would have liked to call Socrates and ask him if the stories were true, but she did not really know where to find him. After leaving London, he had talked vaguely about a trip to Rome and then to the Middle

East. She would have to try to find him. She put down the newspaper as its owner returned from his swim. He stood before her,
his protruding stomach level with her eyes. "Hello." He smiled.
"Please keep it. I have more paper already than I know what to do
with. My name is Smith—paper mills in Oregon."

Helena looked at him coldly. The trouble with these places, she
told herself, is that everyone feels free to talk to anyone else.

She got up and returned to her cabana, removed her bathing suit,
and dressed in green slacks and a white blouse. Then she walked up
to the hotel. The bell captain, happy to be of service to Madame
Satrapoulos, gave her the key to the suite of friends of hers so that
she might use the telephone.

First, she tried Rome, where her husband's office informed her
that he had been there the preceding day, but that he had left for
Baran on the Persian Gulf in his private plane.

She asked the girl at the switchboard to connect her with the airport at Baran—if there was an airport at Baran. Twenty minutes
later, the connection was made. So far as Helena could make out
from the atrocious English of the man at the other end of the line,
Socrates' plane had left the preceding night.

"Where was it going?" she shouted, exasperated by the heat and
the long wait.

"I do not know," came the reply.

Discouraged, Helena hung up. Where could he be? For a moment,
she considered flying to Greece to see for herself if this newfound
mother-in-law of hers really existed, but she abandoned the idea,
knowing that her husband would be furious if she went without
consulting him first. Instead, she called Athens and spoke to Socrates'
valet. He had not seen Monsieur Satrapoulos, the man said, and
added, "But he promised me that he would bring back some cigarettes from Geneva for me."

"Are you certain that he said Geneva?"

"Yes, madame. I'm absolutely certain. The master said Geneva."

Through the half-open shutters, Helena saw a couple, their arms
wrapped around each other, walking down the path toward the
beach.

"Thank you, Niko. Thank you very much."

She gave the operator the number of their apartment in Geneva.
A few seconds later Socrates himself answered the telephone. He
seemed surprised to hear her voice.

"Where are you?" he asked. "At Saint-Jean-Cap-Ferrat?"

"No. Eden Roc, at Antibes. Socrates, I've just seen the news-papers."

"Yes. So have I."

There was a long pause.

"Is it true?" Helena asked.

"What do you think?"

"Is it true or not?" she demanded.

"There's not a word of truth in it."

"Then you have no mother?"

She heard her husband laugh in Geneva. "I never claimed to be an orphan!"

"But neither did you ever mention that you had a family."

"Do you know of any way for a man to be born without having a mother and a father?"

Helena was puzzled by her husband's tone. He seemed amused by the newspaper story. She could think of nothing more to say.

"Helena, I'm in a hurry. I've just arrived, and I have a meeting in a few minutes. Tell me, what is it you want to know? I'll answer any question you ask."

She felt like a fool. She could think of a hundred questions, but none of them were those that a woman should have to ask the man to whom she had been married for five years. Yet they must be asked. She brushed the tears from her eyes and began.

"Is your mother still alive?"

"Yes, she is."

"Is she the woman whose picture is in the papers?"

"No, she is not."

"You're certain?"

"Yes, of course I'm certain."

"Do you know where your mother is right now?"

"Yes."

"Where?"

"She's in Paris, at the Ritz."

"Are you on bad terms with her?"

She heard a sharp intake of breath at the other end of the line. There was a moment of hesitation. Then he answered, "It's true we're not on very good terms."

"What are you going to do to stop these newspaper reports?"

"It's too late to stop them, obviously, since they've already been published. All I can do is make people forget them—by giving them an even more sensational story to talk about."

"Then the lady in the photograph is not your mother?"

"No."

"Do you give me your word?"

"Lena, I give you my word."

"How did all these stories get started?"

"Why don't you ask Kallenberg?"

"Herman?"

"Listen, Lena. Since you like newspapers so much, be sure to buy one tomorrow. And listen to the radio tonight. I'm sorry, but I really must hang up now."

She did not want him to go just yet. She had nothing more to ask, but for reasons she could not identify, she wanted to keep him on the telephone.

"When will I see you?"

"I don't really know. You told me that you were going to New York—"

"I don't feel like going."

"Then why don't you meet me in Rotterdam? I'll be there to-night."

"I—I don't know. Where would I meet you?"

"At the apartment."

"Socrates?"

"Yes?"

"Socrates, do you love your mother?"

He laughed. A strange, sad sound. "I worship her. And I worship you, too! Good-bye, Helena."

Helena held the receiver in her hand. The voice of the switch-board operator brought her out of her reverie. "Have you finished, madame?"

"Get me the desk, please. . . . Hello, desk? This is Madame Sat-rapoulos. Can you charter a plane for me right away? From Nice to Paris. In two hours."

Helena had made up her mind. Since her mother-in-law was at the Ritz, there was no reason on earth why she shouldn't visit her.

Raph Dun was sufficiently vain to repeat anything which might increase his prestige, but he was not foolish enough to reveal the background to the fantastic story spread all over the newspapers. A silence dictated by prudence was a burden he found difficult to bear, since he was not a man addicted to modesty, mandatory or otherwise. He would have loved to boast of his part in the project, to have himself become the subject of an article, or even to have thrown a cocktail party with something like "Raph Dun invites you to celebrate one of the outstanding *coups* of his career, the discovery of Socrates Satrapoulos' mother," on the invitations. Instead, he was compelled to caution his fellow journalists, "Forget that you heard it from me. If you say anything, I'll have to deny it."

He threw the newspaper he had been reading onto the bed.

The telephone rang. It was the editor of *Flash*. "What are you doing this evening at six?" the man demanded.

"I'm busy, Bill. Sorry. And I'll be busy tomorrow night and the other nights after that, too. For a whole year, in fact. I'm going to take some time off. Why?"

"It's about this Satrapoulos business—"

"Yes. Fantastic, isn't it?"

"Yes. It's fantastic, all right. So fantastic that we're going to have to kill Saturday's issue."

"Say that again?"

"You heard me. The whole story is out. Period. Satrapoulos is suing every newspaper and magazine that published it. The photographs aren't of his mother. The whole thing is a put-up job—"

"Come on, Bill! I—"

"It doesn't really matter, in any case. We're going to run another story; this one is about his real mother."

"What real mother?"

"What's the matter, Dun? Are you drunk? I'm telling you that the whole thing was a hoax. We're filing suit against the agency that sold us the story. And it's going to cost them plenty."

"This must be some kind of joke! What makes you think—"

"It's no joke. If you want to see the real mother, go over to the Ritz tonight at six. She's holding a press conference. Do you want to cover it for us?"

"You're sure about this?"

"Absolutely certain. And I'm not asking you to cover it for us because you're such a great reporter, but because you're already at the scene of the crime, so to speak. I have to have the story by midnight. I'm sending Bob for some photographs. Make sure he gets some good ones, will you? And try to be on time."

Dun had turned deathly white. He leaped from the bed and grabbed his pants.

* * *

Helena did not stop at the desk. She crossed the lobby of the Ritz and reached the elevator bank without anyone asking her who she was or where she was going. She was one of those rare women who looked as though they belonged at the Ritz. She could have bathed nude in a public fountain, and no policeman would have dreamed of arresting her or even of asking her where she lived. Instead he would have escorted her to the nearest luxury hotel, knowing, as one knows an eternal truth, that that was where she lived.

On the fifth floor, she asked a passing chambermaid for Madame Satrapoulos' room. The employee, her arms filled with a gigantic bouquet of flowers, glanced at Helena's diamond bracelet and answered: "504, madame." It was a reasonable error, since Athina Satrapoulos and her entourage occupied two adjacent suites, 503 and 504.

Helena thanked her with a smile and proceeded to 504. She stopped before the door, hesitating. Did she have the right to pry into her husband's secrets?

She pressed the doorbell.

The door was opened almost immediately by a liveried servant who peered at her suspiciously.

"Yes, madame?"

"Madame Satrapoulos, please."

The servant made a quick movement as though to close the door. Helena, suspecting that Socrates had given orders to let no one see his mother, spoke hurriedly. "I am Madame Satrapoulos, and I must see my mother-in-law immediately."

The servant tried to explain that Socrates' mother was in the adjoining suite, but Helena did not give him time. She pushed past him and entered the room. What she saw made her gasp. The room had been emptied of its furnishings, except for the lighting fixtures and a few late eighteenth-century woodcuts depicting, appropriately, assorted Roman ruins. Most of the floor was covered by a thick layer of freshly cut hay. In the middle of this artificial pasture was a kind of fenced-in corral. A large blond woman, wearing a nurse's smock, was leaning against the fence. Within the enclosure stood a black goat with small white markings just above its hooves, and, with the goat, an elderly lady, also in black, with white markings around the collar of her dress and wearing a few pieces of tasteful jewelry. The lady was on her knees, milking the goat with an expertise obviously born of long practice. The only sound in the room was the sound of the goat's milk as it streamed into the metal bucket standing beneath its udder.

The nurse was the first to speak. "Madame—"

Helena silenced her with a gesture. "I am Socrates Satrapoulos' wife." She approached the corral fence, her initial astonishment giving way to sympathy for the old woman within the enclosure. "Madame," she said softly in Greek, "I am your daughter-in-law."

Athina did not look at her.

"The wife of your son, Socrates."

Athina, without glancing up, addressed herself to the nurse. "Get that bitch out of here," she said.

Dun stared at the old woman in consternation. How was it possible? The only reasonable explanation was that Satrapoulos had known beforehand of the plot against him. If so, then the chances were that the woman before him was not the real mother.

Athina Satrapoulos was seated in an armchair, still groggy from a massive dose of tranquilizers. She stared blankly at the crowd before her, blinking like an owl blinded by a sudden flash of light. Maria was to her left, the interpreter to her right. Behind her stood Satrapoulos' two bodyguards, on special assignment from Athens. Everyone had received the same instructions: at the first hint of unusual behavior on Athina's part, the conference was to be terminated, using the old lady's fatigue as an excuse. The interpreter had already pointed out in opening the conference that Madame Satrapoulos had been ill, that she was still weak, and that the shock of the scandal, combined with the natural debility of old age, had weakened her resistance.

The interpreter had been chosen by the Prophet of Cascais himself, and the latter had spent two hours of his precious time to instruct him as to his duties before allowing him to board the chartered plane which was to fly him to Paris. The interpreter—a young man with steel-rimmed glasses, short hair, and a neutral expression—had, thus far acquitted himself well. Under the avalanche of questions, he had remained unruffled and expressionless, confining himself to translating queries into Greek and answers into French. His sole contribution to the exchange was to ask Athina the converse of the reporters' questions and to transpose Athina's answers. Had anyone else in Suite 503 been able to understand both Greek and French, this is what he would have heard:

REPORTER: Does she love her son?

INTERPRETER: Why do you hate Socrates?

ATHINA: Because he is rotten to the core.

INTERPRETER: She worships him.

Thus, for two hours, a dialogue of the deaf had been taking place, dozens of questions being asked and then answered precisely as Socrates Satrapoulos would have wished them to be answered. No one except Maria and the two bodyguards was in a position to appreciate the superb performance of the interpreter.

Only Dun, angry at being deprived of his triumph and dreading his next encounter with Kallenberg, sensed that something was amiss. He had remained at the back of the room, waiting for the hoax somehow to be exposed for what it was, for someone to make the fatal slip. Thus far no such thing had happened.

Nonetheless, Raph was unwilling to take it upon himself to intervene, to ask the questions which he felt should be asked. It would be too risky to draw attention to himself or to show too detailed a knowledge of the Satrapoulos affair. He turned to his photographer. "Bob, ask the interpreter to show us the woman's passport."

Bob, with undisguised arrogance, asked the question. The interpreter seemed surprised, then turned to Maria and whispered something. The nurse left the room, to return almost immediately with the passport. She handed it to the interpreter, who handed it to Bob, who passed it to Raph Dun. Dun examined it at length. It was incontestably genuine, and it bore the seals of various countries. He had no way of knowing that the passport had been obtained only two days before, in London, from a pair of forgers whom Socrates had paid a fabulous price to exercise their talents in his behalf. With a sigh of disappointment, Dun handed the document to his neighbor, who started it back on its return trip to Maria.

In the momentary silence which accompanied Maria's acceptance of the passport, a strange sound was heard. Clearly, distinctly, loudly. The bleating of a goat. There was a burst of laughter among the journalists, and everyone looked at his neighbor for confirmation of what he had just heard. Then, all eyes turned to the wall from which the sound seemed to have come, and, from there, they moved to the interpreter.

The interpreter smiled for the first time since the conference had begun. He spread his hands in a gesture of helplessness. "Gentlemen, for an explanation of these sounds, I must refer you to the management of the Ritz. Madame Satrapoulos has had enough questions for one day."

Everyone laughed again, and the reporters and photographers dashed toward the exit.

"He who sows the wind shall reap the whirlwind," the Prophet intoned solemnly, then glanced conspiratorially at Satrapoulos.

The Greek was not impervious to humor when things were going smoothly for him. But he did not know whether or not the Prophet was joking. He had never been able to decide how seriously his guru took himself. There were times when the Prophet, by a remark or a retort, seemed to lower his mask for a second. But Socrates could never be sure.

The Prophet, for his part, had learned long ago that one must never step down from one's pedestal, never refer to one's private life, never show the least sign of uncertainty, never allow a client even a glimpse over the wall which separated them. One must present an impenetrable façade of benevolent solicitude and always be wary of falling into the ever-present pit of personal involvement. Hilary, as the Prophet had been known before his apotheosis, was basically a soft-hearted man, and the necessity to maintain professional detachment was a cause of constant sorrow to him. There were days when he would have liked to forget his tarot cards, to have a drink with a client and talk about literature, philosophy, theology —about anything other than astrological signs and heavenly portents.

"My friend," Satrapoulos said, "your tactics were absolutely masterful from the beginning to the end. I suppose you've seen the newspapers?" He brandished a copy of the *Tribune*, the front page of which carried a headline: BEHIND THE WAR FOR BLACK GOLD.

The newspapers, one and all, in order to make amends for having libeled Socrates Satrapoulos, had been obliged to publish retractions. In these, they punctuated their litanies of recantation with repeated protestations that they had been "misinformed." But they did not say by whom they had been misinformed. The implication was clear that the newspapers had been victims in a merciless war between conflicting petroleum interests. From a scandal, the Satrapoulos affair had now taken on the dimensions of an international *cause célèbre* in which everyone competed to render homage to the Greek's professional integrity. "Rival groups," unidentified, had plotted to ruin him by fabricating the scandalous story of an abandoned mother and an impious son. There followed the editors' apologies and photographs of Athina at the Ritz, "in Paris on a shopping trip," decked out in the jewelry presented to her by Socrates "on a recent birthday." Not only was Socrates absolved of all sin, but now he was actually being congratulated for the dignified and courageous way in which he had comported himself throughout the ordeal to which he had been subjected—an ordeal, the newspapers made clear, manufactured by certain unscrupulous interests which had not hesitated even to take advantage of the editors' good faith.

In truth, Socrates' lawyers had had to threaten the editors with the most terrible reprisals in order to force them to retract. Finally, after tempestuous conferences which had lasted far into the night, the newspapers had submitted, and with rage in their hearts, the editors had ordered the retractions published. The fact that all the newspapers were in the same position offered little consolation. From Rome to Amsterdam and from Munich to Paris, every newsroom resounded with shouted oaths and jangling telephones as the powers of the press focused on the problem of discovering who, precisely, had been the instigator of this incredible hoax. All trails led to the London office SIA—Scoop International Agency—where Mike, immovable as a wall of stone, refused to divulge the name of his informant.

Mike's steadfastness was based not on any particular regard for Raph Dun, but on an inflexible determination to share with no one the ecstasy of revenge. SIA's losses in the Satrapoulos affair were not only the fees that would have to be repaid, but the damage to its credibility which it would require years to repair. And Mike was determined that the punishment visited upon Dun's head would be proportionate to his crime.

"And now?" the Prophet asked.

Satrapoulos smiled. "And now what?"

"What are your plans? What does the future hold for you?"

"Who knows? The world is large, the sea is vast."

"Do you trust this emir?"

"Not in the slightest. He is a fanatic. But I do trust his appetite for money and power. As long as he has the first and wants the second, he will behave himself and respect the terms of our contract."

"That is not enough."

"What do you mean?"

"You must bind him to you so closely that even should he wish to, he will not be able to break with you. Do you think for a minute that Kallenberg is going to give up so easily?"

"No, I suppose not."

"Then you'll have to act very quickly to keep him from overtaking you."

"What can he do now? He's through, finished."

"So you say. Since he has failed to persuade the emir to give him the contract, it is probable that he will try to obtain it by other means."

"What other means?"

"The emir is a man; therefore, he has weaknesses. Your brother-in-law may try to reach him through those."

"I have a signed contract."

"To the Arab mind, a contract is a scrap of paper. Nothing."

"Then what should I do?"

"What sort of power does this emir have?"

"It's essentially a spiritual power, a sort of moral authority over his fellow emirs."

"Based on what?"

Satrapoulos was beginning to see where the Prophet was leading. Very clever, he told himself. "It's based on the emir's ascetic life, his so-called disinterest in material things, his pretended purity."

"Do you see what I have in mind?"

"Vaguely."

"Then you understand that there is always a way to get at a man."

"Yes, of course. But how—"

"First, I must consult my tarot cards to discover the most auspicious moment. Then we will discuss the details of the operation. I can promise you that, this time, the prize will be yours once and for all."

"Perhaps Kallenberg has thought of the same thing."

"Not yet. He will, in a week or so. That is why we must act now."

After the press conference at the Ritz, Raph Dun had decided that it would be best to disappear for a while. He had not even stopped long enough to telephone the Paris airport to discover the flights to Nice. He had simply packed a few summer clothes into the Vuitton bag and taken a taxi to Orly. An hour later, he was flying over the mountains of the Lyonnais, pondering a delicate problem: where would he stay in Nice?

The difficulty lay in the necessity to avoid offending anyone. He knew too many people on the Côte d'Azur, and he was known by too many. No matter which of his friends he selected as his host, there would be a dozen others mortally affronted. He therefore decided to abandon himself to chance, confident that a fortuitous encounter would relieve him of necessity of making a choice.

Life was not easy, Raph reflected. He had thought it more prudent not to contact Mike, knowing that the editor of SIA would demand the return of the money he had paid for the Satrapoulos story. Unfortunately, that money was already in the pocket of the proprietor of the garage where Raph's Ferrari was being held as security for the payment of overdue bills. There was, nonetheless, a way for a man teetering on the brink of ruin to regain his footing. An incomparable, almost miraculous way: the Palm Beach Hotel at Cannes, where Raph had often registered without a penny to his name and without hope of credit and from which he had checked out with all his debts paid and with a healthy bank account to boot. Obviously, the miracle did not always occur on schedule, but at this point, Raph had nothing to lose and everything to gain. A tiny interior voice persisted in saying: but what if you only succeed in getting deeper into debt? But Raph refused to listen. He already had enough trouble without allowing his natural optimism to be tempered.

Kallenberg's personal secretary had called Raph three times in Paris, and three times Raph had disguised his voice and answered that he was Mr. Dun's secretary and that Mr. Dun was away on a business trip. Kallenberg's man had asked him, rather brusquely, to have Mr. Dun call Mr. Kallenberg immediately on a matter of great urgency. They can all go to hell, Raph told himself. After all, he wasn't to blame for the fiasco. Someone had been pulling strings behind the scenes, and Kallenberg was in a better position than Raph to find out who it was.

"Ladies and gentlemen, we are going to land in a few minutes. Please fasten your seat belts."

Through the window, Raph could see the ocean and a long finger of beach stretching like an ocher-yellow serpent against the cobalt blue of the water.

He had barely gotten through the airport gates when he ran into an old acquaintance, Lisa, a girl from a prominent family—hardware of all kinds—but possessed of almost imperceptible brainpower.

"What are you doing here?" Lisa exclaimed.

"I'm just arriving, as you see."

"Are you going to be here long?"

"It depends."

"You're going to Cannes?"

"Maybe. I'm not sure yet."

"Fantastic! Come with me."

"Where to?"

"To Danielle's house. We're bored silly—five girls."

"Danielle who?"

"God, you have a terrible memory. You remember Danielle—"

Raph remembered well enough. Danielle Valberger, one of the beauties of the Côte d'Azur. She had tried to kill herself over Raph and had lived to boast of it. Raph regarded her as someone who took herself too seriously—a type which he abhorred above all others. He had left Cannes after the affair with Danielle, to give the scandal time to die down.

"Yes, Danielle. How is she?"

"Never better."

"Who are the others?"

"Mimsy, Elaine, Marina. With me and Danielle, that's five. Funny, my running into you like this. We were just talking about you this morning. Your article was terrible!"

Raph felt a hollowness in the pit of his stomach.

"What article?"

"The one you did on Harlem."

He had forgotten it. It was as though he had never done anything before the Satrapoulos scandal and as though the whole world must know of his part in that fiasco.

He half sighed in relief.

"What are you doing at the airport?"

Lisa's eyes opened wide. "Oh, God. I almost forgot. Did you see Nicole on the plane?"

"Nicole who?"

"Nicole d'Almerida."

"No, I didn't see her. I wish you'd stop using only first names. How am I supposed to know who you're talking about?"

"Don't play games with me. You know them all. I suppose she missed the plane. All right, let's go."

"Lisa, who told you I would be on this plane?"

"I've never seen a man yet who'd turn down an invitation to visit a harem of five girls."

"Where is Danielle's father?"

"He had to go to Paris. He let Danielle stay home on condition that the rest of us stay with her as chaperones. Wait till they see what I'm bringing home!"

Raph hesitated, undecided.

"Oh, come on, Raph. At least to have a drink and a swim with us. If we bore you, you can always leave. My car's right outside."

[8]

For the past forty-eight hours, the least provocation had sufficed to send Herman Kallenberg into a fit of rage so terrible that it left him exhausted and on the verge of apoplexy. His servants had seen him indulge in such violent outbursts in the past, but never had they seen him in such a state. Everyone stayed out of his sight as much as possible and trembled when duty required them to venture into the Presence.

Kallenberg was still in London when he first saw the newspaper accounts of his personal disaster. The shock had been so great that he had been traumatized into a profound silence at the very moment when an explosion would have been more logical. He had locked himself in his study, stunned by his defeat, incapable of either discerning its causes or foreseeing its consequences. But his withdrawal had been transitory. An hour later he emerged from his torpor and gave orders to locate Dun. When Dun could not be found, Kallenberg charged into Irene's room like an enraged bull and found her lying naked on her bed, a heavy layer of beautician's mud on her face. Kallenberg was not in a mood to require a better pretext to vent his ire. "I'm being ruined!" he screamed at his wife. "I'm being at-

tacked from all sides! Everyone's conspiring against me! And what
do you do? You bury yourself in that goddamned mud!"

Irene all but shivered with delight at her husband's words. He was
in trouble! Someone had gotten the better of him!

"Who's threatening you, dear?" she asked sweetly. "Who's trying
to ruin you? Do tell me."

As she spoke, she rose to a sitting position and groped blindly for
a towel to wipe the mud from her face. Her hand fell upon the white
terry-cloth robe from Dior's that she had removed a few minutes
earlier, and she began to daub at her face with it. Slowly, Herman's
form became visible before her.

"You stupid cow!" Kallenberg shouted, striking her with his fist
in the ribs. "Do you see what you're wiping your face with?"

Wincing with pain, Irene nonetheless took advantage of the opportunity her husband's rage offered to score points in their eternal
game. "Sweetheart, if you're really in trouble," she murmured se-
ductively, "this isn't the time to make love."

Irene's words, combined with his own rage, roused Kallenberg to a
peak of frenzy. He seized one of her breasts and twisted it brutally.
Irene screamed, once. Then with a supreme effort she controlled herself. "Oh, darling," she said. "I love it when you want me so!"

But the pain was too great, and she began screaming, "Bastard!
Filthy pig! Animal! I hope they break you completely. I hope they
take your last penny! I hope they kill you!"

Kallenberg smiled. "Ah, I'm glad to see you're yourself again."

He turned and left the room.

One of the newspapers had headlined its coverage of the Satrapoulos affair: WHO BENEFITS FROM THIS CRIME? But the story
had contained no mention of Kallenberg except to point out that, a
few days earlier, he too had been the innocent victim of an attack
carried out by unknown persons. Was it some sort of extremist plot
to discredit the men who so dominated the international economy?
Was it a political maneuver? A war between rival shipping firms?
Such were the questions the columnist asked. There was no satis-
factory answer to them, since the journalist had no way of knowing
that the victims and the organizers of the two crimes described in
his column were the same people: Socrates Satrapoulos and Herman
Kallenberg.

On that point, at least, Kallenberg's mind was at peace. Satrapoulos was no more suspected of having ruined Kallenberg's Christ-

mas party than Kallenberg was of having exhumed Satrapoulos's
mother in Greece. So far it remained a family affair.

That evening Kallenberg decided to leave for the Côte d'Azur the
following morning. With Irene. He had an estate between Cannes
and Antibes which he seldom visited. A sojourn there would give
him time to lay his plans for revenge. And it would be a good opportunity to play the faithful husband while he mounted his counterattack. He ordered Irene to leave in the morning and assured her
that he would follow later in the day, after he had taken care of
various business matters.

At Nice, his chauffeur was waiting for him at the airport, full of
apologies for having to meet him in a rented vehicle. Kallenberg's
own Cadillac, he explained, had developed a peculiar noise in the
engine, and he had taken it in for repairs.

"When will it be ready?" Kallenberg asked.

The chauffeur looked up in surprise. His master never troubled
himself over such affairs. "It's ready now, sir. I called just before
meeting you. I'll pick it up as soon as I've taken you home."

"No, I think we should pick it up right now."

At the garage, Kallenberg remained on the ground floor as the
chauffeur climbed to the upper levels to get the Cadillac. Five minutes
passed. Kallenberg glanced impatiently at his watch. Ten minutes.
Then, exasperated, he ran up the staircase to find the chauffeur.
On the fourth floor, he found the long Cadillac wedged against
the wall on a curve in the access ramp, unable to move backward or
forward.

Kallenberg ordered the chauffeur out of the car and slid behind
the wheel. He backed a few inches, went forward a few inches, turned
the wheel first to the right, then to the left. But the Cadillac remained approximately where it had been before.

The chauffeur gestured through the window, attempting to direct
his master's efforts to free the car. Kallenberg felt his anger rising.
He was determined to succeed where the chauffeur had failed. He
shouted something at the chauffeur as the Cadillac lurched backward
and smashed against a white Jaguar, ripping off its left front fender.
Ready to explode with fury, Kallenberg threw the automatic trans-
mission into neutral. The front of the Cadillac was now free. He trod
on the accelerator until the engine roared with the full power of its
three hundred and fifty horses, and then slammed the gearshift out
of neutral, intending to put it into forward and move down the ramp.
Instead, he stopped it in reverse, and the car, with a great screeching

of tires, shot backward into the garage, roared across its width, and smashed against the glass wall, tearing through the protective railing that protected it. The vehicle's momentum carried it halfway through the glass, until its rear end was hanging in thin air four stories above the street. Slowly, the angle between the car and the outside wall of the building grew smaller as the weight of the vehicle began to pull it inexorably downward. Screams of panic from the street were audible within the garage. Then, with a resounding clang, the Cadillac's front bumper struck the twisted guardrail—and held.

The chauffeur ran to help his master. He leaned out through the yawning hole in the wall, and below him, through the broken windshield, he saw Kallenberg's face, pale and streaked with blood. It seemed as if he hardly dared move for fear of disturbing the Cadillac's precarious grip on life.

Kallenberg looked up at him quizzically. "It's all right," he said. "Gently, now. It won't fall."

The chauffeur hesitated.

"Here," Kallenberg ordered, thrusting his hand through the door frame. "Take my hand."

The chauffeur did as he was told. Slowly, carefully, Kallenberg pulled himself out of the wrecked Cadillac and climbed into the building. He took no notice of the garage employees, standing mutely in a circle around him. "Hubert," he snapped at the chauffeur, "pay whatever damage there is." Then he wiped his face with a handkerchief and stalked from the room.

Three-quarters of an hour later Kallenberg arrived at his villa in a taxi. Blood was still running from a cut above his left eye. He held out a bill to the driver who had not dared ask any questions of his fare. "Here," he said. "Keep the change."

Irene was in the living room, trying on bathing suits, when Kallenberg entered.

"Herman!" she screamed.

He did not answer but continued on toward the bathroom. She ran after him.

"What is it, Herman? What happened? What did you do to yourself?"

He seemed in a stupor. He did not react even when Irene began wiping his face with a towel.

"Here," she said, "hold this on your forehead. Don't move."

She opened the medicine cabinet and found cotton, alcohol, and a bottle of mercurochrome. She examined the cut above his eye and began cleaning it.

"It's not very deep," she said reassuringly.

Herman, docile as a child, allowed her to do as she wished, and Irene, moved by her gigantic husband's helplessness, felt tears of tenderness well in her eyes. If only he were always like this, dependent on her, willing to accept her help!

"There was an accident," Kallenberg said. "I drove the Cadillac through the wall of a garage, on the fourth story. It's nothing, really."

"That's right, sweetheart. It's only a scratch. Let me take care of it." She had completely forgotten their encounter the preceding evening, the mutual insults, the hostility. Suddenly she was a woman, a warrior's wife. It was her duty to bandage, to soothe, to caress, and to console.

"Now," she said, "go lie down in our room for a while." They had had separate rooms since the first week of their marriage. Yet the term "our room" had come naturally to her lips, as though Herman's accident had wiped out the past.

Without protest, Kallenberg allowed himself to be led into the bedroom. He stretched himself out on the bed while Irene rang for the maid and instructed her to bring a pot of tea and a bottle of whiskey. Then she stood over the bed, stroking Kallenberg's head, running her fingers through his hair and gently rubbing his scalp. It was the first time she had dared do such a thing, and she felt slightly ridiculous. At the same time, she experienced a wave of tenderness and warmth that was new to her. She became aware that it had required only a minor injury to awaken such feelings in her. If he would only give her the opportunity to live for his sake, she would be ready to stand beside him against the world. Instead, their relationship had been one continuous battle, with each of them trying to destroy the other.

Memories suddenly flooded her mind. Ever since her childhood, she reflected, she had been both the victim and the perpetrator of duplicity. Ever since she had been old enough to understand what was going on around her, she had known that her father was carrying on affairs with other women. Why had he behaved one way when he was with his family and totally differently when he was with strangers? And which personality had really been his? She knew now that Ulysses Mikolofides had been a stranger to her, that she knew practically nothing about him. And for the first time, she saw him through eyes that were not those of a fearful, hostile, and rebellious child.

She heard Kallenberg's deep, regular breathing. But he was not asleep. His eyes were open, staring at the ceiling. She looked into those eyes. At the center of the blue-encircled pupils there were flecks of green.

"Herman, I never noticed before. You have green in your eyes." He did not answer.

Instinctively, Irene lay down next to him, raised his head, and passed her arm under it. She pressed against him, suddenly become the protector of her protector, the mother of her tormentor.

"What are you thinking about?" she asked.

He sighed deeply. "I'm worried."

It was the first time he had ever revealed his state of mind to her. She pressed against him even more closely. She had read the newspapers, of course, but there had been no obvious connection between her husband and the stories about Satrapoulos and his mother.

"Is it really serious?" she asked.

"Yes, very serious."

He had answered her! She shivered with joy, even pride. Then she said something without thinking, something stupid which, as soon as she had spoken the words, she was certain would anger him and break the spell: "What sign are you?"

To her amazement, he did not push her away or storm out of the room.

"Taurus," he said. "Why?"

"Nothing," she answered. "I just wondered."

"Do you believe in signs?"

"I don't know. Satrapoulos does. Lena says that he never does anything without consulting an astrologer."

Irene felt Kallenberg stiffen in her arms.

"An astrologer?"

"A seer, a prophet, something like that. A man who lives in Portugal. He's called the Prophet—the Prophet of Cascais."

"Are you sure of that?" her husband demanded.

"Socrates himself told Lena that he wouldn't have married her if the Prophet had advised against it."

Herman raised himself on his elbows, his eyes shining with a new light. "Do you think he's stupid enough to believe in such things?"

"I know he is. He's never in his life signed a single contract without consulting his astrologer."

Kallenberg was on his feet in an instant, an expression of utter joy on his face. He bent and kissed his wife tenderly on the forehead. "Thank you!" he said. "You have no idea how valuable that information is!"

Was he serious? Irene asked herself. Or was it the shock of the accident? Yet Herman was standing before her, calm and smiling, the very picture of a man with a new lease on life.

Athina Satrapoulos was kneeling next to the Hairy One when the nurse left her for a moment to see who was knocking at the door of the adjoining suite. But no sooner was Maria out of the room than the old woman darted toward the door. The nurse had made the mistake of locking it from the inside rather than from the outside. Athina ran down the hallway to the service stairs and plunged down the stairs as fast as she could move, wearing only a black dress and house slippers. She found a door and opened it. It was a closet containing the chambermaids' cleaning equipment and some of their clothing. Athina felt the objects with her hand: a broom, dustcloths, a shopping bag filled with detergent bottles, and a lightweight woman's coat. She put on the coat and emptied the bottles from the bag.

A few minutes later a panic-stricken Maria gave the alarm, but Athina was already walking briskly down the rue de Rivoli. And an old woman in black, strolling down the street in slippers, was not an unusual sight in mid-August, even in the First Arrondissement of Paris.

Athina had nowhere to go and nothing to do. Her only aim was to escape from the place where she was being held prisoner. Nonetheless, she walked quickly, hugging the shade of the arcades, not stopping even to glance into the shop windows. She passed the Place des Pyramides, the Place du Palais-Royal, and continued on until she reached the Sarah Bernhardt Theater, where, for no particular reason, she turned left and reached the Quai de Gesvres.

The air here was dry, dusty, stifling. She stopped only once, near the Pont d'Arcole, to watch an old man feeding the pigeons. She tried clumsily to pet one of the birds, but it scampered away from her hand. The man smiled and said something which she did not understand.

By midafternoon Athina's wandering course had brought her across the Seine, down the Boulevard Saint-Germain and past the rue

Cuvier. She glanced curiously at a barred fence next to the street, then stopped for a closer look at other enclosures, like cages, behind the fence. To her amazement, she saw animals within the enclosures.

She looked for a gate through the fence but found none. She retraced her steps and found the main gate. A man in a blue uniform stopped her.

"Your ticket, please."

Athina looked at him in puzzlement.

"One franc," he said, holding up a single finger to make clear both his meaning and the amount.

Athina shook her head.

The guard concluded, quite correctly, that she did not understand a word of French. He therefore rubbed together his index finger and his thumb in a universally recognizable gesture.

Once more Athina shook her head.

"Money," the guard said loudly and distinctly. "One franc to get in. Do you have a franc?" As he spoke, he tapped the pockets of Athina's stolen coat. There was a jingle of coins. The old woman reached into one of the pockets, then held out her hand, palm upward. There were three one-franc pieces and two twenty-centime coins. The guard took a franc, and called after Athina, "We close at five o'clock!"

Athina joined a group of tourists staring into an enclosure. Farther on, she entered a building which smelled of animals and saw a group of snakes larger than any she had ever imagined existed. How many animals must they eat every day to stay alive? she asked herself.

The thought of food made her hungry, and she spent another coin for a bag of peanuts which she shelled and ate distractedly as she wandered from cage to cage. Maria, the Ritz, and the rest of the world were totally forgotten.

She was watching the lion's cage when a sharp, loud whistle brought her back to earth. Instinctively, she felt an impulse to hide, thinking that the sound somehow signified that her jailers had come to take her back to the Ritz. She looked around in near panic. The people near her were beginning to move slowly toward the exits. Immediately, she set out in the opposite direction, determined not to return to the unknown, dangerous streets of the city. Here she felt safe and at home among the animals. If she could find a good hiding place, no one would ever discover her here.

She passed the last visitors to the Jardin des Plantes: a mother herding her family toward the gate and a pair of lovers walking slowly arm in arm. A guard appeared ahead of her, and Athina slipped behind a brick building as the man drew nearer. Then she was alone. She sat motionless for a long while, hearing the sounds of the city in the distance, like the beating of a giant heart. To the west the sky was still light, but here and there she saw neon signs flicker on.

Then it was three hours since Athina had taken refuge behind her brick wall, and everywhere it was dark. The cries of the monkeys reached her ears, and the screams of the hyenas.

She felt the first pangs of hunger and ventured out onto the dim walks. She sensed the presence of animals around her and wondered vaguely what they ate. She stumbled against something in the darkness. She extended her hand and felt the heavy texture of canvas. Underneath the canvas, her fingers discovered a box containing small paper packages. She knew where she was. It was the candy vendor's stand. Joyfully, she explored its contents: nougats, caramels, peanuts. . . .

After eating her fill, Athina tried to recall where she had seen a faucet. Probably near the lion's cage. Stumbling and groping her way across the lawns, she found the faucet and drank deeply, wiping her mouth carefully on the sleeve of her coat. Then she stretched out on the ground, near a tree, and looked up at the sky. It should have been black. Instead, it had a reddish cast, as though someone had placed a screen between heaven and earth. There were no stars.

Athina slept.

Maria's orders had been quite vague in one respect. If something happened, if Madame Satrapoulos became ill or if anything else unforeseen occurred, she was not to call the police. Instead, she was to notify the manager of the Ritz, who would decide what was to be done. Therefore, after searching the hallways of the fifth floor of the hotel, she returned to the suite and asked the switchboard to connect her with the manager. Her hand trembled on the receiver as she waited, and her legs were so unsteady that she was compelled to sit. Then Monsieur Fouillet was on the line. In English, Maria explained that Athina Satrapoulos had disappeared. There was a choking sound at the other end of the wire. Fouillet saw another scandal looming over the Ritz—newspapers, press conferences, microphones everywhere, glaring lights, raised eyebrows among his clients. . . . He must have been out of his mind to allow that madwoman to stay at his hotel. But how could he have foreseen the trouble she would cause? How could he have known that—that she would bring a goat into the Ritz?

The goat stuck in his mind. "Is the goat still there?" he asked.

Maria was speechless. Athina Satrapoulos had disappeared, and the man was asking about a goat. "I don't give a damn about the goat!" she screamed.

"You don't understand," Fouillet said calmly. "Madame Satrapoulos is a bit, what shall I say? Not deranged, surely; but eccentric. If the goat was important enough to have it brought all the way from Greece, it seems unlikely that she would abandon it. There is a good chance that she will return—that she has simply wandered away."

He's not as much of a fool as I thought, Maria told herself. Athina could not be far away. She would never abandon the Hairy One in a hotel room. She would come back.

Fouillet continued. "While awaiting her return, do you want me to notify the police of her disappearance?"

"No! Absolutely not!"

Fouillet was silent for a second. "Still," he said, "it is my responsibility. . . . Please do not leave your room. I will come up immediately."

He was there a minute later, visibly worried. He questioned Maria closely as to how she had learned of Athina's disappearance. The nurse told him the little that she knew: the old woman had been there in the room; then, suddenly, she was no longer there. It had been that simple.

"Is it possible that she is still in the hotel?"

"No."

"How can you be so sure?"

"Because she hates this place."

Despite the gravity of the situation, Fouillet could not repress a frown. No one in the world could be so jaded or so insensitive as to hate his hotel. "Mademoiselle, please! You are speaking of the Ritz!" Then he added, "I will give orders to have the hotel searched from top to bottom. One can never tell."

"You must not notify the police, no matter what happens!" she pleaded.

"But what if she does not return?"

Maria was in an agony of indecision. Whom should she notify of this unexpected turn of events? She looked at Fouillet in silent appeal.

"Have you received any instructions covering this sort of situation?" Fouillet asked. "Do you know where Monsieur Satrapoulos can be reached?"

No, she did not know. She was crushed by guilt. If Athina did not return, and return quickly, all of Maria's plans for the future would be ruined. She would be dismissed in disgrace.

Fouillet looked at her sharply. "Well, mademoiselle, it is very simple. If Madame Satrapoulos is not in the hotel, and if she does not return within, let us say, two hours, I shall be obliged to notify the police of her disappearance. That is, unless you have another solution to suggest?"

Maria did not answer.

The manager walked to the door and, from that vantage point, launched a Parthian shaft: "If anything happens to that delightful old lady, I am afraid that you will be held responsible." He thought for a few seconds, then added, "For that matter, I have no doubt that you *are*, in fact, responsible."

He closed the door softly behind him, and Maria fell across the bed, sobbing.

Athina awoke with a start. At first, she could not remember where she was or why she was sleeping here, in the open air, rather than in her bed at home. Then she remembered, and she looked around fearfully. The park was as empty and silent as it had been when she fell asleep. She rubbed her arms instinctively, shivering in the chill night air. She rose awkwardly, feeling the pangs of her rheumatism, and made her way to the candy vendor's stand. There, she recalled, she had seen a canvas covering which would make an excellent blanket. First, she passed her hand under the tarpaulin, took a bag, tore open the cellophane, and ate several pieces of candy. Then she lifted the canvas on one side and began pulling with all her strength. The tarpaulin did not budge. She pulled again. The canvas was firmly attached to the framework of the awning above the stand. There was no way for Athina to remove it.

She left the candy stand in search of shelter of some kind, wandering among the animal enclosures, trying to find the birds she had seen during the afternoon. If the birds were able to survive these cold nights, she reasoned, it was because they had shelter of some kind. She would sleep with the birds, in the straw on the floor, and at dawn, she would mingle with the tourists as she had done the preceding afternoon.

She picked her way among the cages in the light of a gigantic red neon sign over the Halle aux Vins. Before her, the walk was barely visible, only a shade lighter than the surrounding darkness, but still sufficiently bright to enable her to find the enclosures she was seeking. There were about twenty of them, stretching along the walk for perhaps a hundred and fifty feet. Each one was composed of a yard or enclosed by bars. Behind this space was a small concrete shelter of some kind. In the wall facing the walk, was an opening just large enough for a human being to slip through. Then, in despair, Athina saw that the gates leading into the yards were padlocked. She tried several of them. They were locked. She began with the first gate and worked her way down the line systematically, giving each padlock a hard tug. There were only three enclosures remaining to be tried when one of the padlocks opened at her touch.

She removed the lock and the gate swung open. She closed it carefully behind her, crossed the small yard, and stood before the opening into the shelter. She could see nothing in the blackness within, but she heard movement—the rustling of feathers. She had disturbed the birds in their sleep. She entered cautiously, her hands outstretched before her. Immediately, she felt the difference in temperature. Inside, it was warm and cozy. She smelled the animal odor within, mixed with something else: a bittersweet scent which reminded her of the smell of the dead whose wakes she had attended in her village. She bent down and picked up a handful of straw. There was no longer any rustling. The birds, she concluded, had gone back to sleep on their perches overhead.

Athina loved birds. At home, she had often tamed them by scattering seeds at her doorstep. Once she had made a pet of a crow. The bird had remained with her for two summers; then, for a reason she had never understood, it had flown away and never returned.

She lay down on the floor of the shelter, then turned until she found a comfortable position. Overhead there was the sound of movement again, a flapping sound this time.

Athina arranged a handful of straw under her head, to serve as a pillow, then removed her slippers and stockings.

Once more, there was a flapping of wings. For a moment, Athina toyed with the idea of stretching out her hand to pet one of her roommates; but for that she would have to stand up again, and she rejected the idea. She was too comfortable in her warm bed of straw.

Who would have thought that so far from her village there would be everything that she loved: grass, trees, food, water, and animals? It might even be that there was someone here who spoke her language. She would try to find someone. Then she would tell him what had happened to her and ask him to help her return to her village. How long had she been gone? It was hard to count the days. . . .

Athina's mind wandered. She was not yet asleep, but she was on the verge of dreaming when a loud flutter of wings overhead brought her back to wakefulness. She listened. The flutter was followed by a loud, dull thump. It could not have come from within the enclosure, Athina assured herself, for the birds were too small to make such a noise.

She opened her eyes. She could see nothing in the darkness.

There was another sound, loud, grating, like two pieces of metal being rubbed against each other. A moment later Athina felt the air move against her face, and something came to rest on the straw next to her. From the impact, she knew that it was something large and heavy. She jumped to her feet, her heart beating wildly, and despite her fear, she stretched out her hand.

There was nothing.

She reached farther, and this time she touched it. Feathers, but feathers on a body so large that it could belong to no bird that Athina had ever seen.

She drew back her hand as there was another flapping of wings and another sound behind her in the straw. She turned quickly, and felt her arm in the grip of something hard, metallic, like a hook cutting into her flesh.

She screamed, once, then smelled an animal stench in her nostrils and felt a hard object brush against her chin, move up her cheek, and then plunge like a dagger into her eye.

Screaming, beating her arms wildly about her head, blinded by her own blood, she stumbled toward the opening which led into the yard, struck her head against the low doorway, and fell, stunned, onto the straw-littered floor. Before losing consciousness, she instinctively rolled herself into a ball in a final, futile gesture of defense. Then they were upon her with a great beating of wings, and hooks of steel tore into her living flesh.

[9]

Maria had spent a sleepless night sitting on the edge of her bed, starting at the slightest sound, waiting for the telephone to ring and for someone to say, "We've found her."

An hour after Fouillet had given up his search of the hotel and informed the police of Athina's disappearance, a man had appeared at Maria's door. She had no idea who he was, and he declined to give his name. He said simply, "I work for Monsieur Satrapoulos. I have informed him of what has occurred. He has asked me to tell you that the matter is out of your hands. I will take full responsibility for the next steps."

Maria had burst into tears.

"However," the stranger continued, "Monsieur Satrapoulos has also asked me to tell you that you should not feel guilty for what has happened. He does not blame you for his mother's disappearance. But he requires absolute discretion. Until Madame Satrapoulos is found, no one is to know that she is missing. Is that understood?"

Maria nodded, muttering, "How terrible! How terrible!"

The man nodded and turned to go. "You are to remain here until I give you further instructions," he said from the open door.

Maria's long night had begun. It was not until eight o'clock the next morning that the telephone finally rang.

"Two policemen are on their way to your room," Monsieur Fouillet said sharply. "Please be kind enough to see them."

Fouillet's telephone call was followed moments later by the arrival of the two men. They identified themselves, then asked Maria to accompany them.

"You've found her!"

The policemen exchanged glances.

"We're not sure that it is Madame Satrapoulos," one of them said. "An hour ago we found an elderly woman at the Jardin des Plantes. She was dead. We'd like you to identify her."

"All right," the nurse said.

An unmarked car was waiting in the Place Vendôme.

"Was it an accident?" Maria asked.

The same policeman who had answered her earlier—he was probably the only one who spoke English—replied, "Yes, an accident. A terrible accident. I'm afraid that it won't be easy to identify her—if it is really Madame Satrapoulos."

No one spoke for the rest of the ride to the morgue. Maria steeled herself for a horrible sight, but before the door of the building, she discovered that she was unable to move another step alone. One of the policemen took her by the arm and led her inside, down a corridor and into an elevator. A few seconds later, the door slid open. A man clad in white was standing waiting for them. He preceded them down another corridor, opened a door, and motioned them into the room beyond. The man pulled a long sheet-covered slab from the wall.

"Please come closer," he said.

The policeman pressed Maria's arm.

"I'd better warn you that it's not a pretty sight," the attendant added. "They really did a job on her."

Maria moved toward the slab, a bitter taste in her mouth.

The attendant pulled back the sheet, exposing what should have been the corpse's face. The flesh was torn, as though pulled off by pincers, and it hung in strips around the empty eye sockets. The body's trunk, where flesh remained—for Maria noted that large pieces of muscle had been ripped away—was covered with similar wounds. Yet, Maria knew that it was Athina Satrapoulos. She herself had dressed that hair, washed those shoulders, dried those arms, and powdered the face which was now so shredded as to be recognizable only by its bone structure. She felt a pressure on her hand.

"Is it Madame Satrapoulos?"

"Yes, I think so." Maria nodded as she spoke.

"I'd like you to look at the clothing she was wearing when she was found." The attendant took a package of clothing from a locker. "Her skirt, her slippers. Stockings, robe . . . and this necklace."

Maria had given Athina the necklace three days before. She reached out and touched the pearls, then nodded again, unable to speak.

The policeman led her to the door. She turned to the attendant. "Who did it?"

She had spoken in Greek, and the man did not understand her. She asked again in English, and this time she addressed the question to the policeman. "Who did it?"

"The vultures," he said and shrugged.

Despite his success, the Prophet was not a happy man. He was sufficiently perverse to regard his motives as noble and exalted, despite the manner in which he earned his living. He was too intelligent not to know that his fortune was tainted and too weak to admit that he had obtained it by reprehensible means. As a consequence, he was constantly assaulted by questions that could not be answered and personal meditations which left him frustrated and discontent.

What disturbed him most, perhaps, was that not once, not a single time, had he ever had a client who was preoccupied with anyone but himself. No one had ever asked him to use his talents for the benefit of a third party. When someone else was indeed mentioned, it was only in relation to the Prophet's client: "Does he love me?" or "Is there another man in her life?"

There were times when the Prophet felt like shouting, "Me! What about me!" But, simultaneously, he understood that this feeling lowered him to the same level as his clients. They came to speak to him of themselves, whereas he would have liked to tell them about himself. He was, after all, like all the rest of them, and he suffered from the knowledge that it was so.

Mario, the Prophet's butler and chauffeur, entered the room carrying a studded chest in his arms, a container not unlike the fabled chests of pirate treasure of which the Prophet had dreamed as a boy.

"What is that?" he demanded.

"It is for you, sir."

"What's in it?"

"I don't know, sir."

"Where did you get it?"

"From a gentleman."

"When?"

"A moment ago, sir. The gentleman is in the vestibule."

"But I have no appointment for this morning. What is this all about, Mario?"

"The gentleman said, 'I have no appointment with your master, but give him this and ask him if he will see me.'"

The Prophet was puzzled. By nature a careful man, he wondered briefly if the chest might not contain a bomb. Such things happened. Perhaps he had given the wrong advice to an abandoned wife and was now to be confronted by an angry husband. Could he be angry enough to kill?

Mario placed the chest on the floor and held out a small key to his master. The Prophet took it and placed it in the lock. He hesitated. Should he order Mario to open the chest? It was an unworthy impulse, and he banished it. Nervously, he turned the key and lifted the lid.

There was no explosion, but what he saw within the chest caused the Prophet to reel back a step nonetheless. He slammed down the lid before Mario had a chance to see the contents.

"You may go," he told the servant. "Ask the gentleman to wait a few minutes. I will see him when I have a moment."

When Mario had closed the door behind him, the Prophet lifted the lid once more. The chest was filled to the brim with gold coins. He smiled. A melodramatic way of introducing oneself, but an effective one.

He looked at the card lying on top of the coins. "Herman Kallenberg." Somehow the Prophet had been certain that the chest was from a woman. But his surprise quickly gave way to panic at the thought that Kallenberg might be here to take revenge for what Satrapoulos had done to him. It was entirely possible he had discovered the part that he, the Prophet, had played in advising Satrapoulos. Yet it seemed more likely that Kallenberg's intentions were peaceable. When someone arrived at one's home with violence in his heart, he did not begin by presenting one with a fortune in gold.

Why don't I study the cards to find out what he wants? the Prophet asked himself ironically. Or better yet, why don't I simply ask him?

He rang for Mario and ordered him to show the gentleman in.

The first meeting between Kallenberg and the Prophet began on an inauspicious note. The Prophet was determined that Kallenberg be the first to speak, and Kallenberg had decided not to open his mouth until the Prophet had spoken. The result was that both men stood in silence, staring at each other across the chest of gold.

The Prophet was the first to waver in his determination, and since he was furious at having wavered, he dispensed with the customary amenities.

"I do not understand," he began, motioning toward the chest. "You are welcome in my house—so long as you understand that it is not a bank."

Kallenberg smiled broadly and extended his hand. "I've heard so much about you," he said, "that I could not forego the pleasure of meeting you. My name is Kallenberg. I'm a shipowner."

The Prophet smiled back. What sort of game was Kallenberg playing? The meanest peasant in the remotest country on earth knew who Herman Kallenberg was. The name was synonymous with unimaginable wealth. The Prophet waited, still smiling.

"May I sit down?"

The two men sat in silence.

Finally, the Prophet began. "May I ask?"

Kallenberg peered closely at the man's face. It radiated warmth, sympathy—and malice. He pointed to the chest. "Is this what you're referring to? It's not important. I was simply playing at being one of the Magi."

"And yet I am not the Infant Jesus."

"I realize that. This small gift—let us just say it gives me pleasure to present it to you."

"I do not understand your reason for doing so." Actually the Prophet understood the reason quite well, but he had regained his composure and was beginning to enjoy the game. What a pity that he would not be able to keep the gold! "You understand, of course, that it is not possible for me to accept your gift."

"Well then, give it to your favorite charity. What I have given, I have given."

"I regret that I must refuse. I cannot accept a gift without knowing the motives of the giver."

"A gift? Did you say 'a gift'? You are mistaken."

"It is the term that you yourself used."

"Then I was in error. I should not have called it a gift. I should have said that it is payment."

"Payment for what?"

"I would like for you to read my fortune in the cards."

"Then you have paid far too much."

"Perhaps I am the best judge of what your services are worth to me."

"Mr. Kallenberg, I am honored by your visit, but I must confess that I am unable to understand you. You announce yourself by sending a chest of gold, which was quite useless since I would have received you, gladly, in any case. You see, in my—profession, I see people every day, people who come to me with problems. I do my best to help them. Now, if you will be kind enough to answer me, I will ask you a straightforward question: What is your problem?"

"I have a family problem."

"I am listening."

"You don't need the tarot cards?"

"The tarot cards are one of the accessories of which I make use, but they cannot give answers to questions which have not been asked."

"Then let me explain. There are times when my affairs puzzle me. I am surrounded by many people, yet I am alone. From all sides, I hear reports that your advice and counsel work miracles. I would like to have the benefit of that advice and counsel for myself. Will you allow me to become one of your clients?"

"Who has spoken to you of me?"

"Everyone. The whole world has heard of you."

"Who, precisely?"

"Someone very close to me."

"Who?"

"My wife."

"And where did she hear my name?"

"From her sister, Helena Satrapoulos."

"I do not believe that I have ever had a client by that name."

"Helena, no. But her husband, Socrates Satrapoulos."

"Are you certain?"

Kallenberg threw up his hands, in a gesture conveying both amusement and irritation. He said, "Mr. Kalwoziac, what do you say we put our cards on the table?"

The Prophet had the uncomfortable feeling that his blood was all rushing into his head and that it would shortly begin to drain through his nose, his ears, his mouth, and even his skull. How on earth could this man have discovered his real name?

"What name did you call me?"

"Kalwoziac. Hilary Kalwoziac. Isn't that your name? Did you expect me not to investigate the background of the man to whom I am about to confide my most intimate secrets? You certainly should understand that I cannot speak of my affairs to any man I chance to meet in the street—"

"I understand," the Prophet answered sourly. He was furious at having been found out and at having Hilary Kalwoziac disinterred and restored to life after he had been buried for so many years. He felt stripped of his defenses, as though he were a priest deprived of his cassock and reduced to the lay state. The future was nothing and did not exist. But the past—

He made an attempt to reestablish himself on a terrain where he would once more have the upper hand. "Mr. Kallenberg," he said, "since you wish to confide in me, let us begin with a general outline of your affairs. I am listening."

"I have told you that I am alone. I need an ally, someone in whom I can confide and who is able to give me advice."

"Advice in what area?"

"Business."

The Prophet smiled ambiguously. "The whole world—which I believe you mentioned a moment ago—believes that your business is flourishing."

"If you only knew! It's a cutthroat business. My success only awakens the malice and jealousy of my competitors. And they stop at nothing."

"Are you referring to a specific incident?"

"Yes and no. Hatred can take so many forms—"

"What, specifically?"

"Someone has tried to sabotage my business, to discredit me."

"Who?"

"My competitors."

"I am certain, Mr. Kallenberg, that you are not a man to turn the other cheek."

"Of course, there have been times when I have given as good as I got. But I don't like that way of doing business. What marvelous things we could accomplish if we did not have to waste our strength protecting ourselves!"

"Can you give me some of the details?"

"It's difficult for me to do. To tell you the truth, I came to you because I hoped you would be able to give *me* the details."

"Your sign is Taurus, is it not?"

Kallenberg stared silently for a moment. "How did you know?"

"If I were not able to see something so obvious, Mr. Kallenberg, you would be wasting your time here. Let us move to my consultation table."

The Prophet rose and walked to the table, with Kallenberg following. The two men sat facing each other.

"Where shall we begin?" the Prophet asked.

Kallenberg made a vague gesture.

"Fine. Let me do it in my own way. At the beginning of our conversation, you mentioned a family problem. Does it have to do with your wife?"

Kallenberg looked at him sharply. "Are you certain that I mentioned a family problem?"

For Kallenberg, the moment of truth had arrived. He must now either retreat or else confide in this charlatan, who, no doubt, would immediately notify Satrapoulos of his visit. How much would it cost to make certain that he would not be betrayed? But what if this so-called Prophet were playing a double game? What if he took the money and still repeated Kallenberg's confidences to Satrapoulos?

Kallenberg did not dare go too far or too quickly. His air of embarrassment was not entirely assumed. "It's a delicate matter," he said. "I've learned, to my sorrow, that family loyalty usually takes second place when there is a great deal of money at stake."

"Continue."

"You see, I had thought that my brother-in-law and I could combine forces, become partners."

"Yes?"

"I hoped that family ties would overcome personal vanity."

"I am listening."

"I was wrong."

There was a heavy silence in the room. The Prophet stroked his tarot cards distractedly. Kallenberg stared out of the window and saw the low green hills studded with black cypresses. He saw the emerald band of the bay. The intense blue of the mountains and the gentler blue of the sky blended harmoniously in the shallow water near the shore.

Kallenberg spoke again, his eyes still on the infinite. "How can I tell you what I must? Most of my troubles have been caused by a man who is already your client!"

The Prophet continued to handle his tarot cards, waiting for what was to follow.

"I am simply putting myself in your place," Kallenberg explained. "I realize now that you cannot advise two men who are in conflict with each other. I suppose I should have given this more thought before coming here. It had not occurred to me that if you took me on as a client, you would have to make a choice. And, obviously, I cannot force you to make that choice. In fact, you have already made it. And I am certain that you are sufficiently free of any attachment to material things to resist any temptation that I might offer."

Furtively, in spite of himself, Kallenberg's eyes moved to the chest still standing in the middle of the room.

The Prophet spoke. "What do you mean?"

"I mean that a man like yourself obviously cannot be bought. That is unfortunate for me. I would do anything to have the benefit of your advice."

"What do you mean by 'anything'?"

"Well, for example, instead of simply paying you for your advice, as I would a barber or a mechanic or a director of one of my companies, I would give you a percentage of the profits from any business that I acquired as a result of that advice."

"I think that you overestimate my talents, Mr. Kallenberg."

"I am certain that I do not. I am talking about a business that brings in millions of dollars in profit. Surely a percentage—let us say, one percent—of such sums would constitute a fair share."

The Prophet sat motionless, expressionless.

"Shall we say two percent?"

"Mr. Kallenberg, I am not a rug merchant. I do not haggle. I am an adviser, a clairvoyant, if you wish. But I am not an informer. To the extent that I do not violate the professional secrecy which is the one inflexible rule by which I am guided, I stand ready to see you whenever you wish, and to accept the three percent, of which you have just spoken, in any business that you acquire through me."

"Did I say three percent?"

"It seems to me that you did. In any event, I most certainly heard 'three percent.'"

Kallenberg knew an expert when he saw one. He did not believe in the stars or in the cards, but he believed in men. And this man was obviously cunning and greedy. He grinned. "Since we understand each other so well, it was ungracious of me not to have said it. Well, then, three percent it shall be."

"Agreed. Naturally, you must take back your chest of gold—"

"I wouldn't think of it. I would be grateful if you would consider these few coins as an advance against your first royalties."

"Since you put it in those terms, I will do as you ask." The Prophet made an effort not to allow his jubilation to show on his face. His voice steady, he asked, "Shall we go on to more serious things? Is there anything that you wish to know?"

Kallenberg leaned forward avidly. "There is a man—the fact that he is a relative of mine is not important, and I don't want to complicate things for you—there is a man who recently succeeded in stealing the most profitable piece of business I had ever seen away from me. Would you—or rather, would the cards—tell me how he did it?"

The Prophet blinked. "My clients usually ask me to look into the future, not the past. However, I will try to do as you ask, in honor of our first meeting. This man, this competitor of yours, describe him to me as completely as you can."

Kallenberg watched as the Prophet began to spread the tarot cards on the table. At that instant, he knew he had won.

There are always irritating formalities to be observed when entering a country, and even a man as powerful as Socrates Satrapoulos was not wholly immune from them. For example, his pilots, before landing, were required to notify immigration officials of the number and identity of the passengers aboard. It was therefore routine that the officials at Paris' Le Bourget airport were informed that Hadj Thami el Sadek, traveling from the emirate of Baran, was about to land on French soil. Immediately, a functionary notified the Ministry of Foreign Affairs. And immediately, the ministry informed the functionary that he must have made a mistake. The Emir of Baran had received a steady stream of official invitations from the French government, and he had invariably declined to accept them. If he had refused to stir from Baran at the behest of the President of the Republic, it was hardly likely that he would do so at the behest of a private citizen, even a private citizen who was a billionaire, like Socrates Satrapoulos.

A flurry of telephone calls followed, and it was finally verified that, indeed, his Highness the Emir of Baran was about to land at the airport. Incredulity now gave way to panic. Second secretaries tried desperately to locate Socrates Satrapoulos so as to obtain information as to the reason for the emir's imminent visit. Others at the ministry took the necessary steps to notify the minister, who was off on an official junket to Libya. The minister's reaction to the news was as pointed as it was violent: "Do whatever you like, but do something! Don't lose this opportunity! Remember, the Middle East is the focal point of all our policies!"

The truth was that no one had the vaguest idea of what to do. It was a situation all but unprecedented in the history of diplomatic protocol. How could a government extend a welcome to a visiting chief of state who chose to arrive totally unannounced, without seeming to interfere in the affairs of a private citizen? This knotty problem was finally presented to the Minister of Foreign Affairs himself, who resolved it with a degree of composure at least equal to the confusion in his mind. A detachment of the Garde Républicaine must be dispatched immediately to Le Bourget, he ordered, along with the Minister of Culture. The latter, however, was to be present only as a private citizen, as though by accident.

Meanwhile, someone had succeeded in locating Satrapoulos. The shipowner was in his car, on his way to the airport, when a telephone call came from the chief of staff of the Premier himself. The Greek, who had plans of his own for the emir, was enraged to learn that the news of his arrival was public knowledge. Stifling his anger, he informed the Premier's office that the emir's visit was strictly personal in nature, and that if he had wished it to be otherwise, he, Socrates Satrapoulos, would have certainly so informed the French government. With that, Socrates hung up. He was certain that if he had stayed on the telephone a moment longer, he would have said things that he would have regretted.

A few minutes later, arriving at Le Bourget, he was sorry that he had not said them, regardless of the consequences. On the verge of apoplexy, he saw a mob of workmen unrolling a red carpet at the VIP gate of the airport while a battalion of uniformed soldiers on horseback were forming in double ranks on each side of the carpet. He leaped from the Rolls and ran through a service entrance, much used by owners of private planes, into a salon specially reserved for these same privileged beings. By telephone, he demanded to be informed as to the exact time his airplane would arrive. He was told that its arrival had just been announced. This, Socrates knew, meant that if he made the least wrong move, all his plans would be ruined. Nervously, he bit through the cigar he had been about to light and began pacing the room, glancing first at his watch, then at the landing strip outside his window. Why did people insist in meddling in his affairs? Why couldn't they simply leave him alone?

Finally, unable to restrain his impatience, Socrates stormed from the room. His car was still waiting for him outside the door. As he climbed into the Rolls, he saw his plane touch down on the landing strip. "Let's go! Drive out there! Quickly!" he ordered the chauffeur.

The car sped to the end of the runway, just as the airplane came to a halt. As Socrates watched, two tall dark men emerged from the aircraft and scanned the runway, as though certain that an attempt was about to be made to assassinate their master. They were followed by the emir, wrapped in an immense jellaba, wearing a turban on his head and with huge dark glasses over his eyes.

The Greek hurried forward to greet his guest. As he led him back toward the Rolls, he explained briefly that the French government had organized a small reception in his honor.

The emir was visibly disturbed by the news. "I'd like to avoid the welcoming committee," he said. "I don't want my fellow emirs to know I'm here—let alone my subjects. How could this have happened?"

"Government intelligence sources, Highness. The Foreign Ministry wishes to welcome an esteemed guest."

"They could not have picked a worse time!"

Satrapoulos shrugged helplessly, then assumed a conspiratorial tone. "Highness," he whispered, "let us see if we can elude them."

Unfortunately, it was necessary for the Rolls to pass before the VIP entry gate in order to reach the airport's only exit. "Drive very slowly," Satrapoulos ordered his chauffeur, "as though you were about to stop. Then, when you are even with the mounted soldiers, give it everything you've got! Put the accelerator to the floor!"

Niki nodded. As the car moved around the corner of the building, he saw the guardsmen and their commander, the latter sitting astride his horse a short distance from his men. A group of men in civilian clothing was milling about near the gate. Judging from their confused faces, they were the welcoming committee.

The commander of the guard saw the Rolls approaching slowly. "Present arms!" he shouted, and his men's sabers flashed from their scabbards.

The emir crouched down in the seat next to Satrapoulos and bowed his head.

Niki followed his master's orders precisely. The car literally leaped forward and sped toward the exit, past frightened horses and shouting men. Satrapoulos looked back for an instant and burst out laughing. It did not take much to outwit a Minister of Culture and a detachment of the Garde Républicaine.

The Emir of Baran was explaining a theory which was original to him. "Among the rosé wines," he said, "the Cliquot 1929 possesses the most body. On the other hand, I would trade every single bottle of your Calon-Ségur for one bottle of Romanée-Con-ti. . . ."

"Highness," Satrapoulos interrupted, "I never expected that you would know more about French wines than I do."

"That is because you are a Greek," el Sadek retorted maliciously. "I know what you are wondering. How can a faithful son of the Prophet defy the laws of the Koran and drink alcohol?"

Satrapoulos raised his hands as if the question had never entered his mind.

"Nonsense," the emir said. "Of course you thought of it. I'll answer the question nonetheless, whether you wanted to ask it or not. The explanation is that the Koran is much more subtle than your Bible. The Prophet knew human nature too well to make laws contrary to man's desires. Thus, it is written: 'Let no man drink alcohol between the rising of the sun and the setting thereof.' Now, you must concede that the wording of the sacred text leaves a certain amount of room for human frailty."

The emir downed another glass of champagne.

Satrapoulos would not have believed that a man could drink so much without falling down dead drunk. He was completely disconcerted by his guest. In Baran, he had known him as a wary, ascetic old man, almost hostile toward strangers. But here, in Paris, the emir was an amusing, learned and cultivated companion.

There had been times during the evening when it had been hard for Satrapoulos to believe that he was in his own house on the Avenue Foch, and not in some third-rate nightclub in the Pigalle area of the city. Except for Socrates himself and the emir, only the servants appeared to belong here. The other guests—all women, all young, and all blond—seemed out of place among the rare antiques, the paintings, the Coromandel screens and the collections of ivory and milk glass. And, indeed, they were. They had been rented for the evening. The proprietor of the rental agency, Madame Julienne, maintained an enormous stock of girls from which to choose, and Socrates had been somewhat perplexed as to the kind of entertainment that the emir might prefer. Finally, he had instructed his secretary to apply the law of contrasts, according to which Orientals prefer blondes, just as Swedes prefer Mediterranean types. And since he had divined a streak of cruelty in el Sadek, Madame Julienne had been alerted of the possibility that her girls might be subjected to some rather distressing attentions in the course of the night. The procuress had replied, haughtily, that her girls were able to handle themselves like professionals in any situation—she had stressed the word *"any"*—so long as they were compensated according to their true worth.

For the moment, the girls were uncertain which of the two men was their client. It might be the small one with glasses, or it might be the Arab, or it might be both. It hardly mattered. The girls knew from experience that the consumption of alcohol in such gigantic quantities was hardly conducive to bedroom gymnastics, and they fully expected to be home early from this engagement. Still, it would be interesting to see which of them would be chosen, and by whom, and for what purpose.

Satrapoulos noted that his guest's hand was under the table, hidden by the cloth, probably in search of a knee or a thigh. The evening was progressing as expected, he noted with satisfaction. It was time to bring it to a crescendo, so that he might have the emir exactly where he wanted him.

"Highness," he said, "I had planned a surprise for you, but I think it may be of a nature which would shock our young guests. Perhaps even your Highness would find it too—"

The emir, his eyes glittering, looked at Socrates expectantly.

"Of course," Satrapoulos continued, "it is not something which you would find offensive. Rather I would hope you would find it amusing."

"What is it? What is it?" the girls shrieked.

"Very well, ladies," the Greek said, "the responsibility is yours. I will accept no blame if the spectacle which you are about to see violates your sense of modesty."

"Well, let's get on with it," the emir said with evident impatience.

Satrapoulos smiled and clapped his hands twice. There was silence, and all eyes turned toward the door, both panels of which swung open to admit four men dressed as Oriental slaves. They carried a gigantic platter, six feet long, which they placed on the floor before their master and his guests. Everyone stared at the platter. It held a large pile of barley seeds, and nothing more.

A fifth man entered, carrying a large sack from which came a chorus of vaguely familiar chirping sounds, like the peeping of a thousand birds. The man knelt alongside the platter and opened his bag. A cloud of baby chicks rushed out and threw themselves ravenously upon the pile of seeds.

Socrates' guests held their breath. The girls seemed mesmerized by the sight of the famished chicks struggling and pushing one another aside to eat their fill.

Suddenly, someone said, "Oh!"

Among the grain, something else had appeared. A bit of human flesh. A nipple.

Another section of breast became visible as the chicks continued to peck with undiminished voracity. Then the curve of a shoulder. Hidden beneath the sarcophagus of grain was a human body, that of a woman. Her thighs were now visible, then a part of her stomach. The human silo moved, and the chicks scattered as a superb brunette rose from the barley seeds and stood upright on the platter. She was nude, very much at ease and confident of the charms which she exhibited, without provocation and without unbecoming modesty, to her applauding audience. She bowed, a faint smile on her lips, and removed a few seeds from her navel. Then, nimbly, she ran from the room as the applause increased in volume.

The emir turned to Satrapoulos. "Most interesting," he murmured. Socrates noted that both of his Highness' hands were now beneath the table, and the expressions on the faces of the girls on either side of el Sadek left no doubt as to the sort of activity in which they were engaged. He could not help admiring the old man's vitality. He himself had drunk in moderation, knowing his own limitations perfectly well and wishing to remain in control of all his actions so as to remain master of the situation. El Sadek, on the other hand, had drunk unbelievable quantities throughout the evening, and yet he remained totally and incontestably sober.

Perhaps he is immune to alcohol. Or perhaps Arabs have no livers.

Satrapoulos, in any event, had arranged to absent himself from the party before the evening reached its true climax. After the meal, one of his servants would call him away on "a most urgent and important matter of family business." Two days earlier he had given strict orders that no one was to know that he was in France. He had not wanted it known that Hadj Thami el Sadek was his guest, and el Sadek, for his part, was even less eager for it to be known. Even the Greek's most intimate friends believed that he was off in the United States.

"Ladies," the emir addressed his fellow guests, "you have been so kind to me that I would like to present you with a souvenir of this evening—that is, if our gracious host will permit me to do so."

Satrapoulos smiled and nodded.

El Sadek called, "Ahmed!"

One of the emir's two giant bodyguards appeared, carrying a soft leather bag. El Sadek took the bag, unfastened the strings which held it closed, and emptied it onto the table. The girls were stupefied at the cascade of precious stones which poured from the emir's hands and rolled on the tablecloth, clicking like marbles.

"A modest token of my appreciation for so much pleasure and so much beauty." The emir smiled. He took a handful of the stones and rolled one toward each of the squealing girls.

A footman bent toward Socrates and whispered in his ear. The Greek frowned and whispered back, "Tell him not to be an idiot! I told him midnight. It's only eleven o'clock!"

"Sir," the distressed servant persisted, "he says that it is most urgent!"

"Tell him to wait until midnight!"

"My brother," the emir said as the footman withdrew, "is something amiss?"

"Nothing serious, Highness. At least, I hope not," Socrates replied. And to himself: He misses absolutely nothing!

The Greek knew his secretary too well to think that the urgent summons had actually been a mistake. Thus he decided to proceed immediately to the second part of the evening's scenario.

"My friends," he said, "I would very much like to show you my house. Highness, if you are willing, we will begin with your quarters. Ladies, I would be happy to hear your opinion of the decorations."

Satrapoulos rose, and his guests followed him down a long hallway hung with red velvet. He opened a door at the end of the corridor and led the emir and the girls into an enormous room, the walls and ceiling of which were lined with mirrors. (They had been installed only two days earlier.) In the center of the room was a bed, but a bed the like of which no one—not even the girls, whose experience with beds was extensive—had ever seen. It was perfectly round, with a diameter of at least twelve feet.

One of the girls squealed with delight. "May I try it?" she asked. And then, without waiting for an answer, she threw herself upon it, as though she were diving into a lake, and bounced on its resilient surface.

"Cathy!" she shouted. "Come try it! It's heaven!"

Cathy joined her friend on the bed, and a wrestling match began, with the two girls laughing and struggling to hold each other down. Thighs were exposed to the crotch as Cathy struggled to free herself from her friend's hold.

Satrapoulos glanced at the emir and saw the old man's small black eyes staring at the bed with an intensity which obviously reflected his inner excitement.

"Highness, Highness!" Cathy called from the bed. "Help me! She's stronger than I am!"

El Sadek looked at Satrapoulos.

"Highness," the Greek whispered, "this house, and all that is in it, is yours. This is your home, to use as you see fit, for so long as you wish. I hope that you will not be offended if I excuse myself. A delicate family matter requires my presence elsewhere, outside Paris. Will you forgive me if I leave you in the company of my friends?"

"Would you like me to accompany you, my brother?"

"I would not dream of asking it, Highness. You must rest and, if you wish, enjoy yourself."

Satrapoulos' last words were all but lost, since there were now six shrieking girls on the bed, their shoes off, struggling in a mass of soft arms and shapely legs multiplied to infinity by the mirrored walls and ceiling.

The emir's lips were now a thin white line in his dark face. With an enormous effort, he tore his eyes from the scene and bowed to Satrapoulos. "Do what you must do, my brother. And Allah be with you."

Socrates bowed in return and repeated: "This house is yours."

In the antechamber, he encountered Ali and Ahmed, his guest's bodyguards. They were smiling. He had never seen them smile before. They bowed low before him, and when they came erect again, their features had resumed their customary impassivity.

Socrates, intrigued, decided to speak to them. "Do you speak English?"

Ali nodded.

"I have had two rooms set aside for your use. Would you like to see them?"

"We will sleep here, outside our master's door."

"Here? On the floor?"

Ali nodded again.

"Your master is in no danger in my house."

The two slaves smiled.

"Is there anything you need?"

Ali shook his head.

"Tell me, you know your master so well, do you think that he has everything he needs? I mean, do you think that he is happy with the companions I have provided?"

The two bodyguards exchanged glances. Their faces remained expressionless.

Satrapoulos' suspicions were immediately aroused. "Don't hesitate to tell me," he insisted, "if there is anything your master requires. I have too much love and respect for him to wish to disappoint him in any way."

Ali and Ahmed remained motionless and silent.

"Please. It's most important. My only wish is for his Highness to remember this night with pleasure. Trust me. I will not betray your confidence. Is it that he does not care for blondes?"

After a moment of hesitation, Ali leaned toward the Greek, who stood a foot shorter than he, and whispered briefly into his ear.

Socrates' eyes opened wide. He seemed taken aback for a moment, but he quickly recovered his composure. "I will see what can be arranged," he told Ali, then nodded to the guards and withdrew.

Satrapoulos' secretary was waiting for him in the library, pacing the floor nervously. "Quickly!" the Greek ordered. "Call Madame Julienne. There is no time to lose! Wait. First, what made you call me away an hour early? I told you to wait until midnight."

"Yes, sir, I know. However—"

"Yes, yes, go on. What is it?"

The secretary cleared his throat, searching vainly for the proper words. There was no way to break the news gently, he decided. "Sir," he said, "your mother is dead."

Socrates, as though he had not heard or understood what the man said, snapped, "I told you to call Madame Julienne. What are you waiting for?"

"Are you going to be in Paris for long?"

"No. I shall only be here for two days."

"Are you here on business?"

"I was invited by a friend."

"Are you celebrating something?"

"Yes. A pact."

The girls were curious as to the identity of this Arab who looked like a poverty-stricken old hermit but who offered them diamonds as other men offered cigarettes.

El Sadek, for his part, was well aware that these six blondes were part of the entertainment, like the dinner and the wines and like this fantastically luxurious house which impressed him not one whit. He wished devoutly that they would shut their mouths and get on with their work instead of asking so many questions beginning with why and how. Yet he experienced a certain reticence. He was not back home in his harem in Baran, and there are certain sexual activities which, like certain wines, travel badly.

"I would like each one of you to tell me her name."

"Brigitte."

"Annette."

"Marie."

"Joëlle."

"Cathy."

"Germaine."

He was sitting on the bed, with his head in the lap of the one called Germaine. The others were around him, so close that each had a part of her body—a hand, knee, thigh, or shoulder—in contact with el Sadek's body. This contact had aroused him to a state of controlled violence, half desire and half fury, which he yearned to release so as to neutralize the power that he felt these hired girls had over him.

"What do your names mean?"

"They don't mean anything. They're just names. Why?"

"In the East, the name given a child has a precise meaning, a meaning which will have a profound effect upon the child's future. It is better to be named Lion than Jackal."

"We don't care about such things in this country."

"Is that so? Tell me, do you know anyone among your friends who is named Judas?"

The girls looked at one another, puzzled.

"All things are written in the Book of Life," the emir intoned.

"Do you believe in fate?"

"What else is there to believe in?"

"Can you predict the future?" demanded the plumpest of the girls.

"Oh, yes!" another one exclaimed. "Read our palms! Read mine first!"

El Sadek was agonizingly aware of a hand, its long nails moving gently in a circular motion, advancing slowly from his knee upward along his thigh.

"In Arabia," he said, making an effort to keep his voice steady, "we have more effective means of foretelling what the future holds."

"What are they? Tell us!"

"The lines on your palm mean very little. The human hand has no secrets. Since it is always bare, it touches impurities. One's fate is indeed inscribed on one's body, but the Prophet, in his wisdom, has decreed that the inscription be made in a secret place."

"Where?"

"I cannot tell you. You will be shocked."

"Tell us! Tell us!"

"Among women, it is in the place that you keep hidden from the eyes of men. It is where the back ends, and the legs begin."

"On the behind?"

"Yes. And also between the breasts."

"Are you serious?"

"I would not deceive you. Is there one among you who would like to know what the future holds?"

"Me!" shouted the one whose hand was on Hadj Thami el Sadek's thigh. "Which place? On the top or on the bottom?"

"Wherever you wish."

Without answering, the girl stretched out on her stomach and raised the bottom of her dress.

"All right," she said. "Tell me what it says."

"You must lower your panties, my dear. Otherwise, I cannot see the inscription."

She obeyed.

El Sadek, his mouth dry, placed an index finger at the base of her spine and moved it downward, slowly, caressingly, tracing the course of an imaginary line.

The other girls were silent, attentive.

"I see a splendid career before you," Sadek reported.

"What kind of career?"

"A career that will bring you wealth," the emir replied, as he reached into his pocket and extracted a diamond which he placed carefully between the girl's teeth. "There. You see that my prediction has already begun to come true. It is the beginning of your fortune."

"It's my turn now," Joëlle said, nervously unbuttoning her blouse. With her hands, she scooped her breasts from her brassiere, holding them out toward el Sadek. "Is this where you can see if I'm going to be rich?"

The emir leaned toward the girl and passed the back of his hand over her breasts. The nipples rose, as though by magic.

"Let me see. How fortunate! It is written that you, too, will be rich! Here, to start you on your way, take this."

Joëlle raised the diamond to her lips, kissed it, then placed it between her breasts.

"What about us?" the other girls asked.

"You all want to know if you will be rich?"

"Yes, yes!"

"All right. But we must organize ourselves properly. I will read the breasts of three of you, and the posteriors of the other three. Now, all of you, lie down."

Obediently, Cathy, Brigitte, and Marie lay on their stomachs, their skirts raised to their hips. Annette, Joëlle, and Germaine lay on their backs, their naked breasts in the air.

"All right. Now, do not move."

El Sadek moved back a step and contemplated the spectacle. It was, he told himself, magnificent.

"Close your eyes," he commanded.

The girls obeyed, listening to discover what the Arab was doing. They heard the clicking of diamonds, then felt stones, cold and marvelous, being placed on various parts of their bodies: on a breast, in a navel, on a hip.

"You will all be rich!" el Sadek proclaimed solemnly, as though the sentence were an exorcism intended to rid him of the spell which bound him to the spectacle of the six women scattered about the bed.

"Come, lie down with us," Marie said softly.

"No, not yet."

"Yes, come," Cathy said, extending her hand and pulling the emir toward the bed with surprising strength.

Instantly they were on him, and he felt their hands everywhere. Some caressed the rough fabric of his trousers while others wandered beneath his shirt.

There was a pause, and Brigitte sat up. "What's the matter?" she asked reproachfully.

"I am not ready yet, my dear. Wait—" He fumbled for his bag of diamonds. "You will all be rich, but you must do as I tell you. Let me see what I have here." He poured the gems into his hand and counted. "There are twenty-four stones left, and six of you. I will divide them equally: four for each of you."

"What do we have to do?"

"Nothing that is not perfectly natural."

"Do you want us to whip you?" Brigitte asked candidly.

"No, only to make love."

"All six of us?"

"Obviously."

"You're a funny man," said Marie. "Instead of reading our palms, you read our behinds, and you tell us that our names are supposed to mean something, and now you want to make love to all six of us. That's never happened to me with anybody before."

"That, my dear," the emir replied sharply, "is because I am not like anybody else."

"I didn't think you were," Brigitte murmured. "A man who is capable of making love to six women—"

"I have no intention of doing so alone."

"What do you mean?"

"To get the stones, you must first have sex with my two body-guards. Oh, you won't be disappointed. I don't think you'll be able to exhaust their potential. . . ."

"Is that all?" Cathy asked.

"Yes. Except—" El Sadek raised his bag and peered into it. "What have we here?" He reached into the bag and drew out another gem. "A twenty-fifth stone," he announced. "I'm afraid that this upsets our arrangements. Obviously, one of you is going to get five stones instead of four!"

"Who?" two of the girls asked simultaneously.

"The one who earns it."

"How can I earn it?" Joëlle exclaimed.

The emir hesitated briefly.

"There are six of you," he explained then. "All six of you are blondes. It's very hard for me to tell you apart. I need some distinctive sign, some mark, that will enable me to identify you."

The girls, despite their greed, looked uneasy.

"What kind of mark?" Germaine asked hesitantly.

"Look," el Sadek replied. As he spoke, he drew a straight razor from his pocket. Its handle of gold, encrusted with rubies, glittered menacingly. "Don't be afraid, my dears," the emir said gently. "All I want to do is to make a tiny mark on each one of you, each in a different place."

"That's silly," Germaine said firmly. "If you want to be able to tell us apart, why don't you mark us with a pen or something like that? If you think I'm going to let myself be mutilated—"

"No, no, my dear! You misunderstand me. I have no intention of spoiling that lovely face! All I'm talking about is a tiny cut, some-where where it will never show. Just enough to draw a single drop of blood."

Joëlle stood. "I'm getting out of here," she announced.

"Wait a minute," Germaine said. "Let him explain." She turned to the emir. "What kind of cut, exactly?"

"Let me show you," el Sadek replied. He pulled up his sleeve to expose his left forearm. The girls would have sworn that the razor did not touch his skin. Yet, where a second before the skin had been unbroken, there was now a drop of blood.

"You see, girls? There's really nothing to it."

"I can't do it," Cathy declared. "The sight of blood makes me sick."

"All right. Who wants to earn this lovely diamond?"

The girls' eyes went simultaneously to the diamond, then to the razor, and finally to el Sadek's penis. The old man's organ was now erect.

"What if it leaves a scar?" Annette asked.

"Nonsense," the emir assured her. "By tomorrow you won't even be able to see the cut."

"And if I let you do it, I get the diamond?"

"Yes."

"All right. I'll do it. But if it hurts, I'm going to scream. Where do you want to do it?"

"What's your name?"

"Annette."

"On your behind. The left cheek."

"I don't see the connection, but go ahead." The girl lay motionless, her eyes shut tightly. She gasped as she felt the cold steel touch her flesh. There was no pain, but she gave a tiny shriek, *pro forma*.

"There," el Sadek said happily. "Now I'll always know that you're Annette. Here, Annette, to reward you for this terrible ordeal—"

He held up the stone for a moment, then threw it to the floor where it rolled under an armchair.

"Now, go get it!"

Annette ran to the chair, threw herself to her knees, and bent down, her posterior in the air. On her white flesh, the drop of blood glittered like a precious ruby.

"You see?" el Sadek said to the other girls. "Tomorrow, she won't even know that she was cut—and she'll have the diamond to remind her of the pleasure she gave to a lonely old man with a bad memory for names. Now, it's not impossible that I could find another extra diamond somewhere if one of you would be interested—"

"I'll do it!" Cathy shouted.

"Very well, my dear. Where do you prefer? Your breast? Your stomach? Or your behind, like Annette?"

"Well, wherever people will see it least, I suppose. My breasts."

El Sadek would have preferred the throat, but he said nothing. He lifted the razor toward the girl's left breast.

"No!" Cathy cried. "I'm sorry. I can't. I just can't."

"Come, come, my child. There's nothing to be afraid of. Look at Annette. Look at her diamond. Wouldn't you like one like it? Don't you want me to be able to recognize you? To tell you from the others?"

As the emir spoke, four automatic cameras were surveying the room from behind the mirrored walls. They had been in operation from the instant that Satrapoulos had opened the door of the suite to show el Sadek his quarters, filming the prologue to the scene which, barring an event unforeseen even by the prescient el Sadek, would now take place. It would be a monumental bit of cinematography, one which, Socrates had reasoned, the emir would no doubt do everything in his power to keep from being viewed along the shores of the Persian Gulf.

There was a knock, and Ali appeared in the doorway. His eyes looking straight ahead, he bowed before his master and spoke briefly in Arabic.

The emir smiled beatifically. He answered in Arabic, then turned to the girls. "I regret, but I fear I must ask you to get dressed," he said.

They stared at him, unable to believe what they had heard.

"Get dressed!" the emir repeated, hissing the consonants. "It has been a most entertaining evening, but now I must give my attention to more serious affairs."

Germaine was the first to find her tongue. "But—but you don't feel like making love?" she stuttered.

"Go! Go!"

"What about the diamonds you promised us?"

"Make love with my guards, and I'll add another to the four stones I promised each of you."

"Call them in," Marie said. She had come to Satrapoulos' house for one purpose, a purpose which neither excited nor revolted her. But now that this was happening to her—or rather, now that nothing was happening to her—she was overcome with a sense of frustration. She felt that she had been duped. It did not help that she was also quite drunk. She began to sob. "Who's going to kiss me?" she moaned. "I want someone to kiss me."

She was sitting on the bed, and Germaine, with the first true tenderness that she had shown that evening, began to stroke her hair gently.

"You'll have to go somewhere else for your kisses!" el Sadek said, his impatience mounting. He dug into his leather bag as the girls watched fascinated, drew out a handful of gems and threw them on the floor. "Here, take these, and get out! Ahmed and Ali are waiting for you."

As though on cue, the two giants appeared in the doorway. The emir spoke to them briefly, then gestured eloquently toward the girls, as though to say: they're all yours.

Silently, Ahmed and Ali helped them gather up their belongings, as el Sadek drummed his fingers impatiently. When the last of the girls had flounced out of the door, el Sadek spoke again to Ali. The giant nodded and disappeared through the door.

The emir sat upon the bed and waited.

There was a light tap at the door.

"Come in!" he said, his heart pounding in his chest.

The door opened wide, and Ali entered accompanied by two boys, aged about twelve, who smiled with professional timidity. El Sadek smiled back. "Come in, my dear children."

Ali disappeared again, eager to take his place at the celebration which had been arranged for him and Ahmed.

The emir approached the boys. "Now, children," he said ingratiatingly, "tell me your names."

[10]

Little Spiro scanned the sky eagerly. For several seconds, he had heard a droning sound, but he had not as yet been able to discover its source. Then, suddenly, he saw it, a black dot growing rapidly larger: a helicopter. It was like the others he had seen in the past few days, except that they had been gray and this one was black.

From his cliff, he watched as the aircraft, after a momentary hesitation, came to rest on the flat ground below. A man clad in black emerged from the helicopter, looked around, glanced at his watch, took a few steps, then returned to the helicopter, where he held out his hand and helped three other men as they stepped to the ground. The men were wearing long white robes. Spiro's uncle had once showed him an engraving of men wearing such robes. The boy remembered his uncle telling him that the men in the engraving had been Turks, and assassins.

There was another droning in the sky, much louder this time. Spiro looked up again. In astonishment, he counted not one, but five more black helicopters. When they passed directly overhead, he ducked instinctively, as though trying to merge himself with the rocks of the cliff. He dared look again as the helicopters settled gently to earth far below, like dead leaves drifting to the ground. More people emerged—both men and women this time. There were handshakes, huddled discussions between various groups, and a universal movement of heads as yet another black helicopter materialized out of the sky and made its descent to earth. Then there were more handshakes and more discussions. Finally, two long black automobiles appeared on the winding stone road which led to the spot where the helicopters had landed. They drew nearer, and there was a pause in the discussions below as eight men emerged from the vehicles. Spiro could clearly see that three of the new arrivals were priests. One of the other five was a short man, dressed in black. He walked toward the other people and said a few words. The groups immediately scattered toward their respective helicopters. Spiro heard the doors slam shut. The engines started, and with a deafening roar, one after the other, the aircraft rose into the sky, heading to the south. Below, there remained only the two black automobiles. Their chauffeurs stood alone, watching the helicopters until they disappeared. Then they climbed into their vehicles and drove away, leaving Spiro alone under the sky, as though nothing at all had happened.

"Tell him, Mama! Tell him!"

Medea Mikolofides did not answer.

Irene insisted. "Go ahead, Mama! You're the only one he's afraid of!"

"For God's sake," Kallenberg groaned, "why don't you leave your mother alone!"

Medea shifted in her seat. After money, the thing she respected most was death and the ceremonies attendant upon death. It did not seem the proper moment to involve herself in Irene's family quarrels. She had no particular affection for her son-in-law, but she had a certain esteem for his business acumen—a quality which she had learned to revere as a girl.

She glanced at the pilot. She was certain that despite the roar of the helicopter's engine, he had not missed a word of what had been said. Irene had never learned that one never aired one's family problems in the presence of inferiors. It was not that Medea had not tried to teach her.

"Nothing for Christmas!" Irene whined. "Not a single blessed thing! Did you see what Socrates gave Helena on the twins' birthday?"

"Be quiet, Irene," Medea snapped, her patience wearing thin. "Have you forgotten the tanker that Herman gave you?"

"That was a year ago. He can keep his tankers for all I care! What can I do with a tanker?"

Kallenberg made a final effort to hold his temper. He contented himself with seizing a fold of flesh on Irene's thigh and giving it a savage twist. Then, to drown out her moan, he laughed loudly and said, "Don't pay any attention to her, Madame Mikolofides. She's upset by the old woman's death. She doesn't mean what she says."

Medea's lips set in a tight smile. She glanced through the window and pretended to be absorbed in the sight of a sailboat, tiny on the broken mirror of the sea, moving toward land. She moved her eyes upward, and in the helicopter to the left, she saw the impassive faces of the three Arabs who, for God only knew what reason, her son-in-law had invited to the funeral.

For some twenty minutes, the seven helicopters flew in tight formation over the sea, at an altitude of three hundred feet. "Go straight ahead," Satrapoulos had ordered Jeff, his pilot. "Not too high, and not too fast. I'll tell you what to do when the time comes."

Jeff was vaguely uneasy. He did not like the idea of flying without knowing where he was going. Moreover, he was concerned that at the last minute, his employer had shifted Madame Satrapoulos from his own helicopter to that in which the three priests were traveling. Jeff was confident of his own ability as a pilot, but he was not so certain that the other pilots could be trusted with Madame Satrapoulos' life. Mechanically, he looked out of the window to see if the others were following him as instructed. He was reassured to see them to his right and slightly to the rear, flying in triangular formation.

Socrates Satrapoulos sat almost motionless for nearly an hour. Occasionally, he glanced out the window at the other helicopters or down toward the waves below. A half hour earlier, they had flown over an excursion ship, and the passengers had waved frantically at the unexpected caravan of helicopters.

Socrates was seething inwardly that he could not be alone in the sky, and the presence of the other helicopters was a reminder that, in spite of himself, there were people who simply could not be prevented from making the trip with him. There was Irene, his stupid sister-in-law; that bastard Kallenberg; and old Medea, his mother-in-law. Then there were the three priests, who were friends of the family, and the three peasants whom he had consulted two days before, as well as Melina, Helena's sister. The two remaining helicopters carried three extremely wealthy shipowners who were Socrates' affectionate cousins and implacable enemies and Hadj Thami el Sadek and his two bodyguards. The emir had insisted upon postponing his return to Baran in order to accompany Socrates.

The entire journey was madness, of course. The final exaction of an old peasant woman, the fulfillment of a wish repeated too often in the presence of garrulous witnesses. And it was Socrates' inescapable duty to honor that wish.

His hands moved over the rectangular bronze casket beside him. It was small, about the size of a sewing box. He would have to open it, however unwillingly. They had already come too far. He hesitated, then removed the tiny padlock and lifted the casket's lid. It required an act of will for Socrates to look at the ashes in the box.

He tried to suppress the sob which rose in his throat, desperately tightening the muscles of his larynx. It was useless. He was racked by a series of spasms which shook his entire body, and he placed one hand within the casket, burying it in the thin layer of ashes which so recently had been his mother's bones, flesh, hair, and blood. He closed his hand in the ashes, raised his fist to the window, and scattered the remains of Athina Satrapoulos over the sea. Then his hand returned to the box and repeated the operation.

When the box was empty, he sat silently for a moment, then spoke into the intercom. "Hover over this spot. And tell the others to form a circle."

By the change in the sound of the engine, Socrates knew that Jeff had executed the order. From his seat, he could see the tense faces of the passengers in the other helicopters: the two peasants, neighbors of his mother, who, two days earlier, had informed him as to how Athina had always wished to be buried. He saw Medea Mikolofides and Melina, the emir and his guards, the cousin-rivals, and the priests. He was certain that Helena was crying, though the distance between them was too great for him to be able to discern the tears. And there was Irene—and Kallenberg. He stared at Kallenberg for a long moment, anger rising in him like lightning. By God, he vowed, he will pay for this, with interest!

Socrates raised the casket, held it out of the window for an instant, then turned it over. The last ashes scattered in the wind and disappeared. Over the roar of the engines, the Greek thought he heard the priests' voices intoning a funeral chant.

He closed the box and set it upon his knees.

"Home," he ordered Jeff.

The helicopter turned, hovering for a brief instant as the others formed a cortege behind it. Then the procession of black aircraft headed northward. The past was dead and buried.

Part Two

[11]

HESITANTLY, almost timidly, the young woman moved the felt-tipped pen toward her client's stomach. Never before had she been asked to do such a thing. And yet her female clients' whims often ran to the bizarre. Those of older women, especially, some of whom wished to allow their gigolos a few moments of illusion before satisfying their passion. There were others, condemned to chastity by their Puritan heritage, for whom their dogs were transformed simultaneously into God, lover, child, and perennial companion. It was not rare to see such a dog promenading alongside his mistress, wearing a coat to match her mink or leopard or persian lamb, its collar set with the same stones as that of the woman, its claws glistening with a polish of the same color.

As the pen moved toward the woman's pubis, she spoke. "Margie, what are you using?"

"A pen, madame."

"What kind of pen?"

"Felt-tipped—a blue one."

"Oh, for God's sake! Are you out of your mind? I'll never be able to get it off! Use an eyebrow pencil or something like that—anything that will wash off. I don't want to be tattooed for life."

Margie fumbled through her supplies for an eyebrow pencil. Covertly, she inspected the nude body of her client. Why on earth would such a woman want to do anything so silly? If only I had that

187

body, Margie sighed—those gorgeous legs, those high, round breasts. The cheeks of the ass were a little too full, maybe, but, after all, men liked them that way.

"Come on, Margie. Don't tell me you don't have an eyebrow pencil. Or maybe you can't draw hearts?"

Margie smiled as she bent over her client and, with exquisite care, began tracing the outline of a heart on the white flesh beneath her thick, dark pubic hair.

She straightened up when she had finished and produced a large mirror from her kit. Holding the mirror at the proper angle, she said, "You'd better look at it before we go any further. I think it's exactly what you want."

"It looks all right," the woman said critically. "Now be very careful during the next part. It takes two months to grow out again, you know."

With long scissors, Margie began snipping away all the pubic hair not within the heart-shaped outline she had drawn. The soft, curled hair fell upon the woman's thighs and stomach as Margie cut.

"Maybe I should save the hair and sell it," Margie joked. "If people knew whose it was, I could make a fortune."

"Maybe you could sell it in lockets," the woman bantered. "In fact, I could give you a whole list of prospective customers."

When Margie had finished clipping the hair, she took a small razor and painstakingly shaved the skin. Then she stood back and inspected her work with professional detachment. She was pleased, and surprised, at the result obtained. Against the woman's milk-white skin, the heart of pubic hair seemed a perfect patch of black velvet. "It's lovely." She smiled. "Look for yourself."

The woman rose and inspected herself briefly in the mirror which covered one wall of the room. "Very good, Margie. You've done a good job. Let me give you a tip: always allow a man to choose the spot where he wants your heart to be located. Now, if you'll get my bill ready—"

Margie opened the door a crack and spoke to an invisible attendant. "Miss Nash-Belmont's bill, quickly!" She turned back to Peggy. "I hope your fiancé will like it." Immediately, she wished she had not spoken. This Nash-Belmont woman, though she seemed to encourage familiarity from subordinates, was unpredictable.

Peggy looked up. "What fiancé, Margie?"

It was too late to take back her words. Margie would have to follow through. She felt her face flush as she said, "I meant, Mr. Fairlane—I—"

Peggy laughed good-naturedly. "Oh, poor Tony. We seem to be less and less engaged every time I see him. In fact, I think that by now we're not engaged at all."

"Oh, that's too bad."

"Oh? Why do you say that?"

Margie shuffled miserably. "Well, Mr. Fairlane is so handsome—"

"Yes, I'll give him that. He's probably the handsomest man I know. I'll tell you what. I'll give him to you if you want him. But I should warn you that he's also the biggest asshole in New York."

Margie did not reply. She left the room wondering how a man could be otherwise when the woman he loved had her heart in her panties.

Three men stood on the stage of the Los Angeles Concert Hall, in a place created for light, crowds, celebration, and music. Tonight Menelas would infuse it with life, to the accompaniment of bravos and cheers. Or else she would consign it to eternal oblivion.

One of the men cleared his throat discreetly, eliciting a venomous glare from Menelas. The general manager, unable to meet those eyes, lowered his own. Twenty years' experience had exposed him to the extremes of artistic temperament. He knew the habits of all the great artists of the day, their foibles, superstitions, and caprices. But this Menelas woman was an original in every sense. Within herself, she seemed to contain all the insanities of all her peers, magnified to infinity.

"Where is the piano?"

The general manager raised his eyes timidly. What could she mean? It was all but impossible to see anything else on the stage. The reflection of its rich dark wood, the glistening ivory of its keys, the inert mass of the professional instrument dominated the vast hall.

"I beg your pardon?"

"I asked where is the piano?"

Overcome by a sense of inadequacy, he pointed toward the piano. Menelas' features assumed an expression of intense surprise.

"That?" She examined it through pinched nostrils, as though it were some alien object, exuding an offensive odor, which she could not bring herself to touch.

"Are you trying to tell me that you expect me to play on *that?*"

"But, madame, Leonard Bernstein, Arthur Rubinstein—"

"Who?"

"Leonard—"

"Silence! Is it a Bechstein?"

"No, but—"

"It is not a Bechstein?"

Menelas turned to one of the three men. "Peter, tell this gentleman that I have no intention of discussing the matter any further. That—that *thing* is not good enough to practice scales on."

The general manager tried once more. "But, madame—"

Menelas cut him off. "Peter," she spat, "we are leaving. We will return when we have a proper instrument on which to play."

"Madame, I beg you! At least try it!"

"You are of the opinion that it is a good piano?" As she spoke, Menelas strode to the offending instrument and smashed her gloved fist down onto the keys three times in rapid succession, raising a cacophonic din which climbed to the dim, remote balconies of the hall.

"You expect me to play Chopin on that? It is out of tune! Do you hear? Out of tune! Very well. No Bechstein, no concert!" She strode majestically from the stage.

Peter, following in her wake, whispered to the distraught manager, "Don't do anything till you hear from me. She's a bundle of nerves this morning. I'll try to calm her down. But, for God's sake, get her a Bechstein!"

Mark was literally physically sick. What had just happened to him was not to be borne. When he was not shooting in the morning, he never got out of bed before 11 A.M. Isabelle, who kept very close track of how he spent his time, usually spent hours in the studio bar, waiting until the shooting was over for the day. Yet there were times when a bridge game lasted far into the night, and on such occasions, Mark took advantage of her absence to indulge in a brief adventure or, when there was nothing else to do, to telephone Helena and ask her to meet him in Paris. Invariably, she came, as she had in this instance.

Helena had taken an apartment in the rue de la Faisanderie. It was there that they met, and it was there, also, that Mark entertained the actresses, French and foreign, who were his occasional companions.

It was a source of constant irritation and frustration to Helena that, when she came to Paris, Mark never spent an entire night with her. Now, at five o'clock in the morning, he rose and began dressing, resigning himself to the invariable dialogue in which he was required to participate:

"Are you leaving already?"

"You know I have to get home."

"Stay a little while longer. Just a few minutes."

"Helena—"

"Put your arms around me."

"Helena—"

"Just once more."

"Do you know what time it is?"

"The time! Always the time! You know how I want to spend a whole night with you!"

"You know that that's impossible." Then, in the oppressive silence which, as usual, followed, he added, "At least for now."

Helena, who was not a really difficult woman, was usually content with the declaration. On this occasion, however, she began all over again.

"Mark, you don't realize—"

"What, Helena?"

"How lonely I am when we're apart."

"So am I."

"Truly?"

"Yes, truly."

"Then why don't you marry me?"

Mark attempted sarcasm. "Because I'm told you already have a husband."

She turned his own weapon against him. "Say the word, just one word, and I'll divorce him. But I know you won't say it. You're too afraid of Isabelle."

He shrugged, thinking: after all, she's absolutely right. Isabelle inspired a feeling of visceral terror in him, an emotion so intense that it required all his energies to avoid looking at, or at least pretending not to look at, the women who looked at him in the street. And to make matters worse, Isabelle's eye, like Cain's, was able to see him even when they were apart.

"You know very well," he answered, "that I only stay with her because I need her money."

"Marry me," Helena pleaded, "and I'll solve all your financial troubles in five minutes."

"What about your children, Helena?"

"They'll come to live with us."

Mark loathed children. The idea of sharing a home with two brats made him actually shiver with revulsion.

"When I'm alone," Helena continued, "I can't help knowing that you share everything with her and not with me. But what about me? What am I to do while you're with her?"

Mark could not have cared less. "Lena," he said, putting on his trousers—another station in the way of the cross which stretched between his underwear and his necktie and shoes—"really, I must go. You know that I have to be on the set early this morning."

There followed another round of entreaties: "Kiss me just once more. Put your arms around me again for just a minute. . . ." Then he fled joyfully into the dawn, like a man who had just been released from prison.

Despite the darkness of the room, Raph Dun recognized Amore Dodino when he entered, escorted by several obsequious waiters and himself escorting a couple who were obviously both American and rich. An incredible cascade of lace tumbled from the collar of Amore's shirt to his waist, swaying as he moved grandly across the room. Raph set his glass down and, without a word to his companion, abandoned her to hurry over to Dodino.

"I had a feeling you'd be here," he said.

"My dear, the whole world knew I'd be here."

Raph laughed. "You're here for the divorce party?"

"No, my dear. I'm taking on-the-job training as a mechanic at the Ford plant."

"Don't do it! They'd probably hire you. When did you get here?"

"Last night. And you?"

"I arrived last night, too."

"I suppose you've come to write all your usual nonsense."

"Not at all. I'm here in an unofficial capacity."

Dodino was pulled down into his chair by the woman he was with. As Raph turned to return to his drink and his girl, Amore managed to blow him a kiss from the tips of his fingers. "You would love this one!" he called. "She's as vulgar as she is ugly and as rich as she is stingy. Definitely your type."

Dodino made a desperate unsuccessful effort to free himself from the woman's grasp.

"Where are you staying?" Raph called back.

"At the Pierre."

"So am I."

"Obviously they've relaxed their standards. . . ."

The few customers in the Barley Mow pub did not look up as the cream-colored Rolls sped by. In Clifton Hampden there was no happy medium so far as transportation was concerned. There was the Rolls-Royce, and there were bicycles, and nothing in between.

As the car moved across a picturesque brick bridge, Irene clapped her hands. "Look! Look! Oh, we're going to love it here!"

Kallenberg did not answer. He had been in a rage ever since leaving London, cursing himself for having given in to his wife's blackmail. Irene never lost an opportunity to take advantage of the feeble power conferred on her by certain familial occasions such as funerals, masses, baptisms, and marriages, a power to which all men, even strong-willed Germans, had inevitably to bow. In the present instance, the occasion had been their anniversary, an ideal pretext for extorting a gift proportionate to the importance of the date to be commemorated. Irene had been extraordinarily generous to herself, Kallenberg reflected ruefully, choosing a country house which, to judge by the price quoted by the broker, must be a veritable castle. In vain Kallenberg had pointed out that they already had houses scattered over the face of the earth. Irene wanted "her house." And as Kallenberg knew, unless he gave it to her, the house would become the focal point of all her real or imagined wrongs for months to come. Yet he had to admit to himself that Irene's stubbornness had one or two points of accidental virtue. Two months earlier Socrates had given Helena a house as a present, at a cost of some hundred thousand pounds. It was situated in the same part of the country as Irene's house, not far from Oxford and Abingdon. That fact had transformed Irene's whim into a matter of prestige, for it was unthinkable that he would refuse his wife anything that Satrapoulos had given to his.

Still, the trip into the country to inspect Irene's house was a tedious chore, especially coming as it did on the eve of a necessary and unwelcome trip to New York. One of Kallenberg's most important customers, Gustave Bambilt—commonly known as Big Gus in the world of tankers—was in the process of divorcing his eleventh wife, Lindy "Nut" Bambilt. Lindy Nut had once been Socrates' mistress, and Kallenberg had never forgiven her for refusing to accord the same privilege to himself. In fact, she had rejected his advances on several separate occasions, to Kallenberg's increasing puzzlement, since he regarded himself as a more attractive man in every way than his brother-in-law.

It was typical of Big Gus Bambilt that, instead of obtaining a quiet divorce, he had felt obliged to throw a party in celebration. His invitation list included anyone who was anyone, and some who were no one, from the world of finance and from the jet set. And Herman Kallenberg, who regarded divorce as a sort of marriage-in-reverse, and therefore a family ceremony, had felt it necessary to bring his wife rather than his mistress to the festivities. For the moment, his plans were to make the best of a bad situation by leaving Irene in New York after two days and, on the pretext of having pressing business, to fly to the Bahamas, where one of his employees would organize a first-class orgy for his benefit. That was all very well, Kallenberg grumbled to himself, but why on earth had Irene chosen the day before their departure for a visit to her goddamned house? Kallenberg had never seen it, but he hated it already. It was impossible for him to renege on his promise to buy it for her, but, by God, she would pay dearly for it.

"Here it is!" Irene squealed. "You'll see! You'll love it!"

The Rolls drew up before a gigantic wrought-iron gate, and the chauffeur gave several blasts of the horn. A man emerged from a small gatehouse built against the ivy-covered wall. The gate swung open majestically, and the automobile moved into an avenue lined by yews and boxwoods.

"Are there servants?" Kallenberg asked.

"Oh, yes. I understand they're absolutely wonderful. Janet, the housekeeper, has worked for—"

"How many servants?"

"I don't know exactly. Six or seven, I suppose."

"You don't know how many servants? I buy you a house, and you expect me to trim the hedges myself? Now, how many are there? Six? Or are there actually seven?"

She looked at him in a manner which suggested an appeal for peace and harmony. "I really have no way of knowing," she said. "This is my first visit."

"This really is unbelievable! You make me spend a fortune to buy you a house you've never even visited?"

"Oh, Herman, look at the river! Isn't it lovely?"

"How many acres does it have?"

"I don't know."

The Rolls continued its stately progress up the avenue through a double row of acacias. Some of the lower branches brushed against the automobile's hood.

"Slow down," Kallenberg barked at the chauffeur.

"I've only seen photographs," Irene said, striving to be conciliatory. "The whole estate is magnificent, but I don't know the exact details as to the size of the grounds or the staff."

Kallenberg's expression was one of complete disgust.

"Look, Herman!"

The automobile had entered an immense clearing, whose lawns began where the avenue ended. In the clearing stood a vast building flanked by four towers. As the Rolls passed, a gardener working on the lawn removed his cap and stared respectfully at his new employers.

Kallenberg, to his infinite regret, was impressed by the majestic edifice before him. There was no denying that the thing had a certain air about it. His irritation increased at the thought that Irene had brought this off by herself, as well as against his opposition. Aware that his wife was watching him, he set his face in an expression of displeasure. At all costs he must avoid letting her know that he liked the house.

"The main building dates from the fourteenth century," Irene informed him.

"Altered and rebuilt in the nineteenth century, no doubt. Don't tell me you actually believe that broker's rubbish. With this kind of white elephant, the only really medieval thing is the plumbing."

Irene, her patience wearing thin, shrugged angrily.

The chauffeur opened the door, and they climbed out of the car. Immediately, they were both struck by the silence. The rare sounds were those of nature, coming as though from a great distance through the clear, crystalline air.

A door opened, and a woman appeared in the main entry. She bowed in welcome, then led them in a tour of the main-floor rooms of the house, with Irene exclaiming in delight over each new wonder and Kallenberg pretending boredom.

The woman said, "If you would like to see the upper stories—"

Irene was already on the staircase. "Aren't you coming?" she asked her husband.

"I'll wait for you outside. I want to get a breath of air."

Without a word, Irene turned her back on him and followed the housekeeper up the broad, noble staircase. Herman went outside and lighted a cigarette. His eyes briefly swept the landscape, and he recognized instinctively that the property was worth more than he was paying for it. It did not displease him to invest his money in land, and he had done so frequently. Land was not like the sea. There were no risks involved. If his entire fleet should sink on that very day, he reflected, he could live out his days in comfort on the revenue from his investments in land.

He heard Irene calling to him from an upper window, but he did not turn his head. He wondered briefly what was irritating him so much, but he abandoned the investigation before it had begun. He was enjoying his ill humor, and he had no wish to resolve or abate it by analysis.

Kallenberg walked to the corner of the house. A hundred yards away he saw a small cluster of buildings and heard the sounds of dogs barking. He walked toward the sounds and discovered a litter of puppies, guarded lazily by their mother. Next to the dogs was an enclosure containing a number of ducks and chickens; and, adjacent to that, a dung pool in which three enormous hogs wallowed in a state of indescribable filth and obvious contentment.

"I thought you didn't like pigs."

Kallenberg looked up angrily, his irritation aggravated by his being discovered contemplating something that he was determined to denigrate systematically. "Are you ready to leave?" he snapped. "Have you had enough of playing the lady of the manor?"

"Oh, Herman, I love it here! The house is divine!"

"Do you really want me to buy this dilapidated old barn? The whole place is falling apart. Even the walls are rotted!"

"I'll never ask you to come here if you don't want to."

"Just what is it you find so fascinating about the place?"

Irene's sweeping gesture took in the house, the grounds, the chickens, ducks, dogs and hogs. "Everything!" she said. "And you know that I adore animals."

"Do you adore the smell, too?" Kallenberg's voice was growing dangerously louder.

"Oh, the animals. I don't mind it. It's a barnyard smell."

Kallenberg's throat tightened in anger. A dark veil descended before his eyes, blotting out the trees, the chickens and ducks, Irene's maddeningly defiant smile, the mud bog, and his wife's dazzling white Dior dress and leaving only a single infuriating vision.

"Well then," he shouted, "since you like it so much—"

He seized Irene's hand, spun her around roughly, then suddenly released her. She fell heavily into the dung pool, among the hogs, which grunted angrily and fled.

Irene wiped her face and eyes. Then she simply sat for a few seconds, too astonished to move. When she finally climbed to her feet, her dress and her person were coated with filth.

Kallenberg stood motionless, contemplating the spectacle, entranced by his act of violence and by the incredible pleasure that he derived from it. It did not even occur to him to wonder what Irene's reaction would be.

When she spoke, her tone was quite normal. "Help me, Herman. You could at least give me your hand so that I can climb out."

He did not move.

She struggled out of the pool on her own, and Herman moved back slightly, half expecting her to attempt to revenge herself. His fears were unjustified. Irene swept past him and strode briskly toward the house. "You'll just have to wait for me." She laughed. "Now I have an excuse to explore the bathrooms!"

[12]

Peggy was reminded of the conversation she had had several days earlier with Scott and of the way he had hesitated when she had described her idea to him. She remembered their exact words. She and Scott had just made love, and they were lying in bed. Scott's head was resting on her stomach, and he was pretending to be listening to an imaginary noise.

"What are you listening to?"

"Shh!"

"Tell me!"

"Be quiet. I'm trying to hear."

"To hear what?"

"Your heart."

"Try a little higher."

"No, it's here. Didn't anyone ever tell you that your heart is located at your navel?"

"Never. But that's not surprising, since most of my lovers were deaf."

"Your resident alien, too?"

"To begin with, he was not my lover, so I don't know whether or not he was deaf. In the second place, Greeks are not aliens."

"What are they, then?"

"Greeks are people who marry the Queen of England. When your silly ancestors were still living in caves, Satrapoulos' people were building the Acropolis."

"You mean he's Jewish?"

"Greek Orthodox, you racist pig."

"That's worse than Jewish. I don't trust him. He's too rich."

"And I suppose you are poverty-stricken?"

"That's different. I am above suspicion. I've never done a day's work in my life."

"I wouldn't brag about it. And, in any case, that phase of your life is over. Daddy's money, Daddy's ideas, Daddy's orders—that's all finished. You're going to have to learn to be your own man, Scott."

"If you think my father wears the pants in my family, you don't know my mother. By the way, you're not trying to become my mother, are you?"

"Don't joke, Scott. I'm very serious."

"What do you see in him?"

"Who?"

"Your Greek."

"Look, I've met him once in my whole life. Do you know what Dodino said about him?"

"Know who said what about him?"

"Amore Dodino, the funniest man in the world—a little French queen. You'll meet him at Lindy Nut's. He said: 'Satrapoulos is as handsome as Croesus.' Now, try to forget that I adore rich foreigners.

If we can get his backing, you'll be President in two shakes of a lamb's tail."

"With his money and your ideas—"

"That's it, exactly. You can thank your lucky stars that you've finally met someone who can do your thinking for you."

"How could I ever have fallen in love with such a domineering woman?"

"Because you have a secret yen to be dominated. Now, are you going to listen to me or not?"

"No. Or rather, tell me again whatever made you become engaged to that fool Tony Fairlane?"

"It's simple. I did it to get even with you."

"What did I ever do to you?"

"You didn't ask me to marry you soon enough."

"Do you still see him?"

"No, not really."

"Never mind not really. Yes or no?"

"Yes. He never gives up."

"Is he still in love with you?"

"You must be joking. Tony only loves himself, as he always has. He's furious that I threw him over. He says that I've made him the laughingstock of the whole country."

"Does he bother you?"

"More than I'd like him to."

"Do you want me to take care of him?"

Peggy's face became serious. "No, don't do anything. I can take care of him myself if he gets too pushy. The only thing I'm afraid of is what he can do to you. If he should make a scandal—"

"Well, then. Maybe—"

"No, forget it. I'll take care of him."

"As you wish. Now, tell me why this Greek of yours might be interested in financing my campaign."

"I never said that he was. I only said that we could try to interest him."

"And if I'm elected, people would say that I bought the election with money from a shady character like Satrapoulos."

"You *are* naïve. If you're elected, do you think people are going to stop and ask how you were elected?"

"A couple of days ago a friend of mine in the Senate told me that your Greek's days are numbered. There's the matter of the oil tariffs and some financial interests which are determined to get him for having screwed them. For openers, the government is going to make him cough up a few million dollars. And that's only the beginning. The big oil companies are after his ass, and they're putting a hell of a lot of pressure on the government."

"Obviously, my Greek needs a friend in high places."

"Do you know anyone shortsighted enough to book passage on a sinking ship?"

"Yes. You. When a man has a billion dollars, he doesn't sink that easily."

"Don't count on me. If it ever came out that there was any sort of connection between him and me, I wouldn't stand a chance of being elected."

"True. But if it doesn't come out, you'll have the election in your pocket. Remember, Satrapoulos is essentially a gambler. To him, you're a thoroughbred whose value is rising. If we approach him properly, he'll go along with us. Since when does money have an odor?"

"His money has a very special odor about it."

"What about the big-business interests that are financing your campaign right now? Do you think they're being run by canonized saints?"

Scott stared at her face for a moment. "Did you know that he's done time in jail?"

"Satrapoulos?"

"Yes, Satrapoulos. Here in New York."

"For what? Drunken driving?"

"Very funny. I tell you that he's more trouble than he's worth."

"Tell me about it."

"They nabbed him a couple of years ago. It goes back to 1945, when there wasn't a single ship to be had in all Europe. Everything had been destroyed in the war, and all the shipowners were bankrupt. All, that is, except the Greeks, including your particular Greek. Before the war, the Greeks usually insured their ships for less than their actual worth, in order to avoid paying high premiums. In 1939 the insurance companies got together and decided that cargo ships and tankers would have to be insured on a contract basis, regardless of their true value. In a sense, it was unjust, because it meant old tubs had to pay premiums on values ten times higher than their real worth. But there was no choice. The shipowners had to go along with the insurance companies or do without insurance. Then the war came along, and when it was all over, who were the first to file claims against everybody in sight? The Greeks, of course. They demanded war indemnities. They demanded that Lloyd's reimburse them for the loss of their ships. And meanwhile, they were demanding that the American government lend them money to rebuild their fleets. To them, the war was a real gold mine—"

"What clever men!"

"Meanwhile, of course, the American shipowners were left out in the cold."

"That's life, isn't it?"

"Yes, other people's lives. My brother's, for example."

"Oh, I'm sorry, Scott."

"That's all right."

"I'm really sorry about William, but you have to be realistic about this. Business just does not come to a halt because there happens to be a war."

"As soon as we had liberated Europe from the Nazis and the war was over, we began selling off our war surplus. Guess who rushed in to bid on our liberty ships?"

"Don't tell me. The Greeks."

"The Greeks. Your Satrapoulos, for example, bought twenty-five of them—for a miserable twelve million dollars. Those ships of ours made him one of the most dangerous competitors of our own American shipping companies. His ships were at sea twenty-four hours a day, seven days a week, almost every week of the year."

"Is that illegal?"

"No, but it irritated the hell out of our own shippers. Then, in 1947, we sold off some more surplus. But this time there was a difference. Only American citizens were eligible to bid."

"That doesn't sound very fair. Is that what you call open competition?"

"Don't worry. Satrapoulos did very well for himself. He organized some American corporations, and bought a few others that were about to go into bankruptcy, keeping only forty-nine percent of the stock for himself, so that the companies were theoretically American-controlled. These companies bought another thirty liberty ships."

"Didn't he pay for them?"

"Forty-five million dollars."

"So what's everyone so upset about?"

"Nothing. Except that the ships brought him fifty times that amount in profit."

"To me, it sounds like a case of pure jealousy."

"Eventually the Treasury Department began an investigation. As a first step, the government impounded eighteen of his ships that were in American waters."

"What an elegant solution. Now who's the crook in your story? I hope he was able to get them back."

"It didn't bother him one bit. The ships were ready for the scrap heap by then, and he had already made an enormous fortune from them. But at that point he made his only mistake. He came to New York to protest the seizure of his ships, and they slapped him in jail."

"For how long?"

"Only one night, unfortunately."

Peggy roared with laughter. "He made fools out of you!"

Scott could not help smiling. What Peggy said was true. The United States had been had by the Greeks in every encounter. "But that's not the end of the story," he continued. "The very next morning he had an army of international lawyers in the courts, and they got him released almost immediately. Still, charges were filed against him for violation of shipping regulations, and eventually there was a settlement. The courts ordered him to place thirty of his ships under the American flag, in such a way that they would be under the control of two American trustees whom he would designate."

"Did he accept?"

"Immediately!"

"Why are you laughing? What's so funny?"

"You haven't heard the best part of the story. He did comply with the court's instructions to appoint two American citizens as trustees. He appointed his two seven-year-old children. It turned out that he had gotten them American citizenship when they were born."

"Scott, be a sport! Give credit where credit is due. The man is a genius. You should take off your hat to him."

"I'll take off my hat to him at his funeral. Now, they're really out to get him. And his brother-in-law, too."

"Kallenberg? That's funny. You know that Kallenberg and Satrapoulos can't stand each other. To make matters even more complicated, they both hate their mother-in-law, Medea Mikolofides."

"It's like something right out of Sophocles."

"That's truer than you know. The family's chief preoccupation seems to be finding ways to get rid of one another. The old lady spends her time trying to undermine her sons-in-law, and their wives spend money as though they were trying to ruin them."

"Nice ladies."

"The wives are stupid, silly women. The third sister is even worse. They say she's a real eccentric, a sort of do-it-yourself mystic. But they don't matter. Socrates Satrapoulos is the important one so far as we're concerned, and you'd better think twice before crossing off a potential ally like him. He's going to be at Lindy Nut's party. Why don't you come, just for an hour? At least you'll be able to see what he looks like."

"Is he really going to be there?"

"Yes, of course. Lindy Nut always invites all her former lovers to her divorce parties."

"Were they lovers?"

"Oh, yes. She was between marriages at the time. It's an old story."

"You have lovely friends."

"Some of yours wouldn't bear close investigation either. Lindy Nut is fabulous! My dearest friend. We've been inseparable for ten years. There's nothing we wouldn't do for each other."

"What makes you so sure that Satrapoulos will be there?"

"You forget that, for love of you, I could teach Mata Hari a few tricks. Have you ever heard of Menelas?"

"Hasn't everyone? She's a singer, isn't she?"

"A pianist, you barbarian!"

"What's the connection?"

"Well, Lindy Nut mentioned that Satrapoulos is a great fan of Menelas, so I suggested she tell Satrapoulos that Menelas would be there."

"I hope at least that she won't play. I can't stand classical music."

"Scott, all the money in your party's treasury wouldn't be enough to pay her for a single recital."

"I knew I should never have stopped taking piano lessons."

Raph and Amore Dodino dropped Rita at her apartment, then took a cab back to the Pierre.

"I'm hungry," Raph said.

"You're a real animal," Amore replied. "Eat, sleep, screw. That's all you think about."

"Can you think of anything better?"

"Better than screwing? No."

"Not even eating?"

"It depends on what you have in mind. I have a very refined palate, and my tastes are literally beyond your comprehension. You are little more than a barbarian. I can see you riding with Attila's hordes, pressing your meat between your thighs—I'd better stop. I'm exciting myself."

The taxi drew up before the hotel. In the lobby, Raph stopped to chat a moment with the night porter, a Frenchman named Leon whom Raph had known for years. Leon was the one man in New York who knew precisely who in the Pierre spent the night with whom. He had often brought food or liquor to Raph's room at four or five o'clock in the morning and found two, three, or even four girls there with him. One night there had been three incredibly beautiful creatures in Raph's bed when Leon arrived with champagne. The girls had not bothered to cover themselves with the sheet, and Leon, who had been married for twenty years to an American girl of the Mormon persuasion, had modestly averted his eyes. On several occasions, Raph had offered Leon large sums of money to dictate his recollections into a tape recorder, but Leon had always declined. He loved his work, and he wanted to do nothing that would endanger his job.

"I'm hungry, too," Dodino said. "Shall we have something before we go to bed?"

"If you like."

"Your room or mine?"

"It doesn't matter."

"Mine, then."

Dodino's quarters were something of a shock to Raph. Rather than a single room, Dodino had a sumptuous suite. "Good Lord," he exclaimed. "How do you do it? Has a rich aunt died suddenly?"

"Even better, my dear. It is all paid for by Lindy Nut. And because I love you, I'll tell you my little secret. There are a lot of people who are willing to pay me to attend their parties."

"Why?"

"Because I'm gay. The ladies find me amusing, and the men know that their wives are safe with me. You, on the other hand, are a constant threat to them. Come, sit down."

Dodino picked up the telephone and ordered breakfast, without bothering to consult Raph. "Some caviar," he said, "you know, the kind with the large white grains. The kind you serve to my friend, Reza Pahlevi—the Shah. And a bottle of Veuve Cliquot '51."

He hung up and turned to Raph. "Is that all right?"

Raph nodded. "I'm exhausted." He sighed.

"Life is difficult when one looks like Tarzan. Is it possible that you're entering the menopause?"

"Not for a long time yet."

"Don't brag. How old are you?"

"That, my friend, is none of your business."

"An answer typical of middle-aged women."

"All right, since you want to know, I'll tell you. I am exactly the same age as you."

"Not really? Well, then, to me, you will always be in the flush of youth."

"Have you looked at me closely?"

"More often than you think."

"And how do I look?"

"You look exactly like my type."

Raph felt a surge of irritation at Dodino's attempt to transform him from a hunter into the hunted. "Come on, Amore," he said evenly. "You know I'm not gay."

"That is precisely why I find you so appealing, you idiot. Haven't you learned that yet? The men who appeal to me are always real men."

"What exactly is a real man?"

"The complete opposite of a fairy."

"And how do you classify yourself?"

"As a homosexual. Etymologically speaking, as a person who is attracted to other persons of the same sex. Do you want examples?"

"No, no examples, please."

"It creates problems, of course. For me to find a man really attractive, he has to be straight. And the less straight he is, the less he appeals to me."

"You always have a mob of men around you."

"Not men. Faggots. But don't pretend to be more stupid than you are. Do you think that you'd be less virile if you let me make love to you?"

Dun was becoming increasingly embarrassed by the direction of the conversation. "Please, Amore, let's forget it."

"What do your sluts have that I don't have?"

Raph laughed. "It's not what they have. It's what they don't have."

"Very smart. I'm going to change my clothes." Dodino disappeared into an adjoining room and returned a minute later wearing a flame-red robe of silk, embroidered in gold. He sat in an immense armchair facing Raph.

Raph twisted uneasily in his chair. "I'm getting hungrier by the minute," he said.

Dodino stared at him in silence. Finally, he sighed deeply and said, "If only you were willing."

"Willing to what?"

"You and I, Raph. What a team we would make. You'd be a rich man."

"Why should I want to be rich? I already live as though I were."

Dodino smiled sadly. "What a pity. Such a lovely boy—"

"Let's drop it, shall we?" Raph said. Then, in an attempt at humor, he added, "I'm not that kind of girl."

"How could I love anyone so common?"

"Thank you."

"I could give you more pleasure than you think possible. With me, you would have everything that you have with a woman—everything except the bother, the jealousy, the hysteria. Raph, listen to me. . . ."

Raph, torn between fright and a wild impulse to laugh, watched as Dodino slid to his knees and crept across the floor toward him. He clutched Raph's hand and loosed a steady flood of words as though afraid that, if interrupted by a moment of silence, his discourse would lose its effectiveness. "Listen, we are in the Middle Ages. . . . A time of courtly love. No, that's silly. We're in the eighteenth century. The time of *Liaisons dangereuses* and Choderlos de Laclos. . . . We are two prisoners in a garrison town and I am your orderly. Shall I remove your boots? I'm on my knees; at your feet. . . ."

Raph tried to withdraw his hand, but Dodino held it with the strength of frenzy.

"Dodino, stop this foolishness, I tell you!"

Dodino's head was now on Raph's knee, and he was caressing Raph's hand. At that precise moment, Leon arrived with the caviar and champagne. Seeing him, Dodino pulled away from Raph, and his movement revealed to Raph that they were no longer alone in the room. At the sight of Leon, he felt himself blush, for perhaps the second time in his life. Leon, meanwhile, focused his attention on the bottle of Veuve Cliquot, from which he was working to remove the cork, and carefully kept his eyes from the two men.

"Leave it," Dodino said. "We'll open it ourselves."

Raph sprang to his feet and strode toward the door.

"But where are you going?" Dodino called after him.

"To bed!"

"What about the champagne? And the caviar? You haven't even tasted it."

"Shove your caviar up your ass!" Raph shouted, then slammed the door behind him.

"What a gross person," Dodino said to Leon. "Did you hear what he said?"

Leon did not look up. "If you wish anything further, sir," he intoned, "please ring."

The Greek studied his reflection in the mirror and made a face. Either the suit was poorly cut or there was something wrong with his figure. The three black alpaca suits which had just arrived from London all looked, as soon as Socrates put them on, like something a small-town merchant would wear to church on Sunday. Yet it was neither Socrates' tailor nor his anatomy that was at fault. The tailor was the best in England, and Satrapoulos was in good physical shape, slender and hard and without an ounce of excess fat. He looked quite passable in a bathing suit, but as soon as he put on a shirt, he looked like a cheese merchant. Why? He shrugged. There was no explanation. There had been a time when he had blamed it on the tailor. Finally, he had resigned himself to the fact that his body had a permanent antipathy to his clothing. He removed the jacket and let it slide to the floor.

He was already irritated at the thought of the party at Gus Bambilt's house. Although there was one consolation. Menelas would be there. Lindy Nut, Gus' future ex-wife, had made a point of telling him so. That in itself was strange. Lindy Nut, with whom he was on terms of affectionate friendship, usually did not bother with such details. In fact, she ordinarily tried to keep him away from attractive women, preferring to keep his admiration exclusively for herself. Their relationship had survived ten years now, and it was as solid as ever. Whenever Lindy Nut was depressed, it was to Socrates alone that she turned for consolation, and when he was depressed, he knew that he would find an understanding and affectionate listener in Lindy Nut. In her most recent marriage, she had had the good sense to take as her husband an oilman who was one of Socrates' best customers.

Socrates glanced at the invitation:

The pleasure of your company is requested at a costume party given by Lindy and Gustave Bambilt on July 22, 1958, at their residence at 127 Park Avenue, at 10 P.M., to celebrate their impending divorce.
Theme: the sea, love, money. RSVP

He threw the card to the table in disgust. It unnerved him to think there were people who celebrated a divorce as others might celebrate a baptism or a wedding. The breaking of the bonds of a sacramental union hardly seemed worthy of festivities. Yet the couple concerned were not exactly venturing into unknown waters. This would be Big Gus' eleventh divorce, and Lindy Nut's third.

Only Americans could be silly enough to do something like this, Socrates assured himself. He did not know whether his offended sensibilities were the result of his upbringing, his background, or his principles. And he did not particularly want to meditate on the matter, for the answer might reopen the question of the armed truce which he had maintained so painstakingly with Helena. For the past two years, they had hardly seen each other, although they both tried diligently to maintain the fiction of a united family. In the first months of their marriage, he had been irresistibly attracted by Helena's youth. Later, she had lost the angular grace of childhood. It had been, he recalled, after the birth of the twins. At first, he had tried to compensate for her lost adolescence by loving her as a grown woman, only to discover that she had matured only in appearance and not in fact. She understood nothing of the consuming need for action which drove her husband. At times, he had tried to explain his goals and the means he employed to attain them, but she had not been interested.

He tried on one of the suits again, hoping against hope that some miracle had taken place. It looked worse than before. On the few occasions that Helena had looked closely at him, it had been to complain that he was badly dressed.

He often wondered if she had a lover. It seemed unlikely. He would have been informed of it if she had. There was that one man, that French actor, whom he suspected Helena found attractive. And of course, he was the one man who did not openly court her, since he was under constant surveillance by his own wife.

One day Irene had dared allude to the possibility that Helena was having an affair by asking whether he was not jealous to see men constantly clustered around his wife. He had answered that he regarded these attentions as the homage paid to the owner of a rare and precious object. Then, on a suspicion, he had had inquiries made into his sister-in-law's activities and discovered, with astonishment, that Irene had had a steady stream of casual lovers—servants, soldiers, even an occasional priest. Socrates had been delighted at the idea of the vain, self-satisfied Kallenberg being cuckolded by the scatterbrained Irene. But there was a darker side to it. If Irene could have affairs so brazenly, was it not equally possible for Helena to do so?

The thought angered and worried him. He paced around the room, then out into the vestibule of the suite which he maintained year-round at the Pierre. As he did so, his eye fell upon a cardboard box addressed to him. He picked it up and tried unsuccessfully to break the string with his bare hands. He went into the bathroom and found a razor blade which he used to cut the cord. Inside the box was his costume: a pirate outfit, consisting of black pants cut off below the knees, a red shirt, and white silk stockings.

He donned the costume and stood before the mirror. The long hoped-for miracle had taken place! The men of Tortuga, obviously, had had bodies quite different from those of the effete snobs who frequented the tailors of Savile Row. He looked positively dashing. The final touch was the black tricornered hat bearing the traditional skull and crossbones. He tried the hat at different angles, studying which position lent him the most ferocious appearance. He returned to the vestibule and found what he was looking for in the umbrella stand: a sabre. He slipped it into his belt. It trailed on the floor behind him. He raised it until the hilt was on a level with his chest. That was better. Uncomfortable, but better; except that he could not bend over very easily.

Socrates drew out the sabre and made a few thrusts at the empty air. It was unbelievable how a weapon transformed a man. Socrates admired himself in the mirror, striking martial poses and dreamed of challenging someone to a duel for the love of a fair lady.

Peggy was lying on her bed, fully dressed. On particularly busy days, she had made a habit of setting aside an hour to rest. At such times she was not to be disturbed. Claudette, her maid, turned away all visitors and unplugged the telephone.

On this occasion, however, Peggy had been in her room only a few minutes when Claudette knocked timidly.

"Madame—"

"Yes, what is it?" Peggy asked sharply.

"It is Mr. Fairlane."

"Tell him to go away."

"Madame, he refuses to go away. He's in the drawing room—"

"Did you let him in?"

"He let himself in."

Peggy jumped from her bed. She would have to put an end to this once and for all. Tony Fairlane apparently could not bring himself to believe that any woman would drop him.

"Where is he?"

"Downstairs, in the drawing room—"

"It's all right, Claudette, I'll go down."

Claudette nodded. "Yes, madame." How could Madame be so cruel? Poor Mr. Fairlane, after all this time. Such a gentleman, too! Why, once he had even brought Claudette a bouquet of the loveliest spring flowers. . . .

Peggy straightened her skirt, patted her hair, and marched down the stairs.

"What are you doing here?" Peggy's voice was cold, severe, even angry. But her anger was directed at herself as much as at Tony. What on earth could she ever have seen in this spoiled, pampered mama's boy? she wondered. Certainly, he was handsome and wildly rich. But he was a nothing in comparison to Scott Baltimore, and he would remain a nothing all his life. Zero. A pretty boy whose widowed mama owned most of the steel in Pittsburgh.

"Peggy—"

"I told you I didn't want to see you again."

Tony laughed. "I know. I know. You're really high and mighty now, aren't you? I hear you're going to be Mrs. Scott Baltimore. Well, you're not married yet!"

"What is that supposed to mean?"

"Never mind what it's supposed to mean. Do you know that his grandfather was a smuggler and a bootlegger?"

"So? What about your own grandfather? A crook and a murderer—"

"Peggy, I'm warning you! I'm not in the mood for your games!"

She glared at him with infinite contempt. "Is that what you came to say?"

"No. I came to tell you that it's not as easy as you seem to think it is. You owe me something! Do you know how much I've spent on you? Half a million dollars! The furs, the jewelry—"

"So?"

"I want it back. All of it!"

"Are you out of your mind?"

"All of it! Do you hear? If you think you're going to make me a laughingstock—"

"You poor fool. I have no idea what you're talking about. If you think I owe you something, then go talk to your lawyer about it. Or, better still, run and tell your mommy!"

"Do you think I'm a child—"

"That's precisely what you are. A stupid, selfish child. And the whole world knows it."

Tony took a step toward her.

Peggy, moving so quickly that Tony was barely able to follow her with his eyes, pulled open the drawer of the end table next to which she was standing. He saw in her hand, pointing at him, not the traditional miniature pistol of the lady-in-distress, but a regulation Colt of the New York Police Department.

"Peggy!"

"Move back." Peggy did not raise her voice, but it was obvious that she was deadly serious.

"Peggy, are you crazy?"

"Move back, I said!"

Without taking his eyes from the muzzle of the Colt, Fairlane moved backward until he was standing ten feet from Peggy.

She lighted a cigarette, inhaled, then blew out a long stream of blue smoke. "All right, Tony, if you really have something to say, now's the time to say it."

Tony, his eyes wide, did not speak.

"Then I'll say it, Tony. You make me want to vomit. You're stupid. You're a silly, ridiculous ass. Everyone laughs at you behind your back. If it weren't for your mother's money, you'd starve in the streets. You can't even screw a woman. Face it, Tony: you're a faggot. You're not even that. All you're good for is to jerk yourself off in front of a mirror."

"Peggy—"

"Shut up! I don't listen to faggots!"

Tony blanched. He gestured helplessly but remained silent.

"Now, Tony, listen carefully to what I'm going to tell you. If ever I see you again, or if ever I hear that you've even mentioned my name to anyone or done anything to harm me, no matter what it is—then I'm going to get you, Tony. Do you understand? No matter where you are, I'll destroy you! As God is my witness, I swear it. Is that clear?"

He did not answer.

Peggy took a step toward him, and he moved backward toward the door.

Peggy raised the gun. "Stop," she said evenly.

Tony stopped.

"Kneel down."

Tony shook his head and smiled, as though it were all a bad joke.

"Kneel!"

Still grinning, Tony knelt.

"Now, take down your pants."

He looked up at her pleadingly. "Lower my pants?"

"Take them down!"

He unbuckled his belt and slid his pants to his knees.

"Take off your belt and push it toward me."

"Peggy, this is ridiculous—"

"Shut up! Do as I say."

Tony thought he saw her finger tighten on the trigger. He pulled his belt from his pants and pushed it toward her.

"Now your shorts."

He hesitated, then pushed down his shorts.

Without taking her eyes from his, Peggy picked up the belt. "Now, Tony, I'm going to give you what all naughty children get. And if you make one sound, I swear I'll kill you."

She raised her arm, and the leather strap whistled briefly before it struck Tony's bronzed posterior. Peggy drew back her arm and struck again and again.

"There," she said at last, throwing the belt at him. "The spanking is over. Now pull up your pants and get out of here."

Tony rose, zipping his pants. As he struggled with his belt, he stuttered, "Peggy, please—"

"Get out!"

He shook his head and moved toward the doorway. As he passed near Peggy, she spat in his face. Then she saw Claudette in the vestibule, staring at her incredulously.

"Claudette," Peggy said, "you needn't bother to see Mr. Fairlane to the door. He won't be coming back."

[13]

Peggy rang Lindy Nut's doorbell. The two women knew each other too well to stand on formality. When one of them wanted to see the other, she simply picked up the telephone and said, "I'm coming by."

Now she walked into the living room and dropped into a chair. "Are you going to give me a drink?" she asked.

Nut took two glasses and a bottle of scotch from the bar.

"Are you alone?" Peggy asked.

"Of course. Why?"

"Gus isn't here?"

"No. Why? What's going on?"

"Nothing."

"Tell me!"

Peggy raised her glass to her lips.

"Do you want some ice?"

"No thanks."

"Now, tell me."

"Am I interrupting something?"

"Don't be silly."

"I mean, with your divorce and all—"

"I've been through enough divorces not to let them disturb my daily routine."

Peggy laughed. Good old Lindy Nut. She never lost her head over anything. She was tall and slender; thirty—perhaps thirty-five. Perhaps a bit more. Peggy had never asked her age, and Lindy Nut had

213

never volunteered it. Even the closest of friends have some secrets. When Nut moved, she seemed to slink. There was something feline about her. Her high cheekbones, her enormous eyes, the way she moved. . . .

"How about another drink?"

"If you're having one."

"All right. Now, what's up?"

Peggy waited until Lindy Nut had handed her a fresh drink. "Are you sure that Satrapoulos is going to be there?" she asked.

Nut looked at Peggy in surprise. "Of course," she answered. "What do you think?"

"Yes, I had almost forgotten. With all your affairs and marriages and divorces, I have trouble keeping them all straight."

"With Socrates it's different. He's neither a husband nor a lover. He's better than either."

"Then why don't you marry him?"

"Why not, indeed? I might just do that one of these days, if I ever have the time."

"Scott is as stubborn as a mule about Socrates. He doesn't even want to meet him."

"What does he have against him?"

"He says Socrates is finished in this country."

Lindy Nut shook her head and smiled. "They've been saying that for years. He's an extraordinary man, you know. If you knew him as well as I do—Well, I'm not sure I want you to. You simply couldn't help falling in love with him."

"Oh, come on, Nut. He's old enough to be my father. No offense intended." Socrates was about fifty, but Gus, Nut's ex-husband-to-be, was seventy if he was a day.

"And none taken. You're right. But what does that matter?"

"It doesn't, of course." Peggy was silent for a moment. "There are a lot of men with money behind Scott," she went on. "I can't understand why he should refuse the support of a man who has more money than any of them."

She glanced through the window. Far below, in the distance, she saw the trees of Central Park.

"But Scott has money of his own," Lindy Nut said.

"You don't understand. Politics and money go together, like eggs and bacon, but we're not talking about a few measly millions. No one man has enough money to finance a political party. It takes practically a national treasury. You have no idea of how many millions of dollars the New American Party has already spent."

"Why are you so set on Scott making a success of politics?"

"Oh, Nut! If you knew him! He was made to be on top. He's handsome, marvelous—irresistible! If you could hear him talk about the things he wants to do! Well, if you're sure that Satrapoulos is going to be there—"

"Yes, I'm absolutely certain. You can take my word for it. Even if he weren't doing it for me, he'd do it for Gus. He needs Gus' business."

"I'm so anxious to have them meet," Peggy said. "They were made to be friends." She hesitated. "What about Menelas? Did you tell him that Menelas was going to be there?"

"I told you I did. Relax, will you? Tomorrow night they'll all be right here in this very room—including Socrates Satrapoulos. There'll be more talent and money per square foot than you've seen in your life."

"Then you're not depressed?"

"Depressed? Why should I be depressed?"

"I mean about your divorce."

"Ha!"

"Well, as you say, you're used to it. How are you coming out of this one?"

"What do you mean?"

"Settlement, alimony—that sort of thing."

"Oh, I've done very well. Let me know when you and Scott are ready to break up. I'll give you a few pointers."

"Scott and I? Don't be silly. I love him too much for that."

Lindy Nut made a face. "It seems to me that I've heard myself say the same thing several times."

"Yes, but with me it's different. I'm not as jaded as you are."

"We'll see. But what are you wearing tomorrow night?"

"It's a secret. And you?"

"It's a secret."

"Nut, are we going to start keeping secrets from one another after all this time?"

"Yes, we certainly are."

Peggy burst into laughter. "Oh, Nut! I adore you! Give me a kiss and let me dash."

* * *

"May I?"

"Why not?"

"After all, I'm still your husband."

Gustave Bambilt smiled apologetically as he spoke. It had never occurred to him that a woman might respond to something other than his money. He always paid his wives, as he did his whores.

He seated his two hundred and forty pounds on the bed.

"It's funny." He sighed.

"What?"

"That we're getting divorced. Why are we?"

"Tell me why we got married in the first place, and I'll be able to tell you why we're getting divorced."

"You're making fun of me."

Lindy Nut did not answer.

"I was at my attorney's office this afternoon," Gus said. "Everything's arranged. You'll get everything we agreed on."

"Good. Have you already picked out the twelfth Mrs. Bambilt?"

He looked at her quickly, to see if she was teasing again. With Nut, one never knew for sure.

"What makes you think there'll be a twelfth one?"

"Oh, Gus, don't try to pull the wool over my eyes. I know you too well. I don't think it's ever occurred to you that a man can do without sex for a few days or even for a weekend."

"Since I've always been a married man, I've never had to find out."

"That's it, precisely. Why do you always get married?"

"Because I don't like to be alone. I got married for the first time when I was seventeen, and I've been doing it ever since."

"Poor Gus."

"What about you? Are you going to remarry?"

"For God's sake—"

"May I?" Gus interrupted. Now he was asking Nut's permission to stretch out on the bed alongside her. She looked at him for a moment and then nodded to signify her acquiescence. It was unusual for Gus to join her in her room once she had retired for the night. Now, however, there was something strange in his attitude, and knowing that Gus had no capacity for deceit of any kind, Nut concluded that he had something he wished to say. She decided to help him along.

"What is it, Gus?"

He raised his head from the pillow and took her hand in his. "Nothing, really. I just felt like talking, that's all."

"Tell me."

"It's not easy. I don't know how to begin—"

"I'm listening."

"Well, it's funny, but by this time tomorrow night we'll be divorced and you'll be a free woman, as they say. We've been married three years, and I still don't feel I know you. Of course, we haven't really seen much of each other, have we?"

"No, not much."

"I've been away so much on business. Why on earth do I work so hard?"

"So that you can meet your alimony payments," Lindy Nut responded without malice.

"I have no children. I'm—over sixty. I'm no longer a young man. Where has it all gone?"

"I don't know."

"It's as though I had never taken advantage of being married to you."

They both remained silent for a long moment, with Gus holding Lindy Nut's hand. "Nut," Gus said, "I have a favor to ask of you."

"What is it, Gus?"

"It's silly, really. You probably won't want to."

"Ask and find out."

"I'd like to sleep with you tonight. In your bed."

She did not answer, and Gus became alarmed.

"Is it all right? I mean, tomorrow it will all be over. I'd like to, just once more. If you don't mind, that is—"

"I'd like to, Gus."

A smile spread over Gus' face, and he rose from the bed and stood like a clumsy child, unsure of his footing.

"Thank you, Lindy! Thank you! I'll go and get my things."

Lindy Nut watched him lumber from the room. I wonder what he's feeling guilty about, she thought. A strange man. In business, he could raid a corporation or drive a competitor into bankruptcy without a twinge of regret. But in love, he always felt compelled to ask for permission.

Scott was not looking forward to informing his mother that he wished to marry Peggy. It was not that he was a stranger to painful necessity and even to necessary violence. His family had had its share, and more, of pitched battles and sudden death. It was a clan given to excess in all things: in its contempt for the rest of the world, in the size of its fortune, in its thirst for power, and in its unbounded loyalty to all its members. Religion itself was practiced with a fervor barely distinguishable from fanaticism, and the family occasionally even used the faith as a hammer with which to batter their enemies. The motto of the Baltimore family, handed down to Alfred Baltimore from his own father, Stephen, was unambiguous: "We, above all others."

Three generations of relentless application of the philosophy thus expressed had brought the Baltimores to the verge of realizing the founding father's dream: that America would one day be governed by his descendants, preferably as *de facto* kings in a theoretical democracy. Scott himself was the heir to that tradition, and even before his birth, he had been regarded as an instrument preordained for its fulfillment. Consequently, nothing had been spared to prepare him for his encounter with destiny.

Before him, his two elder brothers, William and Lewis, had been reared with the same sacrosanct goal in mind. William, however, had been struck down during the war, in France, when his tank was destroyed by German guns. And Lewis, an avid amateur parachutist, had been killed when, in an unwise display of derring-do, he had waited until the very last second before attempting to open a parachute which was fated not to open at all.

The patriarch of the Baltimores was Scott's grandfather, Stephen, founder of the dynasty, who was so indestructible as to seem impervious to illness and death. In his eighty-second year he had insisted on scaling a cedar to trim a few branches which cast an unwanted shadow on his bedroom windows. When he lost his footing and fell to the ground, crushed and broken, it had been assumed, by those who witnessed the fall, that the old man was dead. Yet two years later Stephen Baltimore was still alive, though paralyzed, and still giving orders from his wheelchair.

Scott himself never seemed troubled that his own wishes and desires were never considered. Indeed, the fact that he did not question was in itself a key of sorts to Scott himself, for while he thought of himself as free to lead his life as he chose, he actually lived as others chose for him. He was, in effect, the unsuspecting instrument of his family's overriding determination to dominate. He had barely been old enough to understand when his father had told him: "Scott, one day you will be President of the United States." He had discovered later that the same prophecy had been addressed to his two older brothers, and to the three younger ones, but that knowledge did not disturb him. He understood that one of Alfred Baltimore's seven sons must attain supremacy in his country so that the clan's ambitions might be realized. And he understood, too, that his life must necessarily be one long preparation for the exercise of power, so that he would be ready when the time came for him to assume that power. In case of failure or accident, there were his younger brothers, waiting like the runners in a relay race, ready to grasp the torch before it struck the ground.

This, too, had been part of Alfred Baltimore's plan. In order to increase the odds in favor of the family, he had insisted that his wife bear as many children as possible, and in fact, their union had been blessed with eleven offspring, eight boys and three girls. Five of the children had died—one girl, Susan, who had drowned at the age of twelve, and four boys. John had been carried off by polio at the age of eight, and Robert at fourteen, had killed himself, accidentally, while playing with a loaded rifle. And then there had been William and Lewis.

After the birth of their eleventh child, Virginia Baltimore, Alfred's wife, concluded that she had fulfilled her obligations. Thenceforth, she decided, she would divide her energies equally between her religion and her children's education. The multiple tragedies which had afflicted the family were, in her eyes, heaven-sent trials to strengthen her courage and determination. She was, in fact, a woman of steel, and she was certain that her children were of similar fiber. Very early in life, Scott and his brothers and sisters had learned from her that pain and suffering existed, and since they are part of the order of things, must be ignored if one is to rise above them. They had also learned at her knee that the human race consisted of two kinds of people: the members of the Baltimore clan and the others.

If the children needed proof of these dogmas, it could be found in their own father, Alfred Baltimore, who had been stricken with cancer of the throat. His resistance was such that, at his insistence, he was receiving cobalt treatments three times a week—a regimen that would have felled a healthy horse. He had also undergone an exploratory operation and bore a conspicuous scar on his throat, which he concealed by wearing unusually high shirt collars. For the past several months, his voice had been growing steadily weaker, and now it was necessary for a listener to hold his ear near Alfred's mouth in order to be able to decipher the meaning of those sounds which were never questions but always pronouncements or commands. When people instinctively raised their voices around him, Alfred informed them imperiously that while he might have trouble speaking, he was by no means deaf. All in all, Alfred's infirmity added to the mystery of the colossus with the steel-gray hair and steel-gray eyes. As one bent to listen, he seemed the repository of the great mysteries of life and death, even when his words were no more oracular than a simple comment on the weather.

He was a hard man, certainly, and a pitiless one. Yet with these qualities he combined an instinct for compromise which was the practical application of a favorite axiom he had borrowed from the second Roosevelt: "The best way to defeat an enemy is to make an ally of him." When Scott, at the age of twenty-five, had been elected to Congress—a success owing more to his father's willingness to spend millions than to his own qualifications and credentials— Alfred had enunciated another of his axioms: "The trick to being a successful politician is to look as little as possible like a politician." Scott had accepted his father's dictum as gospel and had applied himself with his customary assiduity to doing as he was told. In politics, his natural endowments were a great help. His tall, slender figure was that of a healthy college boy, and his smile, open and almost naïve, evoked the sympathies both of men, who interpreted it as a sign of innocence and good faith, and of women, who saw in it the appeal of a lost child asking to be mothered. Yet the same blue eyes which had captured the hearts of feminine voters in Scott's native state had been capable, when their owner was but fifteen, of scanning the financial pages of the New York *Times* and, in less than sixty seconds, of enunciating judgments of which men many years his senior would have been proud. Indeed, Scott, with the enthusiasm of youth, had been fond of lecturing his parents' guests—eminent men all, in politics and finance—on matters in their respective fields, until Alfred had found it necessary to admonish his son: "Never make a display of your abilities. If people think you are smarter than they, they will never trust you. Let others believe that they are able to influence you. Remember, the only way to be elected to high office is to seem a little stupid."

Part of the education imparted to Scott by his father had been of a moral nature, at least to the extent that it had taught the young man always to cover his actions with the cloak of morality, humanitarianism, or charity. "When it becomes necessary to eliminate someone," Alfred had instructed him, "you must give the impression that you are acting for the man's own good. If you want to fire someone who works for you, for example, explain that he is overqualified for the job and that he should try to find something more in keeping with the high order of his talents. And if you have to drive a competitor into bankruptcy, take over his business and explain to everyone that you're doing it to keep his personnel from being thrown out of work."

Scott, to his credit, was occasionally scandalized by his father's tactics, but his shock was theoretical rather than practical, a sort of emotional reaction which fed his self-satisfaction without affecting his actions, as though what was involved were the properties in a game of Monopoly rather than real industries and actual human beings. He realized that even in Monopoly, no one plays to lose. Yet his own ambitions lay in a direction other than his father's. His one true desire was to be a writer. This ambition was the only deviation his father and mother tolerated in him, rationalizing that a young man as brilliant as Scott was entitled to one weakness.

Scott glanced at his watch and then ordered the chauffeur to drive faster. It would never do to keep his mother waiting. Actually he was more than a little afraid of her. She had a way of looking at him when she was displeased that made him feel like a naughty six-year-old. How would she take the news? he wondered. Would her rigid Catholicism be able to accept the idea of his marrying a girl of the most impeccable social background but also of almost indecent beauty and considerable worldliness?

Scott himself sometimes found himself aghast at Peggy's blasé attitudes. It had not helped that he had gotten off on the wrong foot at the very beginning of their relationship, by being unable to get back to New York for the dinner interview he had promised her. His secretary's attempts to contact Peggy, first at home, then at the restaurant, had been unavailing. Two weeks later her article had appeared in *Bazaar*, and Scott had been astonished at her ability to strike so close to the truth on the basis of a single conversation with him. He had dropped her a note of congratulations on the piece but had not heard a word in return. Six months had passed before they met again, this time at the Washington home of mutual friends, John and Monica Feydin. The encounter was marked by a singular coldness on Peggy's part. Scott had retaliated by launching into a heated political monologue, which Peggy had ignored totally. By then Monica Feydin, who fancied herself a peerless matchmaker, was in despair. She took heart, nonetheless, when Scott, before leaving, was seen to whisper something in Peggy's ear. She would have been overjoyed if she had been able to overhear their exchange:

SCOTT: The evening we were supposed to meet for dinner—I was stranded in St. Louis. I tried to reach you by telephone.

PEGGY: Really?

SCOTT: Scout's honor. Your article was great. I owe you an apology.

PEGGY: What form will it take?

SCOTT: A drink. Somewhere else, but immediately. OK? What do you say we both leave right now?

PEGGY (after a second's hesitation): All right. Meet me outside, at my car—the black Lincoln.

Ten minutes later Scott found the car. Peggy was there, but so was a young man who was holding her hand in a most possessive fashion. Later Scott discovered that he was a friend who had recognized Peggy's automobile and decided to surprise her when she came out. At the moment, however, Scott had been furious. He had strode off into the darkness, cursing the fickleness of women. Peggy had seen him but had done nothing to stop him.

They met again a year later, through the efforts of the tireless Monica. This time the shoe was on the other foot, and Peggy had broached the subject of their last encounter straight off.

"I think I owe you an explanation for last time," she began.

"Disraeli said, 'Never explain.' "

"I'm not Disraeli, and I'm still dying for that drink you offered me a year ago. I'll be waiting in my car—if the offer still holds good."

"I'll meet you there," Scott promised. But again he had not kept his promise. On his way out, he became embroiled in a political discussion, and an hour later, when he had managed to break away, Peggy's car was gone. A week later he called to apologize and was informed that Miss Nash-Belmont was in Europe for two weeks. Thereupon he made a large note on his desk calendar for precisely two weeks later: "Call Peggy Nash-Belmont." Despite the intensity of his political activities, it suddenly seemed imperative that he see her.

Peggy returned from Europe on schedule, and they met, not once but several times, at irregular intervals and always more or less spontaneously. Neither ever quite knew when the other might suddenly cancel a rendezvous. The first time they danced together, Scott noted with astonishment that politics was the furthest thing from his mind. Peggy's body against his stirred up desires and longings of a violence Scott had almost forgotten. They stood still on

the floor and stared at each other in silence. Then Peggy took him by
the hand and led him out of the room to her car. Still in silence,
she handed him the keys and slid into the passenger seat. As though
by prearrangement, Scott drove toward Park Avenue and Peggy's
apartment. Twice he felt her long fingers move gently along his
thigh.

Two hours later they lay side by side in bed. Not a word had
been spoken since their silent exchange on the dance floor. He
looked at her and smiled. Then he began to laugh: the laugh of a
virile man after a successful act of love. Peggy joined him, and they
laughed until the tears rolled down their cheeks. After a few minutes
they fell silent again. Then Peggy opened her mouth to speak, but
Scott touched his finger to her lips.

"Shhh," he cautioned. "Whoever speaks first is bound to say something silly."

"That's right." Peggy giggled. "You just did."

And so it had begun. Now Scott wanted above everything else to
marry Peggy, and Peggy dreamed of nothing but being married to
Scott.

The chauffeur interrupted Scott's thoughts. "Here we are, sir."

The automobile drew up before the portico of Virginia Baltimore's residence.

"Will you be long, sir?"

Scott reflected for a moment. How long would it take him to announce to a puritanical, principle-ridden mother that her son was
going to marry a woman from another world?

"Don't go away," he instructed the chauffeur. "I'm going to play
the Duke of Windsor. It shouldn't take more than fifteen minutes."

[14]

Socrates decided not to use his own car and instead had the doorman summon a taxi. He was embarrassed by his appearance as he waited outside the Pierre, wrapped in the cloak which partly concealed his pirate costume and the tricornered hat which he held under his arm. In his pocket was a black eyepatch, which he would don before making his entrance at the party. He offered a silent prayer of thanksgiving to his private gods as he climbed into the obscurity of a Yellow Cab and was whisked up Fifth Avenue. He glanced at the hack license attached to the dashboard and read the name "Israel Kafka." Several questions sprang into his mind, but he decided not to ask them. Nervously, he wondered if he would have the courage to approach Menelas. There was something about these great artists which intimidated him. How foolish, Socrates reminded himself. In his way, he was as great an artist as the best of them. . . .

The sound of the cabbie pushing the meter's flag up brought Socrates out of his reverie.

"Two fifty, buddy," Israel Kafka announced.

Socrates felt himself turn scarlet, as though his costume had fallen from his body, leaving him exposed and naked to the stares and whispers of all Manhattan. With an emotion approaching panic, he realized that he, Socrates Satrapoulos, had not a penny on him with which to pay his fare. He had his checkbook, of course, but nothing more.

He climbed out of the cab, stood on the sidewalk before the brilliantly lighted façade of the Bambilt residence, and thrust his hand into his pocket again, feeling desperately for the roll of bills which he was accustomed to carry. There was nothing. It was like a nightmare.

Then one of the Bambilt servants, stationed outside the door of the house, saw his dilemma and hastened to the curb to relieve his embarrassment. Socrates, instead of thanking the servant, glared at him in a fury, in which he was imitated by Israel Kafka, who had received no tip from the man.

Gus Bambilt's home was so jammed with flowers that it was impossible to discern the color of the walls. Roses, orchids, tulips, and lilies were everywhere, transforming the rooms into skillfully interrelated spaces of yellow, red, violet, white, orange, and dark blue.

Big Gus had conceived the idea that his home must be both the symbol and the crown of his achievements. The three stories of the vast building were topped by vegetation which Gus described, in all modesty, as a "hanging garden," but which was a veritable forest. In the center of this mid-Manhattan jungle was a mosaic-lined pool, a hundred feet in length, in which the water was maintained yearround at a temperature of 72 degrees. In cold weather, an immense plexiglass dome covered the pool, maintaining the illusion that one was swimming in the open air.

On the occasion of his divorce, Gus had had the idea—inspired by Nut, to be sure—of decorating the stories of his residence in accordance with the triple theme he had selected for the celebration: the sea (his fortune was based on offshore oil ventures in Alaskan waters), money (which he regarded as an end in itself), and love (which he boasted was the only master he tolerated). He was faithful to reality in the choice of these themes, at least to the extent that he did owe his fortune to the sea and that, although he was a slave to the dollar, he had been held in total bondage and then exploited by the succession of women who had married him.

The main floor, accordingly, was lined with aquariums containing countless living specimens of marine flora. The walls of the second floor were papered in reproductions of hundred-dollar bills. On the third floor the walls were covered by paintings reputed to represent love in its various manifestations. The only worthwhile canvas, a superb Fragonard, depicted a buxom woman playing, on her bed, with a dog which seemed bent on rape. One entire section had been reserved for photographs of Gus Bambilt's eleven wives, the eleventh being Lindy Nut herself. A twelfth frame had been added, empty except for a large, black question mark. Even Lindy Nut's threat of devoting a separate section to photographs of her three husbands had not been sufficient to dissuade Gus from this tasteless display.

All of Bambilt's guests arrived, as instructed, wrapped from head to foot in black cloaks. As each one threw off his or her cloak, there were cries of universal joy or surprise, according to the disguise chosen by the new arrival. Elderly tycoons were dressed in the jumpers and pompons of the French navy, while admirals arrived in the blouses and thirteen-button pants of American enlisted seamen. A fat blonde—Mrs. Firkin, of Firkin Steel—wore a headdress which resembled, however vaguely, the New York Stock Exchange. Many of the other women, all respected and respectable matrons, had succumbed to less obvious longings and were decked out as turn-of-the-century prostitutes, saloon girls, and call girls. One of them was wrapped in a sheet on which had been embroidered, in large figures, her telephone number.

None of Bambilt's female guests, for all their ingenuity, offered the slightest competition to Gus' own wife. For the occasion, Lindy Nut had chosen a costume which was unique and inimitable. Onto a floor-length dress of transparent midnight blue voile, a princely ransom of gold coins—authentic coins, but hollowed out so that Nut would not collapse under their weight—had been stitched. Nut's head was adorned with a tiara which was the envy and despair of every woman who saw it: a semicircle of seven diamonds, six of them weighing twenty carats, and one, the central jewel, weighing well over thirty. With every movement of her body, Lindy Nut's diamonds glistened like improbable stars, and her dress moved against her body like the waves of the sea, creating an illusion which enchanted even Gus. "My God," he exclaimed to his guests, "she's so beautiful that I must be out of my mind to divorce her!"

Socrates, in a state of mingled confusion and rage, made his way into the vestibule of Gus Bambilt's house, where a cluster of guests, all in costume, were milling about. Their masks and cloaks prevented Socrates from recognizing them, but he was certain that they knew perfectly well who he was and what he had just endured. For an instant, he was almost overcome by an urge to flee back to the safety of his suite at the Pierre. For Satrapoulos was not one of those men who pride themselves on never carrying a cent in their pockets. It was true that he was known the world over and that his face and his name alone were sufficient to crush anyone who had the temerity to present him with a bill. Yet the Greek never ventured from any of his many residences without at least two thousand dollars in cash on his person.

It was not that he needed cash. It was rather that the feel of paper money excited him, gave him self-confidence in his undertakings, whether in business or in love. He drew his strength from the feel of his money, and his hand was constantly in his pocket, caressing the roll of bills. Now it was as though he was naked, stripped not only of his clothing but of his power and his defenses against the world.

The feeling of impotence was stronger even than Socrates' will. He darted from the vestibule into the recesses of the lower floor of Bambilt's house, wandering from room to room until he found what he was searching for: a bathroom. He locked the door behind him and then removed a long strip of toilet tissue from its rack on the wall. He folded the paper carefully into a thick wad and placed it into the right-hand pocket of his pirate's trousers. He allowed his hand to linger over the paper, and a look of satisfaction crossed his face. It was silly, Socrates knew, but the thickness of the folded tissue was somehow reassuring. Now he felt ready to face the world.

Lindy Nut Bambilt was ecstatic over her find. She led Amore Dodino from room to room, presenting him to her friends who exclaimed in amazed admiration at his costume. He had come as Elsa Maxwell, or rather, he *was* Elsa Maxwell. Anyone could have padded himself, fore and aft, to the dimensions of the celebrated party giver, but no one else could have imitated so perfectly the waddle like a winded seal, the posture which indicated a precarious balance between the massive posterior and the equally mammoth bosom, the trembling wattles, the hound-dog eyes, or the contemptuous twist of the mouth. Several groups applauded openly when Dodino appeared, delighted at the opportunity to laugh at a person whom, in their hearts, they dreaded.

"My dear," Dodino/Maxwell was saying, "last night at the Windsors', the Duchess—"

There was a stir at the door, and a hush fell across the room. Dodino stopped. Like any experienced actor, he knew when someone was about to step on his lines. He looked toward the door and glimpsed something—something diaphanous, transparent, gelatinous. A monstrous spectacle before which the crowd parted respectfully, as though royalty had entered the room.

Dodino gasped. She was disguised as the Medusa, but he knew her instantly.

She stopped before him and pointed, "Who," she roared, "are you?"

"Elsa!" Dodino shrieked, throwing open his arms. "It's me, Amore! Dodino!"

Elsa Maxwell rushed toward him like a runaway locomotive, her mouth open to bless or to curse according to her whim. But Dodino cut her off. "Elsa, dearest! How lovely you look! How marvelous! So original!"

She was upon him now, her massive arms poised like boa constrictors in the air above Dodino's shoulders. He did not know if she wished to embrace him or to strangle him.

She embraced him. "Dear, dear Dodino," Elsa exclaimed. "Whoever are you disguised as? It's marvelous, of course, but I'm afraid I don't recognize—"

"Why, darling, I've come as a whale!"

"How original! How simply fabulous!" She took him by the arm. "Champagne always makes me thirsty," she bellowed as she led him toward the bar. "Let's have a drink and talk about old times."

The other guests looked at one another in disbelief. Was Maxwell serious, or was she playing a game of her own? The consensus was that she was, in fact, completely oblivious of the nature of Dodino's costume. The confirmation of this hypothesis appeared the following day in Miss Maxwell's column. After a glowing account of the Bambilt party, she concluded: "Despite the terrible tragedy which marred this superb gathering, the Bambilt evening was the most brilliant and exciting of the season."

"Oh, Gus! No!"

"Why not? My entire life is a prison." Gus, his face radiating an excitement undoubtedly heightened by alcohol, made a clumsy pirouette so that Peggy might admire his black-striped convict's costume, then seized a bottle of champagne from a passing waiter. "Here," he shouted, holding out the bottle to Peggy. "Drink! Let's all drink and forget our cares and sorrows."

Peggy took the bottle and swallowed, then threw it over her shoulder, Russian-style, shouting, "To your divorce!"

Gus burst into laughter, "Now," he said, "show me. Have you come as the sea, or as money, or as love?"

"The sea," Peggy answered, lowering her eyes demurely. She let her evening cape slip from her shoulders to reveal her glittering animal trainer's costume.

"An animal trainer? But that isn't related to the sea."

"Of course it is. I train mermaids."

Gus' laughter was joined by that of the other guests within earshot. Then the doors of the elevator opened, and more guests poured into the room. Among them were Menelas, Irene, and Herman Kallenberg.

"My friends! My friends!" Gus roared. "I'm sure you all know one another—or at least recognize one another."

There were embraces and kisses, the latter carefully aimed one inch from the recipient's cheek so as to spare her cosmetics the consequences of such effusiveness.

Gus beamed at Menelas. "But I don't see Mr.—" he began, then stopped himself. Even in his alcoholic haze, he recognized how grotesque it would have been to refer to Peter, Menelas' husband, secretary, manager, and impresario, as Mr. Menelas. He tried again. "I do not see Mr. Gonzales de Salvador."

"He is being punished," Menelas said loftily.

"Drinks! Drinks for everybody!" Gus roared.

The waiters hastened forward with trays of drinks.

"Now, my dear Olympia," Gus said jovially, "let me take your cape so that your splendor may be revealed!"

But Menelas had drawn back amost involuntarily, her face tense, her eyes riveted on Peggy.

"How are you, Miss Nash-Belmont?"

"Well, thank you. And you?"

Irene had removed her wrap to appear in the uniform of an admiral from the First World War. Kallenberg towered over her as Neptune, complete with flowing beard and a papier-mâché trident.

"Now I see," Gus shouted, "why they call you Bluebeard!" Too late, he realized that Kallenberg might not find his little joke amusing. "A bottle for Monsieur Kallenberg," he instructed a waiter, hoping to make amends. Then he shrugged. If Kallenberg was in a mood to take offense, then so much the worse for him. After all, Kallenberg needed Bambilt more than Bambilt needed Kallenberg.

Kallenberg, if he had taken umbrage, gave no sign as he bowed and kissed Menelas' hand.

"Come now, Olympia!" Gus urged. "Surely you don't intend to wear that cape all evening." Without waiting for her to reply, he reached for the cape. For a second, Menelas' eyes grew dark with anger, but she made no move to restrain Gus. He lifted the garment from her shoulders and immediately understood. Menelas stood revealed—costumed as an animal trainer. Gus glanced at Peggy with a helpless expression.

At that moment, Nut arrived and saw the crisis in the making. "Oh, Olympia!" she squealed. "What an absolutely sensational idea! You look simply *divine!*"

Menelas smiled icily.

"Imagine!" Nut continued. "Two animal trainers here tonight. With *you* here, my dear, the animals won't stand a chance. Peggy says she trains mermaids. What do *you* train?"

"Don't worry," Menelas said through clenched teeth. "I'll find someone."

The crowd of guests suddenly parted to reveal Socrates Satrapoulos in his pirate costume.

"Olympia," Nut plunged on in desperation, "surely you know your compatriot, Socrates Satrapoulos. Don't crack your whip at him, my dear. He is absolutely untamable!"

Socrates bowed, wincing from the pain of the saber's hilt pressing against his chest. He had no way of knowing that Menelas interpreted his grimace as an expression of boredom addressed to herself. She glared at him and brusquely withdrew her hand. Socrates, astonished at her obvious anger, moved back a step. Immediately, he felt a pair of hands clasped over his eyes.

"Guess who!" a female voice said.

"Irene, of course. Your perfume is a dead giveaway!"

They kissed, and Socrates stood back to admire her costume. "How marvelous you look, Captain."

"Admiral, if you don't mind."

"How like Socrates," Kallenberg interjected laughingly, "to try to demote you."

"But where is Helena?" Irene asked. "Where is my darling sister?"

Unwittingly, Kallenberg came to Satrapoulos' aid. "Socrates is smarter than I am," he explained. "He has the good sense to leave his wife at home, where she belongs."

"How long did it take you to grow that beard?" Socrates asked his brother-in-law, eager to turn the conversation away from Helena.

"About fifty seconds," Kallenberg answered. "Look!" He gently pulled the Neptune's beard from his face.

"A false god!" Socrates shouted.

"A true pirate!" Kallenberg responded.

"Long live the Greeks!" Gus called. "Everybody drink up!"

Raph Dun bowed ceremoniously before Amore Dodino. "Good evening, *chère madame*."

Amore, in an animated conversation with Menelas, turned his head and gave Raph his most disdainful look. "Well, what have we here? The determined virgin, no less. Have you come to express your regrets for last evening?"

Raph, embarrassed, pretended not to understand. He clapped him heartily on the back and said, "Aren't you going to present me to this divine artist?"

"Don't get your hopes up, dearie," Dodino murmured. "You're not her type." Then he turned to Menelas and, in English, explained: "This man wants me to introduce him to you."

Menelas' eyes swept over Raph. He was one of the few guests in evening dress. (Tailors traditionally are willing to extend credit, but costumers require cash on the barrelhead.) She smiled faintly and turned back to Dodino. "I do not recognize your friend's costume."

"He is disguised as a gentleman, my dear. Do you find him convincing?"

Raph's answer was drowned out by a shout: "Olympia, *carissima!* How marvelous you look!" A man dressed as a crab rushed toward the artist, claws flailing the air.

"Edwin." Menelas laughed. "Edwin Edwards! What an extraordinary costume."

Edwards was not only Menelas' stockbroker, but her financial advisor and occasional host as well. He maintained a splendid residence at Antibes, where he himself scarcely ever stayed but which he generously placed at the disposal of Menelas and her husband between concerts.

"Have you been to France this year?" Menelas inquired.

"No, I've been so busy, unfortunately—"

"What a pity. Such a lovely house, and you're letting it go to waste."

"Not to waste, no. As always, it is at your disposal, for as long as you choose to honor it with your presence."

"Why don't you sell it to me?"

"Dear heart, you know perfectly well that it's not for sale."

Menelas glanced over her shoulder as the crab was speaking and saw Satrapoulos standing directly behind her, obviously listening to every word. Her impression was that he was a small man, too small, and grotesque, too, in his operetta costume. Yet, there was something about him that made it difficult for her to look away, as though she, the animal trainer, had been hypnotized by one of her animals. The Greek, for his part, returned her stare with an intensity which reflected his awareness of the current which crackled between them. Their eyes were locked for what seemed an eternity, but what was in reality no more than two seconds. It was sufficient for them to feel that though they had barely met, each of them knew all, past, present, and future, that was to be known about each other.

Satrapoulos stepped toward Edwards and shook him vigorously by the right claw. "Everything is for sale, Edwin," he said. "Since everything has its price."

"Everything except my house," Edwin protested.

"Everything, including your house," the Greek insisted.

"Well, really—"

"Listen, Edwin. How much is your house worth?"

"I tell you—"

"How much?"

"Since you insist, I paid—let's see, with the improvements I've made—"

"How much?"

"At the very least, I'd say a million dollars."

"Would you sell it at that price?"

"Of course not!"

The Greek held up his hand. "I thought not. Then shall we say two million dollars?"

Edwin was completely taken aback. He had paid five hundred thousand for the property, and it was now actually worth about seven hundred and fifty thousand, and this mad Greek—if he was serious —was offering him two million. On the other hand, owning the property conferred a certain amount of prestige—

"My dear fellow," Edwin stammered. "Really, I—"

Satrapoulos' face was set in an expression which conveyed that he had been quite serious in his offer and that it would remain open only for a few seconds longer. He wanted a simple yes or no, and he wanted it immediately.

Socrates hastened to confirm Edwin's interpretation of his look. "Well?" he asked. "Yes? No? Which is it?"

"Well, yes."

Satrapoulos removed a checkbook from the pocket of his pirate's blouse, then searched vainly through the other pockets for a pen. He turned to the small crowd which had gathered to witness the drama. "Does anyone have a pen?"

Raph Dun held out a pen. Satrapoulos took it and placed his foot upon a chair. Using his knee as a desk, as the crowd gathered closer in unabashed curiosity, he wrote "Two million and 00/100" and the figures representing the same amount. Then, with a barely discernible flourish of triumph, he signed his name to the check and dated it.

"Edwin, to whom shall I make it out?"

"Good heavens—"

"Here, you can fill it in yourself. I'll have an officer of my American subsidiary call at your office tomorrow with a sale contract for you to sign."

The stupefied crab took the check with the tip of his right claw.

"Very good." Socrates laughed. "Offer and acceptance. A meeting of the minds. We have a deal." He held out his hand to Edwards.

The stockbroker took it in his claw and shook it with a fervor which betrayed his complete, unspeakable delight with the sale just concluded.

Socrates, his confidence in himself now restored, leaned toward Menelas and addressed her in Greek. "Obviously, madame, I have no intention of keeping this house for myself. I have bought it because I could not bear to see you deprived of the pleasure of possessing it. Our friend is not a seller of houses. But I am. How much will you offer me for it?"

Before Menelas could recover from her surprise, Satrapoulos set his own price. "Shall we say one dollar?"

Menelas was still incapable of speech.

"You see," the Greek continued, "there is nothing in this world that cannot be bought. Nothing, that is, except genius, and beauty." He bowed. "If you will be so kind, may we have a few words together a little later?"

Menelas nodded dumbly.

Socrates bowed again and turned to go. As he did so, he felt a hand on his arm.

"Excuse me," Raph Dun said. "I wonder—are you through with my pen?" Raph hated himself for having asked, but it was a magnificent gold Parker, the gift of a lady. . . . For all of six years, ever since having served as Kallenberg's accomplice in his attempt to ruin Satrapoulos, Raph had avoided the Greek like the plague. Now, however, the fat was in the fire, and Raph found himself face to face with the man who had every reason to be his enemy and all sorts of means at his disposal to destroy him.

The Greek turned, smiling, "Ah. You are Mr. Dun, are you not? My name is Satrapoulos. I don't believe we've had the pleasure of meeting before, though I am a devoted admirer of your articles. Obviously, there are too many of us for you to know us all."

Raph bowed in confused acknowledgement.

"I am grateful for the use of the pen which has written so many marvelous things," Satrapoulos said, holding out the Parker.

Raph took it. "With your permission," he said, "I'd like to write about what you've just done—"

"Indeed you may. Especially since the transaction actually took place. That is the function of the journalist, isn't it? To relate events as they actually occurred?"

Raph felt his face grow warm.

"Well, Mr. Dun, now that we have met, I hope that we will become friends," Satrapoulos said, smiling pleasantly and having already concluded that it would be more amusing to buy this vicious nobody than to destroy him. "Perhaps you would consider joining my friends and myself aboard my yacht for our next cruise."

Before Raph could answer, Lindy Nut's voice interrupted them: "Socrates!"

She took his arm and drew him away from Dun.

"Come on, now. You absolutely must meet Scott Baltimore. Peggy! Peggy! I've found him!"

Peggy turned. With her, Socrates saw a tall young man with startlingly blue eyes. He, like Dun, was wearing evening clothes. He held out his hand to Satrapoulos, and his smile was blinding. "I knew I shouldn't have checked my sword at the door," he said.

Satrapoulos laughed and shook Scott's hand. He sensed immediately that this young man would go far. He had that indefinable something which some call style.

"Well, what do you think of him?" Lindy Nut asked Socrates. Then, without waiting for a reply, she turned to Peggy. "Don't squeeze his arm so hard. These big ones bruise easily, you know." Then she was gone, shouting that she must find Gus.

"I have heard a great deal about you," the Greek began.

"Not nearly as much as I've heard about you," Scott countered.

"It's not every day that one lone man faces down the United States government."

"From what I hear, Mr. Baltimore, the government had better stop worrying about me and start worrying about you."

"I'm afraid that you've been listening to Peggy's stories."

What a striking couple they make, Socrates thought—beautiful, young, rich, ambitious, intelligent. He banished a twinge of envy at their good fortune.

"This crowd is impossible," Peggy interrupted. "Let's try to find a quiet corner somewhere so that we can talk." She had already spied one, and she led the men toward it without waiting for their acquiescence.

"Are you in New York on business?" Scott asked.

"Not at all. I'm here to celebrate the divorce of my good friends, the Bambilts."

"Indeed?" Peggy said skeptically, "I'll be surprised if you aren't in the middle of some kind of deal. You're like Scott. You never rest for a minute."

The Greek gave an enigmatic smile.

"You see?" Peggy said, triumphant. "Didn't I tell you? What are you doing, buying or selling?"

"A bit of both."

"What?"

"Some property on the French Riviera."

"Who's buying it?"

"That's a secret," Socrates answered solemnly.

"Well, then, who sold it to you?"

Socrates laughed, delighted at Peggy's interrogation.

"That's a secret, too, I suppose," she went on. "Then at least tell me if it was expensive."

"I've just signed a check for two million dollars."

"Not really?"

"Really."

"I'll bet that you're going to sell it for four million."

"Not quite four million, no."

"How much? Tell me."

The Greek hesitated, to heighten the effect of what he was about to say. "For one dollar," he said softly.

Scott and Peggy exchanged glances.

"Is that the truth?" Peggy asked, her eyes round with disbelief.

"My word of honor."

Peggy burst into laughter. "Oh, Scott," she gasped. "Isn't he marvelous? Didn't I tell you?"

"Everybody out to the pool!" Gus' voice rose above the uproar of his guests' conversations. "Everyone out to the pool! We have a surprise for you!"

There was a murmur from the crowd, then a surge outside to the illuminated pool. Gus was already there, waiting for them, standing on a low podium which had been placed before a double screen. Everyone crowded around him, laughing and shouting. The platform, added to Gus' own height, gave him the appearance of a giant, and he towered over his guests.

"All right!" Gus shouted, and, from nowhere, drew two six-shooters. He waved the old-fashioned pistols at his guests and roared, "Nobody move! This is a stickup—I mean, a divorce!"

There was a gale of laughter, the laughter of men who have had too much to drink and the shrieks of excited women.

"My friends! My friends!" The laughter subsided so that Gus could continue. "My friends, three years of total happiness, or almost total happiness, is more than one man, or one woman, can bear. Now, some of you are wondering if Lindy and I have been so happy, why are we getting divorced? I'll tell you why. We've been so all-fired happy that it's either get divorced or go crazy. And that's why we're getting the divorce—before it's too late."

Suddenly, the opening measures of "The Star-Spangled Banner" blared out, and spotlights illuminated an orchestra whose presence had gone heretofore unnoticed.

There was a roll of drums, and Gus shouted, "Lindy and I will now divulge to you, our dearest friends, the secret of our successful marriage!" He paused and shielding his eyes with his hands, searched the crowd clustered around the podium. "Nut? Nut? Where are you?"

"She's here," someone shouted, and Nut made her way through her guests and mounted the podium.

"All right," Gus went on. "Our secret formula is this: when things are going well, keep your mouth shut. When things are going badly, let the other person know about it. Now for the real secret. How do you let him or her know? Like this!"

With a melodramatic gesture, Gus threw open the double screen behind him. Behind the panels were two life-size photographs, one of Gus himself, wearing a suit; the other of Lindy Nut, dressed in a floor-length gown. On each photograph, three red circles had been painted: the first, on the forehead; the second, over the heart; and the third, over the genitals.

"Each circle represents a target," Gus explained. "I want you all to participate in our favorite game. It's called psychodrama. Now, Nut and I are going to show you how we settle our domestic differences."

He drew back a dark curtain beside the photographs to reveal a rack containing two dozen .22 rifles.

"Now, watch!" Gus took one of the rifles, handed it to Lindy Nut, and took another for himself. Then, taking his eleventh wife by her hand, he led her from the platform and into the crowd of their guests, who drew aside to let them pass.

Gus and Nut turned and faced the photographs of themselves. "Ready?" Gus shouted. "Fire!"

Two shots rang out in the sudden silence. On Gus' photograph, a hole appeared in the neck. A large drop of red liquid oozed out of the hole and dripped slowly downward. On Lindy Nut's photograph, a similar wound was visible in the right shoulder.

"You've both missed!" Kallenberg shouted.

"All right!" Gus replied. "Now it's your turn. You try to do better. Everyone gets one shot—and the one who hits the center of one of the targets will receive a very special prize! Fire at will!"

There was a moment's hesitation. No one knew quite what to do. Then a woman's voice called out. "Here, let me be first!" It was Mrs. Firkin—Pittsburgh steel—an obese woman who had never quite forgiven the world for her size. She grabbed the rifle from Bambilt's hand, swung it to her shoulder with a surprisingly practiced motion, and fired. Another hole appeared on Lindy Nut's photograph not far from the center of the red circle on her head.

Mrs. Firkin had broken the ice and set the tone of the game. Now everyone clamored for rifles, and shots began to ring out from all sides as the orchestra launched into the "Intermezzo" from *Cavalleria Rusticana.*

"Go ahead!" Gus' voice rose above the din. "It's only catsup!"

Off to one side, Kallenberg watched the display of vicarious violence with obvious contempt. He noted that though many of the shots struck close to the centers of the targets, not a single bullet hit either of the two photographs below the waist. Whether the shots were fired at Lindy Nut—almost all by women—or at Gus Bambilt, they seemed, by some silent agreement, to be concentrated in the area of the head and chest.

Finally, someone handed Kallenberg a rifle. Without hesitation, he raised the weapon to his shoulder and fired, striking the exact center of the red circle over Lindy Nut's genitals.

Such a roar of laughter arose from the crowd that it was several seconds before Kallenberg could hear the shouts of "He's won! Kallenberg has won the prize!"

Gus mounted the podium again. "Quiet, please!" The roar subsided gradually. "Has everyone had a shot?" he called.

There was a pause, then someone—a woman—shouted, "Satrapoulos! Satrapoulos hasn't fired." Others took up the cry.

Everyone looked at Satrapoulos. Socrates' anger at having become the center of interest in this idiotic game was mingled with a feeling of loathing for the drunken fools and their brainless wives who were shouting his name and of pity for Lindy Nut, who deserved better at the hands of Gus.

His anger was aggravated by the fact that the woman who had drawn attention to him was his own sister-in-law, Irene. He swore silently that the bitch would pay for her insolence.

"My friend," Gus said, holding out a rifle to Socrates, "you are depriving us of the pleasure of admiring your aim."

Socrates stared icily at his host, then pushed the proffered rifle away with his hand. He turned and walked to a trellis nearby and plucked one of Bambilt's famous roses—a perfect white blossom. He climbed the podium, removed his hat, and detached the pin which held the skull-and-crossbones emblem to it. Then he carefully pinned the rose onto Lindy Nut's catsup-smeared photograph. His gesture was followed by wild applause.

"At last!" Gus shouted above the tumult. "A true gentleman!" He gestured toward the orchestra, and the strains of "Over the Waves" drifted through the garden. "The party's far from over!" Gus called. "The grand prize of the evening is about to arrive!" He spread his hands before him, and as though by magic, searchlights swept the sky overhead. Weaving, stumbling, he made his way through his guests toward the pool. He reached the diving board and, to the shouted encouragement of his friends, he began to climb. At the ten-foot board, he paused for a moment, then continued his climb toward the top of the ladder and the twenty-foot board. He hauled himself upright on the narrow, vibrating plank and, miraculously, teetered out to the very edge.

"Gus, no! Come down!" Nut's terrified voice rose from below.

Gus looked down, and at that instant he was filled with the certainty that he was no longer Gus Bambilt. He was a god: omnipotent, eternal, immutable. Below him stood the most powerful people in existence, the most brilliant flowers of international society. And they were his. To each upturned face he could assign not only a name, but a number—the number of millions that the owner of the face possessed. At his feet were millions of dollars, the most beautiful women in the world, the most important men. And he, the god, dominated them all.

"Come down, Gus!"

It was a prayer of supplication addressed to the heavens, and the divinity silhouetted against the sky, drunk first on alcohol and then from the sense of power which filled his heart to overflowing, chose to ignore it. The days of creation were not yet six. He raised his hand slowly, gestured toward the sky, and lights appeared. Then there was a noise like thunder, and a helicopter appeared out of the darkness, descending majestically into the garden as the guests scattered. It landed gently at the far end of the terrace.

Servants bearing torches hurried toward the aircraft while others appeared with a long swath of scarlet carpet which they laid quickly to the door of the helicopter. Then, the door opened, and a girl appeared. She was a statuesque blonde, nude except for three small ribbons attached to the nipples of her perfect breasts and to her blond pubic hair. Gracefully, the young woman walked to the podium and unfurled a banner which read: "I am the grand prize. Who won me?"

"Kallenberg! Kallenberg!" the guests shouted almost as one.

"My friends!" Gus commanded from his perch on the diving board. The guests could not tear their eyes from the grand prize to look at their host twenty feet above the pool.

"Go claim your prize!" a woman's voice urged Kallenberg, and anonymous hands propelled him toward the podium.

Irene grabbed her husband's arm. "Herman," she hissed, her face white with rage, "don't be a fool. You'll make an ass of yourself!"

Herman thrust her aside brutally and strode toward the podium and his prize.

"Look at me!" Gus' voice came painfully from overhead. "Watch! And remember, I'm seventy-two years old!"

"No, Gus! Don't!" Lindy Nut's voice cracked with panic.

The post-factum accounts of what happened next varied as to the details, but all eyewitnesses agreed that two phenomena occurred immediately and simultaneously. Gus Bambilt executed a flawless swandive from the twenty-foot board, and Irene threw herself, eyes blazing and fingernails clawing, upon Herman Kallenberg's prize. As Kallenberg, his beard askew and his trident lost, attempted to separate the squalling, scratching, kicking women, two men, one garbed as Cupid, complete with quiver of arrows, the other dressed as a thousand-dollar bill, dived into the pool after Gustave Bambilt.

Socrates moved quickly to Lindy Nut's side at the edge of the pool. He was in time to see Cupid and the thousand-dollar bill lift Gus' inert body out of the water. Three of the most eminent medical practitioners in America emerged from among the guests: a cardiologist, a brain surgeon, and a specialist in vascular disorders. They felt and probed and listened and nodded sagely, emitting the hums and grunts which are incantations of the medical profession, but still, Gus Bambilt's body lay motionless on the Italian mosaic tile which surrounded the pool.

"Drowned," said the cardiologist.

"An embolism," protested the surgeon.

"We've done all we can," affirmed the specialist in vascular disorders. "There is nothing more to do."

In the ghastly silence which followed these solemn pronouncements, Lindy Nut fell into Socrates' arms, her head pressed against his chest. What if she becomes hysterical? the Greek asked himself in alarm. Then he heard Lindy Nut's soft voice in his ear: "You've got to help me, Socrates. Tell me, right this minute, am I legally a widow or a divorcée?"

Satrapoulos' surprise was brief. Her question was indeed an important one. On the answer rode the fate of tens of millions of dollars and that of Lindy Nut herself.

[15]

"It's been ten years. Did you know that?"

"I know it."

"How has it ever lasted so long?"

Mark clenched his teeth. He was unable to understand his own motives, to say nothing of Helena's.

"Well, time flies so quickly—"

"It's not time that has flown," Helena said vehemently. "It's my life! How much longer do you think I can go on? I haven't the slightest feeling left for him. I see him not more than ten times a year, and even then when we meet, he talks about business. And you. What have you been doing for ten years? When are you going to be man enough to assume your responsibilities?"

Mark winced. The script was familiar to him in all its details and all its possible variations. When Helena began talking about his "responsibilities," it was best for him to pretend not to hear.

She had telephoned him a month after the Bambilt party and asked him to meet her in the rue de la Faisanderie. It had taken no little doing to escape Isabelle's surveillance, but he had come. After all, it was only for a few hours. Helena was en route to Majorca, where Satrapoulos' yacht, the *Pegasus*, was waiting to take on her passengers.

"Mark?"

"Yes?"

"If I got free of him, would you marry me?"

241

Careful, Mark warned himself. We're on thin ice here. To Helena, he said, "You know that I would."

"What about your wife?"

"As soon as you were free again, I'd get a divorce."

"What if she won't let you go?"

"Then I will simply let *her* go," Mark answered, thrusting his chin forward in a gesture of virile defiance. There were times when he believed his own fables.

"Really?"

"Yes, really."

"Will you swear it? Will you swear it on everything that you hold dearest in the world?"

"If you wish. I swear it on your head."

"Not on mine. On yours."

Mark was superstitious, and he made the mistake of not answering immediately.

"Well?" Lena insisted.

"Listen, this is silly! You know I don't like to take these ridiculous oaths. I've given you my word. Isn't that enough?"

"Swear."

"All right, all right. I swear it."

"On your head? Say it. Say: 'I swear it on my head.'"

Mark, trapped, acquiesced wearily. "I swear it on my head."

"Oh, my dearest love!" Helena threw herself upon Mark and covered him with kisses. "You swore, Mark. You swore! Now I'm not afraid anymore. Now I know that you really love me. And I know precisely what I'm going to do."

Mark, thinking only of a way of escaping from the apartment, heard Helena's words without really listening to them. Then their meaning registered in his mind and struck him with the force of a blow to the stomach.

"Helena," he said in alarm, "you don't know what you're saying! What do you intend to do?"

"Be quiet," Helena answered dreamily. "You'll see."

The *Pegasus* lay at anchor at Palma de Mallorca, glistening white in the sun, her brass sparkling. Viewed from shore, she was every inch the model of what a yacht should be. Aboard, Socrates Satrapoulos could hardly believe his eyes. In the passageway outside his suite, he had found a—a turd. It was the only proper word to describe it. It lay there on the polished deck, as incongruous as a rat floating in a bowl of milk.

"Nicholas!" Satrapoulos called for the steward. "Nicholas!"

Within seconds, Nicholas appeared on the stairwell and approached his employer in fear and trembling. Every member of the crew, from the chambermaids to the dishwashers, had battened down their emotional hatches for stormy weather, for the past few days their employer had been in a state of continuous, unrelenting rage. For seven days now the *Pegasus* had been riding at anchor, awaiting the arrival of Menelas and her husband from Venice. Almost hourly, Satrapoulos' radioman was in contact with the artist's pilot, and almost hourly, the pilot was obliged to report that "Monsieur and Madame Menelas are not yet ready to leave." It added considerably to Socrates' irritation that the pilot was unable to grasp the fact that Menelas had taken her husband's name, and not vice versa. When the *Pegasus'* radioman had referred to the couple as Monsieur and Madame Gonzales de Salvador, the pilot had pretended utter ignorance of such beings.

Satrapoulos, as the crew had remarked among themselves, had good reason to be on tenterhooks. The guests he had assembled aboard for the cruise constituted a highly volatile mixture. There was the American widow who had arrived a few days ago and who was, as every sailor knew, their employer's former mistress. Madame Helena had come aboard the same day, and the meeting between the two women had been notably cool. It was a miracle, as the chef remarked to his first assistant, that the Deemount woman had chosen not to accept Satrapoulos' invitation, pleading a prior commitment to Nassau. Obviously, she had brains enough to know that a tempest was brewing. Still, it was strange. Madame Helena had given the crew ample opportunity to observe her jealous rages in the past, yet the whole world, including the crew, knew perfectly well that she had a lover of her own stashed away in Paris. Now, with this American woman aboard, as well as Madame Helena—well, it would be an interesting cruise.

"Nicholas!" Satrapoulos roared. "Come here! Look at this!"

He took the steward by the arm and dragged him to the proper spot in the passageway. "What is this?"

Nicholas leaned over with an air of astonished curiosity.

"This, sir?" he asked, pointing.

"Yes, that!"

"Well, sir, it looks like shit."

"Shit! Shit, you say? What is shit doing here in the middle of the passageway?"

"I don't know, sir. I didn't do it."

"By God!" Socrates swore. "That is all this boat needs, for you to go around shitting on the deck!"

Nicholas remained silent.

"Tell me," Socrates went on, "what do I pay you for?"

"To keep this boat clean, sir."

"So?"

"Well, it wasn't there a few minutes ago."

"Liar! Look at it! It's at least three days old!"

"It's Herman, sir."

There were three divinities aboard the *Pegasus:* the Greek himself, Captain Kirillis, and Herman, Satrapoulos' poodle. Herman was a celebrity of sorts, having sunk his teeth into the legs of the most famous men and women of the twentieth century. Unaffected by fame, he was innocent of snobbery of any kind, and he made no distinction between the white-clad legs of the busboys in the dining room, the pants of eminent statesmen, the shapely contours of Hollywood's greatest stars, and the crocodile shoes of international financiers. He was unpredictable, temperamental, sometimes vicious, and universally feared. Socrates adored him. Herman slept at the foot of his bed and allowed no one to approach his master. Moreover, it was delightful to be able to call him Herman, and Socrates took pleasure in speaking the dog's name and then imagining that it was Herman Kallenberg who gamboled joyfully at the sound of his master's voice.

"Nicholas, clean this up immediately!"

Nicholas bent down and picked up Herman's droppings with his bare hands. "I need a rag," he muttered, and taking his handkerchief from his pocket, he began wiping the deck briskly with one hand while gingerly holding the turd in the other.

The Greek shook his head wearily and turned to go as Helena appeared in the door of her cabin. "What's happened?" she asked. "Why are you shouting?"

"This boat is full of shit!" Socrates snapped. "That's what's happened."

Helena reflected for a moment. "I'm not surprised," she said softly. "Like objects attract." Then she slammed the door.

* * *

Lieutenant Stavenos burst into Captain Kirillis' cabin like a bomb. "The siren, Captain! The siren!"

Kirillis had been instructed to give three blasts of the siren when Menelas came aboard. This, he knew, was a measure of the esteem in which Satrapoulos held her. The only other guest to be so greeted had been Lord Eaglebond, and then only because he had once been Prime Minister. As far as Stan Pickman was concerned, his Hollywood luster as one of the screen's great swashbuckling lovers meant little aboard the *Pegasus*. He had not been accorded a single blast. Everyone below decks had agreed that this was as it should be. Pickman was a great disappointment. True, he was handsome as a god, but that was the extent of any resemblance to the characters he portrayed. He was a businessman like the rest of them, a quiet man who put his money into cattle. He always went to bed before midnight, and never with anyone but his own wife.

"The siren? What about it?"

"She's here, Captain!"

"Are you certain?"

"Captain, she's already on the gangplank!"

"Oh, God! Quick, get everyone up on deck." Kirillis toyed with the idea of having a few words with the radioman concerning his duties but decided to postpone that pleasure. At the moment his place was up on deck.

Menelas' sojourn aboard the *Pegasus*, if the truth be known, did not begin auspiciously. She had barely set foot on deck when Herman, disturbed by the siren, threw himself at the artist and, with obvious determination, began to tear at the leg of her pants suit. Satrapoulos rushed forward and began trying to kick Herman away —or rather, pretending to do so, for he could not bring himself actually to hurt the animal. Two sailors who tried to intervene were promptly bitten. Finally, with much screaming and barking, Herman was separated from his prey and carried below, leaving Menelas, a ghastly smile frozen on her face, standing at the head of the gangplank in her shredded pants.

Satrapoulos bowed. "My dear," he said smoothly, "poodles are notoriously jealous of tigers."

Menelas' death's-head smile remained unchanged as Lindy Nut embraced her and as Helena, while the sailors took Menelas' baggage to her cabin, greeted her more formally. "I am delighted to welcome you aboard my boat," she said, pointing out, by her use of the possessive pronoun, that she, and no other, was mistress on the *Pegasus*.

Pickman kissed Olympia's hand, and Lord Eaglebond greeted her with elaborate compliments, which Menelas returned in kind. They had long been mutual admirers and seemed truly pleased to find themselves as guests together. Socrates beamed at everyone, then turned to Kirillis. "Let's get under way, Captain!"

"Yes, sir." Kirillis saluted smartly.

The party turned from the gangplank as the grating of the anchor chain combined with the muted throb of the engines to indicate that the *Pegasus* was, at long last, coming to life. A detail of seamen moved to the railing to raise the gangplank. Then, from over the side, came the sound of a man's voice, shouting. Everyone stopped. The shouting continued, louder now, the shouter drawing upon his knowledge of several languages to curse the *Pegasus* and her crew in terms which elicited the admiration of even the most experienced of the yacht's hands.

Satrapoulos bit his lip. "Belay that order!" he called.

"Belay that order!" Kirillis roared.

The Greek turned to Menelas. "Dear friend, please excuse me for a moment. I must welcome your husband aboard."

Menelas laughed loudly. "Good God! Poor Peter! I forgot he was with me."

It was midnight aboard the *Pegasus*. The yacht was in darkness except for the four dozen candle flames flickering above the massive gold candelabra. In the soft light, the faces of Socrates' guests, as that of Socrates himself, were cleansed of lines and wrinkles. As though in keeping with the spirit of this ephemeral rejuvenation, dinner had been perfect: the food superb, and the band of gypsy players brought aboard for the occasion romantic in their choice of selections.

There had been much drinking during the early-evening hours. The waiters had been instructed to see that no glass was ever empty. And at dinner there had been champagne and whiskey for the apéritif, Polish vodka with the caviar, a splendid bordeaux with the lobster and turbot, and then champagne once more.

Before dinner, Socrates had allowed his guests to vote on a question of some delicacy: whether or not to dress. The women in the party had expressed themselves unequivocally: "This is a vacation! Let's not dress." Thereupon they had rushed to their cabins to dig out their most elegant little frocks from Dior and Givenchy. In the matter of jewelry, they had showed more restraint, and the gems they wore around Socrates' vast, round dinner table were notable not so much for their quantity as for their size and value. Helena, an acknowledged expert at such games, had confined herself to a single diamond suspended from her neck on a thin platinum chain. Compared to this stone of some fifty carats, Menelas' river of smaller diamonds was almost vulgar, though, as Helena was willing to concede, not altogether unimpressive. Lindy Nut's turquoise earrings were magnificent but, like all things received from the late Gus Bambilt, barely within the bounds of good taste. Alongside such splendors, Nancy Pickman's cincture of worked gold and Lady Eaglebond's miserable little brooch of tarnished silver seemed scarcely worth noticing. And as for that horrid gray serge rag with which the Eaglebond woman had covered herself—

"What would you think of glazed oranges and lemons for dessert?" Socrates asked. "My chef is a positive genius with fruit."

In their sated condition, Satrapoulos' guests would not have noticed if they had been served pea soup for dessert. In any case, their assent was not necessary, for the waiters were already placing the glazed fruit before them as Socrates watched with peculiar intensity. This was the moment he most enjoyed.

Nancy Pickman gave a squeal of astonishment. Everyone turned to her, and Socrates carefully composed his features in an expression of surprise. Nancy reached into her lemon and drew out a ring of magnificent diamonds. She held it up, turned it in the candlelight, her mouth hanging open, too disconcerted to speak. Immediately the other ladies of the party cut open their dessert and, with cries of joy, extracted the treasures concealed within: a topaz bracelet for Lady Eaglebond, diamond earrings for Helena, a pendant of pearls for Nut, and a ruby brooch for Menelas.

Lord Eaglebond applauded, and Peter Gonzales de Salvador followed suit, though in a fury that any man other than himself would dare offer his wife jewelry. Stan Pickman nodded and smiled the smile that had made him the idol of two continents. And the gypsies, flabbergasted at what they had seen, struck up a czardas. Lady Eaglebond, in a rare show of spontaneity, threw her arms around Socrates' neck and kissed him resoundingly. Lindy Nut half rose from her chair to do the same, but then she felt Helena's eyes on her and resumed her seat.

"I propose a toast to our host and hostess," Lord Eaglebond declaimed. He turned to Helena. "Happy the man who can complement the extraordinary beauty of his wife," he said, slurring his words noticeably.

There were expressions of gratitude from all sides as Socrates, beaming, blushed modestly and, in his turn, thanked his guests for the pleasure of their company.

"Madame," Eaglebond now addressed Menelas, "it has been an incomparable evening. It lacks only one thing to make it perfect: Chopin, as only you can interpret him."

Menelas, as the whole world knew, never played except before a vast audience and never without having received an astronomical fee, invariably paid in advance.

"How I would love to play," Menelas exclaimed. "Unfortunately, I have no instrument here."

"Oh, come on," Lindy Nut teased, "would you really play if you had a piano?"

"Of course! With great pleasure!"

Peter shrugged. He alone knew the hours of pleading that it took to extract a few notes from his wife's accomplished fingers, even when it was a matter of meeting her contractual obligations.

"I would never have dared ask such a favor," Socrates interjected.

Helena looked at her husband in barely concealed astonishment. Socrates loathed music in any form. And he particularly loathed classical music. He possessed the most uncompromisingly wooden ear of anyone she had ever encountered.

"How unfortunate that I have no piano," Menelas said softly, smiling at Socrates in a way calculated to engage both Helena and Peter. "Nothing would have given me greater pleasure. . . ."

Socrates raised his hand and gestured to a steward. The man disappeared, and a few moments later a deep rumble was heard. It grew louder, like the sound of an approaching storm. Several crewmen appeared, carrying lighted candelabra. They were followed by others, pulling and pushing at an enormous concert grand piano.

Slowly, Menelas rose from her chair and moved toward the instrument. Her eyes widened in surprise. It was not a Pleyel, or a Rippen, or a Bentley, or a Gaveau, or a Schimmel, or an Erard, or a Schindler. It was a Bechstein. A true Bechstein.

Her hands fluttered over the keys, and at the first sound the company, crew as well as guests, was transfixed. There was no sound, no movement among them as the strains of the great Waltz in G-flat Major rose in the darkness and blended with the faint murmur of the sea.

Lord Eaglebond's eyes were closed in ecstasy and—the supreme compliment—he was no longer sucking on his cigar. Helena and Lindy Nut were both watching Socrates: the former in fury; the latter in consternation mingled with jealousy.

Chopin, indeed waltzes in any key, meant nothing to Socrates. On those few occasions when someone around him had mentioned the name of Chopin, Socrates had had to restrain himself from asking, "How much does he want?" But Chopin in the hands of Olympia Menelas was something else again. Socrates felt that this music had been created for himself alone of all men in the world. Through it, Menelas was saying to him the thousand things that he wished to hear her say. As he listened, he transformed the notes into words and the words into dreams.

He glanced at Helena. Her eyes were on him, her lips pinched in anger. Socrates suddenly felt himself overcome by a desire so intense that he was able to control it only with difficulty. His eyes moved to Menelas. Yes, he had been right. She was saying it. She loved him. She loved only him. With an almost superhuman effort he forced himself to remain seated. Above all else in the world, he wanted to throw himself upon her and take her, there, on the deck of the *Pegasus*.

By six o'clock the following morning the *Pegasus* was well on its way to Ibiza, the first stop of the cruise. At eight o'clock Lord and Lady Eaglebond appeared on deck and were served breakfast—tea for her, an Alka-Seltzer for him. The Alka-Seltzer was followed by a double whiskey, straight, to remove the medicinal taste from his lordship's mouth.

It was a splendid day, and the *Pegasus* moved smoothly through a gentle swell. Lord Eaglebond lighted his first cigar of the day and surreptitiously poured himself another whiskey. His wife looked at him reproachfully.

"George!" she chided.

He looked at his watch. "My dear, you know I never drink before eight o'clock. It's already eight ten."

"Good morning," Menelas greeted their lord and ladyships. "Lovely weather, isn't it?"

"Good morning, my dear. Won't you sit with us?"

Menelas sat, and Peter, who had entered, invisible, in her wake, scurried to take a place beside her.

A moment later Nut arrived, followed by Stan and Nancy Pickman and, finally, Helena.

"Where is Socrates?" Menelas demanded.

"In his office, working," someone answered.

Breakfast passed quickly in small talk about common friends and places. When everyone had finished, Helena asked, "Does anyone feel like lying in the sun?"

"Oh, yes!" Lindy Nut exclaimed. "Everyone does! Let's all put on bathing suits!"

Peter was astonished to see his wife rise with the others. She normally avoided the sun like the plague.

As he did every day, Socrates began by making a list of the telephone calls he would have to make that day. Except, occasionally, for a woman, or perhaps women, there was nothing which could keep him from his business. Indeed, as he was the first to recognize, without his constant personal attention his affairs would almost immediately collapse into a hopeless muddle. His capacity for immediate judgment was so great, and his instinct for the proper decision so infallible, that what would have been folly in others invariably in him turned out to have been a stroke of genius. Even his closest collaborators paled when they heard him give an immediate yes or no to a question that entailed the buying or selling of millions of dollars' worth of goods. Such decisions, had his collaborators been empowered to make them, would have required weeks of careful study and a prolonged weighing of all possible factors before being pronounced.

The fact was that Satrapoulos possessed an intuitive genius for business. There were no more than a handful like him in the world —Kallenberg, perhaps; Paul Getty; and, twenty years earlier, Ulysses Mikolofides, Socrates' own father-in-law. They were, or had been, Socrates' competitors, and he was determined to outdo them all.

"New York is calling, sir," Socrates' secretary informed him.

"Hello? Yes?" Socrates spat into the mouthpiece.

"We have a deal, boss," a voice said curtly. "Everything is ready to be signed."

Satrapoulos hung up with a smile. The day was off to a good start. He was on his way to recouping the outrageous sums demanded by the American government. He was in the midst of a gigantic battle which was half political and half financial, and, whichever way it went, he was in a position to give a jolt or two to the Dow Jones averages. He had enormous influence where it counted most: that is, in the Arab countries, where much of the world's oil, and therefore its energy, was produced. This was wealth and power on a scale hitherto undreamed of by the men who influenced the world's economies.

Through the intermediary of Hadj Thami el Sadek, Socrates had helped the Persian Gulf emirates to free themselves from the yoke of the British and American oil companies, thereby winning the everlasting gratitude of the Arabs and the undying hatred of the Western petroleum interests. But he had not got everything that he wanted. He foresaw that within ten years, world consumption of oil would rise to ten billion tons per year, and that oil would have to come from those same emirates in which Socrates Satrapoulos was so highly regarded. At a word from him, the life-giving flow of oil would be cut off. He had the world, so to speak, by the balls.

Socrates smiled to himself at the metaphor. A picture of Menelas came into his mind. Was she on deck he wondered? Was she perhaps wearing a bathing suit? He yearned to know if her body would fulfill the promise made by the beauty of her face.

"Here he is!"

It was eleven o'clock as Socrates Satrapoulos bounded onto the deck.

"Look at him!" Nut exclaimed. "He looks like the cat who swallowed the mouse. How much money did you make this morning?"

Socrates assumed an expression of childlike disappointment. "It was a bad morning," he said, shaking his head sadly. "I'd be surprised if I made half a million."

Everyone laughed.

"Would you like to go for a swim now," the Greek asked Menelas, "or would you rather wait until this afternoon? I know a marvelous beach on Ibiza. It's completely deserted."

He glanced at Menelas' legs and then, out of the corner of his eye, at Helena. The pianist's legs were absolutely superb. And Helena was beginning to annoy him seriously. The evening before, she had

created a violent scene in his cabin over the gifts he had presented
to his guests. It had ended with Socrates throwing her out bodily
and slamming the door behind her. Had it not been for Menelas,
he would have escaped in his customary fashion, by simply absenting
himself from the *Pegasus* for a few days, then returning in his own
good time, with no questions either asked or answered.

Herman appeared on deck carrying a rubber ring in his mouth,
pranced to Satrapoulos' feet, and dropped the ring. Absently, Socrates picked it up and threw it to the far end of the deck, then began
a conversation with Lord Eaglebond. But when Herman duti-
fully returned with the ring, his master had no more time for games.
The dog barked, but Socrates ignored him. The barking continued
unabated. Finally, Peter Gonzales de Salvador, in order to quiet
the dog, picked up the ring and threw it as far as he could. Herman
took off after it like a rocket, his legs moving so fast that he seemed
to be sliding on his stomach. The ring landed on the far edge of the
deck, wobbled for a second, then rolled over the side. Herman, close
behind, tried to stop in time, failed, and followed the rubber toy
into the sea.

"Oh!" Nancy cried. "Socrates! Your dog!"

Socrates looked up. "Dog? What about the dog?"

"It's fallen overboard."

"Good Lord!" In an instant, Satrapoulos was transformed from
a man of the world into a shaken man. His lips trembling, he ran
to the railing and, without a moment's hesitation, dived into the
sea.

"Man overboard!" Lord Eaglebond shouted.

"All engines stop!" Captain Kirillis ordered, and the *Pegasus*
slowed its forward thrust and moved gently under its momentum.
Everyone rushed to the fantail. Behind, in the yacht's dissipating
wake, they saw a dark figure swimming with surprising speed toward
the vessel's stern.

"He's crazy!" Helena screamed. "He's lost his mind!"

A launch was hurriedly lowered, and two sailors set out to the
rescue. But when they drew near Satrapoulos, they were greeted
with curses. Socrates, clutching Herman to his chest, was determined
to be the rescuer, not the rescued. "Idiots!" he shouted. "Who told
you to lower that boat? Don't you think I know how to swim?"

Nonetheless, he allowed himself and Herman to be hauled aboard
the Chriscraft. A few minutes later, still holding the dog, he stepped
aboard the *Pegasus*, to be greeted as a hero. Someone held out a

glass of scotch which he swallowed in a single gulp. "The water was marvelous!" He laughed. "I didn't feel like waiting till we reached Ibiza."

He saw Menelas' eyes on him, admiration on her face.

[16]

Socrates saw it as soon as the *Pegasus* sailed into the harbor of Ibiza. It was in his berth—the berth which he rented on a yearly basis for the *Pegasus*. An enormous black sailing ship, breathtakingly, stunningly beautiful.

"What is that old tub?" Satrapoulos shouted, irritated that so fabulous a boat belonged to someone other than himself.

"Whatever it is," Helena spat at him, "I wish I were on it."

Socrates stared at the schooner, its elegant, graceful, impossibly tall masts, its perfect lines. The *Pegasus*, admired though it was throughout the world, was a rowboat in comparison.

"It's all right in a marina," he said to his guests, "but it would be impossible at sea. Look at those masts! They're much too tall. Obviously, they're for show. If you hoisted sails up those things, no one could stand upright on the boat."

None of the guests bothered to answer, which only increased Socrates' anger. It was bad enough that his berth was taken by another yacht, but it became unbearable when that yacht was more luxurious, and obviously more expensive, than his own. It was strange that he had never heard of this boat before.

"Captain Kirillis!"

"Sir?"

"Let's drop anchor here. Then take the launch and ask the port captain what the hell he means by giving my berth to another boat."

"Yes, sir."

"George, how about a drink?"

Lord Eaglebond would have accepted, gladly, but he already had a glass in his hand.

"If you'd like," Socrates told his guests, "I know a little restaurant ashore where they serve a magnificent stuffed squid. Nancy, have you ever had squid?"

He could not have cared less about Nancy Pickman's experience with squid, stuffed or otherwise. All he wanted to know was the name of the son of a bitch who had taken his berth—and who had made him look like a peasant in the eyes of his guests.

"Oh, for goodness' sake!" Helena squealed, and rushed to the gangplank. Everyone followed her, except Satrapoulos.

What is that idiot screaming about now? he asked himself irritably. He rose to his feet and followed his guests.

The apparition that rose from the sea before his eyes was as unexpected as it was unwelcome. Climbing up the gangplank, his gigantic bulk obscuring Captain Kirillis below him, was Herman Kallenberg.

Waving his arms, Kallenberg called boisterously, "Ahoy! What are you landlubbers doing on the water?"

"Herman! Herman!" Helena shrieked joyously.

Stupid cow, Socrates said to himself.

"Socrates!" Kallenberg shouted. He was now on deck, standing with his legs braced and his hands on his hips, as though he were commander of a victorious boarding party. "Socrates! Don't tell me you didn't recognize the *Vagrant!* We knew your boat as soon as it entered the harbor. Imagine finding you here! How are you?"

He clapped Socrates on the shoulder and shook hands and exchanged kisses with the guests until the Greek could have sworn that his brother-in-law had multiplied himself by ten for the occasion.

"Well, you old pirate!" Kallenberg roared, turning back to Satrapoulos. "Don't tell me that you're still sailing this old pile of junk!"

Socrates, if he could, would happily have strangled him with his bare hands, in full view of the entire port of Ibiza.

Instead, he laughed. "What a marvelous surprise," he said, trying to sound enthusiastic. "Is Irene with you?"

"Of course. And the whole family."

"How long have you been here?"

"Only two days. We're leaving tomorrow for Capri. How about you?"

"We're leaving tonight."

Helena looked at him sharply. She understood the reason for his sudden change in plans, and she immediately decided to take advantage of his predicament. Until today she had always taken his side in his war with Kallenberg; now she would temporarily become Kallenberg's ally. She was not strong enough by herself to humiliate Satrapoulos as he deserved to be humiliated, but Kallenberg was.

"Why, Socrates," she said, "you told us just a few minutes ago that we were going to stay overnight."

Kallenberg leaped into the breach. "Splendid!" he roared. "Of course you'll spend the night. And you'll all dine aboard the *Vagrant* this evening!"

The blonde rose to her feet when Kallenberg and Satrapoulos entered and, without a word, moved toward the door. The Greek's eyes followed her closely.

"One of your little friends?" he asked Kallenberg when the door had closed.

"My secretary."

"Now I know why Irene complained to Helena that she had insomnia."

"When I hire people to work for me, I don't ask for Irene's approval. Do you ask Helena for hers?"

Socrates did not trust himself to answer. As though it were not unpleasant enough being aboard the *Vagrant*, he was obliged to endure Kallenberg's insolence.

"Tell me," his brother-in-law continued, "how did you manage to lure Menelas into your parlor? Everyone says she's a wild woman."

Satrapoulos remained silent.

"She's a pretty piece, though. Ah, Socrates, if only I had your gift with women!"

Socrates shrugged, uncertain whether or not he should interpret Kallenberg's remark as a compliment.

"What do you think of the *Vagrant*? Would you like a cigar?"

"No, thank you. She's a fine-looking boat. Where did you have her built?"

"Hamburg. Five million, it cost me. The workmen were on over-time wages for six months—three shifts a day, seven days a week. Another three million in works of art. You've seen the Rembrandt nude in the salon? My own discovery—and my secret. All in all, she's the finest yacht afloat, and worth every penny I've spent on her. You see, it is indeed possible to buy beauty, if you're willing to spend the money."

Satrapoulos seethed with rage. Not only was this pompous German ass humiliating him, but he was also lecturing him on the uses of capital. If only there were a way to bring him down a notch or two, to find his Achilles' heel.

"Beauty, my dear Herman, is not everything."

"What else is there?" Kallenberg demanded, taking the bait.

"There is business," Satrapoulos said, removing one of his own cigars from its case.

"Good heavens! How could I possibly want more than I have already?"

Satrapoulos allowed the question to hang in the air for a moment while he lighted his cigar. "There are always new worlds to conquer, Herman," he said finally. "For example, I've just acquired a very interesting new property. Today, in fact."

"What? A new pair of shoes?"

"Not exactly. The Haidoko shipyards."

Kallenberg's astonishment was so great that he was unable to mask it.

The Greek rejoiced in his victory over Kallenberg more than in the actual acquisition of the shipyards, though the latter was no mean accomplishment. There was not a major shipowner in the world who had not tried to buy the Haidoko shipyards when the owner died five years previously, leaving a daughter from a first marriage as co-heir with his widow, who had been his second wife. A codicil to the will held that no property belonging to the estate could be disposed of without the approval of both women. The fact that the daughter was something of a simpleton, and that the widow was prone to hysteria, was not necessarily a fatal obstacle to the sale of the shipyards; but as it happened, the two women hated each other with an all-consuming passion, and it sufficed to have one of them to give her approval to anything for the other to refuse cate-gorically even to discuss it. Offer after offer had therefore been refused, and one by one the bidders had withdrawn in disgust. All except Satrapoulos. For five years, he had kept two full-time agents constantly on the scene, making offers, soothing the widow, and ingratiating themselves with the daughter. Then, a few days ago, Satrapoulos' persistence had borne fruit, though not quite in the way that he had expected. The widow had died in an automobile accident. Hardly had her body been cut from the wreckage when his agents had reached a tentative agreement with the daughter—an agreement most advantageous to Satrapoulos.

"How did you do it?" Kallenberg asked, his voice unsteady.

"Oh, come now, Herman. Do I ask you to tell me all your secrets?"

"Well, at least tell me, was it expensive?"

Socrates laughed. "Not very. A few dollars—and the cost of a sea voyage."

"A voyage?"

"Yes. The widow died unexpectedly, and the daughter became the sole owner. She was eager to sell, for not too much money. And she loves to travel. So I threw in a one-year cruise around the world with all expenses paid. First-class, of course."

Herman shook his head in disbelief.

"You're the first to know about it," Satrapoulos said, looking at his watch. "It will be made public shortly. The contract was signed, I believe, at eleven o'clock, one hour ago, in Tokyo."

With his foot, Kallenberg pressed a button hidden on the floor under his desk. An instant later the door opened and the blonde appeared. Kallenberg said, "All right, Greta. I'll be right there."

He stood. "Will you excuse me for a moment, Socrates? I'll be back in a second."

Satrapoulos leaned back in his chair and puffed contentedly on his cigar. The expression on that bastard's face alone had been worth the price of the shipyards.

Kallenberg returned almost immediately. "Perhaps we should go up on deck," he said. "Our guests are waiting for us."

"But you have to be a witch! How on earth did you find out?"

Despite the elaborate electronic equipment aboard the *Vagrant*, Nut had expected to be barely able to hear Peggy's voice in New York. Still, her impulsive call to her dearest friend had produced unexpected results. Peggy had sounded as though she were in the next room. And also as though she were slightly hysterical.

"Find out? Find out what? I just called to say hello. We're aboard

Herman Kallenberg's yacht, and he has this simply incredible communications center—"

"Then brace yourself, my dear," Peggy Nash-Belmont said from across the Atlantic. "Scott and I were married last night!"

"No! You mean it? Oh, Peggy, tell me all about it, and don't leave out anything! I'm so happy for you! It's marvelous! Fantastic! When are you leaving on your honeymoon?"

"No honeymoon. Scott's in the middle of his campaign. Guess where I spent my wedding night?"

"I can't imagine."

"In a train station, in Warren, Illinois."

"What on earth were you doing there?"

"There was a rally for Scott. Afterward we were waiting for the train in the station, and Scott brought a mob of people over to meet me. Finally, there was only one man left. 'This is Mr. Billcott,' Scott said. 'He's the pastor of the Presbyterian church. He can marry us right here and now.' I thought he was joking, but it was a surprise he'd been planning for weeks. He had arranged everything—the marriage license, all the details. Don't ask me how he did it. Anyway, we were married right there in the train station by that funny little man! I think I cried. Then we rushed to make the train— and it didn't leave. Something was wrong with the engine or something. So we bought a couple of sandwiches, and we found a Coke machine, and we had our wedding breakfast in the station. We sat there all night. I'm so happy I could die!"

"What about his family? How are they taking it?"

"I haven't the least idea. We just got back to New York an hour ago, and I haven't seen anyone yet. Everything has happened so fast."

"Have the newspapers gotten hold of it yet?"

"Absolutely not! That's why Scott wanted a secret wedding in the first place."

"Oh, Peggy, I wish you and Scott could come out here and join us for your honeymoon! It's so lovely!"

"I'd adore it, but it's really impossible for Scott to get away right now."

"Peggy, I'd better get back to the others. I'll call you again in a couple of days. You'll never know how happy I am about you and Scott!"

"Thank you, darling. Listen, we'll be staying here, in my apartment, for another week, at least. You can reach me here."

"Yes. Good-bye, darling."

"Thanks so much for calling."

Lindy Nut hung up, then tapped on the glass door of the communications room to summon the radioman, who had politely withdrawn into the passageway during her conversation with Peggy.

"Madame?"

"There's another call I'd like to make. Also to New York. 751-2743."

"Yes, madame." He busied himself at the elaborate panel as Lindy Nut strummed her fingers on the table. "I have your number," he said after a few minutes.

Nut took the receiver. "Hello. This is Mrs. Bambilt." She looked at the radioman. He rose and left the room again. "Hello, Tom? Lindy—"

The voice in New York spoke for several minutes.

"You're certain?" Lindy asked, her voice quivering with excitement. "Absolutely certain?"

The voice assured her that the court's language had left no room for doubt.

"Oh, Tom! Thank you! Thank you!"

She replaced the receiver, swept out of the communications room and up the stairwell. The other guests were assembled on the forward deck of the *Vagrant*.

"Here she is," Kallenberg cried.

Lindy ignored him. She saw no one, heard nothing. For a moment, she allowed her joy to fill her being, and she exulted in it without reservation. Then she moved toward Satrapoulos and whispered, "Socrates, the most marvelous thing has happened. Today the court ruled that I'm a widow!" Then, without pausing for breath, she rushed on: "And Peggy and Scott were married last night!"

"Oh, Irene. I forgot to tell you. Herman almost drowned today."

"What? Where did you hear that? Herman hasn't been off the boat all day."

"Not your husband. Herman the dog."

Everyone laughed.

"Dogs and women first!" Helena exclaimed.

Lord Eaglebond and Stan Pickman were in animated conversation with Kallenberg's guests, an Italian actress and her German husband. The German, a former Nazi general and now a kingpin of his nation's metallurgical industries, was explaining the tactics he had employed against Eaglebond's armies a quarter of a century earlier.

Kallenberg and Satrapoulos were sitting apart, at Kallenberg's request. "Really, Socrates," he was saying, "you and I are a fine pair of idiots. We're like children."

Here's a new approach, the Greek warned himself. Where would it lead? Had it been generated by alcohol or by the moral defeat Kallenberg had just sustained?

"It's true!" Herman went on. "We spend our time fighting each other. Who profits from it? Not us. Our competitors do. Think of what we could do if we worked together! Who could stand against us?"

"I take it that you're referring to the Haidoko shipyards?"

"Well, yes. That, among other things. You haven't been very cooperative."

The Greek took a long puff on his cigar. He was calm, serene, sure of himself. "Herman, I don't recall that you ever bothered to offer me a share of the profits in any of your own deals."

"Only because I was never sure how you would respond. You seem to forget that it's all in the family."

"The family, my ass! Our family is a group of people united by blood and separated by business. You and I, we married two sisters. So what? Are we better friends than if we had married two women who were strangers? Certainly, it hasn't stopped you from trying to cut the ground from under my feet whenever you thought you could get away with it. The truth is, though, that you've never been able to get away with it."

Satrapoulos leaned forward so that his face was close to Kallenberg's. "I can't really complain. I do the same to you. And I do it gladly, Herman, because you're a piece of shit."

In other circumstances, Kallenberg would have struck his brother-in-law or strangled him. Now he merely smiled. Satrapoulos' words were not insults. They were merely the means by which he was tightening the noose around his own dirty Greek neck.

"It pains me to hear you say such things, Socrates. You and I should be friends. It is at moments like these that you need friends."

"Herman, go fuck yourself."

Socrates spoke with a slight smile on his lip. His bearing radiated confidence, but it was a confidence which had begun to waver. Kal-

lenberg's nemesis, he knew, was his violent temper. He had deliberately provoked him, insulted him grossly, in an attempt to make
him disgrace himself in front of both their guests. Indeed, he had
gone far beyond what was usually necessary to obtain the desired
result. Why, then, was Herman still so calm? Socrates decided to
bring things to a head.

He stood up. "I hear the launch coming. It's late, and we want to
get an early start in the morning. So good night. Thank you for your
hospitality to myself and to my guests. I can't remember when I
enjoyed myself so much."

He turned away and walked toward the other guests. He felt as
though there were a loaded gun pointed at his back, and he almost
cringed.

"Socrates!" The word was like an explosion.

Socrates turned. Kallenberg's face was expressionless, but his eyes
shone with malice.

"What is it?"

"There's something I forgot to mention to you."

Here it comes, Socrates told himself, bracing himself for the
blow he was certain was about to be delivered.

"What time is it?"

Puzzled, Socrates glanced at his watch. "Two o'clock."

"And what time is it in Japan?"

The Greek was like a fish caught at the end of a line. He knew
instantly what Kallenberg would say next, and he was suddenly overcome with nausea.

"What I forgot to mention was that I've just bought the Haidoko
shipyards."

It would have been superfluous for the Greek to ask for explanations. Instinctively he knew that Kallenberg had taken advantage
of the difference in time between Europe and Asia to make the
Haidoko daughter a better offer and had won the prize. Socrates
could not withhold a certain admiration for Herman's boldness. After all, it was his own fault. He had been unable to resist the opportunity to wound Herman, and he had opened his mouth when
it should have remained sealed. He had been unwilling to deprive
himself of the pleasure of parading his latest *coup* before Kallenberg, and the anticipation of that pleasure had caused him to forget
that eleven o'clock at Ibiza was not eleven o'clock in Tokyo. Now
he would pay for it.

"Well," Kallenberg said heartily. "Business is business. Win some, lose some."

Satrapoulos did not reply.

"Come on, Socrates, a man like you knows how to lose gracefully. I think you'll be able to get along very well indeed without those shipyards. In fact, it's even possible that you and I might be able to work out some kind of arrangement—"

The Greek's expression did not change. "I'm listening."

"Maybe we should wait until tomorrow to discuss it."

"No, let's discuss it right now."

"Well, to tell you the truth, now that I have those shipyards, I really don't know what to do with them. They're more of a bother than anything else."

"Which, of course, is why you wanted them so badly."

"Look, Socrates. I want to get rid of them. Let me sell them to you. If anyone is going to profit from them, I'd rather it were you."

"Oh, yes. I had forgotten. The family spirit."

"Yes, the family. And, in the same spirit, you might turn over to me, say, thirty percent of the business you do with the emirates. You see? I'm not as greedy as you thought."

"Herman, go fuck yourself."

"And in return, I'll sell the shipyards to you for exactly what I paid for them. Plus ten percent to cover my expenses, naturally. Now, is that a fair deal, or isn't it?"

"Go fuck yourself!"

"Don't get excited, Socrates. This is purely a business matter. Why don't you take time to think it over? Take until noon tomorrow. Sleep on it. Meanwhile, I'll have the contracts drawn up, just in case you change your mind."

"Go fuck yourself!" the Greek shouted for the third time. He plunged down the gangplank of the *Vagrant* into his waiting launch and signaled the seamen at the helm to pull away. The roar of the engines did not drown out Kallenberg's voice as he cried from above: "Don't forget! Tomorrow, at noon!"

Satrapoulos escorted Menelas to her cabin and bent to kiss her hand.

"Is something wrong, my friend?" she asked softly.

Socrates was taken aback at the unaccustomed gentleness in her voice.

"No, no. Nothing's wrong. Good night." Then, louder, so that the other guests might hear, he added, "Sleep well. By the time you awaken, we'll be on our way."

When the last guest had gone below, Satrapoulos went to the bridge. "I want you to raise anchor at dawn," he instructed Stavenos. "Not later than six A.M. Head northeast. I'll give further orders when I get up."

"Yes, sir. I'll tell Captain Kirillis."

Satrapoulos strode off the bridge and headed for Helena's cabin. It was time to settle accounts. He threw open the door and found her stretched out on her bed, fully clothed.

She rose to a sitting position. "What is it?" she asked.

"It's your fault!" Socrates spat at her.

"What? What's my fault?"

"You're the viper I have nurtured in my bosom. You're a spy for my competitors!"

She looked at him in puzzlement. "Socrates, I'm exhausted. I want to go to sleep. Leave me alone. I don't know what you're talking about."

"I wanted to leave here tonight. You made me stay, just to accommodate that son of a bitch brother-in-law of yours! Do you have any idea what that dinner cost me? Sixty million dollars! Sixty million! But it's not your money, is it? It's mine!"

"Socrates—"

"Shut up!"

Tears welled up in Helena's eyes. With the desperate courage of the weak, she took the offensive. "You have no right to talk to me like that!" she screamed. "You and those whores of yours that you bring aboard my boat!"

"Your boat?"

"Yes, my boat! It's as much mine as it is yours."

"Good! Since it's your boat, you can have it. I'm getting out of here. I'm sick of looking at you."

"Oh, you bastard! You bastard!"

"Lower your voice!"

"I'll scream if I feel like screaming! You're crazy! Insane! You come into my cabin in the middle of the night, raving like a maniac—" Helena burst into tears. "I'm going to tell everyone," she sobbed. "I'm going to tell them how you came in here, how you treat me—"

"How I treat you? You make me lose sixty million dollars, and

all you can find to blame me for is that you don't like my friends!
You're a jealous bitch!"

"I'm going to tell everyone—"

"Who are you going to tell? Who would listen to you?"

"I'll tell," Helena sniffed, "I'll tell—my mother!"

The Greek slammed the door behind him and went up on deck.
He leaned against the railing and stared at the dark water. In the
distance, he heard the music from the nightclubs along the shore
occasionally rising above the sound of the waves. The sky was
aglitter with stars.

I'll be damned if I'm going to let that son of a bitch have his way,
he swore to the heavens. There must be a way. . . .

A half hour later the Greek returned to the bridge. Both Stavenos
and Kirillis were there, studying a chart. "I've changed my mind,"
Socrates said. "We'll wait until lunch to raise anchor. Stavenos, tell
Nicholas to wake me at exactly eight o'clock."

He returned to his cabin, lighted a cigar, and poured himself a
glass of whiskey. It was a little after three o'clock.

At precisely 9 A.M. the next morning, the launch from the *Pegasus*
came alongside the V*agrant,* and Satrapoulos, a black briefcase in
his hand, bounded up the gangplank. Except for a few members
of the crew swabbing down the deck, the boat seemed asleep.

An officer approached Satrapoulos. "Yes, sir?"

"Tell Mr. Kallenberg that I'm here."

"Yes, sir."

Satrapoulos looked around the deck. What a magnificent vessel.
A dream. He looked up at the masts and, in his mind's eye, saw the
sails billowing in the wind.

"Well, Socrates!" Kallenberg's voice boomed. "You're up early!
And dressed for a formal call, too!"

Socrates, without planning to do so, had automatically dressed in
his customary uniform of black alpaca.

"Shall we go down to your office?"

Kallenberg led the way and sat on one side of the vast Louis
XVI table that served him as a desk. He gestured toward a chair on
the opposite side of the table.

Satrapoulos sat. "Do you have the contract?" he asked.

"Naturally," Kallenberg replied, as though surprised at the question.

"Good. Let me see it."

Kallenberg pushed a blue folder across the table. Satrapoulos opened it, removed the papers, and, without glancing at them, ripped them to shreds.

He laughed at Kallenberg's expression of surprise. "Come on, Herman! Did you really think I'd sign that thing?"

"You mean, you refuse my offer?"

"I refuse the terms you've offered, if that's what you mean. That's not the same thing as refusing the deal itself."

"What do you propose?"

"You want thirty percent of my Arabian business. I'll give you twenty percent. You want me to pay you ten percent more for the Haidoko shipyards than you paid for them. Instead, I'll pay you ten percent less."

Kallenberg laughed. "This is unbelievable! You're sitting there, dictating the terms—"

"Take it or leave it, Kallenberg."

"To listen to you, one would think that you hold the upper hand."

"You offered me certain terms. I am making a counteroffer. I refuse to negotiate with a knife at my throat."

"All right. Let's calm down. I do not desire the death of the sinner, but that he be converted and live. Now, listen to me. . . ."

The discussion continued for a half hour, with each of the two men swearing that he would never consent, then consenting. Finally, it was decided that Kallenberg would have thirty-five percent of Satrapoulos' Arabian business and that Satrapoulos would buy the Haidoko shipyards for ten percent less than Kallenberg had paid for them. Greta was called in to take down the terms of the new contract as dictated by the two principals. A clause was inserted, for fiduciary and corporate reasons, which forbade either party from making the contract public before ninety days had elapsed.

Both men read every word of the finished contract.

"Is it right?" Socrates asked.

"Yes."

"Then sign."

"Let's both sign simultaneously."

Satrapoulos shrugged. "All right. You sign one copy, and I'll sign the other. Then we'll exchange copies and sign again."

They did so.

"Good," Kallenberg said, relaxing in his chair. "Now, do you want to know what I offered the woman for her silly shipyards? You had offered sixty million, plus a cruise around the world. I offered exactly the same deal—plus a blank check drawn to the order of the House of Dior! Oh, Socrates! To think that I've always envied you for your understanding of women!"

To Kallenberg's astonishment, Satrapoulos joined in his laughter. "I must say, Socrates," the German observed, "you're taking this very well. Better than I would if I were in your shoes."

The Greek spread his hands in a gesture of dismissal. "As you said last night, a man must know how to lose as well as how to win."

[17]

On the fifth night of the cruise, after a brief visit at Cadaqués so that Stan Pickman might buy a Dali from Dali himself, the *Pegasus* encountered a storm at sea. At first, Satrapoulos' guests were amused rather than alarmed by the rising wind and the giant waves. Then Captain Kirillis asked his passengers to retire to the salon and to stay off the open decks. The meteorological service was forecasting a violent blow, but one of relatively short duration.

Lord Eaglebond was the first to vomit at the table where a lively gin-rummy game was in progress. Nancy Pickman, no doubt encouraged by his lordship's performance, emulated him in short order. Thereupon, her face a pale shade of green, she was escorted to her cabin by her husband, who, before leaving, complained that his own stomach was feeling odd.

Since Lindy Nut had already retired for the night, only Satrapoulos, Menelas, Helena, and Peter were left in the salon. Peter had sworn to himself that, no matter what the provocation, he would never leave his wife alone with the Greek, and Helena, not to be outdone, had taken a similar vow. What was particularly exasperating, however, was that neither Socrates nor Olympia seemed affected by the storm.

Peter, finally, could restrain himself no longer. "Olympia," he said, rising unsteadily to his feet, his face deathly pale, "don't you think we should go to our cabin?"

"Why?" she asked, all innocence. "It's as bad there as it is here."

"Don't you feel well?" Socrates inquired solicitously.

"I feel quite well, thank you," Peter replied and retched.

"Well," Helena interrupted, "you can all stay here if you want to. I'm going to my cabin!" And with that, she ran from the salon.

Peter, to Socrates' surprise, was made of sterner stuff. The diminutive Spanish grandee was leafing through a magazine, sweat pouring from every pore of his face. From time to time, his shoulders heaved significantly. Socrates smiled.

"Why are you smiling?" Peter asked.

"You're holding your magazine upside down," the Greek replied.

"I beg your pardon," Peter retorted with spirit. "It's not my magazine that is upside down. It's your boat." Then he struggled to his feet and dashed toward the door. "Olympia! For God's sake—" he shouted over his shoulder and disappeared.

Socrates and Menelas were alone.

"Are you all right?" he asked.

"Oh, yes. And you?"

"I'm never seasick, perhaps because I've never been afraid of being seasick. But I had no idea that you were such a good sailor."

"I've been in storms before. In the tropics. Storms much worse than this one."

"Were you born in Athens?"

"No, on Corfu."

"Is that where you learned to play the piano?"

"That is where I began, when I was six. My father was a fisherman, and I used to deliver fish for him to a villa at Paleokastrista. The owner of the villa was an American—a quite charming middle-aged man who always gave me candy. I loved the candy, but I loved even more to listen to him play Chopin. I spent hours listening. The poor man, I was the only audience he ever had. He taught me to play my scales. More important, he told me that I had talent."

"A man of discernment, obviously."

"Perhaps. But you know the old saying: genius is ten percent inspiration and ninety percent perspiration. But what are you smiling at?"

"Nothing. Listening to you talk of percentages made me think of—something. Business."

"Do you play any instrument?"

"Not one. I don't even have a very good ear."

"Didn't your parents ever try to interest you in music?"

"My parents—" An image of Athina came into his mind. "My parents—had other interests." How difficult it was to tell the truth. "Tell me," he said, "do you ever lie?"

"Of course, I lie. Doesn't everyone? Don't you?"

"Constantly."

"Is that the truth?" Menelas asked.

They laughed together.

The door opened, and Peter appeared. His face, which had been chalk white, had now taken on a bluish cast. Unable to speak, he gestured wildly, in unmistakable appeal, to his wife, then disappeared again.

"I really should try to do something for him," Menelas said.

Captain Kirillis' head appeared in the doorway. "Sir, may I have a word with you?" he asked Socrates.

"Come in, Captain. You may speak before Madame. What is it?"

"We're taking on water, and we're beginning to list badly. We've been advised by the coast guard to stay away from shore. We would probably run aground if we tried to put in anywhere. I'm afraid that the *Pegasus* can't stand much more of this."

"This blasted boat—"

"It's not the boat, sir. The *Pegasus* is a fine vessel. It simply was not built to withstand this kind of punishment."

"Captain Kirillis, in the very near future I am going to give you another vessel to command."

"Very good, sir. But for the moment—"

Satrapoulos did not hear. He was lost in calculations. With the six million he had saved in his deal with Kallenberg, he would have a new yacht built—a yacht that would put Kallenberg's to shame.

"Sir," Kirillis was saying. "Are all your guests in their cabins? You yourself and Madame—"

"Don't worry about me, Captain. If you can move around in this kind of weather, so can I."

"And if you two can, so can I," Menelas added with a laugh.

"Let's go up to the bridge," Socrates said to her.

"Sir, you can't be serious," the captain protested.

Socrates ignored him. "Olympia, I want to see what's going on," he said. "Will you wait for me here?"

Menelas nodded.

Satrapoulos and Kirillis made their way down the passageway on their hands and knees, clutching at anything that was bolted to the deck. On the bridge, they found Lieutenant Stavenos hanging onto the railing. He heard them enter but did not turn his head.

"How is it going?" Satrapoulos shouted above the roar of the wind.

"Well, we're moving, sir," the lieutenant called.

"Where to?"

"Nowhere," Kirillis answered. "We're circling."

"What can we do?"

"Nothing, except wait for it to blow over," Kirillis answered.

"If the *Pegasus* can take it," Stavenos added.

"Good God!" Kirillis shouted, pointing to the deck below. "Look at that!"

Socrates saw a dark shape sliding on the deck.

"I'll go!" the captain shouted.

"No," Satrapoulos ordered. "You stay here. I'll go!" He struggled for a moment to open the door against the pressure of the wind, then disappeared into the darkness. Kirillis saw him crawl on his hands and knees across the deck. Menelas was clutching the railing, being tossed about like a bundle of rags. She dared not release her hold on the railing to return to the salon, and if she remained where she was, she would certainly be swept overboard.

"Here," Socrates yelled. "Give me your hand!"

She shook her head. "I can't!" she shouted, feeling like a fool. It was as though her hands were bolted to the railing. No command her brain issued could make them release their grip.

Satrapoulos took advantage of a second of comparative calm to release his own hold on the railing and pry her hands open. He placed one of her arms over his shoulders and, still on his knees, turned toward the door of the salon. Their eyes met and held for a second. The look they exchanged said all that had to be said. He felt his shoulder tremble under her hand. He licked his lips and tasted the salt of her hair mixed with that of his own flesh. She leaned her head against his chest, and the faint scent of her perfume intoxicated him.

"Hold onto me," he shouted. "We can make it to the salon."

The storm had no sooner subsided outside than it broke with renewed fury aboard the *Pegasus*. One and all resented Satrapoulos and Menelas for not being sick like everyone else. It was as though the two Greeks had overstepped the bounds of common courtesy or even of common decency. Lord Eaglebond sought to drown his bitterness in Chivas Regal, while Stan Pickman could not forgive Satrapoulos for having invited him on a cruise without having made certain beforehand that the weather would hold. Only Lindy Nut Bambilt was herself. She had slept through the whole thing and had emerged from her cabin the following morning in a marvelous humor.

Peter was the most gravely slighted by Socrates' refusal to vomit during the storm. Not only his self-esteem, but his honor as a grandee of Spain, had been wounded. When the wife of a Gonzales de Salvador was in danger, only her husband was permitted to save her. Satrapoulos, by usurping that function, had offered a grave insult to the Iberian nobleman or at least to his pride. Thus Peter stiffly informed the Greek that he and his wife must be put ashore as soon as possible, at the nearest port.

Satrapoulos knew that it was useless to argue. He ordered Kirillis to make for St. Tropez immediately, rather than for Cannes as originally planned.

Dinner that night was a dismal affair. Helena and Peter, involuntary allies, kept their eyes riveted on Socrates and Menelas, respectively. No one said a word except Lindy Nut. No one ate dessert, not even Lindy Nut. One and all retired early, complaining of headaches or indigestion.

The next morning at ten o'clock, Menelas and Peter debarked at St. Tropez. As their baggage was being loaded into a waiting Cadillac, Peter turned to Socrates, who had accompanied his guests to the dock.

"Thank you for a most agreeable voyage," he said coldly.

"It has been an honor for me to have you aboard," Socrates replied in the same tone.

Menelas extended her hand under Peter's watchful eye. Socrates took it and spoke a few words in Greek. Menelas smiled and nodded. Then she spoke three words in the same tongue.

Peter, already exasperated at his inability to understand the exchange, lost his temper completely when Socrates laughed loudly, then looked at Menelas in a way which admitted of no ambiguities.

"You lecher!" he screeched, leaping at Satrapoulos and seizing him by the front of his shirt. "I'm sick of you and your peasant manners! Just because you have money, you think you can do anything you want! You and your gifts." He pointed to the ruby pin Menelas was wearing on her blouse. "Olympia! Give that back to him!"

The tourists having breakfast on the terrace of Chez Sénéquier nearby perked up their ears.

"What on earth has gotten into you?" Menelas hissed. "Don't be such an ass! Everyone is watching!"

"That little fellow with the glasses," one of the tourists said to another, "isn't that Socrates Satrapoulos?"

"By God, it is! And the woman, it's Menelas!"

"Peter, I beg of you! Don't make a spectacle of yourself!"

"Are they going to fight?"

The tourists left their coffee and rolls to the flies and moved to the dock, where they formed a silent circle around the group from the *Pegasus*.

"My dear fellow," Socrates said to Peter, "this is a ridiculous misunderstanding. Come back aboard the *Pegasus* with me. Let's have a drink and talk this over."

"Never!" Peter shrieked. "I'll never set foot on that floating whorehouse again! Never!"

The tourists moved closer.

Menelas now took the initiative to put an end to the scene. Throwing her handbag into the waiting automobile, she seized her husband bodily around the waist and thrust him roughly after the bag. Instinctively, she raised her hand to the ruby pin to insure that it was still in place; then, with a last look at Satrapoulos, she climbed into the car and slammed the door.

As the automobile moved away, the tourists caught a final glimpse of Peter shaking his fist at Satrapoulos.

By common, silent accord, the guests aboard the *Pegasus* pretended to have noticed nothing. So far as they were concerned, Socrates had simply bid farewell to his departing guests. They made no comments on what had taken place on the dock even among themselves. The Pickmans were to leave the same evening to return to their house in Monte Carlo. Lord and Lady Eaglebond were expected in London the following afternoon—Socrates' plane would fly them to Nice. And Lena, pleading a sudden headache, had disappeared into her cabin.

"This is our last day together," Socrates said. "What do you say we go see the nudists at Levant?"

"Is it far?" Pickman asked.

"About an hour from here," Socrates replied vaguely.

"Could we go bathing there?"

"I'd love to see the nudists," Eaglebond admitted.

"George!" Lady Eaglebond gasped.

"So would I!" said Nancy Pickman.

"I didn't mean to be a wet blanket," Stan Pickman apologized. "It's just that I'm still a little queasy from the storm—"

"Listen," Socrates said, "I have a better idea. We'll go to Tahiti instead! It's much closer—a beautiful beach, packed with nudists. How does that sound?"

"Are we going in the launch?" Lady Eaglebond asked anxiously.

"Oh, let's go by helicopter!" Lindy Nut squealed.

"There's too many of us for the helicopter," Socrates replied. "Besides, what's the *Pegasus* for if not to take us where we want to go?" He gestured toward a waiter. "Tell the captain to weigh anchor and head for Tahiti."

The man's eyes grew wide with disbelief. Everyone laughed.

"No, you idiot," Socrates reassured him. "Not Tahiti, the island; Tahiti, the beach on the other side of this peninsula."

The waiter grinned and scurried off on his errand.

Lady Eaglebond was visibly uneasy. "Have you ever visited a nudist colony before?" she asked.

"I've heard that they're all fat and ugly."

"So much the better," Lord Eaglebond interjected. "I won't feel conspicuous."

"George, surely you don't intend to remove your clothing!"

It took ten minutes for the *Pegasus* to cast off, and another half hour for her to be clear of the port. Her size prevented her from turning easily within the narrow confines of the harbor, and every arrival and departure were torture for Captain Kirillis, who lived in dread of running down smaller craft. Yet Socrates did not mind the delay. There were a hundred people on the pier watching in open admiration and envy as Kirillis maneuvered the enormous yacht expertly toward the open water. Finally, she passed the lighthouse and, at cruising speed, moved majestically along Canoubiers Bay as Socrates and his guests speculated on the nature and habits of nudists.

"Isn't it illegal?"

"Of course it is. But when a policeman shows up on the beach, they put on their bathing suits."

"Are the policemen naked, too?"

"A naked cop isn't a cop."

"Wouldn't it be funny to see a cop disguised as a nudist?"

"Where would they carry their badges?"

Nut touched Socrates' arm. "Where's Helena?" she asked.

"Don't bother about her," Socrates growled. "She's in her cabin, sulking."

"What have you done now?"

"Nothing. She's mad because Menelas and I weren't seasick like everyone else."

"What do you think of Menelas?"

Socrates hesitated, then decided to tell a partial truth: "I think she's unique. I've never met anyone like her."

"I think you're quite taken with her."

"We're almost there," Socrates said, staring toward the beach. "Bring us some binoculars," he ordered a waiter.

Lindy Nut was not to be put off. "Socrates," she persisted, "tell me. You do like her, don't you?"

"What I really feel is disgust—disgust that a woman like that should be married to a nobody like her husband."

"Oh," Nancy shouted. "I see them! I see them!" She pretended not to see Lady Eaglebond's hand outstretched for the only binoculars available at the moment. "They're really naked! Imagine!"

"Let me see," Stan said.

"Wait a minute. Oh, God! That's disgusting!"

"What is it? What are they doing?"

"What a hideous woman! How can she have the nerve to expose herself like that?"

The waiter appeared with an armload of binoculars and distributed them among Socrates' guests.

"I can't see a thing," Lord Eaglebond complained.

Lindy Nut looked at him closely. "Maybe you're holding them backward," she suggested.

"Fat lot of good it would do me either way," Eaglebond moaned. "I'm nearsighted."

"That blonde over there isn't bad."

"Where, Stan?"

"All the way to the right."

"Oh, God," Eaglebond whimpered. "I'm missing it all."

His wife offered her services. "Do you want me to describe her to you?"

"No, let someone else do it. You and I aren't interested in the same things."

"This is most unfair!" Socrates explained in mock indignation. "Everyone can see except George."

"Don't worry about me," Eaglebond replied. "Over the years, I've found that being blind as a bat is more of a blessing than a curse."

"I resent that remark," Lady Eaglebond said. "I'm certain you're alluding to me."

"Not to you, my dear. To politics."

"Listen," Socrates interrupted. "I've found a solution to George's problem. Let's take the launch and go in for a really close look!"

"Yes, yes!" Lindy Nut cried.

"No," Eaglebond growled. "It's kind of you, my dear Socrates, but I'd really prefer to remain here with these comforts." He waved his cigar in the direction of a bottle of Dom Perignon cooling in a bucket of ice. "Why don't you go without me."

"Are you sure you'd rather stay?"

"Absolutely. I'm rather too old and fat for sin."

"I'll stay with you, then," Lady Eaglebond said primly.

"Nonsense, my dear. Go along with the others. It will do you good to see some handsome young men without a stitch on. I'm sure it's been years since you've had the pleasure. . . ."

"How dare you suggest such a horrid thing! Besides I've got my binoculars."

"As you wish," Socrates acquiesced. "George, I promise you a detailed report as soon as we get back. All right, everyone who's going, let's go!"

Socrates, followed by his guests, dashed toward the gangplank under the tolerant gaze of Lord and Lady Eaglebond and climbed aboard the waiting launch. A few seconds later the small craft was speeding toward the beach.

A hundred yards from shore, Satrapoulos signaled the helmsman to cut the engine. From the launch the nudists on the beach were clearly visible.

"It's really shocking," Nancy Pickman said, her gaze riveted to the spectacle.

"You're right," her husband agreed, his eyes moving hungrily from a pair of breasts to a thigh, from a thigh to a posterior. "Skinny-dipping in the privacy of your own pool is one thing, but this—it's too much."

"Are you serious?" Lindy Nut asked innocently.

"Come on, Lindy!" Nancy replied stiffly, without looking away from the beach. "You don't mean to tell me that you actually *enjoy* seeing all those nude bodies."

"I'm not as interested in the nudity as I am in the people themselves."

"Even so, they're nothing but exhibitionists. Can't you see that? Look at that man, for example. The tall, handsome one staring at us—"

The man was standing at the water's edge and looking at the boat. He cupped his hands to his mouth and shouted something, but his words were lost in the wind.

"What did he say?" Nancy asked eagerly.

"I couldn't hear," Socrates admitted.

The man raised his right arm slowly until it was at a right angle to his muscular, bronzed body. Then he placed his left hand on his right arm, slightly forward of the bicep, and, with great emphasis, simultaneously flexed his arm and raised it slightly.

Lindy Nut tittered.

"What does it mean?"

"It means," Socrates said, laughing, "that that young man is not a gentleman."

"Let's go back," Lindy Nut suggested. "After all, they're not animals in a zoo. We shouldn't be out here gaping at them."

Nancy, her eyes never leaving the ungentlemanly Adonis on the beach, retorted, "If they don't want to be stared at, then they shouldn't walk around naked."

The helmsman looked at Socrates questioningly, waiting for a signal to depart. The Greek shook his head. A small crowd had formed on the beach, and some of the people were beginning to shout insults—a few of them audible—at the launch.

Two young men waded into the water up to their waists. One of them shook his fist threateningly at Socrates and his guests. The other cupped his hands to his mouth and shouted, articulating every word with great care. "*Tu mouilles, hein, salope!*"

"Such vanity!" Lindy Nut laughed.

"What did he say?"

"He's inquiring after your health, Nancy," Lindy Nut replied with obvious relish. "He said, 'Are you getting hot pants, bitch?'"

Several other people joined the two boys in the water and began to shout:

"Peeping Toms!"

"Goddamned queers!"

Socrates scowled. "Which one of them said that?"

"If you're so curious," another voice shouted, "why don't you come closer and get a good look?"

"All right," Socrates growled, "if they want us to go closer, we'll go closer!" He signaled to the helmsman. "Go ahead slowly."

The launch moved forward until it was within ten feet of the group of young people in the water.

"All right," Socrates growled, "who called us queers?"

"I did," a chubby youth snarled, his blue eyes flashing. "You have to be some kind of queer to spend your time gawking at people who aren't bothering you."

"Why shouldn't we stare if we want to?" Socrates asked. "It's a public beach, isn't it?"

"It's our beach," the youth retorted. "But since you're so hot to see our asses, why don't you and your friends come up on the beach?"

"All right," Socrates said. Without a moment's hesitation, he slipped into the water. "Anyone coming with me?"

"I'll go," Stan Pickman volunteered in the voice which, in countless Westerns, had signaled imminent doom to murderers and cattle rustlers.

"You look funny in those clothes," one of the boys remarked.

"You'd look funny if you walked down the street naked," Socrates retorted.

One of the girls scowled at him. "The difference is that we don't give a damn."

"If you really don't give a damn, how about coming aboard my boat for a drink?" Socrates said, half seriously. He would have much preferred to have them naked on the *Pegasus* than to be forced to stroll naked with them on the beach.

The girl turned to her friends. "How about it?" she asked.

A moment later four young men and three girls—two of them quite striking—had climbed aboard the launch along with Socrates, Lindy Nut, and the Pickmans.

"Is that your boat out there?" asked one of the girls. "It's really something."

Socrates bowed modestly.

Stan Pickman, vaguely miffed at the awe in the girl's voice, removed his sunglasses.

"Oh, Christ," the chubby youth muttered. "Look, girls, we're in the presence of a star."

"Stan Pickman!" the girls cried.

Nancy cleared her throat softly. She allowed no one to touch her famous husband, but she was always pleased when he was recognized and admired.

When the launch reached the *Pegasus*, Socrates followed his guests, both new and old, up the gangplank. He noted with irritation that his crew's inspection of the girls was as open and unabashed as his own.

"George," he shouted. "I have a little surprise for you!"

Eaglebond, speechless, roared with laughter.

"Champagne for everyone," Socrates ordered, then turned to his young guests. "Would you like a tour of the boat?"

"Oh, yes," one of the girls exclaimed.

"You girls go ahead," the chubby youth said. "We'll wait for you here." He would never have admitted it, even to himself, but he and his friends were intimidated by the splendor of the *Pegasus*. Moreover, they felt ridiculous under the amused stare of the officers and crew in their immaculate, starched white uniforms.

"This way, ladies," Socrates said gallantly. He took the arms of the two more attractive girls. This is life, he told himself. A man must be open to new experiences. So many wealthy men are prisoners of their own image. . . .

It was not until Socrates had reached the aft deck that he saw Helena. She was stretched out on a chaise longue, wearing a bottle-green pants suit from Givenchy's, a magazine on her lap and a glass in her hand. Her mouth dropped open in disbelief as she caught sight of Socrates and the three naked girls.

Socrates stopped short; then, with an effort, he regained his composure. "Girls," he said jovially, "this is my wife. I'm sure she'll be delighted to meet you."

Helena jumped up from her chair. Her mouth snapped shut like a trap; her eyes blazed with fury.

Socrates held out his arms in a gesture of supplication. "Lena, please. You don't understand—"

"Get away from me," Helena screamed. "Don't come near me!" Then she turned and fled.

Socrates read attentively:

> Here at St. Tropez, the Sodom of the twentieth century, we thought we had seen everything. But yesterday morning, we were proved wrong. At ten o'clock, Socrates Satrapoulos, the billionaire shipowner, was attacked by Peter Gonzales de Salvador. Does that name mean anything to you? It is the maiden name of the man who is better known as Mr. Menelas. It seems that, during a cruise from Palma to St. Tropez, Gonzales de Salvador developed a passion of sorts for Madame Satrapoulos. We do not know if the beautiful Helena responded to the Spaniard's attentions, or in what manner, but it is reported that the pair were alone for several hours in the course of a storm which sent *Pegasus'* owner and his other guests to their cabins. Whereupon Satrapoulos is said to have publicly accused his wife of having taken advantage of his transitory nausea to engage in unbecoming conduct with Gonzales de Salvador. And Menelas, not to be outdone, attacked Madame Satrapoulos, accusing her of being a husband stealer. We hear that in the exchange between the two ladies, Madame Satrapoulos suffered severe scratches, while Menelas was bitten several times. . . . At last report, Madame Satrapoulos had left the *Pegasus* to rejoin her children, the twins Achilles and Maria, at St. Moritz. Before leaving, however, she is said to have insisted upon receiving tetanus shots, while Menelas, we have it on good authority, visited another doctor for a rabies injection. It remains to be seen which of the two ladies has actually infected the other. Ironically, Monsieur Satrapoulos is himself widely regarded as the last of the great international rakes, in the tradition of Aly Kahn, Porfirio Rubirosa, and Juan Cappuro. . . .

The Greek crumpled up the newspaper and took a swallow of black coffee. The article was headlined WHEN MILLIONAIRES FIGHT LIKE RAGPICKERS, and it was signed by one J. P. Sarian.

What an ass this Sarian must be, Satrapoulos told himself. How could anyone believe such distortions, let alone write them? The only redeeming sentence in the piece was the line about Satrapoulos' being a man in the classic tradition of Aly Khan and Porfirio Rubirosa. . . .

The rest of it was pure rubbish. Imagine, that pantywaist, Peter, having designs on Helena! And imagine Socrates Satrapoulos as the wronged husband!

He smiled. Perhaps he would send Olympia a gift of some sort, just to irritate Peter.

"Sir"—a crewman interrupted Socrates' reverie—"there's a lady asking to see you."

"What time is it?"

"Ten o'clock, sir."

"Who is the lady?"

"Madame Medea Mikolofides."

Satrapoulos jumped to his feet. Helena had sworn she would tell her mother. . . .

"Why did you let her aboard, you idiot?"

"I didn't, sir. She just came on board."

"All right. I'll take care of her."

Things must be worse than he had thought if Helena had actually called in her mother. When he reached the deck, his mother-in-law stood looking out over the water, her back toward him.

He began gently. "Medea—"

The woman turned. "You bastard!" she spat.

"Medea," Socrates said pleadingly, fingering the roll of bills in his pocket as though invoking their aid in this new crisis.

"What are you doing to my daughter?" Medea demanded, her voice rising to a screech.

A profound silence had suddenly enveloped the *Pegasus*.

"What do you mean, Medea?"

"What have you done to my daughter, you filthy, money-grubbing son of a bitch!"

"What did you call me?" Socrates' voice quivered with mounting fury.

"You heard me! If you think I'm going to allow a piece of filth like you to hurt my little girl! Now, you listen to me. If I hear one more complaint from her, I swear before God that I will destroy you. I'll send you back to the gutter, where you belong! I'll break you, you trash!"

The Greek's rage erupted like a volcano. No one, other than Athina, had ever dared speak to him in such a fashion. He was seized with an all but uncontrollable urge to kill the woman. The boat, the sky, the sea, all dimmed and coalesced into a single mass before his eyes, and he heard his voice as though it came from another mouth, shouting, "Get the fuck off my boat!"

Medea was too enraged to sense the danger. "What did you say, you little turd? You're not man enough to order me off this boat!"

"Get off, you old cunt!" Then he was upon her, his fingers tightening around her throat; a black veil descended upon him, cutting him off from the rest of the world.

"Sir! Sir!" Kirillis shouted, pulling the huge woman away from his employer and placing himself between them.

"Cunt!" Satrapoulos shrieked at his mother-in-law as she leaned against the railing, gasping for breath and clutching at her throat.

Stavenos appeared on deck and seized one of Medea's arms. "Please, madame! I think you had best leave immediately!" He half led, half dragged her away, as Medea struggled to free herself from his grasp.

Kirillis did not release Satrapoulos until the two had disappeared down the gangplank.

[18]

The helicopter settled down at the Nice airport only fifty feet from Satrapoulos' plane. Two minutes later the Greek fastened his seat belt and gave Jeff the order to take off. The plane headed west at first, then made a three-quarter circle and disappeared northward, making straight for Hamburg.

Socrates slumped in his seat, sipping from a glass of whiskey and watching the clouds go by. He shook his head wearily. In the past twenty-four hours, he had been attacked first by a jealous husband, then by an outraged mother. And he had not even been able to enjoy the pleasure of beating either one of them to a pulp.

He removed his glasses and rubbed his nose. He glanced out the window again. The clouds had lost their definition and were now a formless fog.

His head dropped to his chest, and he slept.

The impact of Jeff's landing awoke him. He noted with surprise that he was still holding the glass in his hand. He emptied it in one swallow. The tepid whiskey made him gag.

"Hamburg, sir."

"Thanks for telling me. I could have sworn this was Dakar."

He jumped from the plane and turned to Jeff. "Don't leave the plane," he ordered. "Be ready to take off at a moment's notice. As soon as I'm done here, we're going to Athens. And tell Ceyx to meet me there."

"Yes, sir." In his mind, Jeff decoded the message. It meant: I'm going to be blind, roaring drunk, and I'll need my valet to get me home.

The brass plate next to the impressive entry read: NIEBLUNG UND FUST. Socrates was barely inside the lobby when he was met by a blond giant in a black suit. The man bowed deeply and said, "Welcome, sir! Welcome to Nieblung und Fust. We are expecting you. Please follow me."

On the eighth floor, Herr Fust himself welcomed Socrates with open arms. "Dear Mr. Satrapoulos! Dear friend!"

"Are the engineers here?" Socrates demanded.

"Yes, of course. Just as you asked."

"And the architects?"

"Yes, yes. Everyone. They are all waiting for you. It wasn't easy for me to arrange. Some of them were out of the country. Your telephone call was so unexpected—"

Fust threw open the massive double doors leading into a vast conference room. (Less important customers were accorded only one door.) Twenty men were grouped around a long ebony table. They rose as one at the sight of Satrapoulos. With a lordly gesture, the Greek bade them resume their seats.

"Gentlemen, I am pressed for time, so I will get directly to the point. I want you to build me a ship. No, not a ship. *The* ship. What I want is the most luxurious, the most extravagant, the most magnificent pleasure craft in the world."

He paused. The men at the table looked at one another.

"Can you be more specific, Mr. Satrapoulos?" Fust asked.

"Specific? How can I be more specific? I want you to build me a boat which is unique. If I could describe it in detail, it would hardly be unique, would it?"

"Yes, yes, of course," Fust murmured. "I see—"

"No, you obviously do not see. It's impossible for you to see it, just as it's impossible for me to describe it. I want a boat like no other boat that's ever existed, a perfect boat—perfect from the tip of its mast to the base of its keel. With a swimming pool that can be turned into a dance floor or a skating rink with the flick of a switch. And no cabins. I want apartments—*huge* apartments—instead of cabins. Six of them. No more, no less. The bathrooms will be of marble, with fixtures of gold. . . ."

"What tonnage?"

"What kind of engines?"

"What length?"

"What speed?"

The Greek raised his hand for silence. "Gentlemen, those are details which I am happy to leave in your hands. Are you or are you not the best shipbuilders in the world?"

Fust lowered his eyes modestly. His twenty employees followed his example.

"Very well, then. If you're the best shipbuilders in the world, you should be able to build me the best yacht in the world!"

Herr Fust wrung his hands. "Time, Mr. Satrapoulos! We will need time!"

"Of course, Herr Fust. Time. There is less of it than you think. One week from today, I want the preliminary sketches on my desk. Two weeks from today, I want construction to begin. I don't care how you do it. Work three shifts, and use double or triple crews if you have to."

"Mr. Satrapoulos—"

"Yes? What is it?"

"Mr. Satrapoulos, this is impossible! It will take months just to design such a ship. And we have other customers—we have commitments—"

"I'll give you a check for, let's say, six million dollars as a deposit to cover your initial expenses. What? What was that about other customers?"

Herr Fust bowed his head, as though crushed by the weight of Socrates' deposit. Who could refuse such an order when the Danes

282

and the Japanese were using every trick in the book to lure away the firm's customers?

"Mr. Satrapoulos—"

"No arguments, Fust. Yes or no?"

Fust looked around the table. Not one of his men dared meet his eyes. "I promise you that we will do our best, my collaborators and I—"

"I'm not asking you to do your best. I'm asking you to do the impossible. And I want a direct answer. Can you do it, or can't you?"

Fust stood with his mouth half open, breathing heavily.

"Come, come, man. Yes? No? Which is it?"

"Yes," Fust breathed, as though groaning in agony. He tried to smile but succeeded only in twisting his features into a grimace. "The only thing, sir," he ventured timidly, "is that we can't very well start designing a ship on the basis of a swimming pool that converts into a dance floor—" He assayed a laugh which fell miserably flat.

The Greek looked at him severely. "Herr Fust, this ship will be designed around a swimming pool." He leaned toward Fust. "Do you know anything about art, Herr Fust?"

"Me?" Fust stammered. "You mean paintings and statues and that sort of thing?"

"Yes, that sort of thing, Herr Fust. I want you to act as my agent. Find someone who can buy paintings for my yacht without getting screwed. Masterpieces. You understand? Let's say ten million dollars' worth to start with. That doesn't include your commission as my agent, of course. I want everything lively, gay—nothing depressing. I know I can count on your good taste."

Socrates turned to the men around the table. "Well then, gentlemen, it's all settled." He looked at his watch. "I have to leave for Athens in one hour. I can give you thirty minutes for questions. Who wants to start the ball rolling?"

After a moment's hesitation, the youngest of the engineers spoke up. "I have an idea," he said excitedly. "How about this—"

The most exciting thing about Chez Epaphos was that it was the sort of nightclub where one could expect to meet anyone. Simple sailors rubbed elbows with authentic princes, and denizens of the social world mingled on terms of equality with outrageous transvestites. One night, Socrates recalled, he had seen a famous statesman dancing cheek to cheek with a burly American seaman. There were beautiful women, handsome men, persons of cloudy gender, the very young and the very old. Personalities as burdened with wealth and fame as with years. Cosmopolites in evening clothes. Willowy homosexuals disguised in naval uniforms. Defrocked priests, and a few not yet defrocked. All united in a quest for the unusual and the unexpected in pleasure.

Over this continuous happening presided Epaphos himself, a three hundred pound colossus known as Papa to those privileged to be his customers.

Socrates opened the door of Chez Epaphos and turned impatiently to Ceyx. "Why the hell are you following me? I don't want you in here. Go wait for me somewhere else."

"Yes, sir," Ceyx said servilely.

Papa had already sighted Socrates. "My brother!" he roared, advancing on him with outstretched arms. "My brother!" He threw his arms around Socrates, lifted him bodily from the floor and whirled him around in time to the music of a waltz. Then, suddenly, the waltz ceased and the orchestra struck up the *sirtaki* which always signaled the Greek's arrival.

Everyone in the room began to sing:

> Come here, next to me,
> Time is passing,
> My lips are waiting . . .

"Drinks for everyone!" Socrates cried.

Papa led him to a table which he cleared of an anonymous couple with a wave of his hand. In Papa's establishment, the anonymous always gave up their tables to the famous. And they did it graciously, first of all because they had no choice, and second because they knew that, should the time come, they would enjoy the same privilege.

"What are you drinking, my friend?"

"Chivas," Socrates replied.

"Chivas for my brother!"

Chez Epaphos was not a large place. It consisted of a single room furnished with bare wood tables and uncomfortable chairs with straw seats. Most of the lighting came from candles stuck into bottles. The ample bar had once been the prow of a sailing ship.

"So, Papa. How's business?"

"As you see. Never better. Are you alone?"

"Yes."

"Aha. What would you like? A blonde? A brunette? Fat? Skinny? An elephant? Tell me. All that I have is yours!"

"I'll decide later. Will you have a drink with me?"

"Of course!"

"Straight?"

"Is there another way?"

A quarter of the bottle of Chivas disappeared down Papa's throat. Then he banged his glass down on the table. "Excuse me a minute, my friend. I'll be right back," he said.

Socrates watched the giant move across the jammed dance floor with surprising agility, not once colliding with a customer. He looked around. He loved this packed, intolerably noisy place. It was his refuge and his therapy when he was depressed. It took only one night here to clear his brain. He had brought all his mistresses here, but never his wife. Would Menelas like it? He had no idea.

The table opposite Socrates was occupied by two sailors and three women. One of the men—his strikingly handsome face looked vaguely familiar—caught Socrates' eye and raised his glass to him. Then he turned to the girls and said something that made them laugh. Irritated, Socrates beckoned to the sailor. The man rose and walked to Socrates' table. He was tall and muscular, but he moved with extraordinary grace.

"What are you laughing at?"

"Don't you recognize me, Mr. Satrapoulos?"

"Should I?"

"I'm Eugenio. I was a crewman on your boat until a couple of years ago."

"On the *Pegasus?*"

"Yes. I was the launch's helmsman."

Socrates remembered him. A good sailor, he recalled, but he had reported aboard late on several occasions, and eventually Kirillis had had to fire him. According to Kirillis, Eugenio had ten girls in every port.

"So, what were you laughing at?"

Eugenio grinned. "My friend and those girls over there—I was saying that if I had as much money as you, I'd be drinking Chivas, too."

"You like good scotch?"

"Doesn't everyone?"

"Sit down and have a glass. Boy! Bring another glass."

"Don't bother. There's already a glass here."

THE GREEK

"That's Papa's glass. Get one of your own."

Despite his outward show of conviviality, Socrates felt faintly hostile, or rather, resentful. This young fellow had everything that he himself lacked and had always wanted. He was tall, muscular, and moved with a natural, animal litheness emphasized by his broad shoulders and narrow hips. The eyes which looked at Socrates over the table were ice blue in Eugenio's dark Mediterranean face.

"Can you hold your liquor?" Socrates asked.

"As well as anyone."

"As well as me?"

"Maybe."

"We'll see. Bottoms up!"

Both men emptied their glasses in one swallow.

"All right," the Greek suggested. "Let's do it glass for glass. First you, then me. All right?"

"Okay."

Eugenio emptied his glass again, and Socrates followed his lead.

"You were telling me what you'd do if you had my money. What would you do besides drink scotch?"

"I'd do everything you do."

"What do you think I do?"

"You spend your money. You buy things."

"What things would you buy?"

"Everything."

"Everything?"

"Yes, everything. I don't have anything."

"You have your face, your body."

"I can't buy a boat with my face, or a house, or even a woman."

"You need money for women?"

"For some of them."

The Greek shrugged. "Then leave those alone, and screw those who don't want money. What about the girls with you?"

"What about them?"

"Have you screwed them?"

"I only met them an hour ago."

Socrates poured two more glasses of whiskey. "Another bottle of Chivas," he shouted at a passing waiter.

"*Sirtaki!*" Papa yelled from across the room.

"Why don't you dance?" the Greek asked.

"Why don't you?" Eugenio replied.

"If I dance, will you?"

"All right."

Eugenio untied the red scarf around his neck and handed Socrates one end of it. Holding the scarf taut between them, they moved onto the dance floor and stood facing a line of dancers that had already formed. Everyone applauded as the Greek executed the steps of the *sirtaki* with surprising agility.

"You dance very well," Eugenio commented.

"Why not? Do you think a big bank account causes paralysis?" Socrates asked, removing a bill from his pocket, crumpling it into a ball, and tossing it at the musicians.

When the *sirtaki* was over, the two men returned to their table.

"Another drink? Straight?"

"Straight!"

A waiter passed carrying a pile of plates. The Greek stretched out his leg. The waiter stumbled, and the plates crashed to the floor. There was a round of deafening applause and shouts of "Bravo!"

"More plates for my brother!" Papa roared from behind the bar. "Bring as many as he can break!"

"I'll bet I can break more than you have!" Socrates shouted back.

"It's a bet!" Papa replied. "Start bringing the plates!"

Next to the sale of liquor, the breaking of plates was one of the principal sources of income to Chez Epaphos as well as one of its chief forms of entertainment. So long as someone paid for it, Papa had no objection if his customers destroyed everything in his establishment. On special occasions the very tables and chairs were sometimes reduced to kindling.

"Plates for everyone!" Socrates instructed the waiters, and an orgy of destruction began. Shortly, Papa's shouting, laughing customers were ankle-deep in broken crockery. Two waiters were specially assigned to supply ammunition to Socrates and Eugenio, who competed to see who could build the largest pile of fragments in the shortest time.

Soon there were no more plates.

"Let's start on the furniture!" Socrates cried, seizing a chair and smashing it across the tabletop. Eugenio quickly followed his example, then overturned the table and wrenched off one of its legs. Thus armed, he rushed to the bar and began smashing every bottle within reach. Socrates, not to be outdone, seized a fire ax and attacked the great casks of wine which lined one of the walls. The shrieks of Papa's customers reached a crescendo as dark-red jets of wine spurted to the floor.

When all the casks had been destroyed, Socrates lowered his ax, breathing heavily, beaming and waving at the cheering audience.

"All right, Papa," he gasped. "You be the judge. Who's done the most damage? Me or Eugenio?"

Papa, knowing who would pay the bill, grasped Socrates' hand and raised it over his head. "The winner, and still champion!" he announced.

Ignoring the tumult which followed, Socrates turned to Eugenio. "Where are the girls?" he asked.

"I don't know—over there, against the wall."

"Are we going to lay them or aren't we?"

"I'm ready if you are."

"Do you have a place?"

"I have a room."

"Let's take them there."

"Okay."

"How about your friend? Is he coming with us?"

"Forget him. He's not interested."

"Is he gay?"

"A queen to his fingertips. Wait here. I'll get the girls."

"Oh. Papa! Don't forget to send me the bill!"

Papa shrugged. "What is money between brothers?"

"You old bastard. It'll be a miracle if I don't have it by noon tomorrow."

Eugenio returned with the two girls, and he and Socrates, their arms around each other's shoulders, exited to the sound of a *sirtaki* played by the few instruments which had survived the general devastation. As they pushed their way through the door, Papa pointed to Socrates and proclaimed, in a voice calculated to reach the Greek's ears, "There, my friends, goes a real man!"

Ceyx, like a good valet, struggled desperately to stay awake. Sitting on the stoop of the dingy hotel, he could find neither the strength to wait a moment longer nor the courage to disobey Socrates and go home to bed. He looked at his watch. Five thirty. The first rays of the rising sun were already lighting the street.

If he isn't here in fifteen minutes, Ceyx promised himself, I'm leaving.

Five minutes later Socrates appeared in the doorway. He walked past Ceyx into the street, removed his glasses from the pocket of his jacket, wiped them carefully with a square of white silk, and put them on. Then he looked up at the sky, an expression of utter contentment on his face.

Ceyx wondered what he was thinking about.

The Greek removed his jacket, slung it over his shoulder, and began walking away from the hotel.

"Sir!" Ceyx called.

Socrates turned in obvious puzzlement. "Yes?" Then, recognizing Ceyx: "What do you want?"

Ceyx was dumbfounded. He wanted nothing at all, except to go home and get some sleep. He had been told to wait, so he had waited.

"Do you want me to drive you somewhere?"

"Why? Do you have the automobile with you?"

"No—"

"Then how can you drive me anywhere?"

"There's a taxi stand down the street."

Socrates turned and began walking. Ceyx followed three steps behind.

They found an antique Chevrolet manned by a drowsy driver who, for a fixed sum, agreed to take them to the airport.

During the drive, Socrates did not say a word. At the airport, he ordered Ceyx to pay the driver. The valet handed the driver a bill, telling him to keep the change.

"You must be out of your mind," Socrates reprimanded him, "giving the driver a tip like that. At that rate, you'll never be rich, Ceyx! Now, go get Jeff."

Ceyx found Jeff asleep in the pilot's dormitory.

"Is he back?" Jeff asked wearily.

"Yes. He's waiting for you. He wants to take off immediately."

"Did he tie one on?"

"There's not a stick of furniture left at Papa's."

"Then he must be in good shape."

"I don't know. He didn't open his mouth except to make me pay for the taxi."

"Don't worry about it. You'll get it back, one way or another."

"Don't be so sure. With a skinflint like that—well, come on. He's waiting. It's Geneva this time. God knows why."

I'm finished with Helena, Socrates assured himself. There's no point in going on. But what else is there? Other women bore me. As soon as I've had them, I can't stand to see them again. What am I looking for? The ideal state of affairs, obviously, would be to have the woman I love waiting for me, at home, and at the same time leave me free to screw any other woman that I felt like screwing. Except that when a woman loves you, she refuses to let you screw anyone else. Not that that's ever stopped anyone from doing it.

Of course, it will hurt her if I do it. How would I feel if she went with other men? But what am I supposed to do? I can't live alone, and I can't be satisfied with any one woman. How many women does it take to satisfy me?

I can't be the only man in the world to have such a problem. I wonder what the others do. No one ever says. And what about the children? Will it make them unhappy if I decide to openly live with Menelas? After all, children's happiness is sacred, like motherhood and the flag. Yet, when they're grown, they forget the sacrifices you make for their happiness. They turn their backs on you. I did it to my mother; why shouldn't my children treat me the same way? But if my own mother had loved me, things might have been different between us. Maybe she did love me. Do my children know that I love them? How can they know, since I never tell them that I do? And do I really love them, to begin with?

I wonder how Peter will react. Not that I give a damn. If he wants to keep her, he'll have to fight for her. Then we'll see if he's man enough to keep me away from her. She's never said it in so many words, but I know she'll come with me if I ask her. After all, I have to live my life for myself, and not for other people. I'm going to marry her! Otherwise, what good is all my money? Don't I have the right to be happy, like everyone else?

At that moment, the wheels of Satrapoulos' plane touched ground at the Geneva airport. The Greek had not slept for twenty-four hours, but he did not feel tired. Once, when he was seventeen, he had gone without sleep for five whole days and nights. Yet, with the proceeds from that marathon poker game, he had barely been able to buy a new suit. Today, at the age of fifty-five, he could have been the grandfather of that ambitious young man, except that the prospect of stealing the woman he loved from her husband had had a curiously rejuvenating effect on him.

Helena rushed to the door when she heard the key in the lock. As Mark entered, she threw her arms around his neck even before he had closed the door. "Oh, Mark, Mark," she breathed, "my love! I've done it! I'm through with him! I'm going to get a divorce!"

Mark tried to disengage himself, not quite believing what his ears assured him they had heard. With his right foot, he kicked the door shut behind him. He heard the lock click—like the gates of a prison, closing forever. He was incapable of speaking or of thinking.

"I've really done it. It's all over!" Helena went on. "Now you and I can be together forever!"

Little by little, the horror of what she was saying filtered into Mark's brain.

"Aren't you happy?" Helena asked. "Why don't you say something?"

"Yes, yes," he managed to stammer. "It's wonderful. It's just —just that I'm stunned to hear what you've done."

"As soon as you get your divorce we can find a place for ourselves. Maybe on the Champ-de-Mars. But why wait? Talk to her tonight. Tell her that you want a divorce. Oh, Mark, you do love me, don't you?"

He felt the bile rise in his throat and feared he would vomit. "Yes, of course I love you," he muttered.

"Mark, do you realize what this means? I can hardly believe it! We'll never be separated again! Even when you're making a film, I can be at the studio with you! I can hardly believe it!"

He found it even more difficult to believe than she. He had to do something to bring her down out of the clouds, to stop her. But what? And he had to do it quickly. Isabelle was waiting for him. She was so nervous nowadays. What if she found out? Oh, God! What if Helena telephoned her again?

"Helena, please. Let me choose the moment to tell her."

"But why wait?"

"It would be better, really. Everything is happening so quickly. I didn't expect—"

She stood back and glared at him. "You didn't expect it? We've been talking about it for six years!"

"I know, I know. But you have to understand—"

"Understand what?"

"Just let me get used to the idea. Let's not rush into anything."

"Mark! Mark—"

Now, in order to subdue the terror that was rising in him like a flood, Mark began to shout. "What do you think I am? You drop this bomb in my lap without any warning! You may be free to do as you like, but I have certain responsibilities. I can't just forget ten years of marriage in five minutes!"

"But, Mark, you said—"

"I said, I said! Do you think this is easy for me?"

"Mark, for your sake I've left Socrates, my children, my life, everything. You swore that you would—"

"You're trying to back me up against a wall, and I won't have it, do you understand?"

"Mark!"

"Mark! Mark! Mark! For God's sake, stop saying that! It's all very simple for you! You walk away from your husband, and that's that! You don't even give me any warning of what you plan to do. And now you expect me to act the same way. You're like a child! You have to have what you want right away, and to hell with everyone else. Well, I've had enough of this. I'm getting out of here!"

Before Helena could answer, he was gone, slamming the door behind him.

Helena stood motionless in the center of the room for a full minute, tears coursing down her cheeks. Then she threw herself across the bed, sobbing soundlessly.

The Gonzales de Salvador villa was situated in a quiet residential section on the outskirts of Geneva. On one of the red-brick gateposts, Socrates read "Sonata." All things considered, he told himself, it would have been more fitting to name the house Serenade. He pressed the button on the intercom station at the gate.

"Who is it?" a voice echoed from the speaker.

"Socrates Satrapoulos."

He suppressed an impulse to kick down the gates. It was not necessary. They swung open slowly of their own accord. He plunged up the walk to the house, between the rows of rhododendrons, until he reached the entry. A liveried servant was waiting for him in the open doorway.

"Where is your employer?" Satrapoulos snapped.

"Do you have an appointment, sir?"

"Is he here or not?"

"I do not know whether Monsieur Gonzales de Salvador is here or not, sir. I will inquire."

"Don't bother," Satrapoulos snarled, brushing past the man. "I'll find out for myself."

As he reached the main staircase, the Greek heard the sound of a door opening. "Aurelian," Peter's voice called down. "Who is it?" Then Peter himself appeared on the landing in a cranberry velvet robe. He saw the Greek and immediately turned white as chalk. "If you've come to offer your apologies," he intoned loftily, "you're wasting your time. I refuse to accept them."

"I have nothing to apologize for," Socrates replied. "I've come for your wife."

"What? What did you say?" Peter sputtered.

"You heard me. Where is she?"

"Aurelian, please leave us alone." The De Salvadors did not display their personal problems in front of servants.

Aurelian withdrew, reluctantly.

"Olympia!" Socrates shouted, at the top of his voice.

"You're out of your mind!" Peter shouted back. "She's not here!" His voice rose several decibels between the first word and the last.

"All right. Since you won't tell her I'm here, I'll tell her myself!" The Greek began to move up the staircase. Peter stood at the landing, spreading his arms wide to block the way.

"Calm down, for heaven's sake!" the Spaniard said. "Calm down. Let's sit down for a moment and discuss this. You can't be serious!"

"Olympia! Where are you?" Socrates called, ignoring Peter.

He found her in her room. She had heard his voice when he arrived, and rather than appear or take part in the scene, she had curled up in a corner of her room, waiting in the time-honored tradition of the woman over whom two men have met in mortal combat. She hardly looked up at the Greek as he entered her room.

"Olympia," he said softly, "I've come for you. I want to marry you. If you don't come with me now, I'll come back tomorrow, and the day after, and all the days of my life until you follow me out of this house. I'll wait downstairs."

"You're crazy!" Peter stammered as he followed in Satrapoulos' wake. "Out of your mind! You have no right to do this!"

Socrates turned on him. "Shut up! If you're man enough to fight for her, then do so. Defend her, if she's really yours. Keep me from taking her away from you!"

"I'll call the police," Peter shrieked. "That's what I'll do. You'll pay for this!"

"I hope so," the Greek replied. "No price is too high to pay for such a woman. That is something you've never understood."

Menelas' voice reached them from upstairs. "Aurelian!"

The servant rushed past the two men.

"Do you think for a minute that she'll go with you?" Peter snarled contemptuously, then fell silent.

In a few minutes Aurelian reappeared on the stairs, carrying two suitcases.

"Aurelian," Peter choked, "what are you doing?"

"It's Madame, sir," Aurelian replied helplessly. "She told me to take these to the gate."

Peter rushed into the library and slammed the door. A moment later Menelas appeared at the head of the stairs. As she descended, she caressed the banister of polished ebony as though in a final adieu. She stopped when she reached Satrapoulos and looked at him for a long moment, her eyes boring into his.

"I'm ready," she said.

"Do you want to see him before you go?"

She shook her head. "No. I'm ready to go."

Socrates took her hand and silently led her out into the sunlight. At the end of the walk, outside the gate, stood the Bentley. Beyond it were the roads, the mountains, the sea, the sky, the world.

The orchestra played softly aboard the *Pegasus* as the yacht rode at anchor two miles off Ibiza. At table, one dish followed another and was removed without being touched by either Socrates or Olympia. They sat in silence, not speaking or moving. But above the flickering candles, their eyes met and held. For once in his life, Socrates was not in a hurry to take possession of that which belonged to him. There would be time enough for that. He had seen that Olympia was comfortably installed in a spacious cabin; then he had spent the remainder of the afternoon on the telephone with his offices around the world. The hours had passed gently, unhurriedly, until the coming of twilight.

"You haven't touched your food, Olympia," he said at last. "Aren't you hungry? Would you like something to drink?"

"No. You haven't eaten either. And you've drunk enough for both of us."

"That's true. I haven't done anything for the past two days but drink. When I can't sleep, I drink."

"You didn't sleep at all?"

"Not a wink."

"Aren't you tired?"

"Not at all. I feel as though I could go on forever."

"So do I. I feel marvelous—as though I were floating."

"Perhaps we could go for a walk on the beach. Would you like that?"

"Oh, yes!"

A few moments later they were aboard the launch, speeding toward shore. Well forward in the boat, there was a large, boxlike object covered with a canvas. When they reached the beach, Socrates climbed out first, then helped Olympia disembark. He whispered a few words to Stavenos, and the officer nodded.

Socrates and Olympia were a hundred yards up the beach when they heard the launch pull noisily away from shore. Then the night was silent once more.

Socrates raised his eyes and looked at the sky.

"Do you know the names of the stars?" Olympia asked.

"Yes."

"What is that one called? The one all the way to the left?"

"At the very edge of the sky? That's Arcturus. And directly above us is Cassiopeia. Can you see it? To the right is the Great Bear, and, farther on, the Andromeda nebula."

"What's a nebula?"

"Star dust. Or rather, the debris of a star that has exploded. I'm surprised you didn't know."

"There are so many things I don't know." She took his hand. "You'll have to teach me."

"Do you know how many stars there are in the sky?"

"Well, no—"

"Picture to yourself the surface of the earth, and imagine that it corresponds to the sky. For every square yard of the earth's surface, there are fifteen hundred stars."

"Really?"

"Really. And every one of those stars is born, grows, and finally dies."

"How do they die?"

"They explode, most of them." He laughed softly. "In some ways, I'm like a star."

"Why? Do you feel like exploding?"

"Yes, if I had my choice. I'd rather explode than simply peter out."

She looked at him. In the darkness, she could barely make out his form. He felt her breath on his face as she whispered, "Yes, I'd rather explode, too. Now, at least."

Her hair brushed against his cheek. Socrates gently circled her with his arms, and she trembled against him.

"I want to show you something," Socrates said, and he led her toward the spot where they had landed on the beach. There was a large trunk lying on the sand.

"Do you know what that is?"

"No."

"Your dresses. Your furs. Your jewels. Everything that you brought with you from Geneva."

"What are you going to do with them?"

"I'm going to burn them to ashes."

Menelas' temper was famous the world over, and Socrates would not have been surprised if she had screamed or even struck him. Instead, she sighed softly, as though in relief, and said, "Why?"

"Because tonight is a beginning for you and me. I want to destroy everything that belongs to the past. I want you to come to me stripped of all that you had before, naked as the day you were born."

He walked to the trunk and found a jerrican of gasoline next to it. He emptied the can over the trunk, shaking it to make certain that no fuel remained. He looked at Menelas. "No regrets, Olympia?"

"None, Socrates."

He returned to her side, struck a match, and threw it onto the trunk. There was a great burst of flame which blocked out the stars and threw an eerie orange light over the white sand.

Socrates felt Olympia stir against him. He stretched out his arms to embrace her, but she moved away. He saw her body silhouetted against the roaring fire as she slipped her dress over her head and dropped it at his feet.

"Here," she said. "You forgot this."

"Olympia—"

"And this," she said, pressing something cold into his hand.

He looked down at the pearl necklace, then dropped it onto the dress lying in the sand. After a moment's thought, he bundled the dress and the pearls together and threw them into the low shrubs growing at the edge of the sand.

"So much for the past," Menelas whispered. She took his face between her hands and pressed herself against him. "And now, Socrates, am I naked enough for you?"

Kallenberg threw the newspaper to the floor in disgust. For three months, page one had been filled with stories of Satrapoulos and

Menelas. Satrapoulos and Menelas in Acapulco, Satrapoulos and Menelas in Beirut. Satrapoulos and Menelas in Palm Beach. Satrapoulos and Menelas in West Berlin. Wasn't there any other news in the world, for God's sake? What was there about that insignificant little Greek that so fascinated the press? How much was he paying them for the publicity? If people only knew how this little hero of theirs had been taken by his brother-in-law for millions of dollars. . . .

"All right, Greta," Kallenberg said. "I'll call you when I need you."

Greta smiled. When Kallenberg did not remove his hand from under her skirt, she stood and moved away, gently disengaging herself from his fingers.

When she had gone, Kallenberg spun around in his chair and twirled the dial of the small safe behind his desk. He opened the door and removed a folder marked simply "Baran."

He smiled to himself, then laughed softly. "Now the poor bastard is going to pay," he said aloud.

On the desk before him, he spread out the contract by which Socrates had agreed to cede him thirty-five percent of his business with the Persian Gulf emirates. He scanned it.

Something was wrong, but Kallenberg could not quite put his finger on it. He read the contract again closely. It was all there, just as the two men had dictated it to Greta that morning at Ibiza.

Then he saw it. Or rather, he did not see it. At the bottom of the page, at the spot where Socrates had signed, there was a blank space.

In a panic, Kallenberg held the paper up to the light.

Nothing.

He turned it over.

Still nothing. The space was as empty as though it had never been touched by a pen.

Kallenberg leaped from his chair and rushed into the corridor like a madman, shouting, "Greta! Greta!"

Yet he already knew that it was futile. There was nothing that could be done. By some utterly unexplainable process, he had once more been had by the Greek.

Part Three

[19]

THE taxi took Helena well beyond Marseilles, to the very foothills of the Alps. Even the driver, who prided himself on his knowledge of the countryside, did not recognize the name of the place where his fare ordered him to stop. He knew only that somewhere nearby a group of American hippies—a commune they called themselves—were living like savages. This one looked as if she belonged to them, with her faded jeans and her sloppy sweater. Yet she had paid the fare of fifty-two thousand francs without comment and had thrown in eight thousand extra as a tip. He watched as she strode along the path away from the road, admiring the movement of her legs inside the tight denim pants. When she had disappeared from sight, he shook his head and turned the car back toward Marseilles. Wait until he told his friends about this one.

The first things to strike Helena about the place were the silence and the natural perfume of the air. Occasionally, there was a sound in the grass; a lizard, perhaps, or a rabbit. Without knowing why, she began to run, happy to feel her legs moving freely. How long had it been since she had really run? Not silly, pointless running on asphalt tennis courts, but running like a free being in the open air?

She reached the top of a hill and stopped. Breathing hard, she looked down. In the shallow valley below, she saw the roof of a farmhouse. She noted that several tiles were missing. Just below the overhang, there were windows, their gray shutters peeling with age. She heard the sound of chickens clucking and of guitar music. To the right of the house, a man was drawing water from a well. He was bare to the waist, and he was singing aloud to the music of the guitar.

Helena put down her knapsack and let herself absorb the music, the scent of the air, the beauty of the man's bronzed, muscular back. She felt that this was one of those rare moments in her life when she was at peace with her surroundings. A memory flashed through her mind of another such moment. She was swimming in the Mediterranean, near her husband's yacht, moving up toward the surface, toward the aureoled body of her waiting lover. . . .

She bent down, picked up her knapsack, swung it onto her shoulders, and began walking toward the man at the well. When she was twenty feet away from him, she spoke. "Hello."

He turned. "Hello."

He could not have been more than twenty; a very tall, slender young man. He smiled, and his teeth were like a row of lights in his tanned, bearded face. His light-blue eyes sparkled in the sun, and Helena caught her breath. She had never seen a man as handsome.

She struggled to compose herself. Above all, she must act with authority here. "I've come for my sister," she said in English.

The man put down his bucket. "Who is your sister?" he asked.

"Melina. Melina Mikolofides."

He grinned broadly. "So you're Melina's sister. She's gone to gather some firewood. Would you like a drink of water?"

Helena was suddenly aware that she was dying of thirst.

"No, thank you," she replied coldly.

"Here, have a drink. It's pure water. No chemicals added."

He took her hand and led her toward the well. He handed her a dipper. "Here, drink."

She drank, and the water was so cold that it burned her throat. She swallowed greedily.

"So," the man said when she had returned the dipper to him, "you're the wife of the famous Satrapoulos, the oilman." He burst out laughing, apparently not impressed by Satrapoulos.

"You're five years behind the times," Helena said. "I'm now the Duchess of Sunderland."

His incredible blue eyes mocking, the man bowed low before her. "I beg your pardon, your Grace. I did not know it was you."

She could have killed him on the spot.

"In any case," the man said, "it doesn't make much difference to us whether you're a duchess or a charwoman. Here everyone is treated alike. We're all equal."

"We?"

"There are seven of us. Three girls and four boys. With you, we'll be eight—four and four. A good, round number."

"You're mistaken," Helena replied sharply. "Without Melina and me, you'll be only six."

"What makes you think that Melina wants to leave? In fact, what makes you think that *you'll* want to leave?"

"Where is my sister?"

"Look, why don't you and I declare a truce? Are you hungry?"

"No."

"A minute ago you weren't thirsty, but that didn't keep you from drinking." He picked up the bucket and turned toward the house, and despite herself, Lena followed him. When he reached the doorway, he stepped aside to allow her to precede him. As she passed him, he said softly, "My name is Fast."

Angrily, Irene kicked off her shoes and threw her purse onto the bed. It sprang open, spilling its contents onto the floor. Behind her, her butler and her personal maid exchanged glances.

"Well, don't just stand there," Irene snapped. "Pick up these things!"

Liza, the maid, rushed forward to do as she was told.

"No, no, forget it, Liza. Just leave it. I'll do it myself. Leave me alone for a moment. I'll ring for tea in a few minutes."

Liza knew her mistress well enough to realize that a storm was brewing. She signaled discreetly to the butler, and the two servants withdrew in silence.

Before the door closed behind them, Irene was already fumbling in her purse. She quickly found what she wanted: her pillbox. She opened it, removed three small capsules and threw them into her mouth. She made a face, and opening the door of a small table next to her bed, she removed a bottle of brandy and drank deeply from it. Then she sank onto the bed, moaning in rage and frustration.

Three days earlier she had received a call from her mother in Athens. "Come home immediately," Medea had commanded her. "Take the first plane. Don't ask questions. There is trouble in the family!"

She had felt an impulse to rebel, to say that she would not go, to hang up on the old woman. But habit had asserted itself. "Yes, Mama," she had answered meekly. "I'll come right away."

She had arrived at her mother's house to find Helena already there. Medea immediately launched into an impassioned monologue, pacing the floor in front of her two daughters. "We are disgraced," she cried. "Dishonored! And where there is dishonor, ruin must follow."

Irene and Helena waited for her to continue. Instead Medea walked to her desk and opened a small metal box. She removed a piece of paper from it and waved it at them. "Here," she said, "read this! Thank God your father did not live to see his name besmirched in this way!"

The two younger women leaned over the desk and read the clipping from a French newspaper. It was headlined: SHIPPING MAGNATE'S DAUGHTER IN MAN-MADE PARADISE.

Irene knew instantly that the article was about Melina. Her eyes moved down the page. According to the article, Melina "breaking with the family tradition of hard work and dedication to business, is living an extremely"—the word "extremely" was in italics—"an extremely free life in a hippie commune located in the south of France in which everything is held in common: pleasure, food, sleep, water, and love." Naturally, "love" was also in italics.

"Well?" Medea rasped. "What do you think?"

Irene, in astonishment, realized that the question was addressed to her. It was the first time in her life that her mother had asked for her opinion about anything.

"Before you say anything," Medea continued, "look at these." She removed a stack of clippings from the metal box. "These are from other newspapers and magazines. There's not a newspaper in Europe that hasn't picked up the story from this filthy French scandalsheet."

"Poor Melina." Irene sighed. "How miserable she must be!"

"*She's* miserable, you say? How about me? Listen to me, both of you. Your sister has got to put an end to this foolishness. I want her to come home. And if she won't come of her own accord, I'll send the police to bring her back by force!"

"Do you want us to try to bring her back?" Helena asked.

"Both of us?" Irene added.

Medea was silent for a moment. She looked at her daughters. "What is your opinion?" she asked at last.

Irene was delighted at the opportunity to act as mediator between warring factions of the family. "Mama, I think it would be better if only one of us went. It's a matter of discretion. There would be less chance of only one of us being noticed."

Medea eyed her fixedly. "That's your opinion, is it?"

"Yes, Mama."

Medea turned to Helena. "What about you?"

"I think Irene's right. If we both go, Melina might feel that we're trying to force her against her will, and she'll never come back."

Medea placed both her hands flat on the desk, palms downward. "Then it's decided," she said. "Helena, you will be the one to go."

Irene felt as though a dagger had been plunged into her heart. With a single sentence, her mother had destroyed the sense of importance she had enjoyed so briefly for the first time in her life. Yet she dared not protest Medea's decision, so she attempted to hide her disappointment by saying the opposite of what was in her mind. She turned to Helena. "Mama is right. You're much more of a diplomat than I am. And I have so much to do in London—"

"Forget about going back to London," Medea snapped. "You'll stay here with me and wait for Melina. We have to stick together at times like this."

"But my husband—"

Medea snorted. "Your husband, indeed!"

And so, while Helena went in search of Melina, Irene had spent three days listening to her mother list the faults of Herman Kallenberg and Socrates Satrapoulos, neither of whom, as she confided to Irene, Medea had ever been able to stand. She resented their success in business, and she had never been able to forgive Satrapoulos for divorcing Helena. She regarded their very existence as an insult to her as a businesswoman and as a mother. For three days, Irene had endured Medea's recital of the real and imagined injuries and insults she had sustained at the hands of her sons-in-law. Finally, on the morning of the fourth day, Irene could bear it no longer. In tears, she pleaded with her mother to allow her to return to London, promising that she would telephone her every day and that she would fly back to Athens immediately when Melina returned.

Now she lay on her bed in London, exhausted. She closed her eyes for a few seconds. When she opened them again, her husband was standing at the foot of her bed, looking at her in open disgust.

"Herman," she whimpered. "That woman! She has no heart. She sent Helena to find Melina instead of sending me!"

Kallenberg exploded. "I don't give a fuck about your stupid mother or your bitch of a sister! Something terrible has happened!"

Mechanically, Irene wiped the tears from her eyes with the back of her hand, smearing the makeup across her cheeks. What could be more terrible than what was happening to her? she wondered. First, she had been utterly humiliated by her mother, and now her husband was treating her like dirt.

Melina straightened up with a sigh. "Oh, shit!" she mumbled, rubbing her aching back. She pulled a crumpled pack of Gauloises from her pocket, straightened one of the cigarettes, lighted it, and threw herself down under an olive tree.

God, she said to herself, what am I doing in this place? I wasn't happy playing the grand lady at home, and I'm not happy playing the country bumpkin here.

She inhaled deeply and allowed the smoke to drift slowly out of her mouth and nostrils.

The truth was that Melina had an itch that not even Fast, with his gorgeous body and irritating sarcasms, could cure. It was an affliction from which she had always suffered. She could not bear to deprive herself of any experience. There had been her first cigarette at ten, her first lover at thirteen, her first marijuana shortly thereafter. Her motivation had always been the same: to see what it was like. The irony of it all was that her mother and sisters had always insisted on regarding her as the perennial baby of the family, simply because her rebelliousness made her unpredictable and because she refused to bow to the traditions of the Mikolofides clan. No matter what kind of troubles she had got into—and there had been a variety of them—Medea had always insisted that her daughter was merely being independent, perhaps because it was easier to accept that explanation than to conclude that she was, in fact, unbalanced, or a drug addict, or perverted.

Melina had managed to escape a fate similar to that of Irene, whom she regarded as a brainless mannequin, and of Helena, whom she saw as colorless and insignificant as she was beautiful. But having accomplished that, she was still unsatisfied. Or rather, she had discovered that having escaped Scylla, she was in danger of falling into the hands of Charybdis. Yet she was too proud to go back, to attempt to rebuild some of the bridges that she had burned. Therefore, she pretended, sometimes even to herself, to believe in the adventure she was currently living—in collective love, in far-ranging philosophical theories, even in the benefits of a vegetarian diet. She had become the prisoner of an antisystem which was nothing more than the mirror image of the system she had rejected. There were times, it is true, when she felt that her greatest victory over the world would be to admit that she had been wrong. But at the last moment something always prevented her from doing so.

If it weren't for Fast, she told herself now, I would have gotten out of this place long ago.

She rose, crushed out her cigarette, picked up her bundle of kindling, and slung it over her shoulder. It was time to go back.

Fast was waiting for her at the door of the house, his eternal and eternally ambiguous smile on his lips. She knew instinctively that he had something to tell her. She stopped and dropped the wood to the ground.

"There's someone here to see you," Fast said. "She says you're going to leave with her."

"Who is it?"

"Your sister."

Irene had no idea how long she had remained slumped over her bidet. After Herman's departure, she had wept for a long time before falling into an almost stonelike trance, her eyes vacant. She pulled herself up painfully, ran the hot water full blast into the tub, and staggered over to the mirror—she looked hideous. She drew a small bottle labeled MERCUROCHROME from the medicine cabinet over the sink and drank deeply from it.

She had been in the habit of hiding whiskey in the most unlikely places, in ink bottles, medicine bottles, perfume bottles.

For no reason. No one asked for excuses when she was drunk. She let her crumpled dress slide from her body, stepped out of it, and tried to open the door. She was locked in. She twisted the handle, rattled it—nothing. Herman had imprisoned her. She pounded with both hands on the door, but there was no answer.

She was so stupid! She'd forgotten the bathroom extension, which connected directly with the switchboard. She picked up the receiver: there was no dial tone, nothing. Livid with rage, she threw the phone against the wall, knocking out a tile. Thoughts of revenge stormed through her head. Since Kallenberg behaved like the world's filthiest pig, she'd make him pay!

She flung open the window overlooking the rear of the villa. Not much chance there. The garden was immense, and the servants rarely set foot in it. The chances of escaping weren't worth counting on. Her suite was on the fourth floor, and the outside wall offered no footholds except for the thin iron wires which the ivy climbed. Gasping, she turned and shut off the hot water. The room was filled with steam, which coated each object with a misty sheen. She turned on the cold water, sat back down on the bidet and thought. Beneath her, on the ground floor, were offices and part of the kitchen. It would be the devil's own work if nobody was there now. She had to draw their attention! She returned to the medicine cabinet, set the mercurochrome bottle to one side on a glass table, and began taking things from the cabinet and tossing them out the window, one by one. A huge flask of perfume shattered forty feet below. No reaction. More bottles followed. . . . Where were the idiots? What did she pay them for? She braced herself and wrenched the cabinet itself off the wall. Using all her strength, she carried it slowly over to the window and gave it a shove. Three seconds later came the great crash. She leaned out and heard someone open the door below: Marthe, one of the kitchen maids, gazed up stupidly and spotted her mistress.

"Can't you see I'm locked in?" Irene cried. "What are you waiting for?"

From above, Marthe resembled a melon. The melon rolled out of sight. A few minutes later Albert freed her. She nearly trampled him as she dashed straight for her room, made sure the phone there worked, then feverishly placed her first call.

"Tell me what you're looking for."

"I don't know what you want me to say."

"Say whatever you want," Helena insisted, "and we'll go on from there."

"The opposite."

"What?"

"The opposite. That's what I want. I want to be the opposite of what you are: of what you feel, of what you think, of the people you know and the food you eat. The opposite of what you've made of your life—the dresses and cocktail parties, the sweet old ladies, the sugar daddies disguised as husbands, the endless, boring cruises. And above all, the opposite of our mother."

"What on earth do you have against Mama?"

"Oh, for God's sake, Helena. At this rate, we'll never get anywhere. The trouble is that she's never done anything to me. She's simply closed her mind to the kind of life I want to lead, to everything I love."

"And what do you love?"

"The exact opposite of what you love. Does that satisfy you? Do you even understand what I'm saying? In our family, we are not allowed to marry men. We're supposed to marry titles or bank accounts. And you've done it, because those are the things you love."

Helena did not answer.

"Isn't that the truth?" Melina went on relentlessly. "Isn't that why you married Socrates? And you didn't even choose him yourself. You allowed him to buy you from Mama, as though you were a piece of merchandise. And if he hadn't been rich enough to pay the price, you would have married the first man to come along who was. Then, when you were all settled within the system, you did what everyone else in your world does. You began taking lovers. You people disgust me! You make me want to vomit!"

"Haven't you had lovers?"

"Of course I have, but at least they're men I've chosen for myself. When I see a man who attracts me, I get him. Then, when I've had enough of him, I leave him. It's all honest and straightforward. No lies, no pretenses!"

Nervously, Melina lighted a cigarette. She looked at her sister. Helena was sitting facing her, her face devoid of any expression. There was no way of knowing if Helena had even heard her.

"All right," Melina said in exasperation. "That's enough beating around the bush. Why did you come here?"

"I was sent to bring you home."

"Who sent you?"

"Mama, of course."

"What does she want?"

"Simply for you to come home."

"Why?"

"Because you're her daughter."

"It's taken her a long time to realize that I am."

"She's always known it. You're the one who hasn't always acted as though she were your mother."

"She and I have nothing to say to each other."

"Perhaps *you* have nothing to say."

"I don't give a damn about anything that she has to say."

"Melina, how old are you?"

"Don't you know?"

"I want to hear you say it."

"What kind of game is this? Who do you think you are?"

"You're thirty years old."

Melina reddened with anger. "So what?" she hissed.

"So nothing. Except that you've spent the past ten years 'experiencing life,' as you put it. Don't you think it's time you tried to decide where you are and where you're going?"

Melina was taken aback by the question. This sister of hers, whom she had always regarded as hopelessly empty-headed, was perhaps not quite as stupid as she had thought. She herself had asked the same question with increasing urgency during the past few weeks. And yet the whole purpose of her rebellion had been to discover the meaning of her life.

"I can understand," Helena continued, "that you would reject the kind of life that our family leads. After all, you didn't choose to be born into a family of shipowners. But do you think the rest of us are really happy living as we do? Do you really believe that I've never wanted to run away, as you did? To live my life as I wanted to? But I was always stopped short by one basic question: what kind of life would I have chosen for myself? You see, I have no talent for anything. I can't paint, or sing, or write, or play a musical instrument. I've never had a single brilliant idea in my life. I'm a nobody, and I know it. The only thing I'm fitted for is to be a consumer—to enjoy the accomplishments of other people, and then only so long as they're not too complicated for me to understand."

Melina could not recall ever having heard her sister speak at such length or with such coherence.

"What's the point?" she asked brusquely.

"The point is this: have you broken with your family and your environment in order to be free to create something?"

The question threw Melina into confusion. Her aim was not so much to be right as to appear right, and her method of debating was not to pile up evidence but to demolish her adversaries by ridicule and contempt. But how did one go about destroying someone who confessed that she was nothing?

"What have you created by playing at being a duchess?" she snarled.

"What have you created by playing at being a peasant?"

"At least I don't spend my time going to stupid teas or cruising around the Mediterranean with a bunch of drunks!"

"Perhaps not, but you do spend it gathering firewood and feeding chickens."

"I love doing those things!"

Helena looked at her older sister searchingly. "Do you, Melina? Do you really?"

"Oh, leave me alone! You're too stupid to understand anything. Why don't you lead your life and let me lead mine? Why did you have to come here and stick your nose into my business? Do I try to interfere with the way you live?"

"No, you don't."

"Then why don't you and Mama leave me alone! I could never go back to her. I'd be afraid of becoming like her."

"Do you despise her so much?"

"I hate her! She's everything that I find disgusting in life!"

"And me? Do you hate me, too?"

"I don't know. I hate the kind of life you lead."

Helena stood. "All right, Melina," she said calmly. "I think we understand each other. I'd like to go back to the house now to call a taxi."

"This isn't Fifth Avenue," Melina retorted contemptuously. "We have no telephone."

How can they exist without a telephone? Helena asked herself in honest bewilderment. "All right," she replied. "Could someone drive me to the nearest village?"

"On what? Our cow?"

"You mean you have no automobile?"

"Haven't you understood anything I've said?"

"I'm sorry. All right. I'll walk."

"Don't be stupid. In a few minutes, it's going to be dark. You won't even be able to find the path to the highway."

"I'll manage."

"Not a chance. It's a three-hour walk. Have you ever walked for three hours in your whole life, even in the daylight?" Melina smiled. It would be interesting to see how her bourgeois sister would react in a situation beyond her previous experience. "Come on, Helena. We don't agree on how to live our lives, but that's no reason for you to break your neck trying to get back tonight. Spend the night here with us. It's not exactly Buckingham Palace, but you'll be comfortable enough. Then, early in the morning, I'll walk you to the highway. All right?"

Helena hesitated. "Well," she said finally, "I don't seem to have much choice."

* * *

It was five thirty in the afternoon when the telephone rang, incongruously, almost indecently, at the sacred moment when tea was being served in the great drawing room of Sunderland Castle. Mortimer, twelfth duke of his line, moved his spoon slowly in his cup to dissolve the two lumps of sugar. His mother sat opposite him, turning the pages of the *Times*. The jangle of the telephone brought an expression of disdain to her patrician features. Nonetheless, she put down the newspaper and picked up the receiver. Mortimer, despite his parent's avowed disdain for the telephone, would never have been guilty of the impropriety of denying her the pleasure of answering.

The dowager duchess listened for a moment with a pained expression on her face. Then she handed the instrument to Mortimer as though it were an unclean object.

"It's for you."

The duke took the receiver, as his mother pretended to return to her newspaper.

"What name did you say? Oh, yes. Of course. How stupid of me."

The dowager duchess watched her son from behind her newspaper.

"No," she heard him say, "she's not here."

He listened for several minutes, nodded, and said: "It was kind of you to call, Mrs. Kallenberg." He stumbled over the name, finding it no easier to admit now that such a creature could possibly be his sister-in-law than he had in the beginning. "I will make certain that she is informed."

He replaced the receiver. "Mother, Helena's former husband, Mr. Satrapoulos, has died. Helena's sister Irene has no idea where Helena or her children are. What should I do?"

The taste of vindication was sweet in the dowager duchess' mouth. "My dear Mortimer," she said triumphantly, "how often have I expressed my opposition to this marriage of yours—"

The duke raised his eyebrows. "I'm sorry, but I don't quite see what that has to do with it."

"Only this," his mother replied. "When one marries a divorced woman in defiance of the laws of the church, one must not expect to escape with impunity."

Mortimer shrugged, a gesture which was for him tantamount to open rebellion.

"Mortimer, how old are you?"

"Forty-five, Mother. Almost."

"Very well. You are an adult. Accept an adult's responsibilities. Resolve this problem in any way that you wish."

With a sigh of resignation, the duke settled back in his chair. When one's family antedates the Crusades, when one owns a large part of Lancashire, and especially when one is heir to one of England's great fortunes, one does not argue with one's mother. Particularly when the opinions and prejudices of the mother in question are those that were current at the court of Queen Victoria. The duke had never been able to persuade his mother to accept Helena, and it was unlikely that he would ever be able to do so. The fact that Helena came from a family of tradespeople, however wealthy they might be, was a taint which might fade with the passage of time. But that she was a divorcée was a blot which nothing could ever eradicate. For the Dowager Duchess of Sunderland was an old-fashioned woman with old-fashioned beliefs. It did not seem incongruous to hear her speak of women who divorced and remarried as "living in sin."

The duke sighed again. In their six months of marriage Helena had never ceased to be a problem. When one conferred the strawberry leaves of a ducal coronet on the daughter of Levantine merchants, one could reasonably expect a certain amount of gratitude in return. Helena, however, acted as though it were *she* who had raised *him* from the gutter.

"Well, Mortimer," his mother snapped, "what do you intend to do?"

He dared not tell her what he had just learned from Irene: that Helena, whom he had supposed to be in Athens with her family, had actually been living in a hippie commune in the south of France for several days now. What on earth could a married woman be doing in such a place? And what should he do in such a circumstance?

"Mortimer, do you at least know where your wife is at this moment?"

"Yes, of course," he replied truthfully enough. Then he abandoned the truth. "She's staying with friends of ours in the south of France."

"Well, then, call her on the telephone."

"These friends have no telephone," he replied lamely.

The dowager duchess fell silent, thinking, and Mortimer did not dare disturb her. He waited, as he had waited for forty-five years, for her decision.

"Mortimer," she said finally, "we are members of a family in which duty has always taken precedence over personal inclination. Our duty is clear in this situation. You must go to the south of France and inform your wife of the death of this Satrapoulos person."

"When should I go?"

"Immediately, of course. We will go by air to Marseilles and then rent an automobile."

"We?"

"Obviously. You have displeased me, but that is no reason for me to abandon you. I will order our bags packed. You might try telephoning the airport for flight information."

Mortimer blinked nervously. It occurred to him that his world was about to collapse around his ears.

The island was called Orangine, and it was nothing more than a sandbar held in place by a growth of coral. Its sole native vegetation consisted of eight palm trees, one of which was presently infested by a reddish fungus. Agronomists called in by the Vermeers had stated that this dendrological leprosy was quite common in the Bahamas and that there was nothing to be done about it. Thereafter Hans Vermeer had closely observed the gradual decline of his ailing palm, and as insurance against its eventual loss he had had a hundred more small palms imported, all of which stubbornly refused to grow a single inch in their new home. Hans was staring at them resentfully now when he heard the sound of metal striking wood somewhere nearby. The sound seemed to be coming from the other side of the house. Probably one of the hands repairing a boat. He walked around the house, and what he saw would have made his hair stand on end if he had not had the misfortune to lose it long before. A small blond boy was chopping lustily at the trunk of one of the seven healthy palm trees. An equally blond girl was sitting on the ground, laughing.

"Achilles!" Hans screamed, running forward. "Put down that ax this instant."

The boy turned, saw Hans, laughed, and struck the tree another mighty blow. As he raised the ax again, Hans seized it and pulled it from his hands. It was all the man could do to restrain himself from slapping the child. After all, he told himself, the twins were only here because he had asked their parents to allow them to stay for two weeks.

"Maria, where is your governess? And your tutor?"

"The tutor is with the governess," the girl answered.

"Come with me," Hans ordered, seizing the children by their

hands and leading them toward the house. He found his wife in the living room, sewing. Beyond, in the transparent green waters of the lagoon, he saw his yacht, the *Hankie*, sparkling white in the Caribbean sun. Hans himself was a poor sailor; but his wife adored the boat, and Hans forced himself to accompany her on her endless cruises. It was the least he could do, he told himself. After all, for all his wealth, he had been unable to give her the one thing she wanted more than anything else: children. For the same reason, he indulged her mania for turning all of their residences into vacation colonies for children—other people's children. Fortunately most of them were notably better behaved than these Satrapoulos brats.

"Hankie, do you know what I caught these children doing?"

"No, dear. What?"

"They were cutting down one of the palm trees!"

Hankie patted Achilles' blond head. "You little rascal." She giggled.

"It was so much fun, Aunt Hankie!" Achilles assured her.

"What a lot of fuss over a silly palm tree." Maria sighed.

"Your Uncle Hans sometimes forgets that he was ever a child himself," Hankie explained patiently.

"You shouldn't tell them that," Hans protested weakly.

"Why not? I've never seen such intelligent children!"

"My palm trees—"

"Hans, there are more important things in life than palm trees." She turned to the children. "I'll tell you what. We'll cut them down together!"

Hans walked to the bar and poured himself a whiskey, but Hankie's voice pursued him. "Don't you understand that the children are upset over what's happened in their family?" she asked.

Hans, stricken with guilt, looked at Achilles and smiled. "Achilles," he asked, "what do you want to be when you grow up?"

"I want to own a lot of ships," the child replied enthusiastically, "just like my daddy and Uncle Hans."

Hankie clucked ecstatically. "Did you hear that?" she squealed. "Just like daddy and Uncle Hans!"

"Where on earth is that blasted tutor?" Hans grumbled wearily. "He's paid to take care of these children."

"I told you," Achilles reminded him. "He's with the governess."

"What in God's name is he doing with the governess?"

"He's not doing anything." The twelve-year-old boy sniggered. "He's a faggot."

Hankie's eyes rounded in admiration. "Oh, Hans, did you hear that? Isn't that clever!" She beamed down at Achilles. "What is a faggot, my dear?"

"Don't you know?" the boy asked innocently.

"Of course I know. But I want you to explain it to me."

Achilles looked up at her with the resigned air of an adult who has been asked to state the obvious. "A faggot," he explained with exaggerated patience, "is a man who sucks cock."

[20]

Beside her in the communal bed, Helena heard someone give a half sigh, half cry of joyful release. She bit her lip, wondering who it was. In the darkness, she heard bodies moving, muffled laughter, stifled protestations, and then laughter again. She did not know who the couple were. Occasionally, one of them brushed against her, but it was impossible to tell if it was the boy or the girl.

It was useless to try to sleep. She rose noiselessly, felt her way along the wall to the door and went outside into the bright moonlight. Against a chorus of bullfrogs and crickets, a nightingale was practicing its scales.

Helena slumped onto a large rock near the house and inhaled deeply. How lovely it was to see the leaves of the olive trees glistening darkly in the moonlight. And how utterly impossible that she, the Duchess of Sunderland, the spoiled, adulated, courted darling of international society, should be here on a deserted farm in the middle of the night admiring the olive trees while her sister was being mounted by an assortment of hippies and beatniks—Helena had never been able to understand the difference—only a few feet away. And yet here she was, without a telephone, without servants, without transportation, without even running water, thrilling to the sound of a nightingale. Why? She owned a dozen splendid gardens, in all of which nightingales constantly hymned the night. Why, then, was she hearing its song for the first time in her life?

"I thought that good girls were supposed to fall asleep as soon as they climbed into bed."

Helena spun around on her rock. Fast was standing behind her. She pretended not to notice that he was nude. "Even good girls have trouble sleeping when seven people are making love in the same bed," she said dryly.

Fast passed his hand through his hair. "Where did you get that idea? Eric and Julian are dead to the world, and Melina is so exhausted that she couldn't do anything if she wanted to. Move over!"

Fast sat beside her on the rock. Helena kept her eyes straight ahead, looking up at the moon.

"All this bothers you, doesn't it?"

She did not answer, and after a moment he went on unexpectedly. "Your sister is a pain in the ass," he said.

Helena felt a stab of joy. "Why do you say that?" she asked.

"As though you didn't know. She doesn't belong here any more than she does in your family's bank vault. She's looking for something that she hasn't found yet. And she's also something of a hysteric."

"Not really. Melina is a perfectly normal girl."

"Bullshit," Fast said softly. "You don't believe a word of what you're saying. In fact, you're delighted to hear me criticize her, because you despise her." He scratched his side. "I think it's because you all have too much money."

"People who have never had a cent of their own," Helena observed icily, "always resent those who have money."

"No. It's because money conditions your whole outlook on the world. It becomes the basis on which you judge the people you meet. When we met, I'll bet you said to yourself, 'What an attractive man. What a pity he isn't the president of some corporation.'"

"I never said that you were an attractive man."

"Maybe not, but you certainly thought it. Look me in the eye and tell me that you didn't."

Helena kept her eyes on the moon. There was a long silence. It occurred to her that she knew the answer to the question she had asked herself earlier. If she had heard the nightingale's song for the first time that evening, it was because, for the first time in her life, she had been alone when she listened to it. She had a brief vision of the birdcages she had opened in Paris six years before in a fit of anger at Mark. Most of the birds had been crushed, or stepped on, and had died.

"What are you thinking about?"

She turned toward Fast, careful to keep her eyes on his face. "I was thinking about some birdcages that I opened once."

"The birds died, I suppose?"

"How did you know that?"

"Because freedom is something that must be learned. Some creatures never become accustomed to it. If you raise an animal in the house and then suddenly turn it loose, it usually dies."

"That's more or less what happened."

"You see?"

"Do you always live in these communes?"

"Yes. But they're not what you think they are. Life in a commune doesn't really mean all for one and one for all. It means that everyone tries to use the others to solve his own problems. But it never works, so communes never last. We all drift from place to place, from commune to commune."

"Why doesn't it work?"

"Because of people like your sister. All people in communes are phonies, except those who are trying to find out who they are. And can you think of anyone more boring than someone who doesn't know who he is?"

"What category do you belong to?"

"Both. I'm both at once."

"And are you happy?"

"No."

"What would you like to do?"

"If I knew that, I wouldn't be here now. Or rather, I'm here to find out what I want to do."

"You don't know?"

"I don't have a clue."

"You mean you have no idea of what you want to be?"

"No idea at all. All I know for certain is what I don't want to be."

"And what is that?"

"I don't want to be anything that resembles you in any way."

Helena stiffened under the insult, but Fast appeared unaware that he had said anything amiss. He stood, stretched, yawned, and said, "Good night. I'm going to get some sleep." Then he disappeared into the house.

Through the open door, Helena heard voices. She could not distinguish individual words, but from the tone she concluded that an argument of some sort was in progress. Then Melina appeared in the doorway, bare to the waist. "Did you have a good time?" she spat at her sister. "Do you like the way he screws?"

Inexplicably, Helena felt tears in her eyes.

Irene shivered with joyful impatience. Operation Panic had begun. Sunderland had been unbearably aloof when she spoke to him, but she knew that her call would provoke a chain reaction of events. Was there a husband alive—even an obvious homosexual like Sunderland—who would not be thrown into a frenzy to learn that his wife was living in a commune where free love was the order of the day?

The next call was to Athens. Irene had planned to spend a few minutes building up suspense, but the instant her mother was on the line her eagerness to tell what she knew made her blurt out, "Mama, something terrible has happened! Socrates is dead!"

In Athens, Medea Mikolofides had all she could do to stifle a whoop of joy. Then she made Irene repeat herself three times, each time in more detail than before. Irene went on to say that Kallenberg had already left London for Paris to take care of the details of the funeral. "Above all," she cautioned her mother, "you mustn't let him know I said a word to you. He made me swear not to tell a soul."

"I'm not surprised," Medea said indignantly. "That money-crazy husband of yours wants to keep all the loot for himself."

"However," Irene went on in a submissive tone, "I thought it was my duty to tell you what was going on."

"I'm happy that you did, my child. Now I know what steps to take."

Irene wanted to ask if her mother had news of Helena and Melina, but Medea hung up so abruptly that she did not have the opportunity to do so.

That old bitch! Irene fumed. She didn't even thank me for telling her. Still, there were consolations. Irene stared at the ceiling in her bedroom and conjured up images of all the possible woes that might befall Herman Kallenberg. She rubbed her hands together in delighted anticipation. First, she must call her friends and tell them the news—friends whose husbands were competitors of Kallenberg's.

And to make certain that the information would reach the largest number of people in the shortest possible time, she had already decided that she would swear them all to absolute, undying secrecy.

She picked up the telephone, dialed for operator assistance, and said, "I would like to make a call to the Bahamas, please."

It was true. It was just as Satrapoulos' grief-stricken secretary, François, had said when he called Kallenberg in London in order, as he put it, "to notify the family." The Greek was dying. Kallenberg had seen him, lying unconscious in a darkened room, surrounded by nurses and solemn specialists conferring in hushed tones. "There's nothing more we can do," an eminent cardiologist had assured Kallenberg. "I'd be surprised if your brother-in-law lasts the day."

As the black Bentley sped away from Satrapoulos' palace on the Avenue Foch, Kallenberg slumped in the back seat, lost in thought. There were many things to be done, and the least important of these were the funeral arrangements which Kallenberg had mentioned to his wife. For Kallenberg, over the years and through a series of exceedingly intricate maneuvers, had acquired interests in almost all the enterprises controlled by Socrates Satrapoulos. Indeed, in some of these enterprises, his interest amounted to as much as thirty percent. With the announcement of Satrapoulos' death, there would be panic in the banking capitals of the world. The financial empires of such men as Satrapoulos rarely survive their founders' deaths. There were several options available to Kallenberg in this situation. First, he might acquire Satrapoulos' own holdings. But when, and from whom, and at what cost to himself? Satrapoulos had always regarded himself as immortal, Kallenberg reflected, and it would have been typical of him not to have made arrangements to dispose of his estate in an orderly fashion. It was not unlikely that the Greek's vast fortune would be tied up in the courts for years. Moreover, there would be certain obligations which Satrapoulos' heirs would be required to meet: enormous payments to shipyards, for example, and that business with the U.S. tax people. Of course—and this was a second, separate option—Kallenberg might join forces with his mother-in-law, a course which would provide him with more than enough capital both to acquire all of Satrapoulos' holdings and to meet his obligations. After all, one might be talking about a billion dollars. . . . But it did not seem likely that the idea of cooperating with Kallenberg would appeal to Medea Mikolofides. It would be more like her to grab as much of Satrapoulos' empire as she could for herself and then to do everything in her power to keep her son-in-law from acquiring what was left.

But there was a third way: one which combined the advantages of the first two alternatives and possessed none of their inconveniences. It could work—especially if the news of Satrapoulos' death were kept secret for a while. In such a case, Kallenberg could sell all his holdings in Satrapoulos' business at their present market value. Then, when the news broke and the panic began, he could buy them back at a greatly depressed value—perhaps as little as one-fifth of their present value. With the extra capital this would provide, he would find a way to circumvent Medea and take sole control of the Greek's financial empire.

Kallenberg picked up the telephone, at the same time pressing the button which closed the window separating him from the chauffeur. "Hello, Jack? Listen. Tomorrow, as soon as the exchange opens, I want you to sell everything I own in the Satrapoulos enterprises. . . . Yes, everything! And inform my offices in London, Tokyo, Athens, New York and Stockholm. . . . By tomorrow morning, I want you to have made a complete inventory of my holdings. . . . There is nothing to discuss! Do what I tell you! You don't have to understand why I'm doing it. I'll call you back in an hour."

He replaced the receiver, cutting off the frantic questions of his agent, who seemed convinced that Kallenberg had lost his mind. Kallenberg shrugged. He knew without his agent's reminder, that the sudden dumping of his holdings would alert the financial world that something was brewing. But that was a risk that one had to take. After all, he had not become a billionaire by playing it safe.

[21]

The heat was so intense that Mortimer, Duke of Sunderland, was briefly tempted to loosen his tie. He resisted the temptation manfully.

"Mother," he said, "don't you find it a bit warm?"

"Yes," the dowager duchess replied. "It is."

"Mother, do you think we might open one of the windows, just a bit?"

"Mortimer, you know that I cannot abide sitting in a draft."

Silence.

"Mortimer, this man is driving too fast. Tell him to reduce his speed."

"Mother, we're barely moving."

"I feel ill."

"Shall I tell him to stop?"

"Certainly not. Tell him to reduce his speed."

Mortimer, his exasperation well masked, tapped on the glass separating the French chauffeur from his British passengers and signaled him to drive more slowly. The chauffeur cursed—or, at least, so it seemed to the duke, who, since the partition was closed, could only judge from the man's facial expression. Mortimer gestured again. The Frenchman responded by pressing the accelerator to the floor and the hired limousine lurched forward at a terrifying speed.

"I am definitely not well," the dowager duchess moaned. "Do we have far to go?"

Through the window, Mortimer caught a glimpse of a sign: ROMAINE—10 KM.

"We're almost there, Mother. Do you wish to stop for a while, or shall we continue on?"

His mother shook her head wearily, as though in great and abiding pain. Let us go on, her expression said. I am near death, but I will sacrifice myself for you, my son.

The ancient Austin, as though in response to a mother's prayer, suddenly slowed, then came to a complete stop at the side of the road. Simultaneously, a cloud of steam rose from the hood.

Mortimer, ecstatic over the prospect of a delay, leaped from the automobile and joined the chauffeur as he raised the car's hood. An incredible cloud rose from the engine as he did so.

"It's overheated," the chauffeur said.

"How long will we be here?"

"That does not depend on me, monsieur. It depends on the radiator." The man shrugged and held up his hands to convey his innocence in the affair. "Monsieur insisted on an English automobile," he observed, "and the engines of English automobiles are not built for the French climate."

There was no answer possible, and Mortimer did not attempt one. He returned to his seat.

"What has happened, Mortimer?"

"The engine has overheated, Mother."

"Then let it cool."

"Yes, Mother."

Forty-five minutes later, they were on the road again, moving slowly enough to suit even the dowager duchess, stopping frequently to remove the radiator cap—an exercise which the chauffeur performed with the caution habitually employed in the defusing of a bomb—and to add water to the radiator.

At seven o'clock in the evening, the Austin creaked to a halt at the foot of the road leading to Cagoulet. The chauffeur climbed out and opened the door next to the dowager duchess. "This is it. We are here."

"But where are we? Where are the houses?"

"One moment, Mother. Let me speak to him." Mortimer addressed the chauffeur. "See here, my man, this is not Cagoulet. You were to take us to our destination."

"You're joking. Look at that hill! This car can hardly make it on a flat road. Do you expect it to climb such a mountain?"

"Mother, he says that the hill is too steep for the automobile."

"Mortimer, tell him that I will complain to his employer if he does not immediately take us to our destination."

The duke, greatly embarrassed, turned to the chauffeur and surreptitiously handed him a ten-thousand-franc note. "Let's make a try at it, shall we, old man? My mother has difficulty walking."

The money disappeared into a voluminous pocket. "It's not me," the Frenchman protested, "it's the car."

"Come, now. There must be a solution. As you say in this country, 'The word *impossible* does not exist in French.'"

"I have heard the saying, monsieur. It is a lie." The man reflected for a moment. "The only way is for someone to push the automobile."

"Very well. You drive, and I shall walk behind and, if necessary, push. Shall we have a go at it?"

"If monsieur wishes. When the radiator has stopped boiling."

Twenty minutes later, the Austin began to move up the road to Cagoulet, the chauffeur at the wheel, the dowager duchess in the back seat, and Mortimer pushing and puffing behind.

When the farm finally came into sight, the dowager duchess lowered her window and called out: "Mortimer, get into the automobile. It is most unbecoming for us to arrive in this manner. . . ."

"Well? Well?" Kallenberg shouted into the telephone.

He heard François, in Paris, stifle a sob. "It's all over, sir," Satrapoulos' secretary reported lugubriously. "It's all over."

Kallenberg, by considerable effort, kept himself from shouting "Bravo!" His voice trembling with anticipation, he said, "François, I will be in Paris tomorrow, at two P.M. Leave all the arrangements in my hands."

He hung up and sank back into his chair. The thought that Satrapoulos was dead was not easily assimilated, despite the number of times in the past that Kallenberg had wished the Greek in his grave. Strangely, Kallenberg's elation was not without a certain frustration, as if Socrates had used death as a means of depriving his erstwhile brother-in-law of an opportunity for vengeance. Kallenberg grimaced. How like Socrates to die of a heart attack at sixty. How common. How lacking in style. How totally without imagination. A heart attack, for God's sake!

Kallenberg worked far into the night. At dawn, he took a sleeping pill, but he did not close his eyes. At nine o'clock, the telephone rang.

"It's a disaster, Mr. Kallenberg," Jack's voice whined. "As soon as the market opened, everybody rushed to sell, and nobody is buying." Then, in a tone loaded with reproach: "Sir, you should have told me that Mr. Satrapoulos is dead—"

Kallenberg experienced a wave of nausea. "How do you know he's dead?" he stammered.

"Everybody knows it. There isn't a stockbroker in the world who hasn't heard it in the past hour! Really, Mr. Kallenberg, you should have told us—"

"Shut up!" Kallenberg roared. "I don't pay you to tell me what I should or shouldn't do!"

"Yes, sir. What do you want me to do now?"

"Stay on the line. I want to think for a minute." He set the receiver on his desk and stared at the ceiling. How could they have found out about Satrapoulos' death? Where was the leak? Instinctively, the first name to come to Kallenberg's mind was that of the Greek himself. That was ridiculous, of course. The Greek was dead. Could it have been François? One of the doctors or nurses? A servant? Well, there would be time later for an investigation, and God help the man who had opened his mouth!

"Are you there?" Kallenberg barked into the telephone.

"Yes, sir."

"What are they selling for now?"

"It depends on the enterprise. On the average, I'd say stock in any Satrapoulos company today is worth about one-fifth of what it was yesterday."

Kallenberg groaned audibly. "Is anyone buying?"

"No one is crazy enough to buy now."

Kallenberg strummed his fingers on the desk. It was too early to buy, and it was obviously too late to sell. "Do you think prices are going to drop any more?" he asked.

"It's quite possible. You know the law of supply and demand as well as we do—"

"All right! All right! Never mind the lectures! Shut up and let me think."

A decision had to be made, and immediately. What had happened? It had all seemed so simple. And now his plan had backfired, and Kallenberg himself was in danger of being wiped out.

"Jack? Are you still there?"

"Yes, sir."

"Sell!"

"Mr. Kallenberg, why not wait awhile? This is the worst possible moment—"

"I told you to sell!"

"I think you should wait at least an hour—"

"Do as I tell you, you idiot! Sell!"

"Very well, Mr. Kallenberg. How low shall I go?"

"How should I know? You're on the floor. Do the best you can! What else can you do?"

Kallenberg slammed the receiver down. His shirt was dripping with sweat. He did not have to be a prophet to know what was going to happen. He would be lucky to get thirty cents on the dollar for his shares in Satrapoulos' enterprises.

Two hours later Jack called back to report that, by a stroke of almost unbelievable luck, he had found a group of Latin American banks that were buying—for two-thirds below the previous day's market value of the shares. Every share had been sold. Did Mr. Kallenberg have any further orders?

No. Mr. Kallenberg had no orders. He sat at his desk, his hands dripping sweat onto the polished wood. It could have been worse. It could have meant bankruptcy, ruin, creditors hounding him. . . . At least he had managed to snatch something from the holocaust.

The thought that he would have to go to Paris for the funeral services brought with it a surge of nausea. Yet he had promised to be there by midafternoon. Was that cow, Irene, ready yet?

"Irene!" he shouted with all his strength. He threw open the door of his study and rushed out into the hallway. "Irene!"

His voice echoed through the house, and the servants ran for cover like rabbits on the first day of the hunting season.

"Mortimer, perhaps I should be the one to inform her." Without waiting for her son to reply, the dowager duchess advanced toward Helena, her arms open. It was an unusual gesture on her part. For centuries, the members of the House of Sunderland had faced their crises with arms folded.

"My dear, I have terrible news for you."

The small group gathered at the doorway of the farmhouse were all ill at ease. Mortimer, because he had once again been relegated to the status of a spectator. Helena, because she did not understand what her mother-in-law had said. (The woman, after all, had spoken to her only twice in the six months of her marriage to Mortimer.) The members of the commune, because they did not know what this absurd old woman and her fruity son—everyone had noticed that Mortimer could not keep his eyes off Fast's body—were doing here. And the driver, because he was eager to get back to Marseilles before dark.

"My child, Socrates Satrapoulos is dead."

"Oh!" Helena exclaimed blankly.

That was all. No tears, no drama.

"Your Grace," Helena said, "may I present my sister Melina. Melina, my husband and his mother."

"I thought that, for your children's sake—"

"It was kind of you," Helena interrupted.

"How did it happen?" Melina asked.

With a surge of gratitude, Mortimer realized that the question was addressed to him. Melina had restored to him the individuality habitually usurped by his mother's presence.

"A heart attack," he answered.

The driver interrupted. "All right, what do you want to do now?"

"Helena," Mortimer said, "I've come to take you back."

"And I," Helena answered, "have come to take my sister back to Athens."

"She can ride back with us."

"She refuses to leave."

"I'm going back to the car," the dowager duchess announced.

"It's getting late," the driver remarked.

"Mother, I must have a word with Helena. Can you get to the car by yourself?"

With a gracious gesture, his mother freed him to speak to his wife.

"Are you packed, Helena?" Mortimer asked.

"I only have a knapsack, and there's nothing in it. When is the funeral?"

"Tomorrow, I believe. Should we send for your children?"

"I can't imagine why."

"If we leave now, we'll be in Marseilles in three hours. We can take a night train—"

"All right, Mortimer. Let me get my knapsack."

Helena disappeared into the farmhouse. The members of the commune had scattered, except for Fast, who stood leaning against the doorway.

Mortimer would have liked to talk to Fast at length to find out who he was and what he was. To penetrate the mysterious allure which emanated from him. Instead, he had three minutes; then the brief contact would be lost forever.

"Have you known my wife for long?"

"Only a couple of days."

"I don't know her very well myself," Mortimer stuttered. Then there was nothing more to say about his wife.

"Are you an American?" he asked.

"Yes."

"From what part of the States?"

"From here and there."

The conversation was interrupted as Helena emerged from the house, carrying her bag. "I'm ready," she announced.

"Where are you going?" Fast asked.

Helena and Mortimer glanced at one another. The same thought had occurred to both of them. "To Marseilles," they answered as one.

"Can I have a ride with you?"

"Of course," Mortimer answered quickly.

"But—" Helena began, but Fast had already disappeared into the house. She did not dare look at Mortimer, or he at her, for each was terrified the other might guess what was in his mind.

"Is everyone coming?" the driver called from the car.

Fast reappeared, carrying a jacket over his shoulder.

"Don't you have any baggage?" Mortimer asked in astonishment.

Fast pulled a toothbrush from his pocket. "I've got this," he said.

At that instant, Melina had emerged from the house. "Fast!" she cried. "You're leaving?"

"Yes."

"But—where are you going?"

"I don't know. I'm just leaving."

"Fast!"

"Peace, Melina."

"Fast!"

Fast walked to the waiting automobile and climbed in beside the driver. Helena, Mortimer, and the dowager duchess were already settled in the back seat. The driver started the engine, and the vehicle began to move slowly away in a cloud of dust.

Stunned, Melina did not move. She stood in the late-afternoon sun, repeating over and over, as though chanting a litany, "Fast! Fast! Fast!"

[22]

Yesterday, following a cardiac seizure, Socrates Satrapoulos died at his home on the Avenue Foch here in Paris. Thus far, sources close to the deceased billionaire shipowner have refused to supply any details concerning the circumstances of his death. Since the news became known this morning, however, panic has reigned in the world's marketplaces. . . .

"Ha!" Socrates roared, throwing back the sheets and jumping from bed. "Ha! Those idiots!" He executed several steps of a *sirtaki* on the priceless Oriental carpet, then threw himself across the bed and began reading again:

. . . thousands of small shareholders have been wiped out, and banks all over the world are being besieged by depositors . . . a cabinet meeting to discuss the crisis. . . .

Roaring with laughter, Socrates abandoned his bed and sank into the chair which, only a few hours before, had been occupied by the Orthodox priest—a dirty, ill-smelling man who had come to administer what he believed to be the last rites to a dying son of the church.

"Oh, God," Socrates gasped, "dying seems to be good for a man. I've never felt better in my life!"

Ten days earlier, Satrapoulos had been at Cascais. There was something he wanted to ask the Prophet, but he did not know quite how to go about it. Finally, awkwardly, he had broached the subject:

"Why is it that you never advise me on matters of the heart?"

"Because it appears that your heart belongs only to your business."

"Women and business often go hand in hand."

"What is it you wish to know?"

"I want you to tell me about a woman."

"Tell me. Or rather, do not tell me. I will consult the cards." Kalwoziac spread out the tarots. "She is young," he declared.

"Obviously."

"She is very sheltered. I see her surrounded by walls, by barriers. But it is not she who has erected these walls between you. She is surrounded by many people, but she is bored. Tell me, is this woman well known?"

"Very well known."

"An actress."

"Not exactly."

"It is the woman with whom you are presently living?"

"No. Another woman."

"She is playing a role. Or rather, she is being forced to play a role. What is it?"

"In politics."

"Yes, I can see. And I can tell you that she does not like it. The pressures are beginning to tell on her."

"That's impossible!"

"I see danger and death."

The Greek sat up in his chair. "For her?" he asked in excitement.

"No, I see death around her, but she herself is protected. Is she married?"

"Yes."

"What is your problem?"

"I would like to know if she—likes me. I think she does. She writes me postcards, like a schoolgirl. But by tomorrow she may have a whole nation at her feet."

"Do you see her often?"

"No. Rarely."

"What is it that troubles you?"

"She intimidates me."

"Are you in love with her?"

"I don't know. This all must seem very foolish to you."

"No more so than any other problem concerning love."

The Prophet looked up from his cards. "Later I will consult the cards again and tell you if and when you may approach this woman.

For the moment, however, there is something else I must tell you. Herman Kallenberg came to see me three days ago."

The Greek stiffened. "Will he never leave me alone? I thought that after my divorce, and especially after the way he came out the loser in our last encounter, he'd be more careful in the future. What's bothering him now?"

"He says that you are ruining his life."

"I am only defending myself against him."

"That is not what he meant. He says that you are ruining his life by always being ahead of him. He is compelled to accept second place, whereas everything in him requires that he be first."

Satrapoulos smiled happily.

"Behind your back," the Prophet continued, "he has been buying shares in your enterprises and paying any price for them."

"That doesn't matter. Even if he buys everything that's available, I'll still be in control. I own fifty-five percent of the shares."

"You personally, in your own name?"

"Practically. My two children each have two percent, and Helena has three percent. I have the rest."

"What if Kallenberg gains control of their holdings?"

"Impossible. Achilles and Maria are only twelve, and Helena and I have control of their affairs."

"You and Helena. Can you be certain of her?"

The Greek was usually honest with himself. He admitted that he had not thought of that possibility. If Helena wished, she was in a position to create serious trouble for him. It was at that instant that the idea came to his mind. Or rather, it emerged full-blown, its consequences, means of execution, and advantages all immediately evident. For a long time now, he had felt the need to jettison some of the people he had needed in the past to maintain his power on a firm foundation. Now he had found the way to do so.

"I am not feeling terribly well," he told the Prophet with a smile. "In fact, I wouldn't be surprised if I were to die shortly."

The Prophet shook his head. "That's impossible. I would see it in the cards."

The Greek laughed. "Listen," he said, leaning forward eagerly. "Suppose I died suddenly. And suppose my death was to be a closely guarded secret, but that there was a single, discreet leak. Now I may be dead at that point, but it will be the stock in my businesses that will be buried. Do you follow me? Without me, my business is not worth much. All my capital is tied up in the supertankers that I'm having built. Who would want to take over a business with such debts and obligations? No one. So everyone with stock in the business sells it, knowing that they are going to decrease in value. And then someone buys them up later—"

"Have you chosen the way in which you will die?"

"That is a detail which I am happy to leave in your capable hands."

The Prophet chuckled. "What a splendid idea. But let us not be impatient. We must consider the time at which your death will make mourning most convenient for your friends. . . ."

Mortimer was fascinated by Fast's fingers. They were long, thin, strong fingers. His dirt-encrusted fingernails were broken in several places. Mortimer felt an almost overwhelming impulse to grasp those fingers in his own. What would Fast do? Would he protest? Or laugh? Or would he let Mortimer hold his hand?

"Where will you stay in Marseilles?" Mortimer asked.

"I have no idea."

"At a hotel?"

"No."

"With friends, perhaps?"

"I don't know anybody in Marseilles."

"Will you be staying long?"

"I don't know."

"If you have any—any problem, I have friends in Marseilles who would be delighted to put you up."

"What makes you think I can't afford a hotel?"

"I don't know. But if you'd like, I'm sure I could arrange something."

Fast scowled and looked out of the window.

"Are you a student?" Mortimer persisted.

"Sometimes."

"What are you studying?"

Fast turned around and looked at Mortimer with an air of profound disdain.

"I'm a painter."

"How utterly fascinating! Have you had any shows?"

"No."

"Have you sold anything?"

"No."

"But why not?"

"Probably because nobody likes my work."

"That's difficult to believe," Mortimer said, shaking his head. "It must have some merit to it—"

"No," Fast growled. "It's all shit."

The dowager duchess paled.

Mortimer blushed furiously.

And Helena pursed her lips to keep from smiling.

As Socrates sat in his chair, laughing uproariously, the door opened and Helena entered.

Socrates' hilarity came to an abrupt halt.

Helena stood in the door, her mouth hanging open. Neither of them spoke for a full thirty seconds.

Then the Duke of Sunderland appeared in the doorway. He was followed by François, gesturing in frantic helplessness.

Socrates was the first to regain the use of his tongue. "Would anyone," he said, "like a drink?"

It was the only thing he could think of to say. The sound of his voice enunciating this absurdity struck him as unbearably funny, and he laughed until he was bent double and tears rolled down his face.

Helena looked at him, wide-eyed. Then she snickered, giggled, and finally burst into a tempest of laughter which all but overwhelmed her. She leaned against the wall, helpless in her hilarity. And Mortimer, after a valiant effort to maintain his Britannic impassivity, followed the example of the hysterical Greeks.

At last Socrates managed to make his way across the room where he rang for a servant, then collapsed helplessly onto the bed. The servant appeared, and he managed to gasp out, "Champagne."

The madness lasted for five minutes, after which Socrates, with considerable effort, attempted to master himself. He rose from the bed and approached the Duke of Sunderland, his hand outstretched. "I am delighted to meet you," he said.

His determination to observe the amenities in such a situation served to calm the storm of laughter, and gradually Socrates and his two visitors regained their composure. Over glasses of champagne, the Greek attempted to satisfy Helena's curiosity concerning the exaggerated reports of his death, explaining that the entire episode had been a tasteless prank, obviously devised by his enemies, and that he had every intention of getting to the bottom of it.

Then, in this day of surprises, the door opened again, and François entered. The secretary, his hands fluttering in frustration, was followed by Hankie Vermeer, dressed in mourning. With her were Achilles and Maria.

Achilles rushed forward. "Papa, Papa!" he cried. "Don't listen to them. I only cut down one of their old palm trees!" And Maria ran first to her mother, then to Socrates and threw her arms around his neck.

Hankie Vermeer, meanwhile, had collapsed into a chair from which she listened incredulously while Satrapoulos ran through his explanation once more. "Oh, thank God!" she cried. "Thank God! I knew it wasn't true. Thank God I didn't tell the children why we were coming to Paris!"

There was a sound from the hallway, which Socrates could interpret only as the roar of a wild animal, and Menelas bounded into the room, shrieking, "My God! My God!"

She stopped short and stared through swollen, red-rimmed eyes. "Socrates!" she cried. "You're alive! My God!" Then she threw herself upon him, embracing him, mouthing unintelligible words and phrases in rapid Greek, kissing him on the face, the neck, the hands. . . .

Suddenly, she became aware that they were not alone. She straightened herself to her full height and turned toward the small crowd of friends and relatives. Her features instantly regained their customary immobility, and her poise was impressive.

"Olympia," Socrates said, "may I present Mrs. Vermeer. You already know Helena and Achilles and Maria."

"What handsome children you have," Menelas said to Helena.

"And this is the Duke of Sunderland, my wife's husband." As soon as he had spoken, Socrates realized what he had said. He shook his head and grinned helplessly at the man whom Helena had chosen as his successor.

Menelas, having acknowledged Mortimer's existence, turned back to Socrates. "Now!" she thundered. "You will explain why you chose to frighten me half to death with this stupid joke!"

Once more, Socrates repeated his story while a servant took Achilles and Maria below to regale them with ice cream and cake and while François made arrangements for a suite for Hankie at the Plaza.

Once Menelas had calmed herself, the Greek invited everyone to dinner. Hankie declined, pleading exhaustion, and Helena and Mortimer, to their mutual surprise, simultaneously pleaded a previous engagement. They were supposed to meet Fast at the Ritz, where Mortimer, after providing him with transportation to Paris, had arranged accommodations for the young American. And neither Helena nor her husband had the slightest intention of missing their appointment for so mundane a reason as the resurrection of Socrates Satrapoulos.

The Greek was delighted to have his invitation refused. It would be difficult enough to explain to Menelas, after she had "come half-way around the world," as she put it, why he must be off to Baran the next morning. Perhaps a quiet dinner *à deux*, supplemented by a generous gift—Socrates always kept diamonds handy for such emergencies—would do the trick.

[23]

"Sir, Mr. Kallenberg is here," Mario announced.

The Prophet shrugged. He had been playing a double game so long that a catastrophe was inevitable sooner or later. It seemed that it had now occurred. Kallenberg had called in a rage a few hours before to demand an immediate appointment.

"Very well. Show him in," he said.

Kallenberg stormed into the room, his features set in an expression of furious determination. "You!" he shouted. "I've lost millions! And it's your responsibility!"

"Mr. Kallenberg. . . ." I must play for time, the Prophet reasoned. Perhaps he'll calm down.

But Kallenberg was beyond such games. "Shut up!" he roared. "You've robbed me!"

"Robbed you? I don't understand."

"You told me that he was going to die soon. You told me you saw his death in the cards! Well, is he dead? No! He's alive—alive and laughing at me, with my money in his pocket!"

"Mr. Kallenberg, I told you that he had the mark of death upon him. I didn't tell you—"

"Then you deliberately misled me! What do I know about your goddamn marks of death? All I wanted was for him to die!"

"I had no intention—"

"He's alive, isn't he? Isn't that proof that you deceived me?"

"I did not say he was not alive."

"And to think that I believed you! That I trusted you!"

"Just how did I deceive you, Mr. Kallenberg?"

"By lying to me, that's how!"

Kallenberg was not the first of Satrapoulos' enemies whom the Prophet had misled. This was the first time, however, that he had not phrased his advice in such a way that he could later say that the client had misinterpreted his words. He had been regrettably precise with Kallenberg.

"If you will recall, I told you only that Mr. Satrapoulos was in great danger and that the mark of death was upon him. Did I lie to you in saying that?"

"But he's still alive!"

"Are you blaming me for that?"

"You're goddamn right I am!"

"Mr. Kallenberg, I refuse to assassinate Mr. Satrapoulos merely to substantiate my prophecy. And I have never claimed to be infallible."

"God knows I pay you enough for you to be infallible!"

The Prophet judged that the moment had come for him to defend himself by counterattacking. He assumed an expression of righteous indignation, and rising from his chair, he said, "Sir, you go too far!"

"Don't try to pretend that I've insulted your professional integrity," Kallenberg snapped. "It's not your money that you've lost. It's mine!"

The Prophet remained standing. "In the future, you will lose no more money on my account. This is the last time I will receive you in my house."

"You're not going to get off that easily," Kallenberg said. "You have a lot to make up for!"

Despite the threat in Kallenberg's voice, the Prophet detected something else: a certain ebbing of self-assurance, perhaps caused by the recollection that there were still services that he, the Prophet of Cascais could render. He decided to venture a bit further. "If you feel that I should make reparations, Mr. Kallenberg, I shall do so. I will reimburse you for every cent that you have paid for these consultations."

"You couldn't afford it."

"You think not?" The Prophet pressed the button on his desk, and almost at once Mario's head appeared in the doorway. "Mario, bring me my checkbook."

The Prophet turned to his visitor. "How much do I owe you?" he asked.

Despite himself, Kallenberg was impressed. When someone employed his favorite expression "how much?" he always felt in a disadvantageous position. So he controlled his anger and forced himself to smile.

"Oh, come now," he said. "Let's discuss this—"

The Prophet remained standing, the very picture of outraged innocence.

"Please sit down," Kallenberg said. "I had no intention of offending you."

Slowly, with obvious reluctance, the Prophet resumed his seat.

"I don't care about being reimbursed for the consultations. The money is unimportant. What is important is that you and I together can do a great deal, Mr. Kalwoziac! Let's be practical."

"You don't trust me, therefore it is no longer possible for me to help you."

"I never said that I did not trust you! Or if I did, I did not mean it. When one is angry, one says the first thing that comes to mind. Anyone can make a mistake. I admit that I was wrong."

"If Mr. Satrapoulos is alive," the Prophet said, "it is a miracle. The cards were clear on that point."

The cards, indeed! Kallenberg thought. Still, this charlatan's attitude was puzzling. Could he be sincere? One doubt survived. Had Satrapoulos really died, or had the whole thing been nothing more than an elaborate bit of staging? "Was Satrapoulos actually dying?" Kallenberg asked.

"Can you truly doubt it? Do you have any idea of what was in the cards?"

Kallenberg could not have cared less about the cards. He did not believe in God, and he did not believe in the devil. He was not about to believe in any nonsense about horoscopes and signs. Thus he was astonished to hear himself say, "If you're going to consult the cards for me, then I want you to see what they say about my wife. I'm thinking of getting a divorce."

The Prophet nodded gravely.

Socrates set his papers down and allowed his eyes to wander over the clouds billowing beneath the plane's wings. He sighed. The interview with Hadj Thami el Sadek would not be an easy one. In the past five years, the emir's moral authority in Islam had grown to such an extent that he was now a force to be reckoned with, not only in the oil-rich states along the shores of the Persian Gulf, but throughout the entire Middle East. And the Suez affair, rather than reducing his authority, had actually increased it. El Sadek had contributed so liberally to the Arab cause from the treasuries of the emirates he controlled that Nasser, though roundly defeated on land by the Israeli, British, and French forces, had been enabled to win a major political victory.

During the Suez crisis, the Emir of Baran had offered Socrates a choice: Islam or Europe. That is, oil or no oil. Socrates had chosen Islam—and oil—and he had profited accordingly. At the same time, as he knew very well, he had allowed himself to become a pawn in the fantastic political game being played, a game in which the prize was the virtually unlimited petroleum resources of the Middle East. The principal players were the American and Soviet giants, and their tactics were to overwhelm the Arabs with billions in aid, with shiploads of arms, with declarations at the United Nations, and with all the obfuscatory tactics of the cold war until everyone had lost sight of who one's friends were and who one's enemies.

Predictably, it became known, by courtesy of certain "well-informed sources," that Satrapoulos, along with Kallenberg, Medea Mikolofides, and several other less important Greek shipowners, had sided with the Arabs—which, to London, Washington, and Paris, meant that they were at least the unwitting allies of the Russians. Thereupon in Washington the denizens of Foggy Bottom had sworn a great oath to have Satrapoulos' head. To that end, they had begun a series of legal harassments—impounding ships, freezing funds under various pretexts—which Satrapoulos' army of international lawyers invariably had been able to neutralize with tactics which were at once the despair and the envy of the government attorneys.

As a result of the closing of the Canal, Japan's shipyards were working around the clock to turn out supertankers capable of transporting enormous quantities of oil around the Cape of Good Hope.

Now Socrates smiled sardonically. His Japanese supertankers were doing the job for him. The only ones to suffer from the loss of Suez had been those who had insisted on keeping it closed: the Americans and the British. They had been so terrified of the Soviets using the Canal to ship arms to the Vietcong that they had been blind to another danger, that of pushing the Middle East into the Russian bear's waiting arms. Now Moscow had realized its eternal dream: it had an empire in the Mediterranean, an empire composed of bases —in Algeria, Egypt, and Iraq—populated by "advisers" and "technical experts" of every kind and armed with rockets and radar.

Socrates shook his head. It had been so easy to predict. In fact, he had foreseen it long before anyone else. And it was inevitable that when the Suez Canal reopened, it would be under the control of the Arabs rather than of the Europeans who had built it. And he foresaw, too—in fact, knew it for certain—that, sooner or later, the oil resources of the Middle East would be controlled exclusively by the peoples under whose land they lay.

Actually, he could not have cared less whether the Americans, or the Russians, or the Jews or Arabs, for that matter, won out in the end. Communist or non-Communist, Jew or faithful son of the Prophet, it was all the same. A man was judged not by what doctrine or what country he believed in, but solely by what market he controlled. A reporter had once asked Socrates, "What is your favorite country?" He had replied, "My favorite country is the country which offers the best tax shelter and imposes the fewest commercial restrictions. In other words, a country that understands business."

The only problem was that Socrates, in siding with el Sadek and the Arabs, had been compelled to commit himself further than he would have wished. Now the great cartels were accusing him of treason—as though treason were possible when it was a question of a simple profit—while the Americans were trying to ruin him and his ex-brother-in-law and ex-mother-in-law were trying to steal his business. And to make matters worse, the Emir of Baran was beginning to take himself seriously as a political leader. He was now known throughout Islam as the Great Conciliator, but there was nothing particularly conciliatory about the motto he had adopted: "Arab oil for the Arabs."

It was true that it had been Socrates himself who had suggested the motto. But the methods el Sadek had adopted had come as much of a surprise to the Greek as to the rest of the world. The old emir had immediately grasped that Europe and America were dependent on Arab oil. Therefore, all one had to do to bring the Western democracies to their knees was to turn off the petroleum spigot by suspending production. Then it would be only a matter of time before America's highways were empty and its planes grounded, only a matter of weeks, perhaps, before the Europeans began to freeze in their houses and offices. . . .

But then what would Satrapoulos' supertankers transport?

The Greek removed his glasses and rubbed his nose. Time, of course, would solve all his problems. He had learned from experience that philosophical, ideological, and political options always eventually accommodated themselves, somehow, to economic reality. For the moment, however, he would have to tread carefully. He had expended too much time, effort, and money on el Sadek to risk losing his friendship at this crucial moment in their relationship. Moreover, he was certain that when the final card had been played in the game, the high and mighty Americans and Europeans would have to come to terms with the kinglets of the Persian Gulf—that is, with Hadj Thami el Sadek. Therefore, for the moment it was essential for Socrates to do nothing either to disturb el Sadek or to exacerbate his own already difficult relations with the Americans. After all, if everything went according to plan, Washington would soon be an ally. . . .

It was obviously impossible to do anything with the present American government, but Socrates was counting on the forthcoming elections to change all that. He had contributed heavily to all the candidates with the expectation that whichever of them was elected would reward him a hundredfold for his generosity. Socrates regarded such contributions as long-term investments. They usually paid off, although not always. There was the matter of Scott Baltimore, for example. He had accepted Socrates' contributions willingly enough. But if he were elected, would he turn out to be a friend or an enemy? It was difficult to know.

So far as the Emir of Baran was concerned, Socrates had reason to feel a certain confidence. He had in his possession that superb film in which el Sadek had starred, albeit unknowingly, some ten years before. But this was a weapon to be used only when all else had failed. For Socrates was by nature a peaceable man, preferring negotiation to war and diplomacy to blackmail.

A red light flashed, and Socrates buckled his seat belt and began gathering up his papers. He glanced out of the window, and at the end of the runway, he saw the Grand Conciliator's Rolls waiting for him.

Scott Baltimore was asleep in the next room. Out of deference to him, the small group of his closest advisers which had gathered in the sitting room of the hotel suite kept their voices low. They were exhausted, but there was a problem to be faced, a problem so immediate that they did not dare steal even an hour or two for sleep. Only three weeks remained before the election, and according to the polls, Scott was losing rather than gaining strength. The trouble seemed to be that Scott's campaign had peaked too soon, sooner than these same advisers had foreseen. The handsome young man with the innocent eyes and sincere tone had caught the imagination of the voting public early in the arduous months of the campaign, but it had been difficult to maintain the public's initial enthusiasm. Two weeks earlier Scott had been the clear favorite; had the election been held that day, he would have been elected by a landslide. Now, while he still led the other candidates, his strength was eroding alarmingly.

Post Belidjan shook his head. "We have to do something. Anything."

Belidjan was the brain of the Baltimore brain trust. When no one else was capable of thinking, he thought for everyone else. And it was said of him that when he stopped thinking, he had his most brilliant ideas.

"Anyone have any ideas?" he asked the room at large.

When the silence became intolerable, he spoke again. "If you want my personal opinion, I don't think we stand a chance. We're going to lose our asses."

"I can't think of anything to do that we haven't tried already," said Herb Trendy, the oldest of the group.

"He's already promised them the moon and the stars," someone else said.

"I'm not thinking of promises," Post said softly. "I'm thinking about—about something happening. . . ."

Immediately, everyone's eyes were upon him.

"Well, it probably wouldn't work. It's too risky. And I'm sure Scott would never go for it."

"Come on," Trendy urged. "Let's hear it."

Belidjan, as was his fashion, answered by indirection. "It's the way the Republicans are going at us," he began. "They talk about law and order, and the people like the reassurance of a law-and-order platform. If we're going to get screwed, it's the Republicans who are going to do it. I'm not worried about the Democrats. We've been leaning to the left, I think too much to the left. And it's too late in the campaign to begin backtracking now in order to keep what we have of the blue-collar and Middle America vote. But there's another way. We could do something which would automatically pull us back toward the middle of the road and enable us to keep those votes."

"What, for instance?"

"Well, suppose that, a few days before the election, somebody tries to shoot Scott. I said *suppose*. And suppose the guy who does it turns out to be some wild-eyed leftist who says he tried to kill Scott because he was too far to the right. Then what? Do you think anybody'd vote against Scott because he's a liberal?"

"That's the stupidest thing I've ever heard," Trendy said in disgust. "All you'd lose us is more votes from the left than we'd gain from the right. We'd end up with fewer votes than before."

Another man spoke up, Aaron Bosteld, a psychologist who specialized in unconscious group motivation. "That's right," he agreed. "But there's one advantage you haven't mentioned, Trendy. With Scott dead, we could all go home and get some sleep."

Post shook his head. "You guys don't follow me. The public loves martyrs and heroes. If we can make Scott a martyr, and thus a hero, a few days before the election, we'll have it in the bag. Nobody who intends to vote for Scott now is going to change his mind because somebody tries to kill our candidate, and a lot of people who plan to vote for the other guys are going to vote for Scott instead—out of sympathy for him, or to show that their hearts are in the right place, or for any number of reasons."

There was a long silence.

"I still think it's a dumb idea," Trendy said. "But just for kicks, tell us how you'd go about it."

"The easiest thing in the world. We organize a plot against Scott's life—an assassination attempt. We make sure it fails, of course. There is a big public outcry. Everybody is horrified—and everybody votes for Scott."

"What about Scott? Will he be in on this?"

"You've got to be joking. He'd never agree to it. We'd have to do the whole thing behind his back, for his own good."

"Who will you get to do it?" Bosteld asked.

Belidjan had already noted that Bosteld and Trendy were now speaking, not hypothetically, but practically. The conditionals had given way to the indicative mood.

"I may have someone in mind," he replied, "but it's too soon for that. Before we go any further, I have to be sure that we're all in this together. I want you all to swear that, no matter what happens, nothing that we say in this room tonight will ever be repeated to anyone, under any circumstances. Is that clear?"

"Not even to Scott—later, I mean?"

"No! Especially not to Scott!"

There was a pause. Then, one by one the men nodded their agreement.

Post Belidjan leaned forward. "All right, now listen. The first thing to do. . . ."

The discussion continued for four hours while the intended pseudovictim slept the sleep of the innocent in the next room.

Peggy slammed down the receiver. She had been trying for a half hour to reach Scott in the Midwestern farm community where he was campaigning. It was not that she was particularly eager to speak to him. All she wanted, in fact, was to make certain that he was where he was supposed to be. In an hour, she was to meet the latest of her lovers, a young attaché at the French embassy. His name was Pierre, and when he smiled, he displayed an array of teeth so perfect that she, and half of Washington, suspected they were false.

They had met at a reception which Peggy had attended for the sole purpose of showing off a new gown which had just arrived from Paris. That same night they slept together. Pierre had wondered how such a woman could allow herself to be seduced with such ease. He had heard, of course, that Peggy and Scott were "not getting along," as the Americans said, and that Peggy's amours were as casual as they were frequent. But one heard so many things in Washington and New York that it was hard to know what to believe.

Pierre's information was correct, but not entirely correct. The truth was that Peggy had remained faithful to Scott for an entire year after their marriage. It had taken her that long to realize that she was merely a necessary accouterment in her husband's rise to power. A politician, or rather a statesman, had to conform to certain specifications with respect to background, ideas, morals, and family. Among these was one which called for a wife, preferably an attractive wife. And Peggy certainly filled that specification. The realization had caused the scales to fall from her eyes, and she had begun to see Scott for what he actually was. She saw a man who, among other things, littered his campaign trail with the bodies of the kind of young women who were always available to famous men, especially famous men as attractive as Scott. She had confronted him with the evidence one night, and to her surprise, he had denied nothing. Instead, he expressed amazement at Peggy's failure to understand that such distractions were necessary to relieve the tensions of campaigning.

"Other men drink," Peggy had retorted. "Why don't you?"

"I drink, too."

"I'm not joking, Scott. How would you feel if I started going out with other men?"

He had looked at her incredulously. "You? But that's different. You're my wife."

"Not just your wife. I'm a woman. And as a woman I'm giving you fair warning: from now on, I regard myself as free to do whatever I want."

He had not believed a word of it, of course.

Two days later, when Scott was in Oregon, Peggy had given herself to an old college admirer who had courted her, fruitlessly, for years. And he had been but the first.

There was talk, naturally, but none of Scott's friends or family could bring himself to tell him of Peggy's activities. Finally, her behavior became so open and public that several columnists found the courage to allude to it, though in veiled terms. Thereupon old Mrs. Baltimore "did her duty," as she herself would have put it. Scott's initial reaction was to speak of divorce.

"Impossible," his mother retorted. "In your position, you cannot divorce. You must simply endure." Her tone had left no doubt as to what she herself had endured in her lifetime.

Scott had argued, but without conviction, and finally, he had assured his mother that he would accept her advice.

Only a few days later Peggy herself had brought up the same subject. "Scott," she said, "I want a divorce."

"Why?"

"Because we have nothing in common anymore."

"Nothing?" he asked suggestively.

"I'm no more interested in your body than I am in the kind of life you lead."

"The kind of life I lead may damn well make you First Lady of this country before very long."

"The price is too high. Find someone else—someone who is willing to pay it."

Scott argued, using all the reasons advanced earlier by his mother and adding a few of his own, but it was to no avail. Peggy had made up her mind. She would have her divorce, she announced, with or without Scott's cooperation.

At that point, the patriarch of the Baltimore clan, Scott's grandfather, was pressed into service on his behalf. When he had exhausted all the arguments at his command, and when his throat ached from all the words which his paralysis made it so difficult for him to pronounce, he realized that Peggy would not be moved. Barely able to suppress his rage at the young woman's stubbornness, he then advanced an argument which, in his long lifetime, had never yet failed to make an adversary see the light of reason.

"My child," he began, "it is of the utmost importance that there be no scandal at this point in Scott's career. I know that this very career now prevents you from leading a normal life. I know how lonely you must be when Scott is away and how dull it must be for you to sit at home alone night after night." There was not the slightest trace of sarcasm in his voice. "It is only natural that you be compensated in some way for what you are missing, and I am prepared to offer you that compensation. Tomorrow I will deposit one million dollars to your account: if you will give me your word that, until the elections are over, you will conduct yourself in such a way as to avoid gossip of any kind. Then, once Scott is in the White House, you and I will talk again. It may well be that, by then, you will see things in a different light. I know what I am talking about. All marriages go through these little crises, you know. But, if you still feel you must have a divorce at that time, I will be the first to insist that Scott give it to you. Do you accept my proposition?"

Peggy did not answer immediately. On the one hand, she was indignant that this old man believed she could be bought, but at the same time, she knew a bargain when she saw one. After all, a million dollars for a few months. . . .

"My account is at Chase Manhattan," she replied.

Since that interview, it was not unusual to see her on the campaign trail with Scott, hanging on his arm, the picture of a radiant bride. Her radiance, however, cost Scott dearly. Bills for the most incredible amounts arrived daily from every famous dressmaker on both sides of the Atlantic. Scott protested vehemently, and there were terrible scenes in various hotels all across the American continent.

It was immediately after one such battle that Peggy received an invitation from Socrates Satrapoulos, by way of Lindy Nut Bambilt. The *Pegasus II* was about to set sail on a Mediterranean cruise. Would Mrs. Baltimore honor its owner by spending a few days aboard?

As it happened, Mrs. Baltimore could think of nothing she would like better than to be away from Mr. Baltimore. She accepted and, the same day, flew off to join Socrates Satrapoulos and his guests aboard the *Pegasus II*. She had spent three days on the boat, three glorious days, during which the Greek showered her with the most incredible gifts of jewels. Then, on the fourth day, two men had arrived from the United States. They had had orders from Scott to bring Mrs. Baltimore back to the United States, forcibly, if necessary.

Reluctantly, Peggy had taken her leave of Socrates. "I think I could spend the rest of my life on this lovely yacht," she had told him. Then she had boarded a launch for the trip to shore, thinking, Here at least is a man who doesn't give a damn about the happiness of the people. One woman's happiness is enough for him.

"I tell you that Baltimore has an excellent chance of being elected. Unless we do something immediately, it will be too late."

"Oh, come now. He can't possibly be elected!"

"You think so? Have you heard the little demagogue telling the people all the things he plans to do? How he will strip us of our capital under the pretext of distributing it among the people, all under the guise of being 'liberal'? What he means is liberal with our property. If we allow him to be elected, the country will be ruined economically! And not only the country, but all of us as well."

"Come, now, William. What can we do? This is a democracy. We can't dictate an election. We don't have the means to do so."

"There have been times all through history when those who had power did not hesitate to use it when they were threatened. If he becomes President, then the political system which has made it possible for us to prosper will be finished. The country will be in the hands of the beatniks and the blacks!"

There was a stir among the fifteen men present. The secret meeting was taking place on the fiftieth story of a steel and glass office building in New York. If a bomb had exploded in the meeting room, killing all fifteen of them, the stock market would have been reduced to a shambles and the entire world's economy would have been severely shaken.

William continued speaking, his vehemence unabated. "Do we have the right to allow a man who is motivated only by his own ambition to destroy what we have built?"

"Have we discovered anything that can be used against him?"

"No," William responded. "Nothing at all. Except for his young women and the fact that his wife is a whore."

"What about his campaign team?"

"They're under surveillance night and day. We've been unable to get anything on them."

"There's bound to be something, somewhere!"

"If there is, we had better find it quickly. Time is running out. Gentlemen," William said, "what if we are unable to discover anything? What then? I will tell you: we will be ruined. We must face a basic, brutal fact: it is him or us. We must destroy him, or he will destroy us. If there is no other way, then we must be prepared simply to remove him permanently from the scene, by any means at our disposal—not excluding the use of violence."

William paused to allow the implications of what he had said to be absorbed. There was a heavy silence in the room, followed by a murmur.

He spoke again. "Gentlemen, let me say it plainly. Hundreds of thousands of human beings die every day. Death is as common as life, and as cheap. If Scott Baltimore were to become one of those hundreds of thousands within the next few days, I, for one, would not mourn his passing."

"What are you saying, William?"

"I thought it was clear. I would like to see him dead. In fact, if he does not die, we will be compelled to sit idly by as he plunges us all into ruin."

"What are you suggesting?"

"Since you all refuse to see things as they actually are, I will make it easy for you. I propose that we take a secret ballot on two questions. First, do you wish Scott Baltimore to become President of the United States? Second, if not, are you willing to employ any means necessary to remove him either from the running or from the office itself, if he is elected? That is all. From your answers, I will know what must be done, and I will act accordingly—on your behalf and for the good of this great nation."

[24]

Slim Scobb was carrying a case of beer up from the cellar when his wife called to him. "Slim! There's someone to see you."

She waited for him at the head of the stairs. "I don't know who it is," she whispered.

"All right. You stay with him. I'll be there in a minute." He put down the case of beer and ran down the steps again. From behind a loose brick in the cellar wall he removed a Luger, thrust it into his belt, then carefully arranged his shirt over it before going to meet his visitor.

"Mr. Trendy!"

"Hello, Slim, how are you?"

The three children in the room stared at Trendy. The youngest, an infant of less than two, began to cry.

"Annie, take the kids into the bedroom, will you?"

"Sure, Slim. Can I get you something to drink before I go? A beer, maybe?"

"I'd love a beer," Trendy said.

Annie returned in a moment with two bottles and two glasses. Then she herded the children into the bedroom and closed the door behind her.

"Well, Slim, your kids are growing up."

"The oldest one is first in his class at school."

"Imagine that! How old is he?"

"Twelve."

"How is everything going, Slim?"

"Not too bad. I have a job; night watchman in a garage."

"Do you like it?"

"Well, it's not like the good old days."

"I guess it's not."

"But things are different now. There's Annie and the kids to think of."

"Do you ever see any of your old buddies?"

"No. I don't go out much. I don't like to leave Annie alone."

"There's nothing like married life, is there? The only thing wrong with it is that a man sometimes lets himself get rusty."

"I don't, Mr. Trendy. I still train; sometimes twice a week."

"Are you as good as before?"

"Of course. Why?"

"I was just wondering. You might be looking for a job sometime."

Slim looked hungrily at his visitor. "Do you have something for me?"

"Well, there may be something. If you're man enough for the job."

"Mr. Trendy," Slim said eagerly, "you know me. You know I'd do anything. I haven't forgotten what you did for me."

"I'm sure you haven't, Slim. I'm sure you haven't."

"Is it something—important?"

"Yes. Very important."

"Let me do it for you."

"Not so fast, Slim. You don't know what it is yet."

"Then tell me."

"It's a pretty big job. But then it pays pretty well, too. Enough to let you buy that house in Florida you've always wanted, where the kids can go to the beach and where the weather's always nice. Good schools, too. The best in the country."

"I'm listening."

"The only thing is, if you take this job, it may be awhile before you can see Annie and the kids. You'd have to wait—"

"How long?"

"Well, the longer you're away from your family, the more money you'll be making. Look at it that way."

"How much?"

"Oh, I don't know. I haven't thought about it. How much were you making in the Marine Corps?"

"Just enough to play a little poker and get drunk once a week. But I didn't have a family then."

"What would you say to twenty thousand dollars down and five thousand a month for every month that you're away?"

"How much?"

"Twenty thousand down and five thousand a month."

"You're joking?"

"You know I never joke about money."

"But that's a hell of a lot of money—"

"It's a big job, Slim. Tell me, are you still as good as you were with a revolver?"

"I never miss. Right in the center of the target every time."

"And with a rifle?"

"Even better. I don't think I could miss if I tried."

Trendy smiled faintly. "I know. That's what bothers me. You see, in this particular job, you'll have to miss, but you'll have to make it look as though you wanted to hit the bull's-eye."

Slim's eyes grew large. "I don't understand, Mr. Trendy."

"All right. I'll explain. But first I want to know if you'll go to work on the basis of the offer I've made."

"Oh, sure. You know I'd put my hand in the fire for you, Mr. Trendy. The money's fine."

"OK. Now listen. It's really a simple job. All you have to do is to shoot at a man riding in an open car. But you have to miss him. You see, it's not that hard."

Mortimer and Fast were alone in the vast drawing room of Sunderland Castle. The dowager duchess had left that morning to take the waters, and Helena had just retired with a headache. Mortimer twisted in his chair, uncertain how to entertain so unpredictable and disconcerting a guest.

"Tell me, Fast," he began, "what are you interested in? I mean besides painting. Though I must say, you don't seem to paint a great deal."

"I don't give a fuck about painting."

"I see. But you *are* a painter, aren't you?"

"Sure. And you say you're a gentleman farmer, but I've never seen you plant anything."

"Well, perhaps I'm more a gentleman than a farmer. Fast—"

"What?"

"I'm afraid I don't understand you. May I ask you a question? Are you in love with my wife?"

"Me? You're kidding. That cunt sister of hers was enough for me. I don't want anything more to do with that Gogolifides bunch."

"Mikolofides."

"Whatever their name is. I mean, she's a nice girl, Helena, but—well, I can do without women anytime."

Mortimer felt himself grow faint with pleasure at the ambiguity of Fast's statement. Perhaps he had misunderstood. But perhaps not.

"Are you a pornography buff, Fast?"

"A what?"

"Photographs—you know."

"Do you have any?"

"A few."

"Let's see them."

Mortimer was out of the room for ten minutes. He returned carrying a large leather suitcase. Then he fumbled in his pockets and drew out a key, which he inserted into one of the bag's massive locks.

Fast watched him in amusement. "You're afraid someone's going to steal your fuck pictures?"

"Oh, no. It's because of Mother, you see."

"Mortimer, how old are you?"

"Well—between forty and fifty."

"And you're still afraid of Mama?"

"She's so delicate, you know, so far removed from our generation. She knows nothing about things like these."

"She may be old, but she's human like everybody else. I'll bet that she uses a candle on herself."

"Oh, Fast!"

"Don't tell me it's never occurred to you."

"Oh, Fast! You're trying to shock me."

"Let's see the pictures."

A cascade of photographs tumbled from the antique suitcase. Fast noted, with something less than total surprise, that most of them were of nude males. He looked at Mortimer. The duke, kneeling beside his photographs, kept his eyes on the floor.

"Well, Mortimer—" Fast began, then stopped short in alarm.

At the first word, Mortimer had thrown himself against Fast's legs and hidden his head in his lap, gasping: "Oh, Fast! Oh, Fast!"

"Come on, Mortimer, cut it out!"

"Oh, Fast! I love you!"

Fast tried to extricate himself but, under the weight of Mortimer's body on his lower extremities, succeeded only in allowing the duke to get a firmer purchase on his legs. Oh, God! Fast thought. Now he's crying!

"Please, Fast! Please. I love you!"

"You filthy pigs!"

Fast and Mortimer looked up simultaneously. Helena stood in the doorway opposite them like an avenging angel. "Pigs!" she spat again.

Mortimer climbed awkwardly to his feet. "Helena—"

"There is nothing you can possibly say, Mortimer. I am leaving this house at once!"

The door slammed, and she was gone.

"You dumb cocksucker!" Fast roared.

"Oh, Fast," Mortimer sobbed. "You're so cruel!"

"Sir, Mr. Bert is here."

"Show him in."

Several years before, Bert had been thrown out of the FBI. Bert explained his discharge as being due to the fact that he was too individualistic for Mr. Hoover's taste. The true reason, as William knew very well, was that Bert had been suspected of trafficking in drugs. Yet the man had special talents which made one willing to overlook certain deficiencies in his character. Where anyone else would have run up against a blank wall, Bert had a way of finding a crack and sliding through it, doing what he was paid to do, and then escaping without leaving a trace.

"Well?" William said.

"Something interesting has come up. They sent Trendy to see an ex-Marine—"

"Why?"

"I don't know yet, but I'll find out soon enough. The man's name is Scobb, Slim Scobb."

"So?"

"So, ever since Trendy's visit, Scobb has been spending four hours a day at an underground shooting range on Ninth Street."

"What's the point?"

"Two points. First, Scobb was an expert rifleman in the Corps. In Korea he killed so many gooks they couldn't even keep score. He used to call his shots, like in a pool game. The second point is that you can bet Scobb isn't in training again to go rabbit hunting."

"To kill somebody? But who? Certainly not anybody on their side. Remember, Trendy is Baltimore's man."

"I know that. And that's what's got me bugged. They're cooking up something, I'm sure of it. But what?"

"Are you having Scobb followed?"

"Night and day. By two men."

"Good. Now, I want you to prepare a complete file on this Scobb: his bank account, family, background, tastes—everything. By the way, is it possible that he's been hired as a bodyguard for Baltimore?"

"I doubt it. Baltimore already has all the bodyguards he needs."

"Strange. All right, Bert. Keep your eyes open, and call me if you turn up anything."

Bert turned to go. When he reached the door, he stopped. "Oh, I almost forgot. The file on Scobb—I've already put it together. Here it is." He walked back and placed it on the desk.

Lieutenant Stavenos stood on the afterdeck of the *Pegasus II*, staring grimly out at the sea. Within forty-eight hours, his employer's guests would arrive from New York for a cruise to Puerto Rico, and if today had been any indication of what was to come, it would be a tempestuous voyage. Satrapoulos and Menelas had been at it again, their angry voices punctuated by the sound of breaking glass. This was their seventh day aboard, and some of the crew were making book that, before the cruise was over, Satrapoulos would have dumped the madwoman once and for all.

Stavenos heard a noise behind him. He turned and saw Menelas in a bathing suit, heading toward the swimming pool. She climbed onto the diving board, then seemed to change her mind. She turned and walked toward the railing, climbed over it, and dived into the sea.

As she did so, Satrapoulos appeared on deck. He ran to the spot from which Menelas had dived. "Olympia!" he cried. "Come back! It's dangerous! There are sharks!"

The yacht was not anchored within the protected lagoon, but a mile out in the open sea.

"Come back, I tell you!" he repeated.

Stavenos saw Menelas turn, stick out her tongue, and then continue swimming away from the yacht.

"Cunt!" Satrapoulos muttered.

"Sir," Stavenos ventured, "shall I have a boat lowered?"

"Shut up! Who asked you for advice?" The Greek turned back toward Menelas. "Olympia! Olympia!" he called.

Olympia did not look back.

"I'll show her!" Satrapoulos swore. "Stavenos!"

"Sir?"

"Get four men and follow me."

The Greek led the way to the auditorium and kicked open the door. "Here," he said to Stavenos. "Tell them to throw that fucking thing overboard."

Stavenos and his men exchanged furtive glances. It seemed impossible that their employer, by the term "that fucking thing," intended to designate the priceless Bechstein concert grand standing on a low platform before them.

"Are you deaf?" Socrates asked. "Throw it overboard, I tell you!"

Stavenos set the example by grabbing a massive leg. The four crewmen joined the officer, and slowly the instrument began to move out of the auditorium, onto the deck, and toward that part of the railing which was detachable. The Greek accompanied them, shouting encouragement and instructions and occasionally giving the Bechstein a push with his own hands, until it reached the edge of the deck. The other members of the crew stopped their work to watch this bizarre happening: the gigantic black piano, on a white yacht, ready to plunge into the green water at the least touch.

"Hold it," Satrapoulos ordered. He cupped his hands to his mouth and shouted, "Olympia!"

Menelas was floating on her back two hundred yards to starboard. She turned at the sound of Socrates' voice, stared for a moment at the apparition on deck, then shouted something which was lost in the breeze. Socrates did not answer. She shouted again; then she lifted her arm in a gesture the significance of which is universally recognized.

There were a few muffled snickers from the crew.

Socrates' face was purple. "Overboard!" he snarled.

The Bechstein moved an inch, tottered for an instant, then plunged majestically into the sea with a cataclysmic splash.

[25]

It happened as such things usually happen, through a combination of coincidence and chance. The first person Helena saw upon arriving at London airport in a taxi was Herman Kallenberg.

"Helena!" he called as he emerged from his Rolls.

She tried unsuccessfully to smile. The vision of her husband embracing the man she loved pursued her like a recurring nightmare.

"Helena, what's wrong?"

"Nothing."

"Is your husband with you?"

She did not answer.

"You've left him?"

"Yes."

"Where are you going?"

"I don't know. To Athens, if I can."

"What do you mean, if you can?"

"I mean if there's a plane."

"Why not charter one? Do you want me to arrange it for you? Or better still, use my airplane."

Helena had never paid much attention to Kallenberg when she was married to Satrapoulos. But now his voice seemed so warm, so reassuring, so protective. . . . She saw him speak to his chauffeur. The man saluted, then drove off. Herman returned to her side.

"Come, let's sit down and talk this over. And don't worry. You're not alone. I'm here with you."

A few seconds later, they were sitting in a private lounge reserved for heads of state and distinguished guests. Kallenberg poured two glasses of scotch and handed one to Helena. "Here, drink this. It has a terrible taste, but it will settle your nerves."

She downed the drink in a single gulp.

"Listen, Helena," Kallenberg began, "I can't imagine what's happened, but I can see that you're very upset. I want you to know that you can count on my help and support. Now, if you prefer not to talk about it, I'll understand. But you might feel better if you discussed it with me. Is there any way I can help you? Do you want to talk to me about it?"

"How is Irene?" Helena asked, determined to change the direction of the conversation.

Kallenberg made a face. "Oh, your poor sister. What a problem she is. Maybe we've been married too long—Wait a moment! What am I doing? You're the one with problems, and here I am, about to tell you the story of my life."

Helena assayed a smile. She could feel the scotch beginning to take effect. Herman poured her another glass.

"Where is Mortimer?" he asked.

"I don't want to know where he is."

Kallenberg laughed. "I see we have the same problem," he said.

"Why? What have you done to my sister this time?"

"You should ask what she has done to me."

"You don't look like a martyr."

"I know! That's part of my problem. I'm cast in the wrong role. Tell me, have you and Mortimer had a fight?"

"Everything's over between Mortimer and me."

"Are you serious?"

"Perfectly serious."

"I hope you've given this a lot of thought."

"What's done is done."

"How has he hurt you so?"

"It doesn't matter."

"You see, you didn't believe me when I told you that it would turn out this way."

"What do you mean?"

"When I told you that you and I should have gotten married."

"That would only have provided one more disaster in the family."

"Perhaps not."

A young stewardess entered carrying a bouquet of roses, which she presented to Helena. Herman pointed to the bottle.

"Would you like another?"

"Thank you."

"For what?"

"For the flowers."

"Helena, what on earth is wrong with you? You sound as though you were a helpless animal who had been abandoned."

"That's exactly what I am. But forget me. Tell me about yourself, Herman."

"Oh, things are going about as usual. Socrates is giving me hell, and so is your mother."

"You all act like a bunch of children."

"Perhaps. What a family!"

For the first time since he had known her, Herman had succeeded in establishing contact with Helena. Heretofore the Greek had always stood as an obstacle between them. Today, however, she had become aware of him as an individual, and he felt that she was somehow accessible.

"Lena, I have a suggestion. My personal plane is being readied for you, and of course, it will take you wherever you want to go. But instead of going to Athens, where your mother is going to ask a lot of painful questions, why not spend a few days aboard the *Vagrant*? At least no one will disturb you there. What do you think?"

"Where is the *Vagrant*?"

"At Portofino."

She looked at him pensively. "Herman, I had no idea that you were such a kind man."

He flushed. "There, you see? You can't judge people by their reputations."

"What if Irene finds out?"

"What if she does?"

"Won't she get ideas?"

"Irene always gets ideas."

"Well, it's very tempting."

"Good. That's what I want: to tempt you."

"Good heavens!"

"You know," he said with a small, forced laugh, "the rest of my proposition still stands."

"What is that?"

"That we get married."

"Oh, Herman. Do stop."

"You think I'm joking, but I'm not. I've always been in love with you."

"Be serious."

"I am serious."

Helena sensed that he was indeed. How strange life was. On the very same day on which she left her husband, her former brother-in-law proposed to her.

"I'll tell you what, Herman. As soon as you get home, talk to Irene about it."

"I intend to."

"I'm sure she'll be delighted."

"Not delighted, no. She's jealous of you as it is. Anyway, Irene and I are getting a divorce."

"Really?"

"Yes."

"Why?"

"Why were you and Socrates divorced? And why are you going to divorce Mortimer?"

"You have a point," Helena admitted.

A man in uniform entered the room. "Excuse me, madame. Sir, your plane is ready. Your car is waiting to take you to the runway."

Kallenberg looked at Helena intently. "Well?"

"Well, what?"

"Shall I have you taken to the Vagrant?"

"I'd love it."

"Shall we get married?"

Helena laughed. "Of course I'll marry you!"

"Be serious. I intend to talk to Irene about it tonight."

"I'd love to hear that conversation."

"Why should she mind? She can always marry Socrates."

He saw her recoil. He had gone too far.

"Come," he said. "The plane is waiting."

They rose and walked outside to the car.

"I warn you, Helena. Everything I've told you is true. I intend to speak to Irene about it."

Helena shrugged. It was difficult to tell if the gesture was intended to convey acquiescence or indifference.

"Thank you, Herman, for everything. I'm so happy that I ran into you." Then she disappeared into the automobile.

"I have something new on this Scobb man, sir! He left home last night and flew to New Orleans."

"And?"

"New Orleans is where Scott Baltimore is going to make the final speech of his campaign."

"Yes, yes, I know," William said impatiently.

"Scobb registered this morning at a boardinghouse on St. Charles Avenue—the Columns it's called. Respectable, elderly ladies, retired army officers, that sort of thing."

"Yes?"

"This afternoon, the mayor will welcome Baltimore at the Royal Orleans Hotel in the French Quarter—"

"Never mind the tour of the city. I own a chain of travel agencies for that kind of thing."

"But this is important. Almost immediately after he arrived in New Orleans, Scobb went to an office building opposite the Royal Orleans. He was carrying a package. He went to the fourth floor. He had a key to an empty office. When he came down, he no longer had the package."

"And what was in the package?"

"A high-powered rifle, disassembled, with the serial number filed off."

"How do you know?"

"He had the package with him when he registered at the Columns. A few minutes later he went out for coffee, leaving the package in his room. One of our men opened it while searching his baggage."

"Bert—"

"There's more. The office where he hid the rifle was rented by a New York company three days ago. And, coincidentally, from its window there's a clean view of the exact spot where Baltimore's car will have to stop tomorrow in front of the Royal Orleans Hotel. What do you think of that?"

"Nothing."

"But—"

"But what? Do you expect me to believe that the Baltimore people hired this man to kill Baltimore?"

"Sir, I don't know exactly what's going on, but there's something to this. It can't all be coincidence."

"Maybe this Scobb of yours was hired to protect Baltimore."

"No, it's not that. Baltimore has his own security staff. Four bodyguards who never leave him alone for a second. There's only one possibility that I can see. If I were one of Baltimore's men and I saw his support eroding as the campaign comes to a close, I'd sure as hell want to do something to awaken massive public support on the eve of the election."

"Yes, of course. That's obvious. But what has all this to do with Scobb?"

Bert remained silent for a moment. "Sir," he said finally, "I think there's going to be an assassination attempt. Simulated, of course. A man hired by the Baltimore team is going to take a shot at Baltimore—and miss! Can you think of a better way to gain public sympathy at the last minute of the campaign? Imagine the publicity! Overnight he'll become a national hero, a martyr, but the kind of martyr who miraculously escapes death. The best kind of martyr."

"My God!" William shouted. "That's it. That bastard! What time is it?"

"Nine o'clock."

"What are you waiting for? Do something! Charter a plane! Get your ass down there!"

"And what should I do when I get there?"

"How do I know? Once you're there, you'll think of something. Hurry! There's not a minute to lose."

"Just a minute. I have thought of one thing. We can do it here in New York. According to the file on Scobb, he has a wife and three children. They're the most important thing in the world to him."

"I don't see—"

"Wait. Suppose we get hold of the wife and kids and then tell Scobb that the plan has changed. That instead of missing his target, he must hit it."

"Do you think he's stupid enough to be bought by us?"

"We don't have to buy him—at least not with money. We tell him that if he does as we say, we'll turn his family loose. If not—"

"If he accepts, he'll be signing his own death warrant."

"Do you think that Trendy and his gang plan to let this poor bastard stay alive? He'd be able to blackmail them for the rest of their lives. In this kind of business, sir, there's no room for sentiment."

Between the islands of Guadeloupe and Puerto Rico lie nearly four hundred other islands, many of which are simply unnamed specks on marine charts, stretching out over the hundreds of miles of water bounded by Désirade, Monserrat, St. Kitts, Antigua, St. Martin, Anguila, Sombrero, Nevis, and the Virgin Islands.

The *Pegasus II* was not far from a group of these anonymous islets at the time of the Bechstein incident. Menelas, however, was Menelas, no matter where she was. She had returned to the yacht from her swim as though nothing had happened. Tired but relaxed, she had casually asked Socrates if they might take a closer look at the islands from the helicopter the next morning. She made no mention of the piano. Instantly, Socrates was on guard. He was willing to play her game. He pretended to have no recollection of his anger, but he braced himself for the counterattack that he knew must surely come.

The next morning, over their orange juice, they had smiled at each other, but had remained silent, neither being willing to be the first to speak. An hour passed before Menelas gave in.

"Socrates," she began, "please don't forget that you promised that we would visit those desert islands this morning."

It was a bad sign, Socrates knew. When Menelas said "please," the storm was about to break. He was briefly tempted to ask for an armistice, to promise her a new piano, even to apologize. Instead, he said, "All right. We can go now, if you wish."

An hour later they were in the air, flying at an altitude of about sixty feet. They had passed over three or four of the islands, but Menelas had shown no particular interest in any of them. Gently, Jeff increased the helicopter's speed.

"No, Jeff! Not so fast," Menelas said. "See that island over there?" She pointed to a gray spot in the sea, about three miles to the south. "Let's go there."

Jeff slowed, then turned and headed in the direction she had indicated. Below, a boat was moving slowly through the green water. Jeff brought the helicopter down to thirty feet. From that distance, the boat seemed little more than a rusty hull. There was no one visible on deck.

"How does it stay afloat?" Menelas asked. "It looks as though it's ready to sink."

Jeff laughed. "No, madame. It's a smuggler's boat, camouflaged. It's supposed to look like it's on its last legs. Actually, it has the best radar equipment money can buy and engines that can outrun any police boat in the area."

"What do they smuggle?"

"I have no idea. Weapons, perhaps, or drugs."

Menelas stared at the bizarre craft for a moment, then turned to Socrates. "You know," she said softly, "what you did yesterday was not very nice."

The Greek stared off into the distance, his shirt open, sweat pouring down his chest, his safety belt, for comfort's sake, hanging loose from his seat. It was too hot to fight. He said nothing.

"You know very well," Menelas went on, her voice becoming more strident, "that my piano is a part of myself. If you lay a hand on it, it is the same as striking me in the face. You should have known that I would not allow such an insult to go unavenged."

Something in her tone warned Socrates. He turned to reply, but he was not quick enough. Before he knew what had happened, he felt himself being pushed violently from his seat toward the open door of the helicopter. His momentum was such that he could not stop himself until his body was halfway out of the aircraft, and the sea, which a moment before had been beneath his feet, was over his head. Desperately, he hooked his feet around the legs of his empty seat and clutched at the doorway with his hands in an effort to keep from falling from the helicopter.

It had all happened so quickly that Jeff, sitting with his back to his passengers, had not noticed the incident. Nor did he see Menelas pushing with all her strength to break the Greek's hold on the legs of his chair and pulling to pry loose his fingers from the door frame. Socrates gave several mighty kicks with one of his legs in an effort to defend himself. One of them must have struck its target, for he felt Menelas suddenly release him and fall backward into her own seat, clutching at her breast. With an almost superhuman effort, Socrates pulled himself back into the helicopter and collapsed into his seat, panting like an exhausted animal. Jeff had turned and was staring at him wide-eyed.

Socrates, still out of breath, gasped, "Jeff, land on that island."

A few seconds later the helicopter was hovering over a black sand beach dotted with shells. In the center of the island was a rocky hill covered with a growth of lichen on which a few wild goats were grazing.

The helicopter settled at the far end of the beach. Its blades had barely ceased to revolve when Menelas jumped to the sand and began walking rapidly away. The Greek watched her as from time to time she bent and picked up a shell, examined it closely, then threw it away. The goats, puzzled by this invasion, stood motionless on their hill, watching.

When Menelas was two hundred yards from the helicopter, Socrates turned to his pilot. "Jeff, let's get out of here," he said.

Menelas turned when she heard the engine roar increase in pitch and began to walk hurriedly toward the helicopter. She was still a

hundred yards away when it rose majestically from the beach and began to gain altitude. She was now running, her long white legs sinking into the black sand and leaving a deep imprint. By then the
helicopter was no more than a gray speck moving rapidly northward
in the sky.

The children had stayed home from school that day. It was 10
A.M., and Slim had been gone for two days. He had not told Annie
where he was going. But then, he never did. Invariably he would say
only, "Don't worry. I'll be back soon."

This time he had hesitated briefly, as though he were going to add
something. Then he slammed the suitcase shut, kissed Annie, and
was gone.

It did not occur to Annie to ask him where he was going. In the
years of their marriage, Slim had frequently been gone for several
days at a time without offering explanation. If he had wanted her
to know, she reasoned, he would have told her. She did not complain
because he did not. Like any man, he was entitled to his secrets. He
was a good husband, a devoted father, and a wonderful lover. Annie
was perfectly content with that.

The sound of the doorbell startled her. She hurried to the door
and opened it. A well-dressed man smiled at her.

"Mrs. Scobb?" he asked.

"Yes?"

"Mrs. Scobb, your husband asked me to come."

"Oh? Please come in."

Annie closed the door behind him.

"Mrs. Scobb, I have good news for you. But I can't tell you any
more than that. Slim made me swear I wouldn't spoil his surprise.
I'm supposed to take you and the children to him."

"Take us to him? Where is he?"

"That's what I can't tell you. That's Slim's surprise! He wants you
to pack as few things as possible— Do you want me to help you get
your things together?"

"Well, I don't know. Slim never mentioned anything— Are you a
friend of his?"

"My name is Baden. John Baden. I'm a very old friend of your husband's. We've done a lot of business together."

"Baden?"

"Yes. Wait a second. I have a note here." He fumbled in his pockets
and produced a sheet of paper which he handed to Annie.

She unfolded it and immediately recognized her husband's large childlike script: "Annie, don't ask any questions, and do what Baden tells you. It's a surprise. You'll like it. I love you. Slim."

She looked at Baden. "Will we be gone for long? I mean, what should I do about the apartment?"

"Don't worry about that. Everything is already taken care of. The only thing is, we'll have to hurry. There's a car waiting for us downstairs."

"Well, the children are playing in the bedroom. I'll have to get them ready. . . ."

It never occurred to Annie to question Slim's orders. His note said to do what Baden told her, and that was precisely what she intended to do. She would have liked to tell the woman next door that they were going away, but Mr. Baden seemed in such a hurry that she decided against it.

"How much time do we have to get ready?"

"Oh, let's say ten minutes. You and the kids won't need much."

"All right. I'll hurry," Annie assured him. She went into the bedroom to begin dressing the children for Slim's surprise.

[26]

"I want to tell you something that will amuse you."

Irene speared a pat of butter with a silver knife and spread it thoughtfully on a piece of toast. It was unusual for Herman to join her in her room at breakfast. Obviously he had something on his mind. Normally when he declared his intention of making her laugh, it meant that she was about to be made the victim of one of his vicious tricks. Paradoxically, she was eager to have him get on with it, for she was impatient to be punished for the part she had played in the drama of Satrapoulos' nondeath.

With a shiver of anticipation, she set her face in a smile. After all, she must not let him suspect that she was afraid or that she enjoyed being afraid.

"How nice, darling. Go ahead. Make me laugh."

"I'm leaving."

"That *is* amusing."

"Do you know why I'm leaving?"

"Because you feel like leaving?"

"Precisely."

"When are you leaving?"

"Tonight. As soon as I settle all the details with my attorneys."

"Where are you going? To prison?"

"No. Quite the contrary. I'm breaking out of prison. I'm going to get a divorce."

"Lovely. Do you think you should let your wife know?"

"I'm doing so right now."

Irene felt a wave of nausea sweep over her, but she managed to smile affectionately at Kallenberg.

"So, my darling. Are you angry with me?"

"No, not with you. With myself."

"Naughty, naughty! What on earth could you have done?"

"I'm angry with myself for having put up with a stupid cunt like you for as long as I have."

"Oh, that is wicked."

"Quite apart from being a stupid cunt, you are insane. You should be in a sanitarium."

"Mmm. You can be my attendant and fondle my breasts when you help me on with my straitjacket." As she spoke, she dropped three tranquilizers into a spoonful of strawberry preserves. Usually, she waited until noon before taking her first pills of the day. But this was an urgent case. The most disturbing aspect was that Kallenberg refused to lose his temper, no matter what she said.

"Don't play the coquette, Irene. It won't work. I should have killed you long ago. I didn't, because I know you are so stupid that you're not responsible for your actions. Anyway, you're less alive now than if I had buried you ten years ago."

"That would have been nice, wouldn't it? Then you could have had the wife's money, without the bother of the wife."

Kallenberg went on as though he had not heard. "It should be obvious even to you that, after what you've done, I can't possibly continue to live under the same roof with you. I could put up with your stupidity, but I could never bear treason."

"My, my! Such an ominous word!"

"You may make as many jokes as you wish. We'll see who has the last laugh in this comedy."

"So my little love wants to be free, does he? Have you already chosen your next victim?"

"Yes."

"Do I know her?"

"Of course. It's your sister."

Irene did not understand at first. Perhaps she did not wish to understand. Then she grasped the import of Kallenberg's words. Her nausea intensified, and her heart pounded alarmingly in her chest. With an effort, she managed to control her panic.

"Who, dear?" she asked, her voice almost normal.

"Helena. Your favorite sister. The family pet."

"How devastatingly funny!"

"For God's sake, Irene! Stop buttering that toast. There already are a dozen pieces on the table. Do you intend to eat them all?"

"I'll butter as much bloody toast as I feel like buttering!" She was shouting now, and Herman experienced a joyous tingle. He had finally penetrated her defenses.

"Now, now, dear," he murmured soothingly. "You go right ahead and butter as much toast as your little heart desires. Make a hobby of it, if you like. You're going to have a lot of free time on your hands."

"Do you think I'm going to let you get away with this?" Irene shrieked. "Do you think I'll let you throw me over for that insipid sister of mine? Wait until I tell my mother! I'm going to call her right now—"

"You know where the telephone is, dear. God knows, you use it enough. Why don't you become a telephone operator? Then you could spread your shit over the entire system. You could spy on the whole world—"

"Herman, tell me the truth. Are you serious about this?"

"I've never been more serious about anything in my life. After all, you can always remarry, too. In fact, why don't you marry your former brother-in-law? Considering all the help you've given him, he might be willing to take you."

"Bastard!" Irene snatched up a saucer and threw it at his face. He ducked expertly and grabbed her arms, digging his fingers cruelly into the soft flesh.

"Irene, Irene." He sighed. "How excitable you are! Now calm

down. If you behave yourself, I'll let you come to my wedding. Helena would like that."

Irene snatched one of her hands free and thrust her long nails toward Kallenberg's eyes. He seized the hand in one of his own and with the other slapped her hard across the mouth.

"Do calm yourself, darling. Do you see what you've made me do?"

She broke away from him again and ran toward the door, sobbing wildly. Then, suddenly, she crumpled to the floor and lay still. Kallenberg approached her warily. When he was certain that she was truly unconscious, he raised his foot and kicked her viciously in the stomach. "Here, bitch!" he snarled. "I owe you that!"

Then he opened the door and shouted into the hallway, "Jeanine! Jeanine!"

The chambermaid appeared almost immediately.

"Quickly, Jeanine! Madame is having one of her attacks."

Menelas was beginning to be frightened. What if Socrates didn't return for her? She lay back on the sand, tracing vague designs with her fingers. Watching the helicopter disappear, she had thought he was bluffing. She had been certain he would turn around and come back for her. But as silence gave way to silence, worry turned to anger and anger to panic. Strange thoughts crossed her mind, akin to the thoughts of a person about to die. Shreds of the past: flashes of standing ovations and full houses, men's faces, the visage of that harebrained American who had introduced her to music. The wall of bleached stone in Corfu, behind which she'd hidden when she wanted to isolate herself and know she was alone—the last survivor of a vanishing race. But then, whenever she had succeeded in frightening herself, she had but to peer over the wall to see her house and break the spell.

But there was no wall on this island, there was no house, no one. She was alone, as if in a coffin. In an effort to give herself courage, she shouted as loudly as she could. All that happened was that the goats up on the summit shied in fear. As if seeking company she moved toward them, but was able to get no closer than a hundred yards. She stopped to rest against a cactus and almost fainted. There, flattened against the trunk, was an extra-greenish branch, gnarled and bristling with horny ridges. At its end two eyes, half-hidden beneath heavy eyelids, extended to a thin, forked tongue—an iguana! Shuddering, she avoided the other cacti, each capable of sheltering whole families of iguanas, and she returned to the beach. Only to find the beach, which at first had seemed so deserted, now teeming with terrifying, monstrous crabs. The ripples sweeping the surface of the clear water suggested abundant marine life beneath. She imagined the largest fish devouring the smallest—the eternal, abominable law of nature. Then she began to cry, knowing she couldn't survive one dreadful night spent in this false paradise.

A distant noise roused her from her torpor, and her heart began to pound against her ribs. The throb of a motor, hot and reassuring, grew louder. She scanned the sky nervously, until her eyes, misty with tears, made out a black speck approaching from the north. She only averted her eyes once, to check her watch—during the past four hours she'd died a thousand deaths. Abruptly, as it grew nearer, the speck split in two, one speck above the other, then became two distant objects. The lower was clearly smaller. What would it be. . . . The machine carried beneath its breast a black mass swinging from the end of a cable. Now in the bubble she could see the figures of Socrates and Jeff. They spied her, too. Despite the tempest brewing inside her, she managed to ignore them—conquering her desire to shout, to clap, to wave her arms. She would show them she was no weakling. She was fine where she was and could do without them. So she pretended to toy with some shells, just as if the helicopter weren't revolving right over her head and— My God! It spun away! She leaped to her feet and began to yell as, with a deafening roar, the monster flew over the beach. A half mile away it paused and hovered, thirty feet in the air, and slowly settled toward the sand, inch by inch, until the incongruous object dangling from it touched the ground. She began running like a madwoman as the helicopter, free from its burden, shot up again into the air, and turned north. It wasn't possible! "He" couldn't do this to her. Fifty yards from the large box she stopped, stunned, broken: the pig had brought her piano! She broke into hysterical laughter, which mingled with her tears. . . . The world's most renowned concert pianist abandoned on a desert island in the Caribbean, alone with her Bechstein! Yes, it was a Bechstein! At her feet a small parcel contained blankets, wine, fruit, and canned vegetables. She felt like vomiting. Reeling, she balanced herself with her hand against the instrument's rich mahogany. By reflex more than by intention, she raised the lid of the keyboard and lightly touched the keys. In the open the sound was unusually thin. On the sand lay an envelope. She opened it and read:

Goethe isolated himself on an island for six months to study
Spinoza. Menelas will be able to use her three or four days on
her island to appreciate the subtleties of Chopin. Enjoy the sol-
itude.

—SOCRATES

Weeping, Menelas began distractedly to peel a banana.

There was a quality about Phil which made him uniquely valuable
to his employer—in this case, to Bert. He was that important creature, the average man: average in height, weight, looks, walk. Average even in intelligence. One might encounter Phil a dozen times
a day without recognizing him. He was the perfect tail. To this natural gift for anonymity, he added a dimension of his own. He was
tenacious to the point of monomania, and never in his lengthy career
had he lost sight of the man he was assigned to follow. He did not
intend to let Slim Scobb be the first. He watched as Slim turned
into Iberville Street, walked a half block, and entered a bar. Phil
waited exactly five minutes and followed him.

It was a small place, intimate, cozy. Most of the customers were
drinking beer. He spotted Slim standing at the bar. There was a
space next to him, which Phil quickly filled. "A beer," he told the
bartender.

Phil was not a subtle man. He believed that a straightforward
approach was best. That way a man knew exactly where he stood.
He began speaking, softly yet distinctly, so that no one but Slim
might hear him. "Listen, friend. Listen to what I'm going to tell
you. Don't move, and don't make a sound. Just listen."

He felt Slim give a slight start. That was all. He watched out of
the corner of his eye as Slim took a swallow from his beer, as non-
chalantly as if he had heard nothing.

"Your name is Slim Scobb," Phil said quickly. "You live in the
Bronx. Later this afternoon, you are going to go to Room 472 on
the fourth floor of an office building across from the Royal Orleans
Hotel. You've already taken a package to that room. It contains an
automatic rifle and several clips of ammunition. When Scott Baltimore arrives at the entrance of the hotel, you are supposed to fire
at him and to miss."

In the noise in the bar, Phil's voice was audible only to Slim. Even
if anyone had overheard what he was saying, it would have been
difficult to know who was speaking, since his lips barely moved as
he articulated his words.

"Except, my friend, that you're not going to miss. If you do, you'll never see your wife and children again. Annie and the kids are in our hands, and they're where you'd never find them. Now I'm going to prove that I'm not bluffing. I'm going to walk to that telephone booth over there and dial a number. When you see me talk into the receiver, come to the booth. Annie will be on the line. Do you understand?"

"Bartender!" Slim called. "Let me have another beer."

Phil threw a dollar bill on the counter to pay for his own beer, then walked to the telephone booth.

Slim turned his head and watched the man drop coins into the telephone. What if it was true! He'd kill the bastards! But who were they?

He saw the man look in his direction and nod. It was the signal. He walked toward the booth. Phil let the receiver dangle from the cord and left the booth. Slim entered and picked up the receiver. His hands were so damp that he had difficulty holding it.

"Hello?"

"Oh, Slim—"

"Where are you, for God's sake?"

There was no answer, only a loud sobbing, which suddenly grew fainter. A man's voice said, "All right, you know she's here. If you do as my friend told you, she and your kids will be home again in two hours, safe and sound. If you don't, you'll never see them again. It's your choice!"

"How do I know you'll let them go?"

"You don't. But what would we have to gain by killing them if you do as we say? And what do we have to lose by letting them go? It's a cinch they're not going to go running to the cops."

There was a click, a buzz, then another voice, thin, nasal and impersonal: "Have you completed your call, sir?"

Almost exactly one hour later, an open Lincoln, surrounded by a surging, milling, cheering mob, made its way slowly down the narrow streets of the French Quarter toward the Royal Orleans Hotel. In its back seat Peggy, never relaxing her smile, said to Scott, "God, I'm tired! I can hardly wait to get out of this girdle."

"And I have to piss so bad I can taste it," Scott replied. "Unfortunately, neither of us can help the other with his problem."

As he spoke, Scott waved jovially at the crowd, a broad, happy smile on his face. Peggy glanced at him covertly. What a magnificent specimen, she reflected. The image of triumphant youth, tanned, healthy, handsome, intelligent. . . . Not one of her lovers could have even begun to compare with him. What a pity that he had found it so difficult to reconcile his political ambitions with his love for her.

She waved at a black woman holding a child. The woman looked startled and raised her hand cautiously as though afraid of being rebuked for her insolence. Peggy blew a kiss to the child. The woman's face was transfigured by joy. She lifted the child toward the Lincoln, as though asking for the blessing of the goddess on the head of her offspring. Then she was lost from sight as the automobile moved on. A short distance ahead, Peggy saw the Royal Orleans Hotel looming over the older buildings of the neighborhood.

She looked at Scott again, and as though by inspiration, she suddenly understood something which had eluded her before: she loved Scott, not in spite of his political ambitions, but precisely because he was destined to stand head and shoulders above all men, to be the leader of his nation, the embodiment of its people.

As if he felt her eyes on him, he turned toward her. She reached out and took his hand.

The Lincoln turned to approach the entrance to the Royal Orleans.

Despite the cheers of the crowd, Peggy and Scott did not look away from each other. No words passed between them, but in that instant they understood that all things were possible, that all things could be understood, and all things forgiven. Their hands joined, they silently renewed the promises they had made an eternity before.

At that moment, the first bullet crashed through the windshield of the Lincoln.

It was 4 P.M., as Slim knelt before the window in the office, waiting for the Baltimore cavalcade to appear in the street below. He tried to concentrate on the job before him and to put from his mind the thought that Annie and his children were in those bastards' hands. Through the rifle's telescopic sight he scanned the crowd in the street, singling out first one face, then another from the thousands below, hoping to find the man who had approached him in the bar. If he got that son of a bitch in his sights. . . .

A loud cheer rose from the street. Slim lowered the rifle and peered through the window. Several automobiles, escorted by a detachment of policemen on motorcycles, were moving slowly toward the hotel across the street. The fourth vehicle was a long black Lincoln—a custom job, Slim noted. Its top was down, and two figures were visible in the back seat, waving at the crowd.

He raised the rifle to his shoulder and squinted through the telescope, keeping the Lincoln squarely in his sights as it moved toward the main entrance of the Royal Orleans. It registered dimly in Slim's mind that Scott and Peggy Baltimore were no longer looking at the crowd and waving. Their eyes were on each other, their faces serious, intent on their own affairs. Yes, that was probably it, Slim told himself. People like that, young, rich, in love—what did they know about people like Annie and him?

"Annie," Slim whispered hoarsely. "Annie!"

He squeezed the trigger.

He saw a reddish mass of torn flesh and bone where Scott's head had been.

He saw Peggy's mouth open in a silent shriek of horror.

He looked away. Quickly, he disassembled the rifle and packed it into a small plastic bag designed for golfing equipment. Then he opened the door of the office and emerged into the corridor. Employees from the other offices on the floor rushed past him, their faces fixed in masks of incredulity and dismay. No one seemed to notice him. Careful to walk at a normal pace, Slim moved toward the service stairs. He reached them without being stopped. He plunged down the staircase, not pausing until he reached the second level of the basement. He had memorized the floor plan of the basement of this building as well as those of the adjoining structures. Three more doors, and he would be in a small apartment building fronting on Bourbon Street. Trendy had given him the keys to those doors. Slim felt them in his pocket now. The cold touch of the pieces of metal reawakened hope in him. Maybe, just maybe, there was a chance for Annie and the kids to get out of this alive.

His wife and children's lives were all he could hope for. Even if they let him live after this, Slim knew what his own life would be. He would be a hunted man until the day he died; always a fugitive, living in dread that someday, somehow, he would be found. Yet he had not wanted to kill Scott Baltimore. Until the very last second he had hesitated. It was only when he saw the look of love and understanding which had passed between Baltimore and his wife that his finger had squeezed the trigger—instinctively, almost involuntarily, as though that finger had suddenly assumed an autonomous life of its own and asserted its will in a single, cataclysmic act.

The first door was in front of him. He groped in his pocket for the keys, pulled out one of them, tried to insert it into the keyhole. It did not fit. Cursing, he tried the second key, with the same results. The third key slid into the lock but would not turn.

"Oh, those bastards!" Slim muttered. "Annie . . . Annie, they've trapped me!"

He turned and began running down the corridor, expecting at any moment to come face to face with the man assigned to kill him. Slim had not the slightest doubt that this was the plan. If Trendy had given him the wrong keys, it was for a reason.

His only chance to escape was to return to his point of departure: to the office building from which he had fired. From there he might be able to make it into the street and then disappear into the crowd.

Taking the service stairs four at a time, he reached the ground floor of the building and burst through the door into the lobby.

"Hold it right there!"

Slim froze. A line of policemen stretched across the lobby, blocking the entry. More policemen moved behind Slim to cut him off from the service stairs. One of them tore the plastic bag from his hand while others gripped his arms and forced them behind his back.

"That's the bastard who did it!" a voice shouted. "His rifle's in this bag!"

Slim struggled to break free, but he was unable to move. Then, suddenly, he stiffened as though from an electric shock. Before him, standing in a small crowd of men in civilian clothes, he saw Trendy. Trendy whispered to a small man next to him. Instinctively, Slim's eyes dropped to the man's right hand. It was empty.

The man raised his left hand, and three bullets crashed into Slim's chest.

In his last second of life, Slim saw the man elbow his way quickly through the crowd and disappear.

As the helicopter gained altitude, Socrates felt a twinge of guilt. Perhaps he was being a bit hard on the woman. He looked down and saw her, now only a pale silhouette against the dark sand. He had determined that she would remain there, alone, for a week. But what if she became ill? What if she tried to kill herself? With Olympia, one never knew. He was about to order Jeff to return to the island, when the pilot spoke.

"Sir—" He looked pleadingly at Socrates.

"What is it?"

"Sir, don't you think that maybe—"

That was enough. Socrates' heart hardened once more, and he banished all compassion for Menelas, stranded on her goat-infested island.

"Mind your own business," he snarled at Jeff. "I pay you to pilot my planes. Nothing else!" After all, Socrates reminded himself, she had humiliated him before his crew, not once but twice. And that was twice more than he would allow.

"Sir!"

Socrates' first impulse was one of intense irritation at Jeff. Couldn't the man understand that his employer's personal affairs were none of his business? He opened his mouth to speak, but something in Jeff's face made him hold his tongue.

"Listen to this," Jeff said, handing him his earphones. Above the noise of the engine, the Greek heard a newscaster, his voice quavering, announce that Scott Baltimore had just been shot in New Orleans.

He tore the earphones from his head. "What station is that?"

"Miami."

"Take me back," Socrates ordered.

Ten minutes later the helicopter settled once more onto the beach of black sand, fifty yards from where Menelas stood, tiny, pitiful, waving her arms frantically. She ran to the helicopter and climbed in hastily. Socrates could see that she had been crying, indeed, that she was holding back her tears with great difficulty. She did not speak, nor did he. She reached over, took his hand, and squeezed it. He returned the pressure and said softly, "Scott Baltimore has just been assassinated."

As soon as they reached the *Pegasus II*, Socrates sent a cablegram off to Peggy: STUNNED BY THIS TERRIBLE NEWS. AM THINKING OF YOU WITH ALL MY HEART, AND AM AT YOUR DISPOSAL TOTALLY AND WITHOUT RESERVATION. SOCRATES.

Two hours later, as he sat staring into space, Kirillis handed him a message. To his amazement, it was an answer from Peggy. He read it three times, his hands trembling all the while: THANK YOU. I AM HORRIBLY LOST AND ALONE. I WILL LOOK FOR YOU AT THE FUNERAL.

Part Four

[27]

"NOW, look into my eyes. Your eyelids are getting heavy, very heavy. Your legs seem to be made of lead. Your arms are heavy, heavy, extremely heavy. Your whole body is becoming heavy. You would like to close your eyes. You can hardly keep your eyes open. Your eyelids are so heavy that you can't keep them open. You want to sleep. Sleep. Close your eyes and sleep. Sleep, you are in a deep sleep. You will not awaken until I tell you to do so. Now, get up and sit in this chair. . . ."

"Should I keep my eyes closed?"

Dr. Schwobb sighed in exasperation. "You're not trying," he told his patient, shaking his head. Everything about this man irritated him somehow. First of all, he had insisted on remaining anonymous, which was against all the rules of proper medical procedure. All patients were supposed to begin by stating their full names and addresses. But was this man really a patient? It was hard to decide. Ten days earlier Dr. Schwobb had received a telephone call from Dr. Herbert, the eminent cardiologist. "A friend of mine wants to learn the technique of hypnosis," Herbert had said. "Can you help him?"

Schwobb had answered that he was not a teacher and that he could not afford the time for instruction.

"Yes," Herbert had replied. "I know how valuable your time is. In fact, my friend puts its worth at about five hundred dollars an hour. If that isn't enough, tell me. He's willing to pay anything that you ask."

"Is this friend of yours a medical man?"

"Hardly." Herbert had laughed. "If he were, would he place so high a price on our time?"

An appointment had been arranged for Herbert's friend, and on the designated day a neat little man wearing a black alpaca suit had appeared at Schwobb's office punctually at 10 A.M.

Schwobb began by trying to place things in the proper perspective. "Hypnosis is a therapeutic procedure," he explained, "and there are certain dangers implicit in its use. Before we begin, I would like to know how you intend to make use of it."

The man—Mr. Smith was the name Dr. Herbert had supplied—gave a candid answer: "It's for a woman."

"You want to teach hypnosis to a woman?"

"No. I want to seduce her through hypnosis."

Schwobb threw up his hands in horror. "Really, sir—"

He had intended to point out that he was not a pimp, but a doctor, but Mr. Smith did not allow him to finish. "Perhaps there has been some misunderstanding about your fee, Dr. Schwobb. Dr. Herbert told me, I believe, that it was a thousand dollars per hour. Is that correct?"

Schwobb found the argument irresistible. "Very well," he replied. "Let's begin."

Since then Schwobb had almost regretted his decision. Several times he had tried to induce a state of hypnosis in his patient, but without success. There was something about this man, something within him, which made him proof against suggestion. Still, there was no doubt as to the man's good faith. He was perfectly willing, even eager, to be hypnotized—but only at the conscious level. At the unconscious level there was this mysterious force which invariably surfaced just in time to keep Smith from entering even the first stages of hypnotic sleep. It had even occurred to Schwobb that the man was a specialist of some kind and that Herbert had arranged the whole thing as an elaborate practical joke. But what doctor in his right mind would play practical jokes at a thousand dollars an hour?

Eight times Schwobb had tried to induce a hypnotic trance in Smith. Eight times he had failed. And eight times Smith had handed Schwobb a thousand-dollar bill, discreetly folded, before leaving the office. Now, however, Schwobb was at the end of both his resources and his wits. Money was one thing, and professional integrity was another. He would have to face the fact that he had failed and advise this Mr. Smith to stop wasting his money.

"Listen," he began. "I think we should face the facts. There's nothing I can do for you. I think we should give it up."

"But why?" Smith replied in astonishment.

"I told you. There is nothing I can do for you."

"Doctor, maybe you've been trying to do the wrong thing. I didn't come here to be hypnotized. I thought Dr. Herbert had made that clear. I came to learn how to hypnotize other people. Or at least, another person. How many more lessons will I need before I can do that?"

Schwobb gestured helplessly. "Mr.—Smith, do you really think you need hypnosis to seduce someone?"

"If I didn't think so, would I be sitting here?"

Schwobb cleared his throat. "I mean, Mr. Smith, that you seem to have some kind of inner force—a remarkable force—"

"Yes, yes. I know. It's useful in my business, but it doesn't seem to work in my personal life."

"If I understand you correctly, you want to use hypnosis to make a woman fall in love with you?"

"That would be asking too much. All I want is for you to give me something that will make her notice me, *see* me. That's all I ask. I'll do the rest myself."

Schwobb was silent. Smith's confession of helplessness had restored the doctor-patient relationship in its full vigor. This poor man, whoever he was, had scaled Olympus to seek the aid of the gods. Like any other patient in a doctor's office.

"Very well, Mr. Smith," Schwobb answered confidently. "Now that I understand your problem, I will explain certain techniques that you can use—"

Smith held up his hand.

"Yes?" Schwobb said impatiently. "What is it?"

"These techniques," Smith said. "Remember that no technique will do me any good if I can't get her to see me."

"Yes, yes, I know. But you're not a child, Mr. Smith. Surely you know that there are a thousand ways to get a woman's attention."

"This is no ordinary woman. The whole world is trying to get her attention."

"Don't tell me that if you walked past her naked, with your hair on fire, she wouldn't notice you." Schwobb chuckled over his little joke and glanced at his patient. The man's face was like stone.

"Well, I'm sure it won't be necessary to go to such extremes, Mr. Smith. The important things in catching a woman's attention are the eyes, the voice, intonation, gestures, expression. Tell me, just between us men, what do you want from her? Do you want her to marry you?"

The Greek laughed. "No, never. She will never marry anyone."

"Do you want her to become your mistress?"

"No, not even that. I want her to be my friend. That's all."

Schwobb raised his eyebrows. "I don't mean to pry, Mr. Smith, but do you have any problems of a sexual nature?"

Socrates laughed again. "No, no. Nothing like that! Excuse me for laughing, but I don't think you understand—"

How could he explain to this man that he was consumed by a desire to possess the most revered woman in the United States? And how could he explain that he was awed by her; so much so that the idea of sexual contact with her seemed vaguely incestuous? It was impossible to imagine that the goddess could descend from her altar and lie beside him on his bed. The very thought awakened a feeling of intense guilt in him, as though he had committed an unforgivable sacrilege or uttered a horrendous blasphemy. It was as though he were tempted to sleep with his own mother. . . .

Fast had changed considerably. Helena did not try to determine precisely how, for his metamorphosis was not entirely to her liking. He was as disconcerting and selfish as ever, but his resentments had shifted. He was no longer opposed to the concept of material possessions. In fact, he seemed preoccupied with accumulating money. Thanks to Helena's efforts, Fast's canvases were now hanging in several museums, and he was all the rage among avant-garde collectors. Of course it was somewhat misleading to speak of Fast's "canvases," for he had revolutionized art by introducing an element which past artists—Piero della Francesca, for example—had been able to achieve only through the miserable ruse of perspective. He had, as the critics were now fond of saying, given depth to art. His works were not mere daubs of paint to be hung from walls. They were creations made to occupy a space and a volume in a privileged spot. His first showing, in New York, had made the critics gasp in delight. In a dimly lighted room, he had placed a dilapidated old bed which had come from a public dump in Istanbul. A soiled, suspiciously spotted sheet had been thrown across the bed. Among the spots was a drop of dried, brown blood. "This drop of blood," the catalogue had pointed out, "is from the menstrual discharge of a young woman whose life is linked with that of the artist." The ensemble—the soiled bed and the menstrual blood—was called "End of the Party." The critics had bowed as one before it in reverence and awe. "Fast," one of them had written, reflecting the consensus among his colleagues, "has overtaken and outdistanced Rembrandt."

Once launched on his career, Fast had made giant strides in his work. His latest and most exciting composition was entitled "Women I Have Known" and was a horn-shaped contour of glass filled with thousands of fingernail clippings.

With the attainment of success and fame, Fast had risen above Helena. Now he condescended only occasionally to meet her in New York, in his studio—a converted warehouse beside the Hudson which Helena had bought for him. When they were apart, she bombarded him with telephone calls imploring him to join her or with airline tickets to Paris where the apartment in the rue de la Faisanderie was literally stuffed with Fast's minor works. These had cost Helena enormous sums, for Fast constantly preached that people only appreciated art for which they had paid dearly.

Helena had, in fact, paid dearly not only for Fast's art, but for the artist himself. The cost had included two divorces, the second of which stood unparalleled in the annals of marital estrangements. After her divorce from Mortimer, Helena, too exhausted to swim against the current but motivated also by a desire to irritate her sister and at the same time demonstrate to Mortimer that he was eminently replaceable, had consented to marry Kallenberg. Herman was eager for the ceremony. His union with Helena would have a double advantage. Not only would it enable him to trade his old wife for a new one, without the bother of also acquiring a new mother-in-law, but it would also satisfy his vanity, for it would enable him to feel that he was finally filling the shoes of his ancient enemy, the Greek. So he did everything in his considerable power to expedite the divorce proceedings and his new marriage.

The ceremony had taken place before a hundred guests, and at the wedding breakfast, Kallenberg had handed Helena a black leather box. She had opened it immediately to find inside a diamond necklace—an antique piece which, Kallenberg explained loudly, Louis XV had given to his queen upon the birth of their tenth child.

"Do you like it?" Kallenberg asked eagerly.

"Put it on, put it on!" several voices cried.

Helena slipped it around her neck, and a gasp of admiration rose from the tables. Kallenberg smiled happily. His guests' approval convinced him that he had got his money's worth. He picked up his champagne glass and drained it, then looked at Helena. Her glass was also empty. He beckoned to a waiter. As the man poured, Helena glanced at him. Her heart stopped, and her hand trembled. There, handsome as a god in a waiter's uniform, was Fast. Helena felt suddenly faint, and her heart pounded in her chest as though it would break through its frail enclosure. For a moment, she did not know where she was, or what she was doing there. . . . Then she remembered. She had just been married. But to whom? And why? And why was Fast, the man she really loved, here? She felt a flood of desire sweeping over her, as her eyes remained fixed on Fast's.

"What a lovely dress," her neighbor to the left was saying. Her dress? What dress? She felt naked under Fast's gaze. She made a small gesture, invisible to everyone except Fast. She saw him move away from the table and speak a few words to the headwaiter. The latter shook his head. Then Fast, without looking back, left the room.

". . . Capri, perhaps. Or would you prefer Acapulco?"

"I beg your pardon?"

"Are you all right, Helena? I was asking where you would like to go on our next trip. Do you have any special preference?"

She turned toward him. There was a quizzical look on Kallenberg's face. "Herman," she said softly, "I want to tell you something. I think that, for the first time in my life, I am going to be truly happy."

Enormously flattered, Kallenberg grinned and kissed her cheek.

"I'm sorry," Helena said, rising. "Would you excuse me for a moment?" She walked toward the terrace, smiling mechanically at her guests. Outside, in the garden, she saw Fast, still wearing his waiter's uniform. He seemed to be waiting for her. He stared at her for a moment, then disappeared around the corner of the house. She followed him and saw him enter a long, low building behind the main house: a stable which had been built to accommodate a former owner's racehorses.

She pushed open the door to the stable, peered into the darkness, then stepped inside.

"Fast?"

She felt his arms encircle her, and his lips were upon hers. One of his hands moved to her breast, and she leaned against the wall of the stable, breathing heavily. His other hand raised her skirt and moved caressingly up her thigh. She thought she would die of joy.

"Oh, Fast," she breathed. "I've waited so long. . . ."

She felt him enter her, slowly, gently, and she thrust herself against him with all her might.

The room was suddenly flooded with light.

"I should have known that any woman Satrapoulos married would be a whore," Kallenberg rasped, advancing toward them. He paused to remove a bullwhip from its hook on the wall. He unfurled the whip and sent it whistling toward Fast. Fast ducked instinctively and simultaneously threw himself at Kallenberg, seizing his arm and wrenching the whip from him. Before Kallenberg could recover from his surprise, Fast brought his hand crashing down on the nape of his neck, and Kallenberg crumpled to the floor.

"Come on!" Fast yelled, grabbing Helena's hand and pulling her after him.

A few moments later they were in a car, speeding away from Kallenberg's house.

Fast drove in silence for a few miles, then pulled the car over to the side of the road. He turned toward Helena. "What do we do now?" he asked.

Without knowing why, they both burst into loud laughter.

Later Helena learned that Kallenberg, after regaining consciousness, had returned to the house and calmly announced to his guests that his new bride had become suddenly indisposed. Whereupon the wedding breakfast had continued without her.

After a few days Helena returned to her own house to gather some of her clothing and found this telegram waiting for her: STAY AWAY FROM ME, BUT I WANT THE NECKLACE BACK. KALLENBERG.

Her attorney and Kallenberg's had done the rest. The divorce proceedings had gone on for six months, the minimum interval allowed by law. She had spent the time working to advance Fast's career, thinking that once he was successful, they would be married. Fast, however, thought otherwise. He seemed determined to spend as little time as possible with her, and she was forced to resign herself to seeing him only infrequently. By appointment only, she told herself bitterly. It was a familiar pattern. She had been through it before with Mark Costa. Would nothing in her life ever change except the names of the men she loved?

"How old are you?"

"Let's see," Achilles replied. "This is 1968, and I was born in 1950. That makes me eighteen. I guess. God, how time flies!"

As he usually did when dealing with his son, Socrates vacillated between anger and resignation. He had built the greatest financial empire in the world. He had brought governments to their knees and made presidents and prime ministers tremble. But he was helpless before his own son and heir. He loved him too much.

Achilles knew it and took advantage of it. Despite the deluge of gifts which Socrates lavished upon him and the advantages he derived from his position as the Greek's son, he remained convinced that, somehow, his father was in his debt. Occasionally, he deliberately provoked Socrates and seemed to derive a perverse pleasure from his father's anger. It was as though the father's displeasure soothed the son's resentment. For neither Achilles nor Maria had ever forgiven Socrates for having divorced their mother.

Helena, to her credit, had done nothing to nurture this resentment. Yet neither their mother's indifference nor their father's anger kept the twins from plotting constantly to reunite their parents. Maria frequently asked her father, with an air of sad innocence, "Papa, when are you and Mama going to get married again?"

And Achilles never missed an opportunity to attack Socrates for his interest in other women: "That fat redhead you had last night, the one who kept rolling her eyes at you, what a pig she was!"

The boy's resentment exhibited itself in more than mere words. The evening before, he had tried to drown Menelas in the pool, despite the fact that Socrates' great and good friend had always gone to extraordinary lengths to show her affection for the two children. Menelas was so upset by the incident that she had immediately taken to her bed, and she had not yet left it. She had, however, refrained from telling Socrates that his son had attempted to murder her—an event which the servants described to their master in great detail.

"Why are you concerned about my age?" Achilles asked.

"For a very good reason. When he reaches a certain age, a boy is no longer legally a juvenile. Which means that if he commits a crime, he is prosecuted like any other criminal."

"Oh, come on! A criminal! Because I caused that woman to swallow a little water? She deserves a lot worse than that! She—"

"Achilles! Be careful of what you say!"

"Papa—"

"Shut up! You're going to go straight to Olympia and apologize, do you hear me? Right away!"

"I won't!"

"What did you say?"

"I won't do it. You can kill me, but I won't do it! I hate that bitch!"

Socrates slapped his son across the face, his open hand leaving a vivid red imprint on the boy's cheek.

"Apologize immediately! Immediately!" he thundered.

"Never!"

Father and son glared at each other for several seconds. Neither of them would look away. The Greek was shaken by what he had done. His voice quavering, he said, "Achilles, listen to me. If you do not immediately go and ask Olympia to forgive you, I swear that I will cut you off without a cent."

"Keep your money! I don't want it!"

"Then what do you want?" Socrates shouted.

"Nothing!" Achilles cried. How could he explain to his father that he loved him, but that he loved his mother, too? How could he describe his despair at their separation or his hatred of any woman who took his mother's place? "Papa—"

Socrates, in a rage, was deaf to the unspoken appeal in the boy's voice. "I tell you," he roared, "that it's going to be either you or her!"

His father's words struck the boy like another blow. He shook his head. "No, Papa. No!" He turned and ran from the room.

Irene inspected her face in the mirror. She smiled proudly at the sight of her black eye and the bruises on her chin and forehead. These were her badges of victory. She had reconquered Herman! If she had dared, she would have rushed into the street to display her wounds to the world, so that everyone might know she was once more Herman Kallenberg's unchallenged wife.

On the day that Herman had contracted that ridiculous marriage with Helena, Irene had tried to kill herself, unable to face the prospect of life without Herman's cruelties. But in this, as in so much else, she had failed. A stomach pump had restored her to life, and she had regained consciousness with the same intense nausea with which she had lost it a few hours before.

By the following morning the scandal concerning Helena had become a matter of public gossip. Irene was in seventh heaven. How sweet was vengeance! She had settled back in her bed to wait for Herman to return to her, fully expecting that he would be home by evening.

She had waited for three years. Immediately after his divorce from Helena was final, Kallenberg had married a Texas heiress twenty-seven years his junior. Irene had been disappointed, but not discouraged. Like Penelope, she would wait for her Ulysses. She knew that she and Herman were like—not two peas in a pod or two fingers of a hand, but a hammer and an anvil. Neither could function without the other. She filled her time with public charities and complimented herself on her devotion to the people on whom she inflicted her attentions. Here she was working her fingers to the bone for the poor while that slut, Helena, was living with some disreputable painter, and Melina was smoking marijuana in a hippie commune in Southern California. Thank God there was someone who thought about such things as the family name, and the proper example to be set for one's children.

When Herman had returned—after a nasty divorce from his Texan hussy—Irene did not for a minute believe his explanation that he was concerned about the children. The children had got along perfectly well without him for three years. No. It was not the children he needed, but Irene herself! They were remarried in a simple ceremony under the benevolent eye of Irene's mother. For Medea had not been averse to reacquiring a son-in-law whom she had always loathed. She was an eminently practical woman, and she was aware that with Herman back in the family once again, it would be easier for her to keep a close watch on his business affairs.

And so life went on as before. Irene drank more, and Herman was away from home more frequently than ever. But they occasionally still found time for a good battle, and it was only then that either of them could sleep without the assistance of pills.

Even Herman's women no longer troubled Irene's newfound peace. They were unimportant. She had regained her husband, her position as a married woman, a father for her children, and a comfort for herself in her middle years. She had her scenes, her pills, and her bottles to while away her time. She realized, with a shock, that she was happy.

[28]

The sailor could not keep from laughing aloud when the old woman asked him to dance. The woman insisted: "Just once around the floor, you pretty boy!"

"I'm sorry, lady. I don't like to tango."

The woman rolled her eyes indignantly. "You don't like to tango! You mean you're going to deprive a woman my age of one of her few remaining pleasures in life?"

Her hooked nose and heavy lips were rendered more ludicrous by the elaborate makeup she wore. Her dress was ragged, and her surprisingly muscular legs were covered by black stockings. She smiled coquettishly at the sailor. "How about it, handsome? Think you're man enough to handle me out there?"

The sailor, laughing uproariously, led the woman onto the floor as Lindy Nut applauded.

The sailor leaned toward the old woman and whispered, "Oh, Socrates, this is such fun!"

"I'm glad you're enjoying yourself, young man." Then: "You see, Peggy? I was right. It was wrong of you to shut yourself away from your friends and from the world. You were made to enjoy life and happiness! There is a time for tears and mourning, but that time cannot be extended indefinitely."

The May night was cool, but Socrates had decided to hold the party outside, on the deck of the *Pegasus II*. Somehow, it seemed more festive, with the stars overhead and the shore lights glistening in the distance. Tomorrow Peggy would have to return to her gilded cage in America. Since Scott's death the entire nation had transferred to Peggy the hope and the faith that it had had in its future President. Mrs. Baltimore, in the eyes of the public, was not merely a widow. She had become a symbol of something that might have been.

Thereafter all the things that Peggy truly enjoyed vanished from her life. She could no longer spend hours in the boutiques of the great couturiers, or organize glamorous parties for her friends, or even ask a male friend to accompany her to the theater. On those rare occasions when she ventured into the street alone, it had been necessary for the police to escort her through the mobs of people who gathered around her, some to touch her, others to assure her of their sympathy, a few to swear that they would avenge her husband's death.

Scott's family seemed to think that she should devote the remainder of her life to preserving her dead husband's memory. They were shocked at any suggestion that Peggy might not be willing to play forever the part of a priestess at the altar of Baltimore ambition.

The only one of her friends who had been able to make Peggy laugh was Lindy Nut, for Lindy still treated her as a woman rather than a goddess. Moreover, she often spoke to Peggy of Socrates. The Greek himself often came to visit, invariably bearing gifts. He was considerate, amusing, but the precautions which it was necessary to take on such occasions marred Peggy's enjoyment of them. There were phalanxes of bodyguards and police, and only the chief of the Secret Service knew what else.

And now, suddenly, she was sailing among the Greek isles aboard the *Pegasus II*, the guest of a man who let her do precisely as she wished when she wished, and who seemed to live only for her pleasure. It was like emerging from a tomb into the glorious sunlight.

She smiled as Socrates handed her a drink. "Oh, how lovely it all is." She sighed. "I'd like to spend the rest of my life here, like this."

The Greek wanted to reply that the choice was hers to make, that she had only to say the word. But he did not. It might have seemed presumptuous. Instead, he said, "The *Pegasus II* is at your disposal whenever you wish to use it—with me, or without me."

He thought he heard her say, almost inaudibly, "It would be better with you." But he could not be sure. And he dared not ask her to repeat what she had said. But when she suggested, a few moments later, that they go for a ride in the launch, he was certain that he had heard correctly.

He ordered the small craft lowered into the water and took the controls himself.

When the boat was in the open water with the *Pegasus II* only a shadow in the distance, he cut the engine and moved next to Peggy. They sat in silence, staring up at the stars.

"What are you thinking about, Socrates?"

"About you."

She lay her head against his shoulder. Petrified, he dared not move for fear that if he did so, the miracle would cease.

Peggy placed her hand on his. "What a pity," she breathed.

"Pity?"

"That I can't see you as often as I would like to."

"Do you want to see me often?"

"All the time."

His hands trembling, the Greek took Peggy's face in his hands. To his amazement, she leaned forward and kissed him. He returned the kiss, awkwardly, as though he were committing sacrilege.

Peggy moved away demurely. "Please, madame!" she said. "You'll ruin my makeup."

Her joke served to relax Socrates. He chuckled. "Can you imagine the newspaper stories if the yacht sank and we had to be rescued? You dressed as a sailor, and I as an old woman!"

Emboldened by Peggy's laughter, he rested his head on her breast. She lifted her hand and let it rest gently on his forehead.

Peggy leaned forward and whispered, "Are you certain that no one can see us?"

In the distance, a universe away, the lights of the *Pegasus II* twinkled merrily, like the stars of some improbable constellation.

Socrates had persuaded Peggy to stay for another forty-eight hours so as to enable them to spend an evening in Paris. He was still stunned by the enormity of the victory he had won. It had been totally unexpected. In fact, it had been Peggy who had been the pursuer and he the pursued. The hitherto-inaccessible goddess had been revealed as Diana, the Huntress, and she had brought her victim down.

Socrates hardly expected this miracle to be repeated. Peggy, no matter where she went or what she did, was under constant surveillance. And Socrates was too, for that matter, for Menelas would not let him out of her sight. Not infrequently she refused even to consider lucrative offers for tours so that she might be with him. And when Socrates occasionally urged her not to neglect her career, she hastened to remind him that her professional life must take second place to her private life. Her patent sincerity made him uneasy. Menelas had never spoken of the matter, but he felt that he was under an obligation to formalize their relationship. He was certain that if he suggested doing so, she would not refuse. And so far as Peggy was concerned, she obviously could never agree to live with him. There were too many political factors involved. Peggy was, perhaps, free to be his occasional mistress, but not free enough to become his wife.

He had taken her for a walk along the Seine long after midnight. Peggy had worn enormous dark glasses and a scarf tied around her hair, while he had disguised himself in a cap and trench coat. They were both aware that if a single newspaperman or photographer saw them, they would never again know a moment's peace. Socrates could almost see the headlines. . . .

They were not recognized. Socrates was relieved, but his relief was not unalloyed. In his heart, he had secretly hoped that someone might recognize them. If it had been left to him, he would have shouted it from the rooftops of Paris: "I screwed Peggy Baltimore!" And he was certain that the echo would have come back: "Bravo!" Still, he knew that he could count on the discretion of his entourage, who had certainly discerned that there was something afoot. A world-renowned rake and a beautiful woman do not spend two hours alone in a launch at night just to discuss structuralism. He would have liked to take Peggy on a tour of Paris' nightspots so that the whole world would see her with him, hanging on his arm, laughing at his *mots*.

Well, he told himself, nothing is perfect. He looked at his watch. It was eleven o'clock. Time to go. He had placed his private Boeing at Peggy's disposal for the return trip to America. She would be the only passenger, for Menelas was due to arrive in Paris the following day from a concert in Rio, and Socrates was obliged to remain in Paris. He would have preferred to go to New York. . . .

He rose and knocked at Peggy's door. She opened it, and he was struck again by her beauty and by his own incredible good fortune.

"I'm ready," she said.

"Then we can go."

She hesitated. "I wonder if I'll ever see this house again."

"There is always a way if one wishes hard enough."

As the Rolls turned into the airport, the Greek thrust his hand into his pocket and brought out a small box. He held it out to her, awkwardly, like an adolescent presenting his date with her first corsage. "This is for you. Please don't open it until the plane is airborne."

Why do I play these silly games? he chided himself. A perfect blue-white diamond which had adorned a Hapsburg empress—and which had cost more money than most men make in their lifetimes—this was not something of which he should be ashamed.

"Oh, let me open it now!"

"Absolutely not."

"I'll die of curiosity," Peggy swore.

"Well then, since it's a matter of life and death, you may open it now." He was delighted at her insistence, for he was dying of curiosity to see her reaction. "But," he added, "you'll have to pay for this dispensation."

"All right. What do you want?"

"A kiss."

She threw her arms around his neck and pressed her mouth against his, her tongue darting between his lips. Behind his head, she snapped open the box for an instant and then closed it silently.

"All right," Socrates gasped, "go ahead."

"Maybe I should guess."

"Try."

"Is it jewelry of some kind?"

"Yes."

"Is it made of gold?"

"No."

"I know. It's platinum earrings!"

"No."

"I give up."

"Open it."

She opened the box again, and the incredible diamond burned with a million tiny points of fire in its blue velvet nest.

"Oh, Socrates!" Peggy gasped. "I must be dreaming! It's not possible—"

"Compared to your beauty," Socrates said gallantly, "it's nothing."

"Oh, Socrates!" Peggy threw her arms around his neck again and covered his face with kisses.

The Rolls came to a halt.

"Socrates, when will I see you again?"

"Whenever you wish. Night or day, call the telephone number

I've given you. No matter where I am, I'll have your message ten minutes later, and I'll be at your side an hour later. And may I call you?"

"Of course. Call me every day, please!"

He smiled in the darkness. "All right. Now, don't forget. It's door number eight. They're expecting you. I'm sorry I can't take you to the plane myself. I would have liked to."

"I would have liked it, too," Peggy answered. She kissed him a last time; then she was gone.

[29]

Socrates found Menelas waiting when he returned from the airport. She was seated in the drawing room, a glass of scotch in one hand, a magazine in the other.

"This is a surprise," he said, kissing her with as much enthusiasm as he could muster. "I didn't expect you until tomorrow."

"I came back early. I was lonely without you." She put down the glass and stroked Socrates' cheek.

"How was the concert?"

"The usual. What did you do while I was gone?"

"I made a quick trip to Greece—for a meeting with the architects on a new house on an island I've bought."

"Were you here last night?"

"Yes. Why?"

"Alone?"

"Of course. Why do you ask?"

"When I came in a while ago, I used the elevator. I saw you going down the stairs. I called, but you didn't hear me. I could have sworn I saw someone with you."

"Nonsense. There was no one with me."

"I must have been seeing things."

"Those things happen. Fatigue can do strange things."

"Yes, you're right. That must have been it. Fatigue. All right. Who was she?"

"I've already told you, there was no one."

"Yes, you've told me, you lying Greek asshole! Do you think I'm blind? Who was she?"

"I was alone!"

"You liar! I saw her with my own eyes!"

"Shut up, Olympia! If you've come home to throw one of your ridiculous scenes, you should have stayed where you were."

"You would have liked that, wouldn't you!"

Socrates did not reply, thanking the gods that Menelas had not recognized Peggy. She was perfectly capable of hopping the next plane to Washington and calling a press conference.

"Well, are you going to tell me, or aren't you?"

"What a pity." He sighed, shaking his head sadly.

"What do you mean, 'a pity'? I'll tell you what's a pity. It's that you use this house for your whores while I'm halfway around the world working my ass off to earn a living!"

"It's a pity that you've picked this particular night to accuse me of things that I wouldn't think of doing. I wanted to talk to you tonight about something very important."

"Well, what is it, you liar!"

"I wanted to ask you to marry me."

"To marry you?" Menelas shrieked. "You poor little man! What makes you think I'd ever marry you?"

Disconcerted, Socrates could only stammer, "What? You mean, you won't?"

"That's precisely what I mean! I'm sick of being your mistress, and you want me to become your wife! You must be out of your mind! Do you think for even one minute that marrying me is going to make up for all I've put up with?"

Socrates poured himself a glass of scotch and raised it to his lips. Menelas was out of her chair like a tigress. She slapped the glass from his hand.

"Answer me!" she screamed. "What do you think I am? I didn't ask to come here! You took me away from a husband who loved me!

You brought me here, where I've had to put up with your family and the insults of those brats of yours!"

"I've talked to them about that."

"That's a lie! You've kept your lying mouth shut, that's what you've done! You asshole!"

Suddenly, Socrates had had enough. "Shut up!" he roared, clenching his fists. "Shut up, you filthy cunt! Who do you think you are, you and your fucking Chopin! You piano-playing whore!"

"What? What did you call me?" Menelas sprang at him and locked her arms around his throat, squeezing until Socrates could hardly catch his breath.

With a wrench, he freed himself. "Cunt!" he screamed. "Cunt! Whore! I tell you, you're going to marry me, by God! Do you hear me?"

"Yes," she screamed back. "Yes, yes, yes, you son of a bitch!"

They looked at one another, both gasping for breath. Then, suddenly, Menelas began to sob. She caressed his cheek lovingly, murmuring, "Yes, yes! When, my love, when?"

The Greek could barely restrain his own tears. "A month from today," he whispered. "In London. Is that all right?"

"Yes, my love, oh, yes! Whatever you wish!"

She tore open his shirt and passed her tongue over his chest, then pulled him to the floor with her.

"What about the servants?" he asked.

"Shit on the servants, you bastard." She groaned, and nothing more was said.

Joan stared at him for a moment. "Why did I have to fall in love with you, of all people? I'm old enough to be your mother."

"You would have had to be a child bride."

"No, Achilles, I'm serious. It frightens me. I'm thirty-five years old—"

"That's all right. One day I'll be thirty-five."

"Yes. Seventeen years from now."

Joan was strikingly beautiful, with an extraordinary head of long auburn hair. Achilles was insanely in love with her. He had met her two years earlier and been stricken immediately. At first she had not taken him seriously when he had said he loved her. Joan had just been through her third divorce. She found Achilles amusing, and it was not unpleasant to have a handsome, rich young man mad about one—even if he was only eighteen. Then, one night, she had succumbed to his advances, and her amusement had ended. Achilles might have been a child in years, but in bed, he was a god. Thus, Joan had thrown herself into an adventure which, every morning, she swore she would end the following day. Yet the months had passed, and now she had discovered that she was in love with her child-god.

"If I had a grain of sense," she said, "I'd walk out that door and never see you again."

"Do you really want to be sensible?"

"Of course not."

"Then I have something to tell you."

"What?"

"I want to marry you."

"But you're still a minor!"

"I can wait. But you? Can you wait three years?"

"What do you think?"

"Let's not think. Let's fuck."

"Who is that girl over there?"

"You don't know her, Raph? That's Satrapoulos' daughter."

"Really?"

"Really," the nightclub proprietor affirmed.

"Not very pretty, is she?"

"Any girl with a hundred million dollars is absolutely, indescribably ravishing."

"Is anyone screwing her?"

"I don't know."

"Who are the people with her?"

"Oh, just some boys. They're all from Helliokis' boat. It's docked at Cannes."

"Can you fix me up with her?"

"I don't know. This is only the second time that she's come here."

"Tell her who I am, and say I'd like her to have a drink with me."

"All right, I'll try."

Carlos made his way to Maria's table. Dun saw him bend down and speak to her. She glanced at him, and their eyes met for an instant. She whispered something to Carlos. Carlos smiled.

So far so good, Dun told himself. Maybe there was a story somewhere in this thing. And maybe he'd be able to pay some of his creditors enough to keep them quiet for a while. He looked at Maria again. She had been watching him. Her eyes dropped.

There's gold in that little cunt, Raph assured himself.

"What did she say?" he asked Carlos.

"She says she doesn't want a drink, but that she'd like to dance."

"Oh, Christ! Everyone will say I'm trying to corrupt a minor."

"Well, aren't you?"

"Of course. But I don't want people to say it. Well, here goes." He rose from his chair, noting that Maria was watching him with obvious interest. He was forty-eight, but his wavy blond hair and his chiseled features were still capable of catching the eye of the chorus girl and the Hollywood actress as well as that of the countess—or the billionaire's heiress.

How old can she be? he wondered. Seventeen? Eighteen? It was hard to tell nowadays.

He bowed and smiled. Maria's companions glared at him. She rose and followed him to the dance floor.

"I thought your friends would kill me," he said.

"They will. But not until after this dance."

"Are you on vacation?"

"Are you a newspaperman?"

"Do you live with your parents?"

"What newspaper are you with?"

They both laughed.

"No, I'm not with my parents. I'm with friends."

"A villa?"

"A boat."

"They let you go out alone?"

"Not usually, but I've just murdered my jailer. Are you French?"

"Congolese. I own a banana plantation, but I don't have to be there because my eleven wives are perfectly capable of running it."

"Only eleven?"

"It's a small plantation."

From close, she was not as bad as he had thought. Her body was a bit heavy—it was shamelessly pressed against Dun's own—but her eyes were truly beautiful. And she was obviously no fool.

"Do you know why I wanted to meet you?"

"Yes. I am the woman destined for you for all eternity."

"Don't jump the gun. I wanted to ask you if you've ever posed."

"For photographs?"

"Yes."

"No, never. Have you taken a good look at me?"

"Too bad. You'd make a good model. What's your name?"

"Maria. And yours?"

"Raph. Raph Dun. What's your last name?"

He felt her stiffen in his arms.

"Do you think I'm stupid? You know very well who I am."

"Well—how can you be so sure?"

"Everyone knows who I am. Newspapermen follow me wherever I go. When I was in boarding school, they used to dress up as priests and offer me candy."

"I wish I had my cassock with me. Or at least some candy."

"I'm glad you don't. Now it's my turn to ask the questions. What newspaper are you with?"

"No particular one. I'm a free-lance journalist—a whore. I sell myself to the highest bidder. Are you going to be in Cannes for long?"

"I don't know. How about you?"

"That depends on you. If I can churn out some piece of crap about you, I'll get enough money to be able to stay longer."

"What do you want to know?"

"Do you think we can go to my table without being assaulted by your little friends?"

"I can do whatever I want."

"Let's go."

"You go ahead. I want to get my purse."

"All right. Tell them I'm your father."

She looked him in the eyes for a second. "What a silly man you are," she said.

"Madame, I'm sure you understand that this is very difficult for me. Nonetheless, it is something that I feel I must do. Would you care for a cigarette?"

"No, thank you."

The Greek was uneasy. He had thought to find either a brainless golddigger or a hardened slut. Instead, this woman undeniably had breeding, style, and dignity.

"I wish to speak to you about my son."

"I rather thought so, Mr. Satrapoulos," Joan said.

"It is my duty—my duty—"

"Yes, Mr. Satrapoulos?"

"I must protect him, you understand. He is only a child!"

"And I am not a child. Is that what you wish to say?"

"Not at all—"

"Nonetheless, that is what you are saying."

Socrates shifted in his chair. This was more difficult than he had imagined.

"Mr. Satrapoulos, let's stop playing games. Just what is the purpose of your visit?"

"You must know—"

"I do know. You've come to tell me that I must not see Achilles again. Is that right?"

"I am relieved to find a woman of such understanding."

"I do understand, Mr. Satrapoulos. I can easily put myself in your place. One of the world's great fortunes, and an only son destined to take your place. And here I am, a woman of thirty-five, divorced three times. I could not even bear him a son. If I were you, I would certainly feel as you do. Only—"

"Yes?"

"Only I am not you. And Achilles is not going to fall in love or refrain from falling in love just to please you. Please don't think that I am trying to defy you. I just don't think that you are important in this matter. I have made my choice, and Achilles has made his choice. We love each other."

"Madame, please. If Achilles' father were a clerk, or a lawyer— You know as well as I do that love is not eternal."

"I know it. And that is precisely why I intend to take advantage of it for as long as it lasts."

"Have you considered what's best for him?"

"I am thinking only of him."

"Let us say it does last. When he is a young man of thirty, you will be—"

"An old woman. Is that what you're trying to say?"

"Yes."

"We have a few years before we come to that."

"I have no intention of allowing you to continue seeing him. I have other plans for Achilles, plans which do not include you."

"I'm sure you've spoken to Achilles of these plans?"

"That is none of your business. Surely, you would be the last person in the world to interfere with his future. I must tell you that, if this affair continues, I am prepared to cut him off. You will not have one cent of my money."

Joan looked at him with an air of weariness. "Mr. Satrapoulos, you are so immersed in your own affairs that you are blind to the truth, even when you see it before you. Let me enlighten you. I have not the slightest interest in your money. What is more, I have not the slightest need for it."

"That has nothing to do with it. I tell you that I will not allow Achilles to spend his life with an old woman!"

Joan rose. "Thank you for coming, Mr. Satrapoulos. I don't believe we have anything more to say to each other."

"Just a moment." Socrates took his checkbook from his pocket. "I'm going to sign a blank check and hand it to you. I give you my word that no one will ever know. You may fill in any amount you wish. Any amount—so long as you never see my son again."

He held out the piece of paper on which he had scribbled his signature.

"Here, take it!" He thrust it into her hands.

"Good day, Mr. Satrapoulos," Joan said calmly, holding the check.

The Greek bowed and left. He was waiting for the elevator when a door opened behind him.

"Mr. Satrapoulos?"

He turned.

Joan stood in her doorway. "Mr. Satrapoulos, here is your check." She opened her hand and let the blue rectangle of paper flutter to the floor. "You are a vile, unspeakable man," she hissed. "I forbid you ever to come to my home again."

The door closed. Socrates bent over and picked up the piece of paper. It was the first time in his life that anyone had ever returned one of his checks to him uncashed.

How utterly silly, Peggy told herself. Imagine saying grace over a few lettuce leaves. She looked around the table at the bowed heads of the Baltimore clan. What a change from the *Pegasus II!* Her hand went to her bosom, and she touched the diamond suspended beneath her blouse on a thin chain of gold.

It had been five years since Scott's death, and yet nothing had changed. She was still summoned to spend the summer months at the Baltimore family compound on the Rhode Island shore, still expected to behave as "one of the family," as Virginia Baltimore put it, still expected to endure those dull, unpalatable meals.

The prayer was over, and there was a burst of conversation. Peggy looked at her mother-in-law, and Virginia's steel-gray eyes bored into hers. Then the granite jaw relaxed into the semblance of a smile.

"You seemed far away, my dear. What were you thinking about?"

"I—I was thinking about my future."

Peggy was instantly the center of attention.

"We should all be mindful of what is to come," Virginia said piously.

"I don't mean the hereafter," Peggy said. "I mean the here and now. I was thinking about what I intend to do with my life."

"Indeed? Do you mean New York?"

"No. I mean Europe, but perhaps in this country too, occasionally."

Virginia raised her eyebrows.

"What are you wearing around your neck?" one of her brothers-in-law asked, hoping to steer the conversation away from so explosive a subject.

Peggy unbuttoned the top of her high-collared blouse and showed the great pear-shaped stone.

"Where on earth did you get that?"

"It was a gift from a friend. From Socrates Satrapoulos."

There followed a horrified silence during which everyone was unaccountably fascinated by the contents of his plate. Peggy wondered if it would not have been better to remain silent. Among the Baltimores, Socrates Satrapoulos was viewed as the embodiment of Mideastern duplicity. The feeling was so intense that each member of the family was expected to regard the Greek as a bitter personal enemy. No one ever mentioned that Satrapoulos had contributed heavily to Scott's campaign. No, she had been right to tell them, Peggy decided. Then she made up her mind to go a step further.

"I think I may very well marry him," she announced to the silent table.

Virginia Baltimore raised her hands to her mouth in consternation, and her children exchanged incredulous looks. At that moment, Peggy understood that she had been wrong, that she had never been considered a member of the family. She was a prisoner, serving a life sentence.

Socrates looked sharply at the Prophet. "Am I doing the right thing in marrying again?"

"Whom are you marrying?"

"You know very well that I am going to marry Menelas."

"That is what you tell me. The cards tell me otherwise."

"I don't care what your cards say. I am going to marry again."

"The cards tell me that you will certainly marry again, but not the woman you think you will marry."

"What are you trying to say?"

"I? I say nothing. The cards speak."

"What do the cards say I should do?"

"Do nothing. Follow your own plans, and we will see where they lead. Destiny is not subject to our whims, my friend."

"What do you mean when you say that I will marry, but not the woman I think I'm going to marry."

"Alas, for once I must refuse to tell you everything. You have to know only that the mark of destiny is upon you, that you have nothing to fear, and that the future will surprise you."

"This is all most intriguing—"

"We cannot force the hand of destiny."

"You could tell me a little more," Socrates said and sulked. "You know that I'm not a superstitious man."

[30]

No artist had ever gone so far, and no artist would ever go further. It is true some artists such as Yves Klein—Yves the Mono-chromatic—had covered vast surfaces with a single color—blue or white, red or green, orange or yellow. Others, more daring, had done away with canvas altogether and offered their admirers the opportunity to contemplate an empty frame, explaining that "the artist no longer attempts to restrict your imagination. You are now free to create a work of your own choosing." A Yugoslav painter, inspired and somewhat parsimoniously supported by a Brazilian widow, had had a showing in Munich, in which the sole work exhibited was a mirror in a gold frame. Visitors to the gallery read a notice attached to the frame: "This is a perfect composition. It reflects your own perfection, perfectly." A cleaning woman had broken the mirror, perhaps unintentionally, and the insurance companies had been compelled by the courts to disburse a fortune to the artist.

Fast had outdone even the imaginative Yugoslav who relied on the perfection of others. Fast exhibited perfection itself, as embodied in his own superb naked body. This work of art created a considerable stir at Rome, where on two occasions the police descended upon the gallery and hurriedly threw a sheet over the masterpiece. The left took advantage of the scandal to demonstrate in the streets, and the right, encouraged by the Vatican, demanded that this pornographic exhibition be banned from the city. Finally, the left prevailed. Now Fast spent several hours a day standing on a low column which revolved slowly so that an admiring public, consisting mostly of women, could fully admire the attributes of genius. Helena remained at his side throughout this artistic ordeal, for, jealous as she was, she could not bring herself to abandon her lover to the manifest concupiscence of his Italian admirers.

The gallery closed at 8 P.M., and Fast, who had stoically remained immobile on his column for six hours, rushed for the rest room and urinated blissfully. Then he dressed and, with Helena, made the rounds of the fashionable restaurants and night spots of the Via Veneto.

When Helena tried to persuade him to withdraw his masterpiece from public view, he laughed. "If you really loved me," he said, "you would join me on the column instead of talking nonsense. We could call it 'Artist and Woman.'"

YOUR DIGNIFIED COMPORTMENT IS OUR COUNTRY'S PRIDE. REMAIN AT OUR SIDE IN THE BATTLE WHICH IS ABOUT TO BEGIN. WE HAVE NEED OF YOUR STRENGTH.

The telegram was signed by the figurehead whom Scott's brothers had chosen to lead the New American Party and whom they planned to discard at the proper moment.

The bastards, Peggy thought. All they think about is how to win elections. What did it matter to them that she still had her whole life before her and that she wanted to be free? She could no longer stand the thought of politics. The image of Scott, his head shattered by the assassin's bullet, was with her day and night. She wanted to forget; to forget Scott, politics, America, the Baltimores—especially the Baltimores.

Following her mention of Socrates' name at the Baltimore dinner table, a procession of individual members of the family had made their way to her room, where the family gods had been conjured up: honor, country, the children, the church, duty, and responsibility. Even the sisters-in-law had come, imploring Peggy to do nothing to injure their husbands' careers. Marriage to the Greek, they had said, would ruin the family as surely as marriage to a black.

"Can you imagine the reaction of the press?" one of them had moaned.

"What on earth do you find so attractive about that filthy old man?" the other asked.

She had ordered them out of her room.

They had been followed by a financial emissary who had proposed a bargain similar to that made by the family patriarch five years before. This time the condition was that she undertake not to marry Satrapoulos until after the elections. She had hesitated only momentarily before disdainfully rejecting the offer.

"But you accepted the same offer once before," the emissary objected.

"Yes," Peggy replied, "but times have changed." Compared with the Satrapoulos fortune, the bribe seemed insignificant indeed.

In the midst of all this, Peggy had one nagging worry. The Greek had never really said that he would marry her. What if he did not ask her? And what if *she* asked *him*, and he refused? But that was difficult to imagine. No one said no to Peggy Baltimore. No one ever had.

She touched the Hapsburg diamond. If she married Socrates, there would be others like it, as many as she wanted. And unlimited clothes. And parties every night. No one would be there to talk of duty and responsibility. All this, when she married Socrates. He understood such things, and he loved them, too. It would be a glorious life!

She read the last sentence of the telegram again: WE HAVE NEED OF YOUR STRENGTH. She crumpled the piece of paper and threw it onto her desk. "What about my ass?" she said aloud. "Do you need that, too?"

In order to throw the newspapermen off the track, it had been arranged that Socrates and Menelas would arrive at the church in separate automobiles. Moreover, the Greek would disguise himself—to his own amusement—in a blond wig and matching mustache. The ceremony was to take place in a small Orthodox chapel which had been closed to the public. Only Achilles and Maria had been invited to the ceremony. Both had declined, and Socrates had not insisted, since he was afraid that, if they did attend, there might be some last-minute unpleasantness between Menelas and his children.

Everything seemed ready. Everything, that is, except the bride herself. The evening before the wedding there had been a terrible scene at Socrates' house on the Avenue Foch in Paris. The evening had begun pleasantly enough. The Greek's guests were a group of American shipping magnates whose company was in deep financial trouble. Socrates intended to buy the company, but he would have died before he let his guests know he had the least interest in it. And the Americans, for their part, were consumed with a desire to sell before the company went into receivership. Thus, the stage was set for a transaction which would be of benefit to all.

Menelas greeted the guests warmly, as though they were old friends of the family, and Socrates outdid himself in deploying the charm which was famous the world over. Matters proceeded smoothly until dinner was announced. At table, amid the magnificent crystal and silver glittering under the great chandelier, Menelas played the hostess to perfection. "Since this is your first visit to France," she announced, "I thought it might be interesting for you to have a typical French meal."

With this, two footmen entered carrying a large tureen, which they set on the table so clumsily that a portion of its contents spilled onto the tablecloth. Then, without a word of apology, the two men left the room.

Menelas glared at their retreating backs, then at Socrates, who clenched his teeth in anger. Later he would have a few things to say in the kitchen. He was particularly irritated since the battle plan for the evening depended on a strict adherence to the serving of a particular mixture of wines to his guests. When his guests were half-drunk, he would allow them to broach the subject closest to their hearts. By the time the after-dinner liqueurs were served, he would allow himself to mention a figure, laughingly accept their counter-proposal, and immediately produce a signed contract. Or at least, that was the plan. But if this was an example of the service which was to come, he was already in trouble.

His premonitions were confirmed when, the superb lobster bisque having been consumed, no servants appeared to remove the bowls. He looked at Menelas. She was frantically pressing the button which should have summoned help from the kitchen. From the look of desperation in her eyes and the smile frozen on her face, he surmised that she had been at it for several minutes. He signaled imperceptibly to her, and she rose, excused herself, and left the room.

Socrates chatted with his guests for a few minutes. Then, uneasy at Olympia's prolonged absence, he excused himself, explaining, "There must be some sort of trouble in the kitchen. I'll see what's happened."

His smile disappeared as soon as he was out of the dining room. He burst angrily into the kitchen, ready to curse his servants, and stopped short. The enormous room should have been abustle with cooks, dishwashers, footmen, but there was not a soul in sight.

He heard a moan from behind a counter and hastened to investigate. He found Menelas, stretched out on the floor, her eyes closed, her face waxen. He knelt next to her and rubbed her wrists and shook her head, calling loudly for the servants as he did so. No one came. Feverishly he went in search of a bottle of smelling salts but found none. He returned to Menelas, removed his dinner jacket, rolled it into a ball, and placed it under her head. Then he waited.

A minute later, Menelas stirred, then shuddered.

"My darling!" Socrates said softly. "Olympia! What happened? Speak to me!"

She opened her eyes slowly, looked at him, and then pointed weakly to a sign, scrawled in lipstick on the wall over the ovens:

WE QUIT.

WE HAVE PISSED IN THE SOUP.

Olympia wretched and vomited.

Five minutes later, Socrates returned to his embarrassed guests to explain that Madame had been suddenly overcome by a migraine and that the dinner must perforce be adjourned to Maxim's.

Two hours later he returned home in a rage. The Americans had remained sober throughout the meal, and he himself had not been in the best of moods. Far from having reached an agreement with them, Socrates had parted from his guests in an atmosphere of thinly veiled hostility. He had even refused to accompany them on a proposed foray to a certain well-known house. Now he was in a towering rage as he confronted a partially revived Menelas in the drawing room.

"That was a delightful evening! Thanks to your incompetence, it cost me ten million dollars!"

"My incompetence? They were *your* servants!"

"You hired them, and you're such a bitch that they wouldn't put up with your nagging! That's why they left!"

"How dare you! I've never been spoken to in that way in my life!"

Soon insults, couched in phrases common to the slums of Athens, resounded among the Rubenses and Tintorettos and caused the very pendants of the crystal chandelier to tinkle in horror.

"I'm leaving this house!" Menelas screamed finally.

"Then get the fuck out!" Satrapoulos retorted, forgetting that he was speaking to the woman he was about to marry. "And on your way out, don't forget to piss in the soup!"

As the door slammed behind Menelas, the telephone rang. Socrates ignored it. He would, he decided, spend the rest of the evening at the George V. Or he might go someplace where there would be a few girls to take his mind off his domestic troubles.

The telephone continued to ring. Angrily, he picked up the receiver. "Yes, what is it?"

A small voice, like that of a little girl, answered, "It's me."

"Peggy! Where are you? Where are you calling from?"

"New York. Oh, Socrates. I'm so miserable! You absolutely must help me!"

"Anything, Peggy. Just tell me what you want me to do."

"I want you to marry me."

Socrates jerked the receiver away from his ear and stared at it, as though it might be able to provide answers to the questions which had sprung into his mind. "I'm sorry," he stammered at last. "What did you say?"

"Marry me, Socrates. I've already told my in-laws that you would."

"But Peggy—"

"Don't you want to?"

"I—"

"Oh, Socrates, this is serious. I'm not afraid. Are you?"

"Well—"

"Socrates, my love, yes or no?"

"Oh, yes! Yes, of course."

"When?"

"Just a moment. I can hardly hear you."

He had heard her very clearly.

"When?" she repeated.

He tried to clear his suddenly tight throat.

"Whenever you like."

"Oh, Socrates, you're so marvelous! You've compromised me, you know. Everyone knows about us. The whole Baltimore family. And Lindy Nut, too."

"Oh. Lindy Nut, too."

"Darling, I'm coming to meet you."

"Where?"

"Why, in Paris, of course. We have so many things to talk about, so many things to settle! And, of course, our lawyers have to get together."

"Peggy?"

"Yes, Socrates?"

"Are you serious about this?"

"Oh, yes! I love you! I want to live with you!"

"I love you, too!"

"Oh, darling!"

"I'll call New York immediately and have them get a plane ready for you."

"You think of everything, Socrates."

"Peggy?"

"Yes?"

"I love you."

"Don't move, darling! I'll be there in a few hours!"

He put down the receiver. He had never seriously considered the possibility that he and Peggy might someday marry, but now the possibilities opened by that imminent event began to dawn upon him. The richest man in the world does not marry the most celebrated woman in the world without awakening resentment in a thousand hearts, he assured himself. He thought with delight of Kallenberg's face when he heard the news—poor Kallenberg, who in love as in business had to be content with Satrapoulos' leavings!

What would Achilles and Maria say? he wondered. What could they say! He would tolerate no backtalk from them. Normal children would be proud that their father, at the age of sixty-two, could woo and win the greatest prize in the world. If God were willing, he might live to be a hundred. Perhaps even more. That meant that he had another thirty-eight years ahead of him. Fantastic!

Stunned by the prospect of the happiness that was about to be his, Socrates sank into a chair to contemplate it at his leisure.

[31]

Socrates picked up the house telephone. "Achilles? I want to see you and your sister in my study. Immediately!"

He sat at his desk and put his head between his hands.

A few minutes later Achilles and Maria entered. Achilles, in a cashmere pullover and dungarees, looked like a student. There was a scowl on his face. Maria was wearing a tennis outfit—white blouse, white skirt, white socks, white tennis shoes. She threw herself into an easy chair, and Achilles settled himself on the arm of the same chair.

"I have something important to tell you," the Greek began.

Neither Maria nor Achilles reacted.

"On several occasions, rightly or wrongly, you have chosen to meddle in my private affairs. You behaved atrociously toward the woman I loved, a woman who always treated you with the greatest consideration."

He paused and looked at his children. Their faces were expressionless.

"Because of you, I have broken with Olympia. At the same time, I must respect her for the incredible patience with which she has borne your insults. But that is behind us now. What I want to tell you is this: I am going to marry, and I know that this time you will approve of my choice."

Maria was the first to think she understood what he was saying.

"Oh, Daddy! That's marvelous! You're going to marry Mother!"

Achilles leaped from the armrest and threw his arms around his father's neck. "Hurrah! That's great! *You're* great!"

Socrates struggled to disengage himself from his son's embrace. His face hardened.

"Who mentioned Helena?" he said. "I'm going to marry Peggy Baltimore."

Immediately, his children shrank from him as though he were a leper. Achilles' face was a stony mask. Maria, with tears in her eyes, said, "What? Who did you say?"

"Peggy Baltimore," Socrates repeated. "Can you think of a finer woman in the whole world?"

It was as though they had not heard him. "Come on, Maria," Achilles said casually. "We have time for a set before lunch."

Socrates' face turned red. "That's enough!" he roared. "How dare you try to tell me what I should or shouldn't do! She's a fine woman, I tell you! The most famous woman in the world!"

Achilles and Maria had already left the room.

The giant Boeing was in position for the takeoff when the captain received a message: "Return to the terminal and disembark your passengers."

The pilot and his co-pilot exchanged glances. The pilot scratched his head. He felt the throb of the mighty engines beneath him, ready, at the touch of a button, to hurl the hundred and thirty tons of aircraft toward the sky. He picked up the microphone.

"Captain to control tower. Please repeat the message."

"Control tower to captain. The message is as follows: Return to terminal and disembark your passengers."

"OK. Over and out." He turned to the co-pilot. "Shit! We must have a bomb stowed away in the luggage or a hijacker aboard."

"Do you want me to tell the girls?"

The captain shook his head. "Let's wait a few minutes and see what happens." He grinned weakly. "After all, this is supposed to be nonstop to Athens. And we're going to have a hundred and thirty hopping mad passengers to contend with—"

The radio interrupted him. "Use runway six to return to the terminal; then cut your engines and remain aboard until further instructions. Do you understand?"

"Roger." The captain sighed. "Bob," he addressed his co-pilot, "you'd better tell Lily to make an announcement."

"What should she say?"

"I don't know. I don't give a damn. Let her tell them anything she wants."

A few seconds later the stewardess' well-modulated voice floated over the intercom. "Ladies and gentlemen, we regret that a minor equipment malfunction makes it necessary for us to return to the terminal. Takeoff will be delayed slightly. When we arrive at the terminal, please disembark, making sure that you remove all hand luggage from the plane. Another plane will be ready to take you aboard very shortly. Grecian Airlines regrets this inconvenience—"

Scattered protests were heard from among the passengers.

"Please remain in your seats until the plane has come to a complete stop," Lily continued unperturbed. Then she went forward to the cockpit. "What on earth's going on?" she asked the captain.

"Who knows? Control tower says to go back to the terminal and get all of the passengers off the plane. That's what we're doing."

"What happens then?"

As though in answer to Lily's question, the radio came to life when the Boeing reached the terminal. "Tower to Grecian Airlines flight one twelve. After discharge of passengers, prepare for takeoff in ten minutes. Destination unchanged."

"Grecian Airlines one twelve to tower. Roger. Over and out."

"Is this some kind of joke?" Lily asked in puzzlement.

The pilot shook his head. "If it is, somebody's going to be in big trouble."

The plane drew up near the terminal, and the passengers poured out of the doors, clutching handbags and assorted items of clothing as a crew of men, wearing overalls marked with the logo of Grecian Airlines, began transferring luggage from the Boeing to a line of baggage carts.

From the cockpit, the captain saw three long automobiles pull up near the gangplank. "Who can that be?" he asked.

"It doesn't matter who it is," one of the stewardesses muttered. "The passengers are all mad as hell. A couple of them swore they were going to sue." She paused. "Oh, God! Do you see who it is? The one who just got out of the first car. It's Peggy Baltimore!"

"No wonder! Who are the others with her?"

"I'm not sure, but I think the older woman is her mother. The other one—I've seen her picture in magazines. She was married to that oilman. What was his name? Bambilt, I think. The others look like maids or something."

"Tower to Grecian Airlines flight one twelve. Your instructions are to take better care of your passengers than you've ever taken of any passenger in your life! OK?"

"OK," the captain answered. "Will do."

Lily giggled. "I had forgotten! They're supposed to be married tomorrow! I'd better get out there and meet them!"

"I don't give a shit," the captain growled. "This is the kind of publicity the company doesn't need."

His voice was drowned out by the whistle of the jets as he revved up the engines.

"No," Irene said resolutely. "I won't go. Look at me!"

She pointed to a large purple-blue ring under her eye. "You did this, you know. And now you want to make a laughingstock of me. Well, I won't go, and that's final!"

Kallenberg shrugged. "Suit yourself. I'll go alone."

"No! I forbid you to go!"

"You forbid me?" he said threateningly.

"Yes, I forbid you to go! Think of the family! We're not going to be the guests of the bastard who made my sister suffer so—"

"Your sister is a slut. You hate her yourself."

"You were happy enough to marry her!"

"There wasn't much to choose between the two of you. She's a slut, and you're a cunt. It's in the family blood."

"Socrates has made you look ridiculous all your life! Don't you see that this is just another of his tricks?"

"Why the sudden interest in my welfare?"

"I'm not going! And you're not going either!"

"Shut up! I've had enough! I don't want to hear another word!"

"I'll tell Mama!"

"Irene, look at yourself in the mirror," Kallenberg said contemptuously. "You're an old woman. Too old to be 'telling Mama.' Besides, your mother is as big a cunt as you are—"

Irene settled herself comfortably on her bed. It would be a long session, she knew, but not a very rewarding one. For, appearances to the contrary, Irene and Herman were not fighting. They were simply engaging in their customary early-morning exchange. Even the servants no longer bothered to listen at the door. The dialogue had become so ordinary in the Kallenberg ménage that even the scullery maid knew the script by heart.

The island of Serpentella was the private property of Socrates Satrapoulos. When he had bought it several years earlier, everyone had laughed. Even Satrapoulos, they said, could not turn this stretch

of barren rock into anything but what the gods had always intended
it to be: the home of snakes, scorpions, and spiders. But Satrapoulos
possessed power such as the dwellers on Olympus had never dreamed.
At the touch of his checkbook, an army of horticulturists, engineers,
landscapers, and architects had descended upon Serpentella. For
months, bulldozers had worked to level some parts of the island and
to create hills and valleys on others. Thousands of tons of good earth
had been brought by ship, and this had been followed by shiploads
of flowers and lemon, orange, olive, and eucalyptus trees. But, before any planting had been done, the entire island was doused with
enormous quantities of pesticides and insecticides, so that now one
might search in vain for a single snake, scorpion, or spider, to say
nothing of mosquitoes. A few colonies of ants were the only form of
animal life tolerated by the two hundred people whose sole function
it was to see to the comfort of the master of this artificial paradise.

When the world's journalists had learned of the existence of
Satrapoulos' island, they had flocked to it by air and sea, to see for
themselves and to photograph for their readers, this modern wonder
of the world—and particularly the house, which, they had been told,
was a marvel of opulent simplicity done entirely in the classic Greek
style.

But Socrates would have none of it. The island was guarded by
his private navy, equipped with PT boats so powerful that they
could overtake even a cruiser. Moreover, his sailors had been trained
to answer no questions and to turn away everyone who tried to approach Serpentella on any pretext whatsoever. The newspapermen
had tried persuasion, seduction, corruption, threats, and blackmail.
Finally, they concluded that it was impossible to find out what went
on on Serpentella, and their efforts had fallen off until they became
mere *pro forma* exercises.

On this particular day, the day of his wedding, Socrates had
doubled the number of boats and sailors on guard. The beaches and
the island's interior were under constant surveillance by troops of
private guards, for the evening before *Life* magazine had attempted
to parachute a photographer and a reporter into the dense little
cypress grove near Serpentella's chapel, where the wedding was to
take place.

The news media had not taken kindly to such treatment. Already,
the stories were uncomplimentary. A London newspaper had carried
an editorial on page one, titled PEGGY, AREN'T YOU ASHAMED? And

others had been no more generous: SHE'S MARRYING A MAN OLD ENOUGH TO BE HER FATHER, and THE IDOL HAS CLAY FEET, and even SCOTT BALTIMORE'S WIDOW DISGRACES AMERICA. Of the hundreds of stories and articles which had already appeared, only two or three bothered to point out that the marriage was solely the affair of the parties concerned and that they were accountable to no one for their actions.

"Socrates," Peggy said, "I would like you to meet my mother."

He took Janet Beckintosh's hand as the old woman—she was the same age as her prospective son-in-law—regarded him severely.

"Do you promise that you will make my daughter happy?" she demanded.

Socrates, overcome with emotion, nodded dumbly and finally succeeded in stammering, "Yes, I swear it."

Then Peggy thrust her two boys toward Socrates. "Darlings, kiss Socrates!"

Socrates bent to kiss the elder, who submitted silently. The younger, however, began to cry and took refuge against his mother's miniskirt.

"Christopher," Peggy snapped. "What's gotten into you?"

The child's sobs grew louder.

"You'll see," Peggy went on, her voice softening. "You'll love it here. It's the most beautiful island in the whole world. You're going to be so happy here, darling!"

After dinner that night, Socrates led Peggy into his office. Two men were waiting for them. One was tall and cadaverously thin; the other, short and grotesquely plump. The tall one was Peggy's attorney; the short one, Socrates'. Both were counted among the most talented members of the legal profession, and both had worked like slaves for the past six months, assisted by a battery of lesser lights, to devise the most extravagant marital agreement ever conceived by the mind of man.

Everything, even the unforeseeable, had been foreseen. Death. Accidents. Possible separation. Sickness. The education of the children, the number of their bodyguards, the nationality of their governesses and tutors, their allowances. One section of the contract dealt with the possibility of either party being afflicted with insanity; another, with the possibility of both going mad simultaneously. The various infirmities to which human flesh is heir, including impotence, were treated alphabetically, and the medical experts to be consulted in each case were named. There were lists of residences and clauses specifying when the couple might visit each of them and for what length of time. A special fund was established upon which the bride might draw for her pedicures, manicures, massages, beauty treatments, stockings, and underwear. Another for her outer clothing. In addition, Peggy's right to receive an annual stipend of one million dollars was clearly set forth in the section titled "Miscellaneous Expenses." The following section, however, was not so restrictive. It conferred upon Madame Satrapoulos-to-be the absolute right to purchase, at her husband's expense, an unlimited amount of jewelry at any or all of the three jewelers named in the agreement: one in London, one in Paris, and one in New York. Peggy, in other words, was being handed a blank check to cover the most expensive items in the world.

Such stipulations constituted Part One of the agreement. It ran to ninety-two single-spaced pages, plus a sheaf of amendments and riders. Part Two comprised thirty pages, also single-spaced, listing, in general terms, all the worldly goods of the respective spouses. Of these, twenty-eight pages covered Socrates' corporations, companies, partnerships, consortiums, tankers, banks, airlines, paintings, real property—everything he owned anywhere in the world, from his yachts to his garters.

Peggy did not wish to read the instrument, but at Socrates' insistence, her attorney turned the pages for her and pointed out the salient features of the agreement, including the stipulation that, in the event of Socrates' death, she was to receive the sum of one hundred and fifty million dollars, that being the amount, as everyone had recognized, which would be necessary to keep her in reasonable comfort to the end of her days.

"Now, if you will sign," Socrates' attorney suggested, offering his own gold pen.

"Socrates," Peggy said, "what about the number of weekdays that we're to occupy separate bedrooms?"

"Page seventy-two, Section fifty-one," the tall attorney whispered, riffling the pages of the contract.

Peggy took the pen and signed in a large, juvenile hand, under the spot where Socrates had already affixed his signature.

The two attorneys shook hands, and Socrates embraced his bride-to-be.

"You have nothing to worry about, my dear," he said. "Everything, absolutely everything, has been taken into account."

Socrates had insisted that the marriage ceremony be celebrated according to the Greek Orthodox rite, and the tiny chapel of Serpentella was stifling. A mere two dozen guests had been able to squeeze themselves into the building, and sweat dripped indiscriminately from the faces of both ladies and gentlemen as the sun rose in the sky and the temperatures climbed.

The Greek stood before the altar, a candle in his left hand, Peggy's hand in his right. The resident priest of Serpentella—Socrates' personal priest—was assisted in the ceremony by an archimandrite from the monastery at Corfu. Behind Peggy, who was also carrying a lighted candle, her two children, Christopher and Michael, stood quietly, staring in fascination at the magnificent beards of the two priests. Socrates' offspring, Achilles and Maria, were in the nave with the rest of the guests. Socrates had only been able to force them to attend by making direct threats. Close by them Lindy Nut was radiant in a white Givenchy gown, although inside she was torn between joy at the marriage of her dearest friend, and resentment at the loss of a man whom she had occasionally hoped to transform into a husband for her own use. Peggy's mother, Mrs. Arthur Erwin Beckintosh, stood next to Lindy Nut, still wearing the dazzling smile which she had assumed the previous evening, at the precise moment when Socrates and Peggy had signed the agreement by which the Greek endowed his new bride with an incredible percentage of his worldly goods. . . .

"The servant of God, Socrates," the archimandrite intoned, "is united in the bonds of matrimony to the servant of God, Peggy, in the name of the Father, the Son, and the Holy Spirit."

Outside, in the blistering sunlight, milled the throng of guests for whom there had been no room in the chapel.

"I'm surprised that you were able to crash this one," Amore Dodino hissed.

"Gate-crasher, yourself," Raph Dun retorted. "I'm an official guest!"

"Of course. I had forgotten. You belong to the legion of her former lovers."

"Hardly. I'm here at the direct invitation of the daughter of the happy groom, in my capacity as *her* future lover."

"My dear, could you actually bring yourself to screw that fat little thing?"

"Why not?"

"If I were going to sell myself, I'd choose her brother. He's *so* much more attractive."

A joyous shout acclaimed the newlyweds as they emerged from the chapel. The guests threw handfuls of rice and sugar almonds. It was an ancient Greek custom—the rice for fertility, the sugar almonds for happiness. There were comments concerning the couple's chances for the latter and snickers over their capacity for the former. No one of them—not even Kallenberg, who had tried vainly to discover the details of the property agreement between the happy couple—was aware of Clause Nine of the contract: "In no event will Peggy Satrapoulos be expected to bear children of this union."

Despite the solemnity of the occasion, Barbudo, Socrates' private secretary, approached his smiling employer and placed a piece of paper into his hand. Quickly Socrates slipped the paper into his pocket before anyone had noticed it. He waited until Peggy had been swallowed up by a crowd of her friends before casting a discreet glance at it. It was a cablegram consisting of but five words: I HOPE YOU BOTH CROAK.

It was unsigned.

The Greek smiled. Menelas had remembered him, after all.

Part Five

NOT far from Mykonos, there is a tiny island known as Ixion. Ten years earlier, Herman Kallenberg had bought the entire island from the Greek government for the sum of two million dollars. Since then, he had spent another four million to transform it to his taste. He had only one goal: to equal, and preferably surpass, the island of Serpentella.

He had succeeded to the extent that those who had been guests on both islands were hard put to say which they liked the better. Indeed, they all lived in mortal dread that one day either Satrapoulos or Kallenberg might put that very question to them. It was universally agreed, therefore, that no one would ever mention Ixion in Satrapoulos' presence and the name Serpentella would never be spoken in Kallenberg's.

Irene was sitting alone in the great white house. Alone, that is, except for the thirty-odd servants employed to look after her comfort. She had just finished consuming the half bottle of whiskey which she had found essential to dispel the gloom engendered by her children's departure for London an hour before.

Suddenly, the sound of a helicopter penetrated the room. Irene hurried to the window in time to see Herman emerge from the aircraft. He held out his hand to assist another passenger to disembark: a tall blond girl whom Irene had never seen before.

Irene quickly passed a comb through her hair, donned a dressing gown, and lay down on her bed clutching a book. When Kallenberg entered the room a few moments later, he found her in a state of obvious concentration on the contents of the work.

"Ah, here you are."

"So you're back?"

"You mean you didn't hear the helicopter landing? Have the children left?"

"Yes, awhile ago. Are you alone?"

"What business is it of yours?"

"Nothing. I was wondering about dinner—"

"I am dining with a friend."

"Without me?"

"Yes, without you. You make me lose my appetite."

"Who is this friend of yours?"

"No one of any concern to you. A new employee. She speaks four languages. And her measurements are thirty-eight, twenty-four, thirty-six."

"Where did you find her? In a whorehouse?"

"Precisely, my darling. A whorehouse is the only place on earth where I can be sure of not running into you. They'd never let you in. You'd scare away the customers."

Irene's voice rose. "I want you to get that slut out of this house! If you don't get rid of her, I will!"

"Marina is going to dine with me—alone. We have things to discuss. Now, one more word and I'll lock you in your room."

He drew the key from the lock inside the room and then inserted it on the side of the door facing the hallway. Irene, terrified that he might actually carry out his threat, threw herself on him. Kallenberg laughed, certain of victory. Irene stepped back, raised her foot, and kicked him in the groin, screaming, "Here! Here's a present from me to Marina!"

Herman gave a roar of pain and rage. "Bitch! You'll pay for that!" He advanced on her, clutching his genitals with one hand, his face contorted by pain.

In her haste to escape, Irene stumbled and fell to the floor. Instantly Kallenberg was upon her, kicking viciously at her stomach, her chest, her legs.

Finally, Kallenberg stopped, afraid that she might lose consciousness. He bent over her and slapped her twice hard across the face.

With an effort Irene lifted her head, moistened her lips and tried to speak.

". . . a doctor. . . ."

Her head fell forward, and she lay flat on the floor, tremors sweeping through her body, breathing painfully, her eyes half-closed and puffy. Seating himself on the bed, Herman, out of breath, caressed his leather belt with his fingers. He smiled delightedly.

"Speak louder, my darling. . . . Did you say you need a doctor?"

Irene again roused herself up from her stupor and shook her head violently. She swallowed and pronounced painfully, ". . . the doctor's report . . . you'll go to prison. . . ."

Kallenberg pouted, as if heartbroken.

"You see how difficult you are? I do everything to make you happy, and still you complain!"

Actually, at the point of exploding from nervous tension, Irene had deliberately goaded her husband until he had beaten her. After all, he hadn't made love to her for weeks. After she had excited him with her injuries and by letting him rain blows on her, Irene had thought Herman would take her, make love to her, as in the good old days. She moaned and rubbed her neck painfully.

Solicitously her husband inquired, "Can I help you with anything? Do you want me to beat you some more? Or would you prefer a drink?"

"You . . . will go . . . to prison!" she managed to croak.

Kallenberg assumed a shocked expression.

He rose and moved toward the door. As he passed Irene he pretended to trip over her, which enabled him to give her yet another kick in the ribs.

"Oh . . . I'm sorry, my love! . . . I'm sorry!"

He backed out of the room, an expression of sincere desolation on his face. Irene sank her head into the carpet and sobbed with rage and pain. She loved being beaten, as long as inevitably, as a finale, her tormentor would have the decency to screw her. But not one without the other. With great difficulty she groped for the bedside table and managed to knock a metal container off it. She poured a quantity of pills into her hand and swallowed them.

Her last thought before she lost consciousness was: "This time Herman has really gone too far."

Kallenberg hurried through his dinner with Marina and through the "discussions" which followed. He was not feeling well. His genitals ached from Irene's well-aimed kick, and he was in a foul mood. He retired to his study as soon as he could, leaving Marina to her own devices. He had barely settled into his favorite chair, with a sigh of relief, when there was a knock at the door. It was Allan, his valet.

"Sir, you must come immediately. Jeanine has found Madame on the floor in her room!"

"On the floor, you say?"

"Yes, sir. Unconscious."

Kallenberg rose and followed the servant.

"Please, sir. Hurry. Jeanine is very worried."

Jeanine rose as they entered. Tears rolled down her cheeks. "We have to do something immediately, sir. Call a doctor—"

"Come now, Jeanine. This isn't the first time you've seen Madame during one of her attacks."

Herman picked Irene up in his arms and carried her to the bed. Her skin seemed unusually cold, but he thought he detected a faint pulse. Very faint.

"Get me some smelling salts. I'll try to bring her around. Irene! Irene! Can you hear me?"

He slapped her lightly on both cheeks, with no result other than to move her head limply from side to side.

"Irene! Irene! Allan, where are those salts? Jeanine, get the nurse."

"The nurse isn't here, sir. Madame gave her a holiday this morning."

Irene's eyelids seemed to flutter momentarily.

"You see? She's coming to. Irene! Let's lay her flat so that she can rest. And Allan, call Dr. Kiralles. Tell him to come quickly. I'll send the helicopter for him. He knows how to handle things like this."

Ten minutes later Allan returned. "Dr. Kiralles is not at home, sir. I've left word for him to call you immediately when he returns. Shall I call Dr. Salbacos?"

"What I want, above all, is for everyone to refrain from telling anyone about this, do you understand? Since Dr. Kiralles will be back shortly, we will wait. To save time, tell the pilot to leave for Athens immediately."

Jeanine hesitated. "And what about Madame, sir?"

"We'll stay with her. Have you anything better to suggest?"

"No, sir."

"If she moves, call me. I'll try to reach Dr. Kiralles myself."

He went to his study and dialed the number. He was told that the doctor had not yet returned. Nervously, he tried to call Dr. Salbacos only to be told that the doctor had just left on a call.

He returned to Irene's room a half hour later to relieve Jeanine and found her in tears again.

"Well?"

"Madame is dead, sir." She began sobbing uncontrollably.

Allan entered the room. "I've reached Dr. Kiralles, sir. He'll be here as soon as he can."

"It's too late. Too late. She's dead," Jeanine howled.

An hour later Kiralles and Salbacos arrived almost simultaneously. Together they examined Irene's body. Kallenberg breathed a sigh of relief that Kiralles had come. The doctor was one of his oldest friends. Kallenberg had contributed generously to his clinic. . . .

Dr. Salbacos looked up from the body. "Did your wife have an altercation of some sort before her death?"

"You're referring to the bruises on her face. I'm afraid I'm responsible. I slapped her while I was trying to revive her. Allan and Jeanine saw me."

The two servants nodded vigorously. "Oh, yes, sir," Allan said. "As soon as Jeanine found Madame, the master did everything possible to revive her."

Dr. Kiralles removed the empty pillbox from Irene's hand. "Poor Irene," he said softly. "Apparently she was unable to overcome her depression."

"She was extremely depressed," Kallenberg agreed. "Our children have just returned to London."

"My poor friend. Alas, we are powerless to prevent suicides."

Salbacos raised an eyebrow. "Doctor," he asked, "have you examined the bruises on Mrs. Kallenberg's face?"

"I've already told you," Kallenberg interrupted, "that I slapped her in an attempt to revive her. My servants have already stated the same thing."

Kiralles shook his head. "Poor Irene," he murmured. "It takes more than a few slaps to shake off an overdose of barbiturates. Now, Dr. Salbacos, if you will follow me, we must make out the certificate of death. It is quite obviously a case of suicide. Don't you agree?"

"Of course, doctor," Salbacos answered, his face expressionless. "Obviously."

"Why don't you marry me?"

"Everyone would say that I'm after your money."

"What money? To keep me from living with you, Papa has cut off my allowance."

"Yes, but you'll be an heiress someday. People talk, you know."

"I don't give a damn about people, Raph. We have our own lives to live."

"I'm too old for you."

"Bullshit. Why don't you try talking to Papa?"

"He would say that I'm old enough to be your father."

"So what? All his girls are young enough to be his daughters. Even Mama."

"That's different. He's rich, and I'm poor."

"Raph, please try talking to him. It might just work."

"But why, Maria? What good would it do? He looks on me as a poor newspaperman without enough talent to be able to earn even a few million a year like everyone else."

"Suppose I ask him to see you? Will you go?"

"Why not?"

"All right. I'll do it."

Raph smiled to himself. The girl was really in love with him! For two years they had been living together, moving from hotel to hotel, always one step ahead of Raph's creditors. His hope was that Satrapoulos would tire of the scandal and beg him to marry Maria and become his son-in-law. If he intended to do so, however, it would have to be soon. Even the credit extended to Raph on the strength of Maria Satrapoulos' known passion for him had its limits. And there was not much time left from another angle also. Time was passing, and Raph was nearing fifty.

"Mr. Dun, I have agreed to see you only because my daughter insisted that I do so. I will not try to hide from you that I hold you in utter contempt."

"May I ask what you have against me, sir?"

"My feelings are not at issue here, Mr. Dun. Why did you wish to see me?"

"Maria didn't tell you?" Dun asked, flustered.

"Tell me what? That she is living with you? I deplore it, but I cannot prevent it. You are merely the latest in a long line of bullfighters, racing car drivers, and embassy attachés. I suppose a newspaperman was inevitable."

"I am not interested in the past."

"And yet the past is the key to the future."

"Nor am I interested in history lessons. I came here to ask your permission to marry your daughter. In view of your attitude, however, I will not do so. I will simply inform you that we are going to be married."

"Congratulations. I suppose you want to borrow money to buy her a wedding dress?"

"Mr. Satrapoulos, I cannot allow—"

"Don't get on your high horse with me, Dun! I know you for what you are: a fading playboy who's looking for a sinecure for his old age."

"*I* am a fading playboy? Have you looked at yourself lately?"

The Greek seized Raph by the lapels of his jacket, tailored in Rome by Chiffonelli and still not paid for.

"Listen to me," Satrapoulos rasped. "You are a pimp, a gigolo, an asshole journalist, and a son of a bitch! If I didn't put a bullet in your skull twenty years ago, when you indirectly caused my mother's death, it was because I didn't want to dirty my hands with a piece of shit like you!"

"Your mother?" Raph stuttered. "What do I know about your mother?" How on earth did he find out? he wondered.

"Get your ass out of here," Socrates shouted. "And remember this: what should have happened to you twenty years ago might still happen—today, tomorrow, next week. Anytime! And who would mourn for you, you miserable son of a bitch!"

[33]

"Achilles, is that you? This is your Uncle Herman. Can you hear me?"

"Yes. I hear you."

"Then listen carefully, because this is very important. The great loss I've just suffered has made me stop and think about many things. There's something I feel I must tell you. Something—something so terrible that I never thought I would mention it to a living soul. But my poor darling wife's passing has given me a new perspective on things."

"Yes. I'm listening."

"Your father is a strange man, Achilles. But I'm sure you've noticed that yourself?"

"Yes."

"But you don't know how strange. Has he ever mentioned his own mother to you? Has he ever told you anything about the dear woman who was your grandmother?"

"No."

"Haven't you ever asked, Achilles?"

"No."

"You're not a very curious young man. I remember when you were a child, you used to play on our boat— you were curious then, Achilles, always asking me and your Aunt Irene why the sea was blue, why the stars twinkled. Do you remember, Achilles? Oh, if only I could bring back those days—"

Achilles heard a curious sound, like an inexpertly articulated sob.

"Are you there, Achilles?"

"Yes, Uncle."

"We loved you very much, you know, your Aunt Irene and I."

There was an expectant pause. Achilles remained silent.

"Achilles, I want you to do something for me and for yourself. I want you to ask your father why he left his own mother in poverty. And ask him to tell you how she died. Do you know how she was buried?"

"No."

"Then ask him to tell you that, too."

Achilles said nothing.

"One more thing, Achilles. You know how much your poor dead aunt loved you. God has taken her from us. But I know she's looking down on us, on those she loved on earth. And I want you to know that nothing has changed with me so far as you are concerned. If there's anything you need—advice, money, help of any kind—then I'll always be there, ready to do whatever I can for you. I know how unfair Socrates has been about Joan, for instance. If there's anything I can do, anything at all, let me know. Do you understand?"

"Yes, Uncle. Thank you."

Achilles put down the receiver. What on earth could Kallenberg have really wanted?

He shook his head. So many strange and puzzling things were happening all at once. Irene had died only a month ago, and, since then his father had thrown Maria's boyfriend out of the house and somehow forced him to stop seeing her. Then he had tried to do the same thing with Achilles and Joan. There was nothing that he hadn't attempted. He had threatened to disinherit Achilles. And when that didn't work, he had tried to buy off Joan—Joan, for God's sake, who preferred blue jeans to evening dresses and pea coats to mink!

He looked at his watch. It was time to go. He was irritated that his father had insisted upon one more meeting, that he would have to tell him no once more. And he was angry at himself for having listened to those monstrous insinuations of Kallenberg's.

Why didn't people just let him live his life? What did he care what Socrates had done? What did all this have to do with Achilles Satrapoulos? He had never asked anything more out of life than to be left alone.

Furiously, he slammed the door behind him and started down the stairs.

There was a long silence as their eyes met. Both men sensed that the battle about to be joined would be decisive and that no quarter would be given.

Socrates launched the attack. "You poor fool!"

Achilles said nothing.

"You think you're a man because you're screwing a woman old enough to be your mother!"

"As I recall," Achilles replied calmly, "all your wives were young enough to be your daughters."

The blow was so direct that Socrates pretended not to have been hit. Never had Achilles spoken to him in such a manner! He ignored the remark and expanded on his original thought: "Not only is she old, divorced, and worn-out, but you're supporting her!"

"I suppose it's a taste I inherited from you."

The Greek leaped from his chair. "Shut your mouth! You're a fool! She knows it, and she's trying to take you for everything she can get! Are you out of your mind? Do you think I'm going to let you spend my money, the money I've worked for all my life, on that whore?"

"I don't ask you how you spend your money, do I?"

Socrates' eyes opened wide. "Since when do I have to account to you for what I spend? Are you supporting me, or am I supporting you?"

"You may be supporting me," Achilles answered, his voice steady, "but I need more than money to live."

"You little asshole! Don't you see that Joan would leave you in an instant if you didn't have money?"

"And if you were broke, how long would Peggy stick by you."

Achilles experienced a pang of guilt as he saw his father place his hands over his face and stand motionless for a few seconds. He was tempted to apologize, but he resisted. He knew he was too weak to afford the luxury of guilt.

"Papa—"

Socrates did not answer.

"Papa," Achilles repeated.

Socrates spoke as though he were alone in the room. "Your sister has taken up with a gigolo. She's a girl, after all. But you're a boy— my only son. I wanted something else for you. I have plans for you—"

"I'm sorry, Papa, but I can't live my life for your sake, and you can't live yours through me. But that's not really what I wanted to say."

The Greek looked up, intrigued. "What is it?"

"For years, Maria and I wondered about certain things. You were always away, and Mama wasn't with us often. Sometimes we heard the servants talking. . . . I know that you didn't accumulate your fortune by behaving like an altar boy. But there are things I'd like to know."

"Go on," Socrates said.

"I'd like to know about my grandmother."

"Why? She's dead. You and Maria were only two when she died."

"That's just it. I won't tell Maria if you don't want me to, but I'd like to know. Is it true that you let her live in poverty?"

"Who told you such a thing?"

"Does it matter?" Achilles asked. "Is it true or not?"

"Yes, it's true," the Greek shouted. "So what?"

"But why?"

"What business is it of yours? Do you know what I had to do to get where I am today? I was born poor! I've seen what life is like on the other side of the tracks! You've never known anything but luxury all your life, and you have the nerve to ask me for explanations? How dare you try to judge me! No one has that right! Now, get out of here! Go to your Joan!"

"Papa—"

"Don't 'Papa' me! You think you're a man! Well, act like a man. Solve your own problems!"

"I'd never let you starve to death."

"All right. Since you must know, I'll tell you," Socrates said sharply. "You are going to discover from what an illustrious line you descended. You may not know it, since you're an American citizen, but I was born on the outskirts of Smyrna, in a windowless wooden shack with a piece of canvas for a roof. In Turkey, the Greeks were considered the Jews of Asia Minor. They were aliens, foreigners. Occasionally, when the Turks didn't have enough to do killing each other, they massacred us. In Greece we were hated too—because we had left Greece. When I was six—the same age at which you were given your first sailboat—I saw four of my uncles hanged just for being Greeks. And they weren't the only ones who died. Those who weren't hanged died of famine or pestilence. We were so poor that your grandmother used to cook a cabbage in a pot of water and say it was soup! One cabbage lasted us for three days. Well, I swore that I'd have my revenge. I swore that I'd never be poor, that I'd do whatever I had to do to escape the poverty and the massacres—"

He paused for a moment to catch his breath. Achilles did not dare interrupt to ask questions.

"I left home when I was little more than a child," Socrates went on, "and signed on to a freighter as a galley hand. I stayed on that ship for three years. Then, one day, we docked in Venezuela, and I jumped ship. I don't even know if they noticed I was gone. But there I was in Caracas, without a cent in my pocket. But I had the will to make my way. Eight years later I had my first million! And I didn't steal it! I earned it! Three days a week I didn't sleep. I had a job during the day and a job during the night. I didn't spend money . . . I saved it. I thought, I listened, and I learned. And I met a great many people. Someday I'll tell you about it, when we're both calm. But for the moment, I tell you that it's true about your grandmother. When she died, I hadn't seen her for over thirty years."

"Where is she buried?"

"I scattered her ashes in the sea. It was what she had always wanted. You know, once she moved to Greece, she only left her village once, and that was to go to Paris, to stay at the Ritz—and to die. And she died because of that son of a bitch Kallenberg! He was responsible for her death!"

"He was the one who suggested that I ask you that question, Papa," Achilles confessed timidly. "He called me yesterday and said to ask about my grandmother."

"That bastard! I knew it!"

"Papa, you said you didn't see your mother for over thirty years. Why?"

"I'll tell you. But I won't offer any explanations. You must accept me at my word, do you understand?"

"Yes, but I'd like to know."

"All right. I was six years old at the time—" He hesitated. He was the last witness to what he was about to describe. All the others were dead. He looked down at his hands and made an effort to steady his voice. "When I was six," he continued, "after seeing my uncles hanged, I saw my mother raped by a gang of Turks. There were at least thirty of them. After that, as young as I was, I could never look at her without hearing her screaming. . . . I have always wished that she had died then. I could not bear to see her. Do you understand?"

Achilles rose from his seat and silently clasped his father's hands in his. They stood without speaking for several seconds. Then Achilles, his face chalk white, fled from the room.

Achilles tried to compose himself as he pulled into the airport. He parked his car, then walked into the administration building. He found Jeff in his office, alone. Jeff had been one of his father's first pilots, and he had remained in the Greek's employ ever since. He was now president of a subsidiary of Socrates' airline which specialized in air-taxi service. Jeff had given Achilles his first flight training, and there had been a strong bond between the two men ever since.

"Jeff," Achilles began, "I have a favor to ask you."

"Go ahead."

"Are we buddies?"

The aging old pilot smiled. "What is it this time? Do you need money, or is somebody's husband chasing you?"

"You were my father's pilot when he scattered my grandmother's ashes in the sea, weren't you?"

Jeff's face went blank immediately. Satrapoulos, many years before, had ordered him never to speak of that episode. To anyone.
He was fond of Achilles, but he was terrified of the old man.

"Who told you that?"

"Let's not play games, Jeff. I'm not a child any more. I've known
about it for years. Papa told me about it the day I turned twenty-
one."

"It was so long ago," Jeff replied lamely. "I don't remember. I
may have been the pilot. In fact, I suppose I was."

"Tell me where it was, Jeff. I want to see it."

"Well. . . ."

Three-quarters of an hour later Achilles was flying over the route
which, twenty years earlier, Athina's funeral cortege had taken on its
way toward the open sea. The old Bonanza air taxi he had nagged
Jeff into letting him take moved gracefully over the villages below.
Then it turned and moved out over the water, following the course
laid out by Jeff.

Now that he was alone, Achilles felt the emotion that he had suppressed during his father's account of his experiences well up in him.
He had always thought of himself as having no past to speak of. And
yet he had suddenly discovered that he had emerged from a violent
background—violence, madness, murder, rape, and bloodletting. He
felt strangely tied to those mysterious events which had taken place
before he was born, but which had affected every phase of his existence and of which he was one of the consequences. Since he had not
lived those experiences or fought those battles, he found it difficult
to understand that men could fight over money or that they could
struggle to acquire a power which was more imaginary than real.
For what was real in life was not bills of lading, or accounts, or tankers, or oil. What was real was the sun, the waves, the sand, Joan's
hair. . . .

He flew in a straight line for thirty minutes, then circled down
toward the water, reducing the plane's speed to the minimum. In
his mind's eye, he saw his father and his mother as they must have
been twenty years before, and he saw, too, the handfuls of ashes
being scattered in the wind. Tears came into his eyes.

Shit! Something was wrong with the engine. The right wing
dipped toward the sea. Achilles pulled back on the stick, and the
Bonanza steadied itself and rose a few feet. Then it seemed to
pause and hang in midair for an eternity before it plunged nose-first

into the sea. There was no time for Achilles to unfasten his safety belt or to send out a Mayday signal.

Jeff had waited two hours for Achilles to return. Then, in a panic, he had gone to Satrapoulos and related, word for word, his dialogue with the boy. Immediately, the Greek had been galvanized into action and organized a search party. Then he went up in his own helicopter to direct the operation. He' knew that his son was a skilled pilot, and he felt that the boy must have been able to bring the old Bonanza down in a belly landing and escape before it sank. The fact that there had been no message was probably due to Achilles' haste to get out of the plane before it went down. Therefore, he was probably somewhere in the open water, waiting for a rescue party. There was no danger, actually, since Achilles was an expert swimmer, capable of remaining afloat for hours. The only problem, then, was to find him.

At 5 A.M. dawn broke, and a blue mist seemed to rise from the sea. A few moments later the sun appeared in a cloud of gold.

By 8 A.M. nothing had been found.

At 10 A.M. a message was received from a reconnaissance plane. An oil slick had been sighted.

Socrates flew immediately to the coordinates given by the pilot. He saw it, a dark area in the blue water, perhaps a hundred yards across. He asked that a sounding be made. The answer came back quickly: forty-five hundred feet. It was practically impossible to raise a sunken plane from that depth, even if it were possible to find it.

Since he considered it most unlikely that Achilles had gone down with the plane, Socrates concluded that he must be in the water nearby, and he gave his orders accordingly. The Greek naval officers attached to the operation exchanged glances, but no one offered a contrary opinion. The commanding officer ordered the area to be divided into sectors and searched thoroughly.

Meanwhile, the Greek demanded that preparations be undertaken to raise the aircraft from the bottom. He ignored the objections raised by the officers and ordered, "Don't lose any time! Begin immediately! Work day and night!"

By nightfall of the first day no trace of Achilles had been found. It was decided to continue the search in the darkness, with the help of gigantic floodlights. At the same time, specialists worked frantically to pinpoint the exact location of the sunken Bonanza.

By nine o'clock Socrates had been without sleep for forty-eight hours. Over the years, he had spent many sleepless nights in the pursuit of wealth and power, he reflected. Now such objectives seemed pitifully unimportant. The indescribable fear which gripped his heart suddenly enabled him to see clearly what had eluded him throughout his life: the only real treasure for man, the treasure he invariably ignores because he regards it as his due, is life itself.

Long after midnight, an officer handed Socrates a message. It was signed "Kallenberg," and it read: TERRIBLY WORRIED. AM WHOLLY AT YOUR SERVICE IF I CAN BE OF HELP IN ANY RESPECT.

The Greek did not bother to crumple the telegram. He simply let it fall from his hands.

[34]

It was not until the afternoon of the third day that the wreck was found. As soon as the Greek heard the news, he took off in his private plane for Portugal, leaving orders to have the hull of the Bonanza raised immediately. He was certain that Achilles' body would not be in it. There were known cases of shipwrecked sailors surviving for as much as two weeks without food and water in weather far worse than this.

Before entering the Prophet's house, he instructed his chauffeur that he was to be called immediately if there was any news. Then he went inside.

The Prophet received him in silence.

"The cards," Socrates whispered, seating himself.

He watched the stiff rectangles fall, certain of their verdict: Achilles was alive.

433

Still the Prophet did not speak.

"Well?"

"There is not much hope," the Prophet said softly.

"I am not interested in hope, but in knowledge. Give me a yes or no. Now!"

"You know that it is not I who answer you."

"Is my son dead? Yes or no!"

"Be patient. I cannot tell for certain yet. There are other things here—"

The Greek pounded the table with his fists. "For the last time," he shouted. "Is Achilles alive?"

The Prophet hesitated for three interminable seconds before he decided to reveal what he had seen in the cards.

"No," he answered. "He is not alive."

Socrates jumped to his feet, sweeping the cards to the floor with his hand. The Prophet glanced down and saw that, once more, their message was clear: death.

"Charlatan!" Socrates cried. "I don't believe you! You know nothing! Achilles is alive!"

The Prophet did not answer.

Socrates ran from the house to the waiting Rolls. "Take me to the airport," he ordered. Then he picked up the telephone and spoke to the radioman on his plane. "I am going to hold a news conference tonight at seven o'clock, at my house in Athens. I want to make a public statement in the presence of the Archimandrite of Corfu! Notify him immediately. Now, repeat what I've told you."

The officer repeated his orders.

"Good. Now, get ready to take off. I'll be there in a few minutes."

Angrily, he swore to himself that he would never again set foot in Cascais.

Kallenberg examined Medea's face closely. My God, he told himself, she looks more like an old lizard than ever.

Medea stared back. There was no trace of warmth in her eyes. She had consented to receive Kallenberg only when he had spoken the magic words: urgent business. She had been listening to him for a half hour now, and she had hardly been able to bring herself to speak to him. This, after all, was the man who had taken her two daughters from her without bringing happiness to either.

"Come now," Herman said. "You and I are alike. We're both real-ists. Are we going to sit around and not try to hold onto what we've worked so hard to get?"

"We're talking about my grandson," Medea said.

"And my nephew! Don't forget that. But we have no real proof that he's dead."

"There is little hope that he will be found."

"Stranger things have been known to happen. But by the time Achilles is found, it may well be too late. Our competitors will have destroyed us by then!"

"Exactly what is it you want?"

"Satrapoulos is distraught, and he is letting his affairs go to ruin. If he falls, he'll drag us down with him. He owns forty-nine percent of Persian Petroleum. You have twenty percent. I own twenty-one percent."

"Who owns the other ten percent?"

"Six people. A Frenchman has three percent. Two Englishmen each have two percent. And then there are three industrialists who each have one percent."

"So?"

"They are all willing to sell. I've offered them five times what their interest is worth. If you're willing to combine your holdings with mine, I'll buy theirs. Then you and I will have control."

"How much for me, and how much for you?"

"Half and half," Kallenberg assured her. "We'll form a new cor-poration. Of course, you'll share the cost of buying the stock of the minor shareholders with me."

"Are they ready to sell now?"

"As soon as I give the word."

"Poor Socrates. How sad for him."

"Terrible, terrible! But as soon as he recovers from his depression, he'll realize that we've acted for his own good, and he'll thank us."

"How ungrateful men are. Do you think the stock can be trans-ferred tomorrow?"

"Of course, if I have your approval. Our success depends on how quickly we can move."

"Very well. You have my approval. You know that I am doing this solely for the sake of my grandchildren."

"How could I possibly think otherwise?"

Kallenberg was delighted. Not only would he make Satrapoulos bite the dust, but he would also play a dirty trick on the old witch.

He had offered the minority stockholders only twice the value of their holdings.

He had no way of knowing that the "old witch" was equally pleased. When the time came to sign the contract, she intended to refuse to pay her part of the purchase price for the stock. Kallenberg would then be obliged to pay the full sum himself—a matter of some two million dollars. She owed him that, she told herself self-righteously, for the way he had treated her daughters.

The vast drawing room of the Satrapoulos house in Athens was jammed with reporters and photographers from every major newspaper and magazine in the world. As Socrates entered, a sudden hush fell over the room. Perhaps it was the presence of the tall, cadaverous monk with the flowing beard which elicited the respect, or at least the silence, of the normally cynical gathering.

The priest and Peggy took seats behind a small table, while the Greek remained standing.

"Gentlemen," Socrates began. "I would like to begin by presenting Monseigneur Corybantes, Archimandrite of Corfu. The archimandrite has been kind enough to offer himself as a witness to what I am about to tell you. I wish to thank him for his kindness in being here, and also for allowing the White Virgin"—he gestured toward a small statue standing on a pedestal to his right—"to be brought here from the monastery at Corfu.

"You see before you, gentlemen, a broken man. I have a son, as you know. An only son, named Achilles. At this moment, I do not know where he is. I do not even know if he is among the living. Yet his life is more precious to me than my own."

"That fucking hypocrite," a reporter at the back of the room whispered to his neighbor.

"Shut up," the neighbor replied. "Don't you have any respect for anything?"

"This is what I want to say to you," the Greek continued. "If God has called my son to Himself, I intend to retire from worldly affairs. My wife is in complete agreement with me on this point."

There were incredulous looks on several faces in the room, and smiles on others.

"But if by some miracle of God's grace, through the intercession of the White Virgin, I find Achilles alive, then I take a solemn oath, with the Archimandrite Corybantes as my witness, that I will convey all my worldly goods—I repeat, *all* my worldly goods—to our Holy Mother the Church. And on this point also, my wife is in complete accord with me.

"Gentlemen, thank you for coming here this evening. I can only add that the search for my son will continue."

The Greek glared ferociously at Lewis. "What do you want?" he demanded.

"It's very important, sir." The secretary had the look of a frightened dog, but he stood his ground, blocking Socrates' way.

"Can't you see that I'm with the archimandrite?" Socrates snapped.

"Sir, it's extremely urgent."

"What can be more important than what I am going through at this moment?"

"I know, sir," Lewis persisted. "But—"

"But what?"

"It's about Persian Petroleum—"

"Have you lost your mind? I've just announced that I'm withdrawing from the world, and especially from business! How dare you speak to me of Persian Petroleum!"

"It's Mr. Kallenberg, sir."

"Kallenberg? What about him? Speak up!"

"And Madame Mikolofides—"

"Yes, yes! Go on, man! For God's sake, out with it!"

"They've joined forces. They're trying to ruin you!"

"Impossible. They hate each other!"

"That may be. But they're buying up the shares of the minority stockholders with the intention of becoming the majority stockholders."

The Greek turned chalk-white.

"Oh, the bastards! Are you certain?"

"Absolutely certain, sir."

"They dare do this to me at a time when I am dying of grief!"

"That is precisely why they are doing it, sir."

"Well, they won't get away with it, by God! I'll put a stop to this —if only out of respect for Achilles' memory. What can we do?"

"There are two shares still free. If we can stop them from acquiring those, then control of the company will remain in your hands. Have I your permission to act?"

"Yes, yes, of course, my boy. You have my full authorization to do whatever must be done. Shoot down those vultures for me!"

Since eight o'clock in the morning they had been at work, raising the downed plane inch by inch toward the surface. The crane operators had warned that they might not be able to raise the hull completely out of the water. It was a very delicate operation. One slip and the plane might break free from the hoists and be lost forever in the depths of the sea.

Socrates stood bareheaded in the blazing sun on the deck of one of the boats supplied by the Greek navy. His eyes did not leave the steel cables as they wound, with maddening slowness, around the giant spools. There was no sound except the squeaking of the pulleys and the macabre cry of the gulls.

Suddenly, a red buoy appeared on the surface among the waves. It signified that the plane had reached the level of the diver who held the deepest station. In a half hour Socrates would know if the wreck contained the body of his son.

A diver emerged on the surface next to the buoy and signaled frantically. Immediately, the crane operators slowed the ascent.

Behind Socrates on the deck Helena and Peggy, the old wife and the new, stood side by side, not speaking, clutching the railing.

A shrill whistle sounded, and the small craft in the area moved away and formed a wide circle around the three taut steel cables.

Beneath the surface, Socrates could see an immense indistinct gray form. His boat alone had not moved at the signal. The captain had wished to obey, but Socrates had given him a look so commanding that he had not dared give the order to move away from the center of operations.

The tail of the airplane emerged from the water, its markings clear in the sunlight: GAL—Grecian Airlines.

A few minutes more and the cockpit would be visible.

"Stop!" an officer shouted.

The plexiglass of the cockpit glistened in the sun. Its interior, however, was strangely clouded. It was impossible to see within.

The crane operators locked their hoists in position, and another team set to work to insert giant buoys under the wreck so as to hold it on the surface.

Before they could slide the first buoy into place, the Greek stretched out his hand from the deck of his boat and touched the wing of the plane. His hand closed on it, and he hoisted himself from the boat onto the wing. A sailor leaped forward to stop him, but Socrates riveted him to the deck with a glance. Before anyone else could intervene, the Greek was moving cautiously along the wing on his hands and knees.

"Sir!" the captain shouted. But Socrates did not hear. No power on earth could prevent him from doing what he must do in order to know.

Under his weight, the hull of the plane began to shift in its precarious cradle of steel. Now no one dared intervene. The slightest additional weight on the plane might cause it to be lost forever.

Slowly, the Greek climbed from the wing onto the hull, slipping and sliding on the slippery aluminum skin of the aircraft. Yet he reached the edge of the cockpit, and, not finding a foothold on the hull, he straddled the plexiglass dome and clutched it with his arms in order to steady himself.

"Sir!" the captain shouted again. "Slide down to the wing and come back to the boat. Let your specialists do it!"

This time Socrates heard him. In a rage, he made a violent gesture which almost caused him to lose his balance. Peggy gasped.

There was a deafening grinding noise, and the hull shifted slightly.

The Greek wiped his forehead. He would have to try to open the cockpit. Lying flat against the dome, he reached down toward the handle, touched it with his fingertips, then leaned on it with all his weight. He felt the dome move slightly; then it swung open.

On the deck of the boat, Helena was crying silently. Peggy's eyes were dry, but the tension visible on her face expressed her anguish more eloquently than any tears. She saw her husband lean forward in a final effort to see into the interior of the cockpit. Then he disappeared into it as though he had been swallowed by some incredible monster from the depths. With a terrible, final noise, the cockpit door swung shut behind him. At that precise instant, the tailfin, to which one of the three cables was attached, gave way, and the end of the hull plunged into the sea in a cloud of spray. Almost simultaneously, the wing seemed to crumble like paper, and the cable which supported it snapped and whipped into the air with a loud whistling sound. A second later, the third cable gave way.

No one had time to move, or even to scream, as the plane disappeared, nose-first, into the depths.

Peggy looked away, emitted a loud moan, and bit her knuckles until they bled. When she forced herself to look again, the sea was empty.

EPILOGUE

HERMAN Kallenberg wiped his forehead with a silk handkerchief embroidered with his initials. The heat was stifling in the chapel, and the clouds of incense nauseated him. Not even the excitement of his own marriage ceremony could reconcile him to his discomfort. This was, after all, his eighth. He might eventually surpass the record set by Gus Bambilt years before: eleven marriages. It was enough to stir a man's ambitions. With Satrapoulos out of the running, Kallenberg reflected, he might make a try at it.

It had been a year since Kallenberg's erstwhile brother-in-law, and perennial nemesis, had died. His bones still lay in the ocean, in forty-five hundred feet of water. For his widow had refused to allow another attempt to raise the hull which served him as a coffin. The authorities had respected her sorrow and had bowed to her wish. What had been born of the sea had now returned to the sea, Herman reflected. First the mother, then the son of the son, and finally the son himself. It was all very depressing, but there were moments when Kallenberg had difficulty in repressing a smile as he thought of the unbroken chain of mourning which had afflicted his family. After all, he himself was still alive and in perfect shape. It would be senseless to allow such lugubrious thoughts to invade his soul and upset his digestion.

For Kallenberg's appetite had not diminished with the passage of time. He still ate and drank with the capacity of a giant. And he still continued to amass fortunes, nibbling away at the vast financial empire of his former mother-in-law, Medea Mikolofides. At eighty, Medea refused to die, refused to delegate her power, and, by holding so tenaciously to life, succeeded only in poisoning everything around her. Or at least so it seemed to Herman.

Kallenberg raised his eyes to the ravishing form of the woman who, in a few moments, would become his wife. She was slender and tall for a woman, but a tiny figure compared to Herman himself. Seen from a distance, the couple looked like a father in the company of his little daughter.

To celebrate the marriage, the Archimandrite Halirrhotios himself had been imported from Istanbul. With money in one hand and a bit of goodwill in the other, it is always possible to reach an understanding with the servants of the Most High. A special decree, which constituted a milestone in canon law, had stipulated that Herman, by the fact of his bereavement, had regained his virginity and was once again as pure as an adolescent. Irene's death had, so to speak, wiped out all of Herman's preceding divorces, and made it possible for him to be married in the church.

"Who is that old owl over there?" Dodino asked, motioning toward a thin, bald man of considerable age.

"You mean you don't know?" Raph Dun replied. "That is the famous Prophet—Satrapoulos' astrologer!"

"A fat lot of good he did poor Satrapoulos. If I were Kallenberg, I would be careful."

"People say that Kallenberg also consults him."

"Well, my dear, no one ever accused Kallenberg of being the cleverest man in the world. That reminds me. How is your own charming, fat little fiancée?"

"Maria? I haven't seen her since her father died. She really wasn't my type at all. Money is all right, but one mustn't pay too high a price for it. Can you imagine me spending my life with that little butterball?"

"Please, Raph, do try to be a gentleman. . . . Oh, look at the bride! Isn't she lovely! And look at the size of the candle she's holding! Does that have any particular significance, I wonder?"

"Calm yourself, Dodino. It's a consolation to see that you, at least, never change."

"Of course not. Why should I change? Life goes on, as always."

In the sudden silence, the Archimandrite Halirrhotios cleared his throat discreetly. He was about to pronounce the sacred formula which would transform the bride into Herman Kallenberg's eighth wife. His superb bass voice rose majestically under the vaulted ceiling of the chapel as he enunciated the moving ritualistic phrases of the Orthodox liturgy.

"The servant of God, Herman, is joined in the bonds of matrimony to the servant of God, Peggy. In the name of the Father, of the Son, and of the Holy Spirit."